GOLDEN AGE
WHODUNITS

OTTO PENZLER, the creator of American Mystery Classics, is also the founder of the Mysterious Press (1975); Mysterious-Press.com (2011), an electronic-book publishing company; and New York City's Mysterious Bookshop (1979). He has won a Raven, the Ellery Queen Award, two Edgars (for the *Encyclopedia of Mystery and Detection*, 1977, and *The Lineup*, 2010), and lifetime achievement awards from NoirCon and *The Strand Magazine*. He has edited more than 70 anthologies and written extensively about mystery fiction.

GOLDEN AGE
WHODUNITS

OTTO
PENZLER,
EDITOR

AMERICAN
MYSTERY
CLASSICS

Penzler Publishers
New York

Published in 2024 by Penzler Publishers
58 Warren Street, New York, NY 10007
penzlerpublishers.com

Distributed by W. W. Norton

Cover image: Andy Ross
Cover design: Mauricio Diaz

Paperback ISBN 978-1-61316-542-3
Hardcover ISBN 978-1-61316-541-6
eBook ISBN 978-1-61316-543-0

Library of Congress Control Number: 2023922350

Printed in the United States of America

9 8 7 6 5 4 3 2 1

GOLDEN AGE
WHODUNITS

CONTENTS

INTRODUCTION

This is the fourth collection of Golden Age mystery stories in the American Mystery Classics series, preceded by *Golden Age Detective Stories*, *Golden Age Locked Room Mysteries*, and *Golden Age Bibliomysteries*. It is a series that appears to be successful and for which I have every hope that it will continue until politicians are regarded as symbols of virtue.

The so-called Golden Age of detective fiction, often described as being the years between the two World Wars, more accurately began with E.C. Bentley's *Trent's Last Case* in 1913 and has never really ended, since the many elements that loosely define the books that we regard as of the era continue to be employed. In addition, many of the greatest authors of the Golden Age continued to write for many years after the end of World War II (1945). Some of the best and most popular works by Agatha Christie, Ellery Queen, Rex Stout, Mary Roberts Rinehart, and others were produced in the 1950s, 1960s, and even 1970s.

Any definition of Golden Age mysteries will be a poor one because there are so many books that would never be regarded as part of our understanding of what we think we mean. But, as noted in another context, we know it when we see it. Remember, Dashiell Hammett and Raymond Chandler wrote detective stories in the 1920s and 1930s, yet they are unlikely to be thought of as Golden Age writers in the way that Queen, Christie, John Dickson Carr, and Dorothy L. Sayers, among many others, are.

The puzzle is generally the mainstay of these writers, the *raison d'etre* of their tales, without being overly concerned with the psychological make-up of the killer, nor are they overtly attempting to take political, sociological, or philosophical positions, as is Hammett, for one example.

Among the characteristics that we expect to find in an ideal Golden Age story are a detective, whether a member of the police, an amateur who happens upon a crime and thinks it would be interesting or great fun to solve it, or a private investigator who, in those between-the-war years tends to have a remarkable ability to solve crimes that baffle the police. Equally noteworthy is the number of law enforcement representatives who give private eyes access to crime scenes, various records, and even assign low-ranking members of the force to assist them, often attaining the apotheosis of their profession by being showered with praise and thanks from the top-ranking cops and agents.

To satisfy our desires for a proper Golden Age story we need a murder and, no matter how violent it may have been, the details are spared the reader. We can read about someone being shot or stabbed or bludgeoned, but we are seldom witnesses as the crime is generally carried out off-stage without granular descriptions of blood, guts, and brain matter splashed across the wall.

Another expectation of Golden Age stories is that the author will have played fair with the reader. If there is a puzzle to be solved, there must be clues to enable the reader to follow along, just as the detective does. It is a rare mystery story that is solved by the reader before the detective has nabbed the murderer but it is a tribute to the author when readers acknowledge that it's their fault for not have spotted the clues that are enumerated when the denouement arrives, generally in the form of a gloating speech by the brilliant detective who sweetly and subtly tells his audience (and, by proxy) how dim the reader is because they were not smart enough to have spotted all those so-obvious signs of the suspect's guilt.

There is great satisfaction in a good, fair-play detective story in which the peace and comfort of a community is ripped apart by a heinous crime, often apparently inexplicable and frightening to those in the general vicinity and, if the author is good at the job, to readers. What a relief it is when a familiar detective, or one whose attributes have been trumpeted by the author, arrives at the scene!

We expect justice to be done in a Golden Age crime story and are rarely disappointed. The fact that such an outcome is less certain in much of contemporary crime fiction is one of the attractions of the novels and stories of what was a simpler, safer time—or so we like to think.

Another significant difference between today's crime fiction and the stories of the 1920s, 1930s, and 1940s is the changing language that has evolved into a more sensitive pattern of usage. There may be a great disparity between the attitudes of people nearly a century ago and there are commensurate differences in words in the context of gender, race, and ethnicity. Occasionally, casual use of words before WWII may be offensive to the modern reader but these have not been edited out or rewritten. It is a disservice to the authors who worked in one era to be judged in a different one and absurd to bring today's tastes and preferences to the language of fiction written before most of us were born

The current volume has many of the era's most beloved detectives, including Ellery Queen, Hildegarde Withers, and the Great Merlini, as well as some of the most popular authors of the day who did not regularly feature a series character, such as Mary Roberts Rinehart, Frederic Brown, and Melville Davisson Post.

This volume also features some of America's greatest authors who are not generally thought of as mystery writers, including F. Scott Fitzgerald, Ring Lardner, and Stephen Vincent Benét. While mystery, crime, and suspense may not have been the primary focus of the majority of their work, just wait until you read their distinguished contributions to the literature!

Otto Penzler
New York
October 2023

THE AMATEUR OF CRIME
Stephen Vincent Benét

Although he died young, Stephen Vincent Benét (1898-1943) was quite prolific in several literary forms, most notably poetry, for which he won two Pulitzer Prizes, the first in 1929 for the long narrative history of the Civil War, *John Brown's Body*, and posthumously in 1944 for the unfinished *Western Star*, a narrative based on the settling of the United States.

He had writing credits on more than fifty published or dramatically produced works, included eight posthumous in the four years after his death.

Benét was devoted to writing and had his first book, *Poetry—Five Men and Pompey* (1915), six dramatic monologues in verse, published when he was only seventeen. While he favored poetry, Benét also wrote novels, plays, and short stories, one of the latter being his most famous and enduring work, "The Devil and Daniel Webster" (1936).

This fantasy was for decades required reading in every grade school in America and served as the basis for numerous plays and a 1941 motion picture starring Edward Arnold and Walter

Huston. It tells the story of a farmer who sells his soul to the devil and changes his mind, resulting in a jury trial pitting the great orator against Satan ("Mr. Scratch" in the film). Benét was a co-writer of the screenplay with Dan Totheroh.

Among his plays was the libretto for an opera based on "The Devil and Daniel Webster" and, perhaps most successfully, one for which he is not at all known, *The Bat*, based on *The Circular Staircase* (1908), a novel by Mary Roberts Rinehart. The stage play made its debut in 1920, with credit for its authorship going to Rinehart and Avery Hopwood but, in fact, it had been ghost-written by Benét. It has been staged relentlessly since then and has served as the basis for several motion pictures, the best-known being *The Bat Whispers* (1930), starring Chester Morris and Una Merkel.

"The Amateur of Crime" was originally published in the April 1927 issue of *The American Magazine*.

The Amateur of Crime
Stephen Vincent Benét

AND WHAT IS *your* hobby, Mr. Scarlet?" queried Mrs. Culverin kindly of her shyest guest. Her long, pendent earrings of antique crystal winked like tiny stars as she turned upon him the full battery of her celebrated smile.

"Murder," said the owlish young man in the English dinner-jacket, serenely. Mrs. Culverin gave a slight, pleased scream.

In a day of hostesses who were famous for rules, and hostesses who were notorious for breaking them, Mrs. Culverin achieved unique celebrity as a hostess who seemed to recognize no rules at all. At the moment she was opening her Long Island house for the summer, and the company gathered to celebrate the event could hardly have been more diverse had Mrs. Culverin deliberately planned it so. But Mrs. Culverin never planned anything deliberately.

This particular house party included, among others, Prince Mirko, of Ruritania, head of the Ruritanian debt commission to the United States; his extraordinarily beautiful wife; Baron Kossovar, the Ruritanian Ambassador; Daisy Delight, the cinema star; a bishop; a banker; a bandmaster; the most celebrated dance expert of the moment; two débutantes; the woman's Olympic diving champion; a blind pianist; a Mr. Lang, who was vaguely spoken of as a big-game hunter, and Peter Scarlet—the last, a pink-cheeked youth with surprised, mouse-colored hair which, together with his enormous horn rimmed spectacles, gave him much of the innocent downiness of a very young owl.

Mrs. Culverin could not remember exactly what he did, or exactly why she had asked him; but, as she was often in the same quandary about many of her guests, the fact perturbed her not at all. He neither smoked opium in his bedroom nor attempted to secrete small articles of silverware about his person—and as these were the only two social solecisms her generous heart admitted, she felt satisfied enough with him, whoever he might be.

But when he spoke of murder, she viewed him with a new and acquisitive eye. So far, it must be admitted, her Long Island housewarming had leaned perilously toward the verge of failure. The bishop, though a liberal bishop, had lifted episcopal eyebrows at the dancer. The banker had insisted on talking statistics. The Olympic diving champion had had too much of a cold to exhibit her skill—and the Ruritanians had been so freezingly polite to each other that a pall of gentility had descended upon the whole assemblage. Mrs. Culverin suddenly remembered, with that vagueness that characterized her memories, having heard of some tiresome, political feud between Prince Mirko and Baron Kossovar.

Now, however, young Mr. Scarlet's unexpected admission of his unusual hobby seemed to give her a heaven-sent opportunity of redeeming her dinner party. She raised her voice to carry to the end of the table.

"How quaint!" she said, with relish. "Mr. Scarlet knows all about murders—or murdering—which was it, Mr. Scarlet? Do tell us lots about them, anyhow!" And she patted him approvingly on the arm.

The young man, thus abruptly singled out as the object for the stares of the whole company, looked more owlish than ever. A faint pink flush mounted slowly toward his ears.

"Mrs. Culverin flatters me," he said, looking at his plate. "I don't know all about murders—or murderers, either. But, yes, I am—interested in them."

"You are a detective, Mr. Scarlet, yes?" queried Prince Mirko, in his careful English.

"No, Your Highness. Merely an amateur of crime."

The princess laughed—a long, beautiful ripple of laughter. "An amateur of crime!" she said, giving the words a foreign twist. "Think of it, Mirko! At his age—an amateur of crime! But I thought you were—what is it?—undergraduate at an American university, Mr. Scarlet?"

"I am, Madame. I'm going back to college Monday," muttered Scarlet, obviously abashed. "But, well—you ought to start in young at any profession, oughtn't you? And—I've had certain opportunities, in a way. At least, my father was in the diplomatic service, so we traveled around a lot when I was a kid—"

A pleased expression crossed Prince Mirko's face: "If I am

right, your father was *chargé d'affaires* at our capital, Mr. Scarlet—let me see—in my father's time?"

Scarlet nodded rapidly. "Yes, Your Highness. I was only so high, then; but I remember your father." He smiled. "I used to be terrified by his beard."

"And Baron Kossovar—you remember him too?" asked the prince, with an acid smile.

"I'm afraid not, sir," said Scarlet pleasantly. "I think Baron Kossovar was away from Ruritania at the time."

"I was in exile—a very unjust exile," said the tall baron, coldly. His glance and Prince Mirko's were two rapiers clashing together. Again a constraint fell on the party.

"But, Mr. Scarlet, do tell us all about your murders!" said Mrs. Culverin brightly.

Scarlet grinned boyishly: "They aren't really my murders, Mrs. Culverin. I've just studied a bit—thing fascinated me. I mean—the queer kinds of people who are murderers, and the even queerer kinds who are murderees."

"Murderees?" breathed Mrs. Culverin. "Murderees?"

"Yes—that's what Pearson calls them, in his book." His spectacles flashed. "The people who seem just born and bound to be murdered. Who have the same irresistible attraction for a murderer that—a nice, plump goat has for a hungry tiger."

"I think it's all perfectly horrid!" said Mrs. Culverin delightedly. "Do go on!"

"Well," said Peter Scarlet, "there was the Jamison case, in London. Mrs. Jamison was an ideal murderee. She had an acquaintance, Mrs. Wheen. She knew Mrs. Wheen hated her. She often said so to her friends. She even said, several times, that she was sure Mrs. Wheen would murder her if she got a chance.

And yet, for some unfathomable reason, she kept on going to tea with Mrs. Wheen until, finally, of course, Mrs. Wheen did murder her."

"Served her right," said Mrs. Culverin, with a beaming smile. "I'm sure, if I ever got the idea that anyone would murder me, I—I'd never so much as ask them to dinner again!"

A general chuckle followed her pronouncement. But Peter Scarlet stuck to his guns. "You wouldn't—because you're not a murderee," he said. "Most people aren't—most people never contract elephantiasis, either. But there is a certain proportion of people who do both, and a very definite proportion. Of course,"—he spread out his hands—"there are the normal, casual murders, too. But I'm talking of this one peculiar tendency."

"And you think," said the somber Mr. Lang, "that you could diagnose—a tendency to be murdered, in an otherwise normal person, as a doctor could diagnose illness in a person who looked perfectly well?"

"That's what I'd like to do," said Peter Scarlet ingenuously. "Oh, I know it sounds fantastic, especially from me. But if you could do that and safeguard the murderee, as modern science safeguards the diabetic, why, half our present murders would never occur at all!"

Mrs. Culverin struck in. "But this is marvelous!" she said, her eyes very wide. "Just like numerology and reading your fate in tea leaves, only so much more exciting! Do tell us, dear Mr. Scarlet, because you can, of course—are any of us—murderees?"

Peter Scarlet looked very unhappy. "I couldn't, honestly," he managed to reply at last. "I mean—even if some of you did have murderee tendencies—well, you'd allow a doctor some time for a diagnosis and some rather intimate information, wouldn't you? Well—" He obviously did not wish to go on.

Mrs. Culverin, however, was insistent. "But you could just give us a hint?" she persisted. "The tiniest hint! It would be too wonderful!"

Peter Scarlet's eyes roved nervously up and down the table. "Well—" he said dolefully, and paused.

"You need not be afraid to say it!" said Prince Mirko, abruptly, with unexpected grimness. "I know there would be rejoicing—in many quarters—if I were to die by violence."

"And there are others whose murder would please certain men in my country. Myself, for one," said Baron Kossovar instantly. Again his eyes and the prince's met, with the impact of steel upon steel. The princess's hand went nervously to her breast.

Scarlet did his best to smooth over the awkward moment. "Any statesman's life is always at the mercy of a fanatic's bullet," he said, with a little bob at both Ruritanians. "But, oddly enough, if I had to decide at first glance upon the one person in this room who stood the likeliest chance of meeting a violent end, I should select—Mr. Lang!" he ended unexpectedly, with a nod in that gentleman's direction.

Mr. Lang gave a slight but definite start. For a moment his eyes blazed with anger. Then he gave a loud laugh—and the tension in the room relaxed.

"Not bad at all, for getting out of a hole," he said, still laughing: "I suppose you could be murdered by a lion—if you'd want to call it that—and my last trip out from Nairobi—" He plunged into a big-game reminiscence, and the talk grew general again.

"Only, I wasn't thinking about lions," murmured Peter Scarlet to his plate. But no one at the table overheard him.

Some time later, after the ladies had left the room, Scarlet found himself near the banker.

"You nearly put your foot in it then, my boy," said the latter, in a low voice, glancing down the table at Prince Mirko and Baron Kossovar. "You know what this Ruritanian debt commission means, I suppose?"

"I know the prince and the baron are old enemies," admitted Scarlet, "and that the baron is supposed to look for a return of the monarchy—in Ruritania—while the prince is entirely committed to the new republic."

"Just so," said the banker. "And if Mirko succeeds in his mission, he and the republic win—and Kossovar's political future isn't worth *that!* On the other hand, if he fails, the republic will undoubtedly go to pot, and Kossovar will be the power behind the return of the throne. The way things are at present, the prince seems sure to win, too," he added thoughtfully. "He's going down to Washington, Monday, to clinch it."

On their way to the lesser drawing room where the Royal Russian Midgets, especially brought down for the occasion, were to perform their celebrated though Lilliputian feats of acrobatics before the dancing began, Peter Scarlet was accosted by the saturnine Mr. Lang.

"What the dickens did you mean by picking me out as a likely target for murder?" he queried, in a tone whose attempted lightness was not wholly successful.

Peter Scarlet looked at him steadily. "I wonder," he said. "Have you ever shot a Lipmann's gazelle, Mr. Lang?"

Mr. Lang seemed both amazed and piqued by the odd query. "Lipmann's gazelle?" he said. "Well, I have, as it happens—managed to bag a brace near Victoria Nyanza. But what the deuce has that got to do with my being murdered?"

"It might have a good deal, under certain circumstances," said Peter Scarlet cryptically, and turned away.

He watched with apparent interest the agile feats of the Russian midgets, and the little pantomime of "Beauty and the Beast" that concluded their performance. But within his mind, all the while, certain dim, half-remembered pictures were beginning to take on form and color and perspective. He shook his head, wearily—the pictures weren't very pleasant pictures; and yet he must fit them together, somehow. Only he couldn't quite recollect a few of the most important ones—yet.

At the end of the little entertainment, as the Blue Boy Blue Blowers began to blare out their invitation to the dance from the larger ballroom, he unobtrusively sought the princess.

She looked drawn and tired—the continual friction between her husband and the baron was obviously telling upon her. He made some compliment, to which she replied mechanically; then his glance fell upon an ornament in her hair.

"I am glad you still keep up the old Ruritanian custom, Madame," he said.

She laughed a little. "The dagger, you mean? Yes—all our girls pin their hair with a little dagger on feastdays—you must remember." She withdrew the small, needle-pointed, silver stiletto from the dark coils of her coiffure, so that he might examine it. "It is a family thing," she said, the weariness returning to her face. "You must have seen many like it in Ruritania."

Her expression changed, she lowered her voice. "Did you mean what you said tonight—that Mr. Lang was in greater danger of his life here than my husband?" she asked with a sudden, queer intensity, as they paused on their way to the door.

Peter Scarlet looked at her with an expression of humble surprise. "I didn't say quite that," he said embarrassedly. "Do you mean that you have any reason to suspect that . . . your husband is in danger here?"

She made a nervous, pathetic little gesture with her hands.

"Oh no, no, no!" she said hurriedly. "Oh no—it is impossible—impossible—and yet—"

Baron Kossovar came up to them. "May I have the honor of the first dance, Madame?" he asked, bowing profoundly as the princess replaced the dagger in her hair.

The evening wore on, the Blue Boy Blue Blowers outdid themselves in miracles of syncopation; at last Peter Scarlet found himself ready for bed. Alone in his room, he undressed for the night. Then, with the same neat, unhurried swiftness, he dressed himself completely again. It was no use—he couldn't sleep till one question at least had been decided in his mind. He left his room and, walking with a singular lack of noise for so ingenuous and blundering a young man, made his way toward the wing of the house where the Ruritanians were quartered.

Prince and Princess Mirko's suite was on the second floor; Baron Kossovar's, above, on the third. The house itself was a curious example of architectural misalliance between Long Island and Spain. Odd, useless balconies jutted from it at unexpected corners; there was one at the end of the corridor which Scarlet now traversed, and another, he knew, outside the princess's bedroom.

As Scarlet came down the corridor, walking more loudly now, a low voice challenged him suddenly. "Who's that?" said a fierce whisper.

Scarlet stood perfectly still. "It's Scarlet, Mr. Lang."

There was a sound of breath taken in. "How in—" said the low voice. Then it changed its tone. "I thought your room was in the other wing of the house," it said.

Scarlet smiled to himself in the dim shadows of the corridor. "I thought yours was too, Mr. Lang," he said easily. "But I felt restless, couldn't get to sleep."

"So did I," said Lang, unconvincingly. "Well—I suppose we'd both of us better get back to bed."

"I suppose so," admitted Scarlet, strolling on to the end of the corridor. He stepped out upon the balcony for a moment and glanced up.

"H'm," he said, "that iron stair must go to the third-floor balcony. Convenient little dingus for a burglar, wouldn't you say?"

"Infernally convenient," admitted Lang, with a certain tenseness. "Well—" This time his hand fell definitely upon Scarlet's shoulder, and the latter permitted himself to be led back toward his own wing of the house. Mr. Lang paused outside a door halfway down the Ruritanian corridor.

"Well, here I am," he said. "Good night, Scarlet. And I wouldn't go wandering about at night if I were you. It isn't done—take the word of an older man."

Scarlet seemed entirely unperturbed by the rebuke. He walked noisily back to his own room and waited there for some time. Then he emerged again, slipped up to the third floor, retraced his way to the Ruritanian wing, and concealed himself on the third-floor balcony. He had hardly done so when the tall figure of Baron Kossovar ascended from the second floor and entered his quarters. Scarlet smiled, and devoted his attention to another point. A little while later his vigil was rewarded by a curious sight that gave him much food for thought. But it was not until half an hour at least had passed that he heard the scream from the second floor.

Twenty seconds later he was outside the door of Prince Mirko's suite—but the mysterious Mr. Lang was there before him, now rapping upon the door with a sort of muffled fury, now trying to force the lock with what looked suspiciously like a skeleton key.

He saw Scarlet and wheeled. A revolver glittered suddenly in his other hand. "You infernal meddler—" he began furiously, motioning him back; but Scarlet continued to advance.

"Oh, shut up!" he said, somewhat tiredly. "I know you're a detective—known it for hours. You get in that room—I'll keep the others back."

Lang gave him one sharp, very searching glance, then turned back to his work with the key. After a moment the lock yielded—the door flew open.

Scarlet, glancing in at the room over Lang's shoulder, felt the bristles at the back of his neck begin to rise. Prince Mirko of Ruritania lay on his face in the middle of the luxurious sitting room, dead, with the hilt of a silver dagger protruding from his neck. The princess knelt beside him. Her hands were stained with his blood, her eyes were staring, and the silver dagger ornament was gone from her hair. A tiny handkerchief lay on the floor, and a little white dog ran in circles about the body, moaning and whining.

As Scarlet was turning away, the princess succeeded in rolling the body over on its back. There was a curious incision on the dead man's forehead—two little slashes that formed a capital T.

When the initial confusion of the event had somewhat subsided, a strange court of inquiry met in the disfigured sitting room. Luckily, Mrs. Culverin's house was huge, and many of the guests had not been aroused at all. Those who had, Peter Scarlet sent back to bed again, with the news that Princess Mirko's maid had suffered a minor accident. As for Mrs. Culverin herself, she had risen to the crisis astonishingly, and she now sat patting Princess Mirko's limp hand with a certain sturdy kindliness that made Peter Scarlet like her better than he ever had before. Baron Kossovar, Lang, and Scarlet completed the party.

Mrs. Culverin rose at last. "Well, Mr. Lang," she said, "the matter is entirely in your hands. I'll do and say whatever you tell me. Meanwhile, I'll go back to my room, unless, Your Highness, you—" She turned to the princess.

"No," murmured the latter weakly. "No, thank you. You are very kind. But—"

"I know," said Mrs. Culverin. She gathered her wrapper about her. "Oh, one thing," she said to Lang, "if I might make a suggestion?"

"Yes, Mrs. Culverin?"

"You'll find that young man useful," she said, indicating Scarlet. "His talk about murders may be all bosh—but he knows Ruritanian." She swept away.

Lang turned to Scarlet. "You do speak and understand Ruritanian?"

Scarlet nodded. "Yes, I've kept it up fairly well."

Lang considered. "Well, I suppose you'd better stay," he said at last. "Only—no interference—no amateur detecting! And, naturally, if your father was in the Service, you understand the gravity of—"

Scarlet's face was very grave. "I do. And I shouldn't think of—interfering. But—I could make a suggestion? If one occurred to me?"

"You could," said Lang grimly. Scarlet's spectacles blinked.

Lang turned to the baron and the princess. "I have no wish to put impertinent questions," he said, with a good deal of dignity. "But you must realize, as I do, the very delicate position in which this murder has placed not only everyone in this house but the Governments of two countries. Prince Mirko was in this country under the protection of the United States. He was murdered while under that protection. Naturally, in view of the diplomatic issues involved, this inquiry cannot follow the normal course of such inquiries. But—I take it you both are willing to help me in finding the murderer?"

The princess stared at him, dry-eyed. "My husband's murderer must be found," she said in a dry, toneless voice.

Baron Kossovar stiffened. "Prince Mirko was my political enemy," he said; "but I am no less anxious than you, Mr. Lang, to find his murderer."

Lang received their statements gravely. "Thank you," he said. "Now—you'll pardon me if I'm frank—there are three ways in which Prince Mirko might have been murdered: He might have been murdered by an intruder from without. He might have been murdered by a servant or a guest. Or—"

"Say it," said the princess, in a dry, terrible voice. "He might have been murdered by me, his wife."

"Or me," said Baron Kossovar rigidly.

Lang made a little bow. "I regret the necessity," he said; "but we must take every supposition into account. First: the intruder from without. In the first place, my men—and they're skilled men—have been guarding the gates and so forth since Prince Mirko's arrival. It would have been practically impossible for an intruder to get past them. In addition,"—he stepped toward the window—"the windows of this room and of Prince Mirko's bedroom were all locked on the inside when we found the body; and it is a sheer fifteen-foot drop from the windows to the ground."

"Also," said the princess, still in that toneless voice, "I had locked the door from my part of the suite earlier in the evening. When I unlocked it again, it was to find my husband dead." She shuddered.

"I remember," said Lang noncommittally. "You wished to be alone?"

"For a time, yes—my husband and the baron were talking business; I did not wish to disturb them. Then later, I heard the dog barking and came to say good night to my husband—and then—"

"Yes," said Lang. "But even supposing the intruder had flown through the walls and got in—how did he get out? We made a thorough search. Of course he might have jumped from one of your bedroom windows, Princess, supposing you did not lock the door as you say you did."

"I did lock the door," said the Princess. "And—my maid, and myself, of course, were in our part of the suite the whole time. He could not have concealed himself or escaped."

"Exactly," said Lang. "Therefore, if there was an intruder, he is still here. But he isn't here. Therefore, Prince Mirko was not murdered by an intruder from without."

He paused. The logic of his explanation seemed inevitable. Scarlet took the opportunity to emerge from his silence.

"May I ask a question?" he said diffidently. Lang nodded.

"You didn't hear any sound of a struggle—a fall—either you or your maid?" he queried owlishly.

The princess seemed greatly perturbed. "No," she muttered. "That is strange—strange—yet the door was thick."

"Very thick," said Scarlet agreeably. "I wonder you heard the dog through it. Yet you did hear the dog barking."

The princess moved her hands. "Yes," she said weakly. "But that was the first we heard. It is—strange—yes, strange!"

It did not seem so strange to Lang. By the expression on his face it obviously seemed either impossible or untrue. But he resumed his questioning, with a scrupulous, heavy fairness.

"Then," he said, "we come to the valet and the maid. The valet's room did not communicate directly with the rest of the suite. I saw him go out before Baron Kossovar came to talk with

Prince Mirko. He could not have entered again without my seeing him. So we may dismiss the valet. As for the maid—you insist, Princess, that she was under your eye all the time?"

"I do," said the Princess, in a ghost of a voice.

"Very well," said Lang. "Then we must dismiss the maid. As for another guest, or servant, getting in from the corridor—I was there on guard. I would have stopped and questioned anyone who came."

"Yes," said Scarlet; "you stopped and questioned me."

"And so you come to us," said the princess bluntly. Her voice rose. "Oh, it is terrible—terrible!" she said. "You suspect me—you have reason to suspect me! My husband is killed with the little dagger I wear in my hair—I do not hear him killed, though I hear a dog bark afterward—you find me beside his body when you come—you find a handkerchief too, a woman's handkerchief—you find—" her voice broke—"the mark on his face—And yet, I swear before God, I did not murder my husband!"

Baron Kossovar rose, his eyes burning. "But if you must suspect her, you must suspect me more!" he cried. "I was with him and we were talking, sometimes angrily, till half an hour before you found him dead. I had reason to kill him if I wished. I might have killed him—pretended to say good night to him at the door, so you could hear me and think he was still alive, and then gone back to my room, to be aroused by the news of his murder!"

"Only," said Scarlet quietly, "in that case, after you had said good night to the dead man, the dead man got up and locked the door after you."

"Well, he might have had strength enough left to do that," said the baron impatiently. "Or it might have been done somehow else or—" Then his head drooped suddenly. "No, it is useless," he said; "I did not kill Mirko; I cannot pretend I did. But you should not suspect her, when you have better reason to suspect me."

"Ah, my friend, you are very noble," said the princess, lightly touching his hand with hers.

"You're both noble," said Scarlet dispassionately; "but you're both very silly. There is another possible murderer that Mr. Lang has not mentioned."

"And that is?" said the latter with a dangerous calm.

"Mr. Lang," said Scarlet demurely. "He might have got in with his masterkey after the baron left, murdered the prince, relocked the door, and—"

"But what reason would I have to murder Prince Mirko?"

"Oh, you might have had a dozen reasons," said Scarlet airily. "But you didn't. Because you wouldn't have used a dagger. You'd have shot him—or killed him with your hands—in the good old Anglo-Saxon way. On the other hand," he continued reflectively, "Madame is a Ruritanian and might very possibly use a dagger—especially this one." He lifted the stained weapon delicately from the table. "But Madame asserts that she lost her dagger-ornament earlier in the evening and did not see it again till she found it in her husband's body."

"Yes," said the princess desperately, "that is true. The dagger fell from my hair. I do not know where. I do not know how. But at first, when I found it again"—she shivered—"I did not see how it could be mine."

Scarlet blinked. "I see. And then—the handkerchief." He replaced the dagger and took up a tiny square of fine linen. "Obviously not a man's handkerchief, from its size, and"—he sniffed it—"scented. But Madame asserts that the handkerchief is not hers, that she found it beside the body."

"Yes, I have never seen it before. It is not mine," said the princess, in the voice of an automaton, staring down at her feet as if she saw them already enmeshed in the net which Scarlet's diffident sentences slowly wove about her. Scarlet went on:

"Third point. The slash on the prince's forehead—the slash like a capital T. Well, that rather points to the baron, on the whole. At least, Mr. Lang, who has had great experience with Italian criminals, has informed us that a similar T-shaped slash is a common occurrence in political assassinations—the 'T' being for 'Tradditore' or 'Traitor.' Now, the baron's political views might easily lead him to consider the prince a traitor to their mutual country. On the other hand, the T might be a blind—employed for the purposes of argument by Madame. Curious clues all of them; and yet the most curious thing of all is—that every one points in the same direction—"

"I'm afraid they do," said Mr. Lang heavily. "Princess Mirko—" he began in an official voice.

"But I did not murder my husband!" said the princess, with a terrified gasp.

"One moment," said Scarlet bashfully. "Think of the nature of the wound. The prince was a tall man—the wound was high on his neck and slanted down—such a wound as would suggest a tall assassin—woman or man. Now the baron and madame are both tall, but—"

"Stop!" said the baron suddenly. He turned to the princess. "It's no use, Nadja," he said. "One of us must speak to protect you. Gentlemen—Prince Mirko's wife was not even in this suite when her husband was murdered. She was on the balcony of my suite; I had asked her to come there—to talk of a private matter—"

The princess put her head in her hands with a gesture of utter defeat. "Oh, Stanislas, Stanislas!" she sobbed, "you have ruined everything. They will never believe me now!"

"Yes; I think that clinches it, if that's true," said Lang with austere triumph. "Gives a better motive than politics. And they both killed him. Princess Mirko—"

But Scarlet cut in before he could finish his sentence. "Oh, what the baron says is true enough," he said briskly. "I saw and heard them from the other balcony. Only your deduction's wrong Lang. It wasn't a love affair—she went because she was worried about her husband. But why do you keep on calling her 'Princess Mirko'? She isn't really Princess Mirko, you know," he went on in tones of shy patience.

The princess raised terror-stricken eyes to his. Lang gasped.

"You mean that woman isn't the prince's wife?"

"Oh, yes; she was the prince's wife, right enough—she merely isn't and wasn't Princess Mirko. Have you never heard of a morganatic marriage? If she had been a princess," he concluded thoughtfully, "the murder, most probably, would never have been committed."

"I don't see why?" said Lang, with the air of a baited bull. "And I don't see why it makes any difference whether the princess was a princess or not. Someone murdered Prince Mirko—if it wasn't this woman here—what woman was it?"

"No woman murdered Prince Mirko," said Scarlet quietly.

"A man, then? What man? The baron?"

"Nor was the murderer of Prince Mirko a man, as we think of men."

"Well, then, in heaven's name, what was it?" cried Lang, in a sort of fury. "A ghost that walks through the walls? A gorilla? An act of God?"

Scarlet's eyes, behind his spectacles, danced with little points of light. "On that point," he said, with deceptive meekness, "I should like to take the evidence of the dog." He turned quickly to the princess. "The little white dog your husband was so fond of," he said. "The dog we found running about when we came in—do you remember when he was brought back to your suite this evening?"

"Why, yes," said the princess, with obvious bewilderment. "Stepan, the valet, brought him up from the kennels when we came back after the dancing; my husband liked to have him in his room at night."

"Ah," said Scarlet, obviously laboring under some mounting excitement. He flung open the door of the princess's room and whistled. The dog came bounding in, ran about for a moment, sniffing, then, lifting his head toward the ceiling, gave a long, doleful howl. The princess burst into tears.

"What in thunder do you think you'll get from the dog?" queried Lang. "And we know he's tracked up the carpet," he added as Scarlet stooped to examine certain dull red paw marks on the floor. Scarlet straightened up, his whole body alive and tense. "Yes, we know he's tracked up the carpet," he said, in a voice like a trumpet; "but what we don't know is how he tracked up the wall!" And he pointed at a spot on the glazed wallpaper above a tall painted wardrobe—a muddy spot, near the ceiling, that looked singularly like the imprint of a dog's muddy paw.

For a moment none of the others could believe their eyes— and the world seemed to slide and alter into a distorted and monstrous cosmos, where a little white dog could run up a wall like a fly, and a tall prince might be struck dead with a dagger wielded by neither a man's nor a woman's hand. Then Scarlet threw open the doors of the painted wardrobe. There was nothing there but an overcoat on a hook, some hats on a shelf above, and a large leather hat trunk beside the hats.

"We've looked through that wardrobe already," called Lang.

"No," said Scarlet; "you've only looked at it. For instance,"— he shook out the overcoat—"here are the same kind of paw marks there are on the wall, only here the marks are bloody. While, as for the hat trunk—"

The dog burst into a fury of barking that drowned the rest of the sentence.

"For heaven's sake!" shouted Lang, in a final exasperation, "you don't expect to find the murderer of Prince Mirko inside a brown leather hatbox, do you?"

"That," said Scarlet, quite unruffled, "is precisely what I expect to find!"

He started gingerly to lift the hat trunk down from its shelf. As he did so, its lid popped open like the lid of a jack-in-the-box, and something bright and tiny struck at his eyes. There was an intense little scuffle for an instant; then Scarlet was holding out for Lang's inspection a kicking, fighting little creature hardly three feet high. The thing was grotesquely disguised in the stage-garb of a midget Beast, and its distorted lips poured forth a stream of denunciation in a hissing, clucking language that Lang did not understand.

"Permit me to present the murderer of Prince Mirko," said Scarlet, with a boyish flourish.

"Well, I'll be—" said Lang, with a long whistle. "One of those Russian midgets that played the pantomime! But what is he talking—Russian?"

"No," said Scarlet pensively, "Ruritanian. He's telling the princess—if we may give her her title—that she was always a bad sister to him, and he's glad he killed her husband; and she's telling him she hopes he hangs, if he *is* her brother. You see, the whole was what one might call a family affair," he added, with a touch of embarrassment.

Some time later, over cigarettes and full glasses, Lang and Peter Scarlet watched the dawn brighten the window of the latter's chamber, and discussed the extraordinary events of the night.

"But I don't see yet—" said Lang, and paused.

"Oh, I was very lucky," said Scarlet. "Very. Knowing Ruritanian—and some of the previous story. And then, hearing the princess and the baron on the balcony. Though, of course, the minute I saw the weapon I knew the baron hadn't committed the crime."

"Why?" said Lang, with heavy patience. Scarlet considered. He flushed.

"Sounds absurd—my trying to lay down the law to you," he said. "But—the baron had motive enough; but he wouldn't have killed that way. He might hack his enemy to bits with a cavalry saber; he wouldn't stab him with a toy. It wasn't in character—as I'd heard of it, and knew it in other Ruritanian nobles of his sort."

"The princess might have stabbed, though," said Lang thoughtfully.

"Oh yes—she'd be a stabber, if she'd be anything," agreed Scarlet promptly. "But I also happened to know that she was devoted to her husband. In fact, she'd as much as told me that she was worried for his safety, earlier in the evening. I know now she was worried on two counts: Baron Kossovar, and the brother she thought she'd recognized among the midgets. She wasn't quite sure it was he—she hadn't seen him for years and he was made up as the Beast in the play. That was the real reason she had her talk with the baron above—though the baron used to be in love with her, right enough. She wanted to try and find out if the baron had recognized any of the midgets, either. She didn't dare ask her husband."

"Why not?"

"Well, that's a long story. I'll cut it as short as possible. But they *are* blood brother and sister."

"That beautiful woman and the little deformity? It seems incredible."

"Not as incredible as it sounds. There have been numerous cases—one or two normal children in a family of giants or dwarfs, and vice versa. But Nadja was the only normal one in her family, except for a brother who died. The other two were midgets—two brothers. The family were small farmers, but proud as Lucifer. They'd been great people, long back. Well, Mirko came along and fell in love with Nadja, so much in love he was ready to make her is morganatic wife; but he couldn't stick her family—one can see why. And she was in love with him; so she married him. But her being willing to be his morganatic wife struck her family in their sorest point—their pride."

"They got ready to make trouble; and Mirko, very quietly, had them shipped to England—saw they got an allowance, but were never to come back to Ruritania. This was just the midget brothers, the old people were dead. So the midget brothers—they hadn't thought much of Nadja when they had her; in fact, they'd been pretty spiteful to her; but now she was their wronged sister—they were going to get Mirko if they ever had a chance. Then the war came along, and one brother died. The one who was left organized a troupe of performing midgets—when Mirko's allowance stopped coming after Ruritania was invaded by the Germans—and brought them over to America after the war."

"And—he got into the room—"

"With the help of the others. Bribed them, probably. You saw them do their living tower on each other's shoulders. Well, they did it for him under the window, and it was just high enough to get him up to the window sill. The window was open—the valet locked it later. Then our friend hid on top of that wardrobe—he's an excellent acrobat for his size—and he probably swarmed up to the shelf by way of the overcoat and so on. That was how he got the mark on the wall. It looked like a paw mark because he was still wearing his Beast's costume from the pantomime—perhaps for a blind, perhaps because he didn't bother to change."

"While the marks on the carpet?"

"Were some of them his and some of them the dog's. The handkerchief was his, too; it was scented, because, like many midgets, he was very vain. And the dagger that actually killed Mirko was his—one of a pair of family heirlooms. The princess was speaking the truth when she said she lost hers—it fell from her hair while she was on Kossovar's balcony. She got up there without your seeing her, by the same sort of little stair there was on the balcony you and I visited. And her maid was waiting for her on her own balcony. That's why neither of them heard the prince fall when he was killed—or cry out, if he did."

"I see; and, of course, the actual attack was entirely unexpected."

"Entirely. The little fiend waited with monumental patience till the prince was alone. Then, at some moment when the prince passed fairly near the wardrobe, he jumped at the back of his neck like a striking snake. You see, we deduced that, because the wound was high and slanted downward, it must have been made by someone tall. But put a short man on stilts and he's as tall as a giant. Our friend, with the aid of the wardrobe, was much taller than the prince. Then, when he'd killed his man, he marked him with the T—used his own pocketknife that time."

"T for traitor?"

"No; that was where your Italians misled you. The Ruritanian word for traitor begins with a J. But the Ruritanian word for seducer does begin with a T—and that was what he meant. That was what finally put me on the right track—that and the dog."

"I couldn't see why you made so much fuss about the dog!"

"I didn't see it for a long time—and then everything hitched together, with a sort of flash. The dog hadn't been there when the midget first got in the room, he was brought into the bedroom by the valet when the Mirkos returned. And he stopped our little murderer from getting away by the bedroom window—his friends must have been ready to catch him in a blanket or something. Your men wouldn't have found them, except by great luck; they were too small.

"Well, after the murder, the midget made for the bedroom and the dog jumped at him—there are paw marks on the bedroom door. He couldn't get to the window—the dog wouldn't let him—so he scuttled back to the wardrobe, climbed up the overcoat, and stowed away in the hatbox. The dog found his master's body and stopped to whine at it; then he turned back to the midget, who had shut the wardrobe doors from the inside and was safe. But the dog kept barking—and the next minute or so, the princess came back and heard him. Then—you know the rest."

Lang smiled a trifle dubiously. "And I used to have a fairly good conceit of my own reasoning powers," he said somberly. "Well—but there's just one more thing—"

"Yes?"

"For heaven's sake tell me how I gave myself away to you—on the big-game-hunter stuff. It passed everyone else."

Scarlet blushed to the tips of his ears. "Well, there had to be somebody like you guarding Prince Mirko," he said. "And you were the likeliest candidate—the rest were too old or too flabby. So I tried you on the murderee idea. Naturally, if you were what I thought you were, you'd run into more chances of being murdered than the rest of us. And you played up marvelously—but you couldn't help blinking for just a second. So then I asked you about Lipmann's gazelle—and when you said you'd shot a couple I knew, whatever you hunted, it wasn't African big-game!"

"But what the dickens is the matter with Lipmann's gazelle?" queried Lang heatedly. "Isn't it an animal you shoot? It sounded all right."

"Old man," said Scarlet a trifle sadly, "it isn't an animal at all, at least to my knowledge. I made it up that minute—out of my own little head!

BLACK MURDER
Anthony Boucher

Despite having a very long and successful career in both the mystery and science fiction genres, all of Anthony Boucher's detective novels were published in the 1930s and 1940s, beginning with *The Case of the Seven of Calvary* (1937), which was followed by four novels featuring Los Angeles private detective Fergus O'Breen, including *The Case of the Crumpled Knave* (1939) and *The Case of the Baker Street Irregulars* (1940). As H.H. Holmes, he wrote two novels in which an unlikely detective, Sister Ursula of the Sisters of Martha Bethany, assists Lieutenant Marshall of the Los Angeles Police Department: *Nine Times Nine* (1940) and *Rocket to the Morgue* (1942), which was selected for the Haycraft-Queen Definitive Library of Detective-Crime Mystery Fiction.

However, Boucher, the pseudonym of William Anthony Parker White (1911-1968), better known under the pseudonyms he used for his career as a writer of both mystery and science fiction, had numerous other accomplishments. Under his real name, as well as under his pseudonyms, he established a reputation as a first-rate critic of opera and literature, including general fiction, mystery, and science fiction. He also was an accomplished editor, anthologist, playwright, and an eminent translator of French, Spanish, and Portuguese, becoming the first to translate Jorge Luis Borges into English.

He wrote prolifically in the 1940s, producing at least three scripts a week for such popular radio programs as *Sherlock Holmes*, *The Adventures of Ellery Queen*, and *The Case Book of Gregory Hood*. He also wrote numerous science fiction and fantasy stories, reviewed books in those genres as H.H. Holmes for the *San Francisco Chronicle* and *Chicago Sun-Times*, and produced notable anthologies in the science fiction, fantasy, and mystery genres.

As Boucher (rhymes with "voucher"), he served as the long-time mystery reviewer of *The New York Times* (1951-1968, with eight hundred fifty-two columns to his credit) and *Ellery Queen's Mystery Magazine* (1957-1968). He was one of the founders of the Mystery Writers of America in 1946. The annual World Mystery Convention is familiarly known as the Bouchercon in his honor, and the Anthony Awards are also named for him.

"Black Murder" was originally published in the September 1943 issue of *Ellery Queen's Mystery Magazine*; it was first collected in *Exeunt Murderers* (Carbondale, Illinois, Southern Illinois University Press, 1983).

Black Murder
Anthony Boucher

IN PEACETIME the whole Shaw case could never have happened. As Officer Mulroon said later: the first attack would have been passed off as natural illness, and besides there never would have been a first attack.

But police work in the spring of 1943 was full of cases that could never have happened in peacetime. Detective Lieutenant Donald MacDonald (Homicide, L.A.P.D.) was slowly becoming reconciled to the recruiting officer who had dissuaded him from joining the Navy. He was necessary here on his job, even though he sometimes wished that he were back in a patrolman's uniform. His plain clothes did draw occasional sardonic stares.

Even the stripe and a half of Lieutenant (j.g.) Warren Humphreys made him uniform-conscious and reminded him of his frustrated enlistment. But the slight bitterness was effaced by the knowledge that in this case the Navy had had to turn to him because he was a trained specialist who knew about murderers.

"We don't believe in coincidence in the Navy," Lieutenant Humphreys had barked over the phone. "When I'm sent out here to pick up specifications on a sub detector, and find the inventor's suddenly come down with an attack having all the symptoms of arsenic poisoning, I want police action. And quick."

Lieutenant MacDonald remembered when Warren Humphreys had been his favorite political commentator, and hoped that he diagnosed poisonings more accurately than he had the strength of the Red Army.

Apparently he did. At least the police doctor made the same snap diagnosis after an examination of the comatose inventor, and commended the naval officer for his prompt administration of a mustard emetic followed by milk of magnesia.

"Best I could do with what's in an ordinary house," Lieutenant Humphreys said with gruff modesty. "Got to know a thing or two about poison treatment in Naval Intelligence. You never know . . ."

"You've made a good start; he ought to pull through. Keep him quiet and give him lots of milk. I'll send out a male nurse. You can call the lab about six, MacDonald. I'll try to have a full report on these specimens by then."

It was now one forty-five. Humphreys had arrived at one and phoned the police almost immediately. The attack, which the household had taken for ordinary digestive trouble, had struck Harrison Shaw at twelve-thirty, after his usual lunch: a tartar sandwich and a bottle of beer.

"The dietetics boys'd say he had it coming to him," MacDonald observed.

"But it was what he always ate, Lieutenant," the blind man said. "And it seemed to sustain his energy admirably—enough at least to interest the Navy, if not to bring in any marked practical rewards."

The slight note of bitterness toward the—professional habit made him think "deceased"—toward the victim caused Mac-Donald to look at the blind man more closely. He saw a tall, lean man of fifty, with a marked resemblance to the poisoned inventor save for the sightless stare and the one-sided smile that never left his face. He wore a gray suit of unusually fine tailoring and unusually great age.

The suit was like the house. One of those old family mansions in the West Adams district near U.S.C. You saw it from the outside and expected sumptuous furnishings and a flock of servants. You came in and found a barn, and not a servant in sight.

"Let me get the picture straight," MacDonald said. "The medical report was the first essential. Now that that's given us something to sink our teeth into, pending the lab analysis, there's plenty more to cover. I gather you're Mr. Shaw's cousin?"

The blind man went on smiling. "Second cousin, yes. Ira Beaumont, at your service, Lieutenant."

"You've been living with Mr. Shaw for how long?"

"Mr. Shaw has been living with me for some three years. Ever since I inherited this house from a distant relative of ours. He felt, and with some justice, that he had as great a right to the inheritance as I, and I was glad to give him some of the space I could not possibly use up in this white elephant."

"And the rest of the household?"

"First my cousin's mother came to look after him. Then his laboratory assistant joined our happy household. I began to feel a trifle like the old woman who is so horribly moved in on in the play *Kind Lady*."

"That's all in the house?"

"There was a couple who cooked and kept house, but we could not compete with Lockheed and Vega in wage scales. Mrs. Shaw now takes their place." He rose and crossed the room to a humidor. "Do you gentlemen care for cigars?"

"No thanks, not now." MacDonald noted admiringly the ease with which the blind man moved unaided about his own house. There's something splendid about the overcoming of handicaps . . . a splendor, he reflected, that we'll have many chances to watch in the years to come. . . . "Then Mrs. Shaw prepared your cousin's lunch today?"

"As usual. I believe you'll find her in the kitchen now; I know she'll be thinking that the family must eat tonight, whatever has happened."

Lieutenant Humphreys tagged along. The prospect of a Watson from Naval Intelligence somewhat awed the police detective.

"There can be only one motive," the Naval Watson muttered.

"Somebody had to keep him from delivering those specifications to me. And if you can find them, officer, I'd almost be willing to write off the murder as unsolved."

"We don't even know yet that they're lost," MacDonald pointed out. "When Shaw's himself again, he may hand them straight over."

But Humphreys shook his head. "They're good," he said cryptically. "They wouldn't slip up on that."

There was a sudden slam of a door as they entered the kitchen. Mrs. Shaw, MacDonald thought, was almost too good to be true. Aged housedress, apron, white hair and all, she was the casting director's dream of Somebody's Mother. But at the moment she was nervous, flustered—almost guilty-looking.

Wordlessly the Lieutenant crossed the kitchen and opened a pantry door. He saw, at a rough count, a good hundred cans of rationed goods. He laughed. "You needn't worry, Mrs. Shaw. This isn't my brand of snooping; I shan't report you for hoarding."

Mrs. Shaw straightened her apron, poked at her escapist hair, and looked relieved. "It's really all for the good of the war," she explained. "My boy's doing important work that'll save thousands of lives, and he's going to get what he wants to eat whether somebody in Washington says so or not. Why, if he was a Russian inventor they'd be making him take it."

"We didn't see a thing, did we, Lieutenant?"

Humphreys made a gruff noise. It was obviously hard for him to resist a brief official lecture.

"Now about this attack of your son's, Mrs. Shaw . . ."

"I just can't understand that, Lieutenant. I simply can't. Harry never was a one to complain about his food. He liked lots of it, but it always set right fine."

"Mr. Beaumont said he always ate this same lunch?"

"Yes, sir. A white bread sandwich with raw ground round, with a little salt and Worcestershire sauce, and some slices of raw onion. And he drank beer with it. I can't say I'd cotton to it myself, but it's what Harry liked."

"Where was the beer kept?"

"In a little icebox in his laboratory. He always opened it himself. All I did was fix the sandwich."

"And bring a glass for the beer?"

"No. He liked it out of the bottle, just like his father before him."

"And where did you keep the meat, Mrs. Shaw?"

"I didn't. I mean not today. It didn't get kept anyplace. I didn't get out to shop till late and I bought it down at the little market on the corner and brought it right back here and made the sandwich."

"And the onion?"

"I peeled a fresh one, of course."

"And the salt and the sauce?"

MacDonald impounded the shaker and bottle indicated. "We'll analyze these, of course. Although no one would take the chance of leaving them here in the kitchen where anybody might. . . . And what did you do with the sandwich after you made it?"

"What should I do, officer? I took it right up to Harry and now he's . . . Oh, officer, he is going to be all right, isn't he?"

"He will be. And you can thank Lieutenant Humphreys here that he will."

"Oh, I do thank you, Lieutenant. I didn't know what to think at first with Harry so sick and you running around here and wanting mustard and things, but now I see the good Lord sent you to save my Harry."

Humphreys looked relieved when MacDonald cut through her embarrassing gratitude. "Thank you very much, Mrs. Shaw. Now do you know where we'd find your son's assistant?"

As they walked down the long empty hall to a crudely improvised laboratory, MacDonald said, "Did you ever see such deliberate suicide before?"

"Suicide? But great Scott, man, you don't mean that Shaw—"

"Lord no! I mean Mrs. Shaw. She's told a specific, detailed story that doesn't leave a single loophole. Unless analysis turns up something in those seasonings, there's only one person who could conceivably have poisoned Shaw. And that, by her own admission, is his mother."

The assistant, so far nameless, introduced himself as John Firebrook. He was a little man with a thick neck and a round, worried face. "I don't believe it, Lieutenant," he began flatly. "Nobody could want to kill a fine man like Mr. Shaw. It must have been something he ate."

"Sure. It was with Mrs. Crippen too."

"And there are too many people at large in this world," the naval officer added, "who think killing fine men is just what the doctor ordered. Especially fine men who invent sub detectors. And how much do you know about that detector, Firebrook?"

"I know the principles, of course, sir. I helped to work them out, though Mr. Shaw didn't trust even me with the final details. You remember the man recently who made a seventy-nine cent bombsight out of junk? Well, ours is not perhaps quite in that class, but comparable. It consists of

(censored)

Humphreys nodded happily. "Brilliant, Firebrook. Brilliant. What we need is men like Shaw who can make something out of apparently nothing. If this lives up to expectations, I think the Navy can promise him plenty more jobs."

"If the Navy will promise us a decent laboratory and materials, we will be happy. It's fine to make something out of nothing, Lieutenant, but it is nice to work with something too. We have kept hoping that Mr. Shaw would receive a large sum of money from a great-uncle; but the old gentleman has defied all the statistics of life-expectancy. If this detector is a failure . . . I do not know what will become of us," he added simply.

"Do you know where these specifications are?" MacDonald asked.

"I do not. We could not afford a safe that would be any real protection. Mr. Shaw had his own plans which even I did not know."

"It'll be simple," said Humphreys. "Call your men, Lieutenant, and we'll search the whole place, starting with this lab."

"No!" said Firebrook sharply.

"And why not?"

"You see this laboratory? It is cheap, it is insufficient. But it is in perfect working order. I keep it so. I will not have hordes of police trampling through it and destroying that order."

"Even with warrants?" MacDonald murmured.

"Even with warrants." Firebrook's little eyes flashed. "Gentlemen, you will not search this laboratory."

The officers stared at him for a moment, but his defiant gaze was steady. "My, my!" Lieutenant Humphreys said at last. "The racial passion for order . . . Very well. You'll be seeing me again—Herr Feuerbach."

And that was the end of the first phase of the Shaw case.

There was nothing more that Lieutenant MacDonald could accomplish at the rundown mansion of Ira Beaumont until he had the report from the laboratory and could talk to the inventor himself. He stationed Mulroon to watch the sickroom pending the arrival of the police nurse, and Shurman and Avila to guard the outside of the house. Lieutenant Humphreys appointed himself part of the guard too.

"I'm not leaving this house till I hear from Shaw's own lips where the specifications are. And I'm keeping an eye on that German."

MacDonald drove slowly back to headquarters. He didn't like this Shaw business. It was too wrongly simple. There was only one possible suspect, and that one was impossible.

Greed can do strange things to people (was there a lead in that legacy expected from the great-uncle?), and perverted political fanaticism can do even stranger; but could a mother kill her son even from such motives? Worse yet, psychologically, could she kill him by means of her own food, while she calmly broke all rationing regulations to provide him with that food?

He didn't like it. And he found, as he mused, that he had overshot headquarters. He was driving out North Main Street. He was, in fact, just about opposite the Chula Negra Café.

Lieutenant MacDonald grinned at himself. It was that kind of a case, wasn't it?

The Noble scandal had been long before MacDonald's time on the force. He'd gathered it piecemeal from the older men: a crooked captain who had connections, and a brilliantly promising detective lieutenant who'd taken the rap for him when things broke, losing his job just when his wife needed money for an operation . . .

Nick Noble had been devoted to his wife and his profession. When both were gone, there was nothing left. Nothing but cheap sherry that dulled the sharpness of reality enough to make it bearable. Nothing but that and the curious infallible machine that was Nick Noble's mind.

That couldn't stop working, even when Noble's profession no longer needed it. Present it with a problem, and the gears meshed into action behind those pale blue eyes. A few of the oldtimers on the force were wise enough to know how invariably right the answers were. Twice MacDonald himself had seen the Noble mind trace pattern in chaos. And this was just what Noble would like: only one possibility, and that impossible. The screwier the better.

Screwball Division, L.A.P.D., they called him.

He was in the third booth on the left, as usual. So far as MacDonald had ever learned, he lived, ate, and slept there . . . if indeed he did ever eat or sleep. There was a water glass of sherry in front of him. His hair and his skin were white as things that live in caves. A white hand swatted at the sharp thin nose. Then the pale blue eyes slowly focused on the detective and he smiled a little.

"MacDonald," he said softly. "Sit down. Trouble?"

"Right up your alley, Mr. Noble. A screwball set-up from way back."

"They happen to you." He swallowed some sherry and took another swipe at his nose. "Fly," he said apologetically.

MacDonald remembered that fly. It wasn't there. It never had been. He slipped into the seat across the booth and began his story. Once the Mexican waitress came up and was waved away. Once the invisible fly returned to interrupt. The rest of the time Nick Noble listened and drank and listened. When MacDonald had finished, he leaned back and let his eyes glaze over.

"Questions?" MacDonald asked.

"Why?" Nick Noble said.

"The motive, you mean? Humphreys thinks spy work. He must be right, but a mother . . ."

"Uh uh." Noble shook his head. "Why questions? All clear. Let Humphreys hocus you. Awed by the gold braid you wanted, MacDonald."

The detective shifted uncomfortably. "Maybe. But what do you mean? What's clear?"

Nick Noble turned sideways and slid his pipestem legs from under the table. "Come on," he said. "Take me out there."

He didn't say a word on the drive out Figueroa. His eyes were shut: not glazed over, as they were when he worked on a problem, but simply shut, as though he were done with it. He opened them as they turned off the boulevard. In a moment he said, "Almost there?"

"Yes. We turn again at the next, then we're there."

"Stop here," Nick Noble said.

MacDonald was beginning to wonder what he'd let himself in for. Conferences at the Chula Negra were one thing, but . . . He pulled up in front of the small market and said, "What goes?"

"Need some meat," Noble said. "Supper. Come on in."

MacDonald followed, frowning. At least this was a clue as to how Noble lived outside the Chula Negra . . . The butcher's counter was sparsely filled. Not so bad as before rationing, but still not overflowing.

Nick Noble said, "I wanted about a pound of ground round."

The butcher had red hair and a redder face. "Don't know's I've got any left to grind, but I'll see. Got your red stamps?"

Noble's face fell as he groped in his pocket. He muttered something about his other suit.

The butcher said, "Sorry, brother."

Nick Noble said, "It's what the doctor said the baby ought to have . . ." He took out a wallet and held it open. It was far from empty.

The butcher said, "Hold on, brother. With a baby . . ." He went into the refrigerating room.

MacDonald stared at the greenbacks in the wallet. It wasn't possible that Nick Noble should flash such a roll.

The butcher came back with a package in heavy paper. He didn't weigh it. He said, "One pound. That'll be ninety cents."

Noble's pale eyes rested on the posted list of ceiling prices. "Kind of high," he said.

"Take it or leave it, brother."

Nick Noble took it. As he turned to go, a woman came in with a heavy shopping bag. She said, "Frank, I'd like to ask you about that meat I got in here yesterday. My husband's been . . ."

Frank began talking loudly about the meat quota problem. Nick Noble went on out. On his way he stopped at the grocery department and picked up a quart of sherry.

Back in the car he handed the meat to MacDonald. "Lab," he said. Then he went to work on the seal of the bottle, and broke off to swat at the fly.

MacDonald grinned. "The Noble touch! So you've done it again. Black market, huh?"

Noble nodded. "Food poisoning symptoms pretty much like

arsenic." The bottle glurked and its contents diminished. "Mother hoards for son. She'd buy on black market for him too. But she poisoned him. Same like woman's husband."

"'All clear,'" MacDonald quoted. "I guess it is. Humphrey's profession gives him a naturally melodramatic outlook, and it sucked in the doctor and me. We expected poisoning, so we saw it. The lab tests'll be the final check. All clear but one thing: how come you have all that folding money?"

"Oh," said Nick Noble. "Sorry." He handed over the wallet.

MacDonald felt in his own empty pocket and swore good humoredly. "In a good cause," he said.

He was still grinning when they drove up to Ira Beaumont's mansion. Shurman wasn't in front of the house as he should have been. Instead he answered the door. His broad face lit up. "Jeez, Loot, we been tryna get you everywheres."

"It's all O.K., Shurman. All cleared up. There never was an attempt at murder."

"Maybe there wasn't no attempt. But somebody sure's hell did murder Mr. Shaw about fifteen minutes ago."

It was the first time MacDonald had ever seen Nick Noble surprised.

This was the most daring murder that MacDonald had ever encountered or heard of. The murderer had slipped up behind Mulroon, on guard before the sickroom, and slugged him with a heavy vase. Then he had entered the sickroom and slit the throat of the sleeping invalid, leaving the heavy butcher knife (printless, MacDonald knew even before dusting it) beside the bed.

It was a crime as risky as it was simple, but it had succeeded. Harrison Shaw would contrive no more somethings out of nothing for the Navy.

"The method doesn't even eliminate anybody," MacDonald complained. "The knife was sharp enough and the vase heavy enough for even a woman to have succeeded. And that damned wheeze Mulroon has from his cold could've guided the blind man. Method means nothing."

"Motive," said Nick Noble.

The motive seemed indicated by the scrawl on the plaster near the bed. At first glance it looked like blood. A closer examination showed it was red ink. The bottle and a pastry brush (taken from the same drawer as the butcher knife) lay under the bed. The scrawl read:

So sterben alle Feinde des Reiches!

Firebrook had translated this as, *Thus may all enemies of the Reich perish!* The mere fact of his knowing the language had caused Lieutenant Humphreys to glower on him with fresh suspicion.

"And so what?" MacDonald complained when he and Noble were alone again with the body of Harrison Shaw. "So he is a German and his name used to be Feuerbach. That doesn't convict him."

Nick Noble said nothing. His pale blue eyes studied the room.

"What have we got?" MacDonald recapitulated. "Nobody in this house alibies anybody else. And it must be one of them. Avila and Shurman swear nobody came in. One of three people is a Nazi agent who took advantage of Shaw's illness and the confusion to steal his plans and now to kill him so he can't reproduce them. Mrs. Shaw, the assistant Firebrook, the blind cousin Beaumont: one of these three . . ."

"Four," said Nick Noble. He stood teetering on his thin legs. One hand swiped at the fly. Then his eyes fixed on the wall inscription and slowly glazed over.

He rocked back and forth while his last word echoed in MacDonald's mind. Four . . . That was true. There was a fourth suspect. And who had planted the notion of murder in the first place? Who had forcibly established himself in this house? Who had created the very confusion by which—

"Lieutenant!" It was Firebrook in the doorway, and his round face was aglow. "Lieutenant . . . !" And he thrust a set of papers into MacDonald's hands. "I did not wish your men to search, but myself I can search and respect the order of things. I have searched . . . and found!" MacDonald's eyes lit up. "Then at least the killing was in vain. We've got the detector! Humphreys will have to see these," he decided, his momentary suspicions rejected as absurd. "Come on, Noble."

Nick Noble took a swig from his bottle before he followed. His eyes had come unglazed now.

"In this room," Lieutenant MacDonald announced, "is a traitor." He looked around the shabby room. The naval officer was happily absorbed in contemplating the recovered plans. Firebrook looked as though his pleasure in the discovery was fading at the realization of the death of the man he had worked with. Mrs. Shaw was crying quietly and paying no heed to anything. It was impossible to read the sightless eyes and permanent half-smile of Ira Beaumont.

But it was Beaumont who spoke. "Isn't it obvious who the

traitor must be, Lieutenant? Mrs. Shaw is a dear sweet woman who knows nothing of the world beyond her kitchen and her family. Lieutenant Humphreys is an officer of Naval Intelligence. I lost my sight in the Argonne; that does not predispose me toward our country's enemies."

"I'm afraid, Mr. Beaumont, we need some proof beyond what you think obvious. We have a traitor here, and he is a traitor who failed. He killed Shaw, and to that potential extent harmed our war effort. But the plans of Shaw's detector he has failed to find."

"Did he?" Beaumont insisted. "Is Lieutenant Humphreys certain that those plans which he holds—?"

"Well, Lieutenant?" MacDonald asked.

Humphreys grunted. "Can't be positive till they've been checked by experts. Seem damned plausible, just the same."

"Beaumont's right," said Nick abruptly.

No one had been paying any attention to him, beyond the first obvious glance of wonder as to why the detective lieutenant should drag along such a companion. Now all the faces turned to him. The blind man's smile widened with gratification. He said, "Thank you."

"Beaumont's right," Noble went on. "Obvious who's traitor: Nobody."

The room gasped. Lieutenant Humphreys snorted.

"Private murder. Clear pattern: Humphreys started spy scare; murderer took advantage."

"But the scrawl on the plaster . . . ?" It was Firebrook's question.

"Proves it. Clumsy trick to mislead. Swastika wrong."

"*Ach so . . . !*" Firebrook made a click of belated realization.

"Wrong?" MacDonald asked.

"Pencil," Nick Noble said.

The officer handed him pencil and notebook. He drew for a minute, then showed the results as he spoke. "Old Indian swastika was straight. So's swastika on wall. Like so:

alle Feinde

Nazi swastika slants. Always slants. See any pictures. If Nazi made wall scribble, it'd have to be:

alle Feinde

So fake."

"You're right," Humphreys said grudgingly. "Should've seen it myself. They always slant like that."

Beaumont, unable to see the illustrations, looked puzzled.

"So who'd go wrong?" Nick Noble went on. "Who but man who's never seen Nazi swastika. Heard about swastika, naturally thought it same as old Indian. Man who hasn't seen anything since long before there were Nazis ... since Argonne."

Even the half-smile was gone from Ira Beaumont's face. He said, "Nonsense! My cousin was, I confess, a burden to me, but I was willing to tolerate him for the work he was doing. Why should I kill him?"

"Check," said Nick Noble to MacDonald. "Great-uncle Shaw was expecting fortune from. See if Beaumont's next of kin."

MacDonald knew he wouldn't have to check. The momentary twist of Beaumont's lips, the little choking cry of realization from Mrs. Shaw were enough.

"If not spy, who else but Beaumont?" Noble went on. "Only possible pattern. Humphreys total stranger. Mrs. Shaw devoted to son. Firebrook too likely to know right swastika; besides wouldn't pull German fake pointing straight at him. Who else?"

Ira Beaumont regained his smile. "Lieutenant, your drunken friend is amusing enough, but you surely must realize what pure tosh he is babbling."

"Must I?" said MacDonald.

"Of course. I defy you to arrest me."

As MacDonald hesitated, Nick Noble spoke. "O.K. Don't. Withdraw police. Leave him here."

MacDonald's eyes opened in amazement at the advice. Then he looked at the faces in the tense room.

They were all fixed on Beaumont. Humphreys was thinking, *He killed a man who could help the Navy.* Firebrook was thinking, *He killed my friend and tried to frame me for it.* Mrs. Shaw was thinking, *He killed my son.*

Ira Beaumont could not see the faces, but he could feel them. He could think of a blind man left helpless and alone with those faces when the police guard was withdrawn.

He rose slowly to his feet. "Shall we go, Lieutenant?"

As the wagon took away Beaumont, with the aching-headed Mulroon and the rest, MacDonald and Noble climbed into the Lieutenant's car.

On the seat lay a package wrapped in heavy butcher's paper. Nick Noble pointed at it. "Another murderer for you."

MacDonald nodded. "That butcher, plus Humphreys's suspicions, set the stage for this murder all right. And God knows what else the black market and the racketeers behind it are responsible for. Black market? Black murder . . ."

He held the butcher's parcel in his hand and stared at it as though it were a prize exhibit in the Black Museum. "I may not have had the heart to report Mrs. Shaw's hoarding, but it'll be a pleasure to turn in that market. And to see that the first part of this case gets enough publicity to cut some ice with the meat-buying public."

Nick Noble uptilted his bottle. "I'll stick to this," he said. "Safer."

His pale blue eyes closed as MacDonald drove off.

CRISIS, 1999
Fredric Brown

One of the most ingenious mystery writers ever to put words on a page was also an amazingly prolific writer of short stories and novels. Fredric William Brown (1906-1972) claimed that he wrote mysteries for the money, but science fiction for the fun; he is equally revered in both genres.

Born in Cincinnati, Ohio, he attended the University of Cincinnati at night and then spent a year at Hanover College, Indiana. He was an office worker for a dozen years before becoming a proofreader for the *Milwaukee Journal* for a decade. He was not able to devote full time to writing fiction until 1949, although he had for several years been producing short stories; he was a master of the form for which he is much loved today, the difficult-to-write short-short story, generally one to three pages, which generally had a surprise ending.

Never financially secure, Brown was forced to write at a prodigious pace, yet he seemed to be enjoying himself despite the work load. Many of his stories and novels are imbued with humor, including a devotion to puns and word play. A "writer's writer," he was highly regarded by his colleagues, including Mickey Spillane, who called him his favorite writer of all time; Robert Heinlein, who made him a dedicatee of *Stranger in a Strange Land*; and Ayn Rand, who in *The Romantic Manifesto* regarded him as ingenious.

After writing more than 300 short stories, he finally produced his first novel, *The Fabulous Clipjoint* (1947), for which he won an Edgar. His best-known work is *The Screaming Mimi* (1949), which served as the basis for the 1957 Columbia Pictures film of the same title that starred Anita Ekberg, Philip Carey, and Gypsy Rose Lee.

The bizarre story in this collection is, amusingly, set in the past—1999—though it was a futuristic detective tale when it was written a half-century earlier. It was selected for the 1950 edition of *Best Detective Stories of the Year* by David C. Cooke.

"Crisis, 1999" was originally published in the August 1949 issue of *Ellery Queen's Mystery Magazine*; it was first collected in *Space on My Hands* (Chicago, Shasta, 1951).

Crisis, 1999
Fredric Brown

THE LITTLE man with the sparse gray hair and the inconspicuous bright red suit stopped on the corner of State and Randolph to buy a micronews, a *Chicago Sun-Tribune* of March 21st, 1999. Nobody noticed him as he walked into the corner superdrug and took a vacant booth. He dropped a quarter into the coffeeslot and while the conveyor brought him his coffee, he glanced at the headlines on the tiny three-by-four-inch page. His eyes were unusually keen; he could read those headlines easily without artificial aid. But nothing on the first page or the second interested him; they concerned international matters, the third Venus rocket, and the latest depressing report of the ninth moon expedition. But on page three there were two stories concerning crime, and he took a tiny micrographer from his pocket and adjusted it to read the stories while he drank his coffee.

Bela Joad was the little man's name. His right name, that is; he'd gone by so many names in so many places that only a phenomenal memory could have kept track of them all, but he had a phenomenal memory. None of those names had ever appeared in print, nor had his face or voice even been seen or heard on the ubiquitous video. Fewer than a score of people, all of them top officials in various police bureaus, knew that Bela Joad was the greatest detective in the world.

He was not an employee of any police department, drew no salary nor expense money, and collected no rewards. It may have been that he had private means and indulged in the detection of criminals as a hobby. It may equally have been that he preyed upon the underworld even as he fought it, that he made criminals support his campaign against them. Whichever was the case, he worked for no one; he worked against crime. When a major crime or a series of major crimes interested him, he would work on it, sometimes consulting beforehand with the chief of police of the city involved, sometimes working without the chief's knowledge until he would appear in the chief's office and present him with the evidence that would enable him to make an arrest and obtain a conviction.

He himself had never testified, or even appeared, in a courtroom. And while he knew every important underworld character in a dozen cities, no member of the underworld knew him, except fleetingly, under some transient identity which he seldom resumed.

Now, over his morning coffee, Bela Joad read through his micrographer the two stories in the *Sun-Tribune* which had interested him. One concerned a case that had been one of his few failures, the disappearance—possibly the kidnaping—of Dr. Ernst Chappel, professor of criminology at Columbia University. The headline read, NEW LEAD IN CHAPPEL CASE, but a careful reading of the story showed the detective that the lead was new only to the newspapers; he himself had followed it into a blind alley two years ago, just after Chappel had vanished. The other story revealed that one Paul (Gyp) Girard had yesterday been acquitted of the slaying of his rival for control of North Chicago gambling. Joad read that one carefully indeed. Just six hours before, seated in a beergarten in New Berlin, Western Germany, he had heard the news of that acquittal on the video, without details. He had immediately taken the first stratoplane to Chicago.

When he had finished with the micronews, he touched the button of his wrist model timeradio, which automatically attuned itself to the nearest timestation, and it said, just loudly enough for him to hear "Nine-oh-four." Chief Dyer Rand would be in his office, then.

Nobody noticed him as he left the superdrug. Nobody noticed him as he walked with the morning crowds along Randolph to the big, new Municipal Building at the corner of Clark. Chief Rand's secretary sent in his name—not his real one, but one Rand would recognize—without giving him a second glance.

Chief Rand shook hands across the desk and then pressed the intercom button that flashed a blue not-to-be-disturbed signal to his secretary. He leaned back in his chair and laced his fingers across the conservatively small (one inch) squares of his mauve and yellow shirt. He said, "You heard about Gyp Girard being acquitted?"

"That's why I'm here."

Rand pushed his lips out and pulled them in again. He said, "The evidence you sent me was perfectly sound, Joad. It should have stood up. But I wish you had brought it in yourself instead of sending it by the tube, or that there had been some way I could have got in touch with you. I could have told you we'd probably not get a conviction. Joad, something rather terrible has been happening. I've had a feeling you would be my only chance. If only there had been some way I could have got in touch with you—"

"Two years ago?"

Chief Rand looked startled. "Why did you say that?"

"Because it was two years ago that Dr. Chappel disappeared in New York."

"Oh," Rand said. "No, there's no connection. I thought maybe you knew something when you mentioned two years. It hasn't been quite that long, really, but it was close."

He got up from behind the strangely-shaped plastic desk and began to pace back and forth the length of the office.

He said, "Joad, in the last year—let's just consider that period, although it started nearer two years ago—out of every ten major crimes committed in Chicago, seven are unsolved. Technically unsolved, that is; in five out of those seven we know who's guilty but we can't prove it. We can't get a conviction.

"The underworld is beating us, Joad, worse than they have at any time since the Prohibition era of seventy-five years ago. If this keeps up, we're going back to days like that, and worse.

"For a twenty-year period now we've had convictions for

eight out of ten major crimes. Even before twenty years ago—before the use of the lie-detector in court was legalized, we did better than we're doing now. 'Way back in the decade of 1970 to 1980, for instance, we did better than we're doing now by more than two to one; we got convictions for six out of every ten major crimes. This last year, it's been three out of ten.

"And I know the reason, but I don't know what to do about it. The reason is that the underworld is beating the lie-detector!"

Bela Joad nodded. But he said mildly, "A few have always managed to beat it. It's not perfect. Judges always instruct juries to remember that the lie-detector's findings have a high degree of probability but are not infallible, that they should be weighed as indicative but not final, that other evidence must support them. And there has always been the occasional individual who can tell a whopper with the detector on him, and not jiggle the graph needles at all."

"One in a thousand, yes. But, Joad, almost every underworld big-shot has been beating the lie-detector recently."

"I take it you mean the professional criminals, not the amateurs."

"Exactly. Only regular members of the underworld—professionals, the habitual criminals. If it weren't for that, I'd think—I don't know what I'd think. Maybe that our whole theory was wrong."

Bela Joad said, "Can't you quit using it in court in such cases? Convictions were obtained before its use was legalized. For that matter, before it was invented."

Dyer Rand sighed and dropped into his pneumatic chair again. "Sure, I'd like that if I could do it. I wish right now that the detector never *had* been invented or legalized. But don't forget that the law legalizing it gives *either* side the opportunity to use it in court. If a criminal knows he can beat it, he's going to demand its use even if we don't. And what chance have we got with a jury if the accused demands the detector and it backs up his plea of innocence?"

"Very slight, I'd say."

"Less than slight, Joad. This Gyp Girard business yesterday. I know he killed Pete Bailey. You know it. The evidence you sent me was, under ordinary circumstances, conclusive. And yet I knew we'd lose the case. I wouldn't have bothered bringing it to trial except for one thing."

"And that one thing?"

"*To get you here*, Joad. There was no other way I could reach you, but I hoped that if you read of Girard's acquittal, after the evidence you'd given me, you'd come around to find out what had happened."

He got up and started to pace again. "Joad, I'm going mad. *How* is the underworld beating the machine? That's what I want you to find out, and it's the biggest job you've ever tackled. Take a year, take five years, but crack it, Joad.

"Look at the history of law enforcement. Always the law has been one jump ahead of the criminal in the field of science. Now the criminals—of Chicago, anyway—are one jump ahead of *us*. And if they stay that way, if we don't get the answer, we're headed for a new dark age, when it'll no longer be safe for a man or a woman to walk down the street. The very foundations of our society can crumble. We're up against something very evil and very powerful."

Bela Joad took a cigarette from the dispenser on the desk; it lighted automatically as he picked it up. It was a green cigarette and he exhaled green smoke through his nostrils before he asked, almost disinterestedly, "Any ideas, Dyer?"

"I've had two, but I think I've eliminated both of them. One is that the machines are being tampered with. The other is that the technicians are being tampered with. But I've had both men and machines checked from every possible angle and can't find a thing. On big cases I've taken special precautions. For example, the detector we used at the Girard trial; it was brand-new and I had it checked right in this office." He chuckled. "I put Captain Burke under it and asked him if he was being faithful to his wife. He said he was and it nearly broke the needle. I had it taken to the courtroom under special guard."

"And the technician who used it?"

"I used it myself. Took a course in it, evenings, for four months."

Bela Joad nodded. "So it isn't the machine and it isn't the operator. That's eliminated, and I can start from there."

"How long will it take you, Joad?"

The little man in the red suit shrugged. "I haven't any idea."

"Is there any help I can give you? Anything you want to start on?"

"Just one thing, Dyer. I want a list of the criminals who have beaten the detector and a dossier on each. Just the ones you're morally sure actually committed the crimes you questioned them about. If there's any reasonable doubt, leave them off the list. How long will it take you to get it ready?"

"It's ready now; I had it made up on the chance that you'd come here. And it's a long report, so I had it microed down for you." He handed Bela Joad a small envelope.

Joad said, "Thank you. I won't contact you till I have something or until I want your cooperation. I think first I'm going to stage a murder, and then have you question the murderer."

Dyer Rand's eyes went wide. "Whom are you going to have murdered?"

Bela Joad smiled. "Me," he said.

He took the envelope Rand had given him back to his hotel and spent several hours studying the microfilms through his pocket micrographer memorizing their contents thoroughly. Then he burned both films and envelope.

After that Bela Joad paid his hotel bill and disappeared, but a little man who resembled Bela Joad only slightly rented a cheap room under the name of Martin Blue. The room was on Lake Shore Drive, which was then the heart of Chicago's underworld.

The underworld of Chicago had changed less, in fifty years, than one would think. Human vices do not change, or at least they change but slowly. True, certain crimes had diminished greatly but on the other hand, gambling had increased. Greater social security than any country had hitherto known was, perhaps, a factor. One no longer needed to save for old age as, in days gone by, a few people did.

Gambling was a lush field for the crooks and they cultivated the field well. Improved technology had increased the number of ways of gambling and it had increased the efficiency of ways of making gambling crooked. Crooked gambling was big business and underworld wars and killings occurred over territorial rights, just as they had occurred over such rights in the far back days of Prohibition when alcohol was king. There was still alcohol, but it was of lesser importance now. People were learning to drink more moderately. And drugs were passé, although there was still some traffic in them.

Robberies and burglaries still occurred, although not quite as frequently as they had fifty years before.

Murder was slightly more frequent. Sociologists and criminologists differed as to the reason for the increase of crime in this category.

The weapons of the underworld had, of course, improved, but they did not include atomics. All atomic and subatomic weapons were strictly controlled by the military and were never used by either the police or by criminals. They were too dangerous; the death penalty was mandatory for anyone found in possession of an atomic weapon. But the pistols and guns of the underworld of 1999 were quite efficient. They were much smaller and more compact, and they were silent. Both guns and cartridges were made of superhard magnesium and were very light. The commonest weapon was the. 19 calibre pistol—as deadly as the .45 of an earlier era because the tiny projectiles were explosive. And even a small pocketpistol held from fifty to sixty rounds.

But back to Martin Blue, whose entrance into the underworld coincided with the disappearance of Bela Joad from the latter's hotel.

Martin Blue, as it turned out, was not a very nice man. He had no visible means of support other than gambling and he seemed to lose, in small amounts, almost more often than he won. He almost got in trouble on a bad check he gave to cover his losses in one game, but he managed to avoid being liquidated by making the check good. His only reading seemed to be the Racing Microform, and he drank too much, mostly in a tavern (with clandestine gambling at the back) which formerly had been operated by Gyp Girard. He got beaten up there once because he defended Gyp against a crack made by the current proprietor to the effect that Gyp had lost his guts and turned honest.

For a while fortune turned against Martin Blue and he went

so broke that he had to take a job as a waiter in the outside room of a Michigan Boulevard joint called Sloppy Joe's, possibly because Joe Zatelli, who ran it, was the nattiest dresser in Chicago—and in the *fin de siècle* era when leopard-skin suits (synthetic but finer and more expensive than real leopard skin) were a dime a dozen and plain pastel-silk underwear was dated.

Then a funny thing happened to Martin Blue. Joe Zatelli killed him. Caught him, after hours, rifling the till, and just as Martin Blue turned around, Zatelli shot him. Three times for good measure. And then Zatelli, who never trusted accomplices, got the body into his car and deposited it in an alley back of a teletheater.

The body of Martin Blue got up and went to see Chief Dyer Rand and told Rand what he wanted done.

"You took a hell of a chance," Rand said.

"Not too much of a chance," Blue said. "I'd put blanks in his gun and I was pretty sure he'd use that. He won't find out, incidentally, that the rest of the bullets in it are blanks unless he tries to kill somebody else with it; they don't *look* like blanks. And I had a pretty special vest on under my suit. Rigid backing and padded on top to feel like flesh, but of course he couldn't feel a heartbeat through it. And it was gimmicked to make a noise like explosive cartridges hitting—when the duds punctured the compartments."

"But if he'd switched guns or bullets?"

"Oh, the vest was bulletproof for anything short of atomics. The danger was in his thinking of any fancy way of disposing of the body. If he had, I could have taken care of myself, of course, but it would have spoiled the plan and cost me three months' build-up. But I'd studied his style and I was pretty sure what he'd do. Now here's what I want you to do, Dyer—"

The newspapers and videocasts the next morning carried the story of the finding of a body of an unidentified man in a certain alley. By afternoon they reported that it had been identified as the body of Martin Blue, a small-time crook who had lived on Lake Shore Drive, in the heart of the Tenderloin. And by evening a rumor had gone out through the underworld to the effect that the police suspected Joe Zatelli, for whom Blue had worked, and might pick him up for questioning.

And plainclothesmen watched Zatelli's place, front and back, to see where he'd go if he went out. Watching the front was a small man about the build of Bela Joad or Martin Blue. Unfortunately, Zatelli happened to leave by the back and he succeeded in shaking off the detectives on his trail.

They picked him up the next morning, though, and took him to headquarters. They put the lie-detector on him and asked him about Martin Blue. He admitted Blue had worked for him but said he'd last seen Blue when the latter had left his place after work the night of the murder. The lie-detector said he wasn't lying.

Then they pulled a tough one on him. Martin Blue walked into the room where Zatelli was being questioned. And the trick fizzled. The gauges of the detector didn't jump a fraction of a millimeter and Zatelli looked at Blue and then at his interrogators with complete indignation. "What's the idea?" he demanded. "The guy ain't even dead, and you're asking me if I bumped him off?"

They asked Zatelli, while they had him there, about some other crimes he might have committed, but obviously—according to his answers and the lie-detector—he hadn't done any of them. They let him go.

Of course, that was the end of Martin Blue. After showing

before Zatelli at headquarters, he might as well have been dead in an alley for all the good he was going to do.

Bela Joad told Chief Rand, "Well, anyway, now we *know*."

"What do we know?"

"We know for sure the detector is being beaten. You might conceivably have been making a series of wrong arrests before. Even the evidence I gave you against Girard might have been misleading. But we *know* Zatelli beat the machine. Only I wish Zatelli had come out the front way so I could have tailed him; we might have the whole thing now instead of part of it."

"You're going back? Going to do it all over again?"

"Not the same way. This time I've got to be on the other end of a murder, and I'll need your help on that."

"Of course. But won't you tell me what's on your mind?"

"I'm afraid I can't, Dyer. I've got a hunch within a hunch. In fact, I've had it ever since I started on this business. But will you do one other thing for me?"

"Sure. What?"

"Have one of your men keep track of Zatelli, of everything he does from now on. Put another one on Gyp Girard. In fact, take as many men as you can spare and put one on each of the men you're fairly sure has beaten the detector within the last year or two. And always from a distance; don't let the boys know they're being checked on. Will you?"

"I don't know what you're after, but I'll do it. Won't you tell me *anything?* Joad, this is important. Don't forget it's not just *a* case; it's something that can lead to the breakdown of law enforcement."

Bela Joad smiled. "Not quite that bad, Dyer. Law enforcement as it applies to the underworld, yes. But you're getting your usual percentage of convictions on nonprofessional crimes."

Dyer Rand looked puzzled. "What's that got to do with it?"

"Maybe everything. It's why I can't tell you anything yet. But don't worry." Joad reached across the desk and patted the chief's shoulder, looking—although he didn't know it—like a fox terrier giving his paw to an airedale. "Don't worry, Dyer. I'll promise to bring you the answer. Maybe I won't be able to let you keep it."

"Do you really know what you're looking for?"

"Yes. I'm looking for a criminologist who disappeared well over two years ago. Dr. Ernst Chappel."

"You think—?"

"Yes, I think. That's why I'm looking for Dr. Chappel."

But that was all Dyer could get out of him. Bela Joad left Dyer Rand's office and returned to the underworld.

And in the underworld of Chicago a new star arose. Perhaps one should call him a *nova* rather than merely a star, so rapidly did he become famous—or notorious. Physically, he was rather a small man, no larger than Bela Joad or Martin Blue, but he wasn't a mild little man like Joad or a weak jackal like Blue. He had what it took, and he parlayed what he had. He ran a small night club, but that was just a front. Behind that front things happened, things that the police couldn't pin on him, and—for that matter—didn't seem to know about, although the underworld knew.

His name was Willie Ecks, and nobody in the underworld had ever made friends and enemies faster. He had plenty of each; the former were powerful and the latter were dangerous. In other words, they were both the same type of people.

His brief career was truly—if I may scramble my star-nova metaphor but keep it celestial—a meteoric matter. And for once that hackneyed and inaccurate metaphor is used correctly. Meteors do not rise—as anybody who has ever studied meteorology, which has no connection with meteors, knows. Meteors fall, with a dull thud. And that is what happened to Willie Ecks, when he got high enough.

Three days before, Willie Ecks's worst enemy had vanished. Two of his henchmen spread the rumor that it was because the cops had come and taken him away, but that was obviously malarkey designed to cover the fact that they intended to avenge him. That became obvious when, the very next morning, the news broke that the gangster's body had been found, neatly weighted, in the Blue Lagoon at Washington Park.

And by dusk of that very day rumor had gone from bistro to bistro of the underworld that the police had pretty good proof who had killed the deceased—and with a forbidden atomic at that—and that they planned to arrest Willie Ecks and question him. Things like that get around even when it's not intended that they should.

And it was on the second day of Willie Ecks's hiding-out in a cheap little hotel on North Clark Street, an old-fashioned hotel with elevators and windows, his whereabouts known only to a trusted few, that one of those trusted few gave a certain knock on his door and was admitted.

The trusted one's name was Mike Leary and he'd been a close friend of Willie's and a close enemy of the gentleman who, according to the papers, had been found in the Blue Lagoon.

He said, "Looks like you're in a jam, Willie."

"——, yes," said Willie Ecks. He hadn't used facial depilatory for two days; his face was blue with beard and bluer with fear.

Mike said, "There's a way out, Willie. It'll cost you ten grand. Can you raise it?"

"I've got it. What's the way out?"

"There's a guy. I know how to get in touch with him; I ain't used him myself, but I would if I got in a jam like yours. He can fix you up, Willie."

"How?"

"He can show you how to beat the lie-detector. I can have him come around to see you and fix you up. Then you let the cops pick you up and question you, see? They'll drop the charge—or if they bring it to trial, they can't make it stick."

"What if they ask me about—well, never mind what—other things I may have done?"

"He'll take care of that, too. For five grand he'll fix you so you can go under that detector clean as—as clean as hell."

"You said ten grand."

Mike Leary grinned. "I got to live too, don't I, Willie? And you said you got ten grand, so it ought to be worth that much to you, huh?"

Willie Ecks argued, but in vain. He had to give Mike Leary five thousand-dollar bills. Not that it really mattered, because those were pretty special thousand-dollar bills. The green ink on them would turn purple within a few days. Even in 1999 you couldn't spend a purple thousand-dollar bill, so when it happened Mike Leary would probably turn purple too, but by that time it would be too late for him to do anything about it.

It was late that evening when there was a knock on Willie Ecks's hotel room door. He pressed the button that made the main panel of the door transparent from his side.

He studied the nondescript-looking man outside the door very carefully. He didn't pay any attention to facial contours or to the shabby yellow suit the man wore. He studied the eyes somewhat, but mostly he studied the shape and conformation of the ears and compared them mentally with the ears of photographs he had once studied exhaustively.

And then Willie Ecks put his gun back into his pocket and opened the door. He said, "Come in."

The man in the yellow suit entered the room and Willie Ecks shut the door very carefully and locked it.

He said, "I'm proud to meet you, Dr. Chappel."

He sounded as though he meant it, and he did mean it.

It was four o'clock in the morning when Bela Joad stood outside the door of Dyer Rand's apartment. He had to wait, there in the dimly luminous hallway, for as long as it took the chief to get out of bed and reach the door, then activate the one-way-transparent panel to examine his visitor.

Then the magnetic lock sighed gently and the door opened. Rand's eyes were bleary and his hair was tousled. His feet were thrust into red plastic slippers and he wore neonylon sleeping pajamas that looked as though they had been slept in.

He stepped aside to let Bela Joad in, and Joad walked to the center of the room and stood looking about curiously. It was the first time he'd ever been in Rand's private quarters. The apartment was like that of any other well-to-do bachelor of the day. The furniture was unobtrusive and functional, each wall a different pastel shade, faintly fluorescent and emitting gentle radiant heat and the faint but constant caress of ultraviolet that kept people who could afford such apartments healthily tanned. The rug was in alternate one-foot squares of cream and gray, the squares separate and movable so that wear would be equalized. And the ceiling, of course, was the customary one-piece mirror that gave an illusion of height and spaciousness.

Rand said, "Good news, Joad?"

"Yes. But this is an unofficial interview, Dyer. What I'm going to tell you is confidential, between us."

"What do you mean?"

Joad looked at him. He said, "You still look sleepy, Dyer. Let's have coffee. It'll wake you up, and I can use some myself."

"Fine," Dyer said. He went into the kitchenette and pressed the button that would heat the coils of the coffee-tap. "Want it laced?" he called back.

"Of course."

Within a minute he came back with two cups of steaming *café royale*. With obvious impatience he waited until they were seated comfortably and each had taken his first sip of the fragrant beverage before he asked, "Well, Joad?"

"When I say it's unofficial, Dyer, I mean it. I can give you the full answer, but only with the understanding that you'll forget it as soon as I tell you, that you'll never tell another person, and that you won't act upon it."

Dyer Rand stared at his guest in amazement. He said, "I can't promise that! I'm chief of police, Joad. I have my duty to my job and to the people of Chicago."

"That's why I came here, to your apartment, instead of to your office. You're not working now, Dyer; you're on your own time."

"But—"

"Do you promise?"

"Of course not."

Bela Joad sighed. "Then I'm sorry for waking you, Dyer." He put down his cup and started to rise.

"Wait! You can't do that. You can't just walk out on me!"

"Can't I?"

"All right, all right, I'll promise. You must have some good reason. Have you?"

"Yes."

"Then I'll take your word for it."

Bela Joad smiled. "Good," he said. "Then I'll be able to report to you on my last case. For this is my last case, Dyer. I'm going into a new kind of work."

Rand looked at him incredulously. "What?"

"I'm going to teach crooks how to beat the lie-detector."

Chief Dyer Rand put down his cup slowly and stood up. He took a step toward the little man, about half his weight, who sat at ease on the armless, overstuffed chair.

Bela Joad still smiled. He said, "Don't try it, Dyer. For two reasons. First, you couldn't hurt me and I wouldn't want to hurt you and I might have to. Second, it's all right; it's on the up and up. Sit down."

Dyer Rand sat down.

Bela Joad said, "When you said this thing was big, you didn't know how big. And it's going to be bigger; Chicago is just the starting point. And thanks, by the way, for those reports I asked you for. They are just what I expected they'd be."

"The reports? But they're still in my desk at headquarters."

"They were. I've read them and destroyed them. Your copies, too. Forget about them. And don't pay too much attention to your current statistics. I've read them, too."

Rand frowned. "And why should I forget them?"

"Because they confirm what Ernie Chappel told me this evening. Do you know, Dyer, that your *number* of major crimes has gone down in the past year by an even bigger percentage than the percentage by which your convictions for major crimes has gone down?"

"I noticed that. You mean, there's a connection?"

"Definitely. Most crimes—a very high percentage of them—are committed by professional criminals, repeaters. And Dyer, it goes even farther than that. Out of several thousand major crimes a year, ninety percent of them are committed by *a few hundred professional criminals.* And do you know that the number of professional criminals in Chicago has been reduced by almost a third in the last two years? It *has.* And that's why your number of major crimes has decreased."

Bela Joad took another sip of his coffee and then leaned forward. "Gyp Girard, according to your report, is now running a vitadrink stand on the West Side; he hasn't committed a crime in almost a year—since he beat your lie-detector." He touched another finger. "Joe Zatelli, who used to be the roughest boy on the Near North Side, is now running his restaurant straight. Carey Hutch. Wild Bill Wheeler—Why should I list them all? You've got the list, and it's not complete because there are plenty of names you haven't got on it, people who went to Ernie Chappel so he could show them how to beat the detector, and then didn't get arrested after all. And nine out of ten of them—and that's conservative, Dyer—*haven't committed a crime since!*"

Dyer Rand said, "Go on. I'm listening."

"My original investigation of the Chappel case showed me that he'd disappeared voluntarily. And I knew he was a good man, and a great one. I knew he was mentally sound because he was a psychiatrist as well as a criminologist. A psychiatrist's *got* to be sound. So I knew he'd disappeared for some good reason.

"And when, about nine months ago, I heard your side of what had been happening in Chicago, I began to suspect that Chappel had come here to do his work. Are you beginning to get the picture?"

"Faintly."

"Well, don't faint yet. Not until you figure how an expert psychiatrist can help crooks beat the detector. Or have you?"

"Well—"

"That's it. The most elementary form of hypnotic treatment,

something any qualified psychiatrist could do fifty years ago. Chappel's clients—of course they don't know who or what he is; he's a mysterious underworld figure who helps them beat the rap—pay him well and tell him what crimes they may be questioned about by the police if they're picked up. He tells them to include every crime they've ever committed and any racket they've ever been in, so the police won't catch them up on any old counts. Then he—"

"Wait a minute," Rand interrupted. "How does he get them to trust him that far?"

Joad gestured impatiently. "Simple. They aren't confessing a single crime, even to him. He just wants a list that *includes* everything they've done. They can add some ringers and he doesn't know which is which. So it doesn't matter.

"Then he puts them under light waking-hypnosis and tells them they are not criminals and never have been and they have never done any of the things on the list he reads back to them. That's all there is to it.

"So when you put them under the detector and ask them if they've done this or that, they say they haven't and they *believe* it. That's why your detector gauges don't register. That's why Joe Zatelli didn't jump when he saw Martin Blue walk in. He didn't know Blue was dead—except that he'd read it in the papers."

Rand leaned forward. "Where is Ernst Chappel?"

"You don't want him, Dyer."

"Don't *want* him? He's the most dangerous man alive today!"

"To whom?"

"To *whom?* Are you crazy?"

"I'm not crazy. He's the most dangerous man alive today— to the underworld. Look, Dyer, any time a criminal gets jittery about a possible pinch, he sends for Ernie or goes to Ernie. And

Ernie washes him whiter than snow and in the process tells him *he's not a criminal.*

"And so, at least nine times out of ten, he quits being a criminal. Within ten or twenty years Chicago isn't going to *have* an underworld. There won't be any organized crimes by professional criminals. You'll always have the amateur with you, but he's a comparatively minor detail. How about some more *café royale?*"

Dyer Rand walked to the kitchenette and got it. He was wide awake by now, but he walked like a man in a dream. When he came back, Joad said, "And now that I'm in with Ernie on it, Dyer, we'll stretch it to every city in the world big enough to have an underworld worth mentioning. We can train picked recruits; I've got my eye on two of your men and may take them away from you soon. But I'll have to check them first. We're going to pick our apostles—about a dozen of them—very carefully. They'll be the right men for the job."

"But, Joad, look at all the crimes that are going to go unpunished!" Rand protested.

Bela Joad drank the rest of his coffee and stood up. He said, "And which is more important—to punish criminals or to end crime? And, if you want to look at it moralistically, *should* a man be punished for a crime when he doesn't even remember committing it, when he is no longer a criminal?"

Dyer Rand sighed. "You win, I guess. I'll keep my promise. I suppose—I'll never see you again?"

"Probably not, Dyer. And I'll anticipate what you're going to say next. Yes, I'll have a farewell drink with you. A straight one, without the coffee."

Dyer Rand brought the glasses. He said, "Shall we drink to Ernie Chappel?"

Bela Joad smiled. He said, "Let's include him in the toast,

Dyer. But let's drink to all men who work to put themselves out of work. Doctors work toward the day when the race will be so healthy it won't need doctors; lawyers work toward the day when litigation will no longer be necessary. And policemen, detectives, and criminologists work toward the day when they will no longer be needed because there will be no more crime."

Dyer Rand nodded very soberly and lifted his glass. They drank.

THE FLOWERING FACE
Mignon G. Eberhart

Like her creator, Mignon G(ood) Eberhart (1899-1996), Susan Dare is a mystery writer. She also happens to be a dazzling beauty and is charming, romantic, fearless, and gushily emotional—but comes upon real-life murders with alarming regularity.

Eberhart was once one of America's most successful and beloved authors, ranking behind only Agatha Christie and Mary Roberts Rinehart as the third-bestselling female mystery writer in the world from the 1930s into the 1960s. She enjoyed a career that spanned six decades and produced sixty books, beginning with *The Patient in Room 18* (1929) and concluding with *Three Days for Emeralds* (1988).

Her first five books featured Sarah Keate, a middle-aged spinster, nurse, and amateur detective who works closely with Lance O'Leary, a promising young police detective in an unnamed Midwestern city. This unlikely duo functions effectively, despite Keate's penchant for stumbling into dangerous situations from which she must be rescued. She is inquisitive and supplies O'Leary with valuable information. Five films featuring Nurse

Keate and O'Leary were filmed over a three-year period in the 1930s.

Many of Eberhart's stories were published in the now-forgotten periodical *The Delineator*, an American women's magazine founded in 1869 as *The Metropolitan Monthly*; the name was changed in 1875 and it ran until 1937 when it was merged with *The Pictorial Review*. At one point, Theodore Dreiser was the managing editor and wrote articles guiding women as consumers.

"The Flowering Face" was originally published in the May 1934 issue of *The Delineator*.

The Flowering Face
Mignon G. Eberhart

THERE WAS a knock and then another knock, and Susan Dare left a murder half completed and went to the door.

The murder—that particular murder—was, however, entirely fictional. The caller was Katherine Vandeman, who said, "Darling," breezily, entered with a rush and then saw the sheet of paper on the typewriter.

"Oh, my dear," she said contritely. "I've interrupted you. Sorry. But I had to see you."

She rushed on breathlessly: "We are going up on French Crescent today. And we want you to go along. Now please don't say you can't."

Susan hesitated, and Katherine came closer to her so that Susan caught a whiff of cigarette smoke and lemon verbena, curiously mingled. Katherine Vandeman was a tall woman, angularly built; there was about her a kind of hard, bright surface which made people feel that she was herself hard and superficial.

Only her eyes, to Susan, were like bright clear holes through a stage curtain, for they were sober and clear, and somehow let you through to the Katherine Vandeman who was behind all that brightness and loudness and hardness. Her eyes and, amended Susan, the way she cared for and nursed her invalid brother-in-law. His name was Cecil Vandeman, he was perhaps ten years younger than Katherine and had been, since the death of Katherine's husband, her only close personal tie. Thinking of him Susan said:

"Who's we?"

"Cecil," said Katherine, bright eyes looking past Susan. "Norman Bridges. Sally Lee Sully. You."

"How's Cecil?" asked Susan because it was the customary inquiry. Katherine was slow about replying.

"We've had another specialist," she said finally. "I'm not altogether sure that I agree with him."

"He doesn't think Cecil is worse?" said Susan quickly.

"Oh, no, no. He thinks—or says he thinks—there's definite improvement." Katherine pulled off her gloves slowly. "You'll go with us, won't you? We'll drive up to the inn, then leave the car and take the trail to the top. It isn't much of a climb—two hours, perhaps. And Norman just telephoned the weather bureau and says it will be clear."

She looked again into Susan's eyes and caught the indecision. And quite suddenly she said in a still voice that had lost all its bright vivacity:

"Please come, Susan Dare."

There was something urgent, something indefinably compelling about it. Susan said lamely: "But there's a friend of mine coming from Chicago."

"Who?" said Katherine.

"His name is Byrne. Jim Byrne. I had a note this morning—written sort of hurriedly." Susan fished among the papers on the table and found a sheet of yellow copy paper with a few scrawled lines on it—"Dear Susie: Have an unexpected weekend and am coming down to stay at Hunt Club. Find two good riding horses and don't plan any work. Arrive Thursday or Friday night ten o'clock train. Have greatest regard for you and your stories but kindly do not mention six-letter word meaning to destroy by violence in my hearing. Jim."

"He's just finished reporting the Blank case," said Susan explanatorily. "It must have been pretty awful."

"Reporting. Why, that's—" Katherine stopped abruptly.

"Yes, that's the Jim Byrne."

"Oh—oh, yes, I see. I remember his name now. Well—we shall be home before ten. But you might leave a message at the Hunt Club, just in case we are delayed. Tell him—" Katherine hesitated again. "Tell him to join us—if he wants to. We'll stop for you after lunch. Goodbye, my dear."

Susan didn't really know Katherine Vandeman very well, although the Vandeman place, a huge old Southern home with stables and bluegrass meadows, lay in the valley only two miles distant from Susan's own small cabin. Susan knew in a vague way that Katherine's husband, considerably older than Katherine, had left his widow a sizable chunk of the Vandeman money. She knew, too, that Norman Bridges, a lawyer and an old friend of the Vandeman family, was, in a rather prolonged and desultory way, a suitor of Katherine's.

They called for Susan shortly after noon. Katherine at the wheel of her long convertible coupe, with Cecil beside her and Norman Bridges's tweed shoulders beside Sally Lee Sully's green sweater in the rumble.

Sally Lee Sully, a slim, dark-eyed girl with the sweet languid loveliness of a magnolia, waved prettily to Susan. Norman Bridges's white teeth flashed below his dark mustache, and Cecil got out slowly, unfolding his slender length and explaining to Susan that the seat was wide enough for the three of them if Susan didn't mind a little crowding.

Afterward Susan tried desperately to recall anything at all significant that was said or done during the trip to French Crescent. But there was nothing. Katherine drove furiously with bursts of speed and sudden brakings which threatened to send her passengers through the windshield but somehow never did.

They wound higher and higher. The road became narrow and the hairpin curves sharper. Great expanses of sky and space would appear suddenly ahead and then would vanish as the car swerved, and be replaced by a tangled wall of pines and mountain growth.

It was perhaps four o'clock when they reached the inn, from which only a footpath continued to the mountaintop. Katherine parked expertly in the space reserved for cars. And it took expert parking. They had emerged upon a small plateau backed by the steep rise of the mountain but dropping suddenly away upon sheer space and distance with only a little line of white stones to mark that irregular, precipitous edge. Katherine turned, backed, turned until Cecil, looking rather pale said: "That's enough, K. You're only a few feet from the edge.

Katherine stopped at last, and Susan took a long breath of relief and Cecil slid out of the car. He turned and smiled, holding out his thin hand to Susan to help her. "Are your legs cramped?" he asked.

"A little," said Susan, "I've kept my foot on a brake that wasn't there practically all the way up the mountain."

"I know," said Cecil. "One does when K is driving. She—" He stopped so abruptly that Susan glanced up into his thin young face and followed the direction of his gaze. Norman Bridges had climbed down from the rumble seat and was holding up his arms for Sally Lee Sully. He was laughing, his white teeth flashing and his face red from the wind, and Sally Lee, blown and lovely, was looking down and laughing, too, so that her eyes were half-closed and darkly shadowed. As she stood above them her green sweater and knitted skirt clung to her body like wet cloth to a clay model and outlined breast and hips and slim young waist against the dull sky. Still smiling gently she brought up one knee in order to step over the side of the car and poised there for an unforgettable instant, one lovely line of grace flowing into another.

The instant that she stood there against the sky became sharp and terribly clear. The still, pearly sky. The pines. The consciousness of space and a plateau and a precipice at its edge, and a great spreading valley below.

And Norman Bridges holding his strong arms up toward Sally, with the laugh on his face becoming fixed while Sally Lee Sully poised there with her beautiful body against the sky.

Katherine banged the heavy door of the car, and the scene dissolved. Sally Lee slid into Norman's arms. Somebody cried: "What a view!" And Katherine was walking away from the car, and they had all turned to look out across space and valley.

"Don't go too near the edge," said Katherine sharply to somebody and Susan realized that she was speaking to Cecil and that, insensibly drawn, they had all drifted toward the little line of stones that marked the edge of the cliff.

Susan stepped nearer, resisting her inborn dread of high places, and looked over. A sheer drop of how many feet—a hundred—three hundred? She couldn't guess.

"Over here," said Cecil to Susan, "is the Crescent. At the right. Just behind the car." She turned at his gesture toward the car again. "It's really just a ravine but it's so sharp and sudden that it's like a gash. It's a queer sort of thing—like a cleft in the face of the plateau. Probably made in some past geological age by a mountain torrent, though it's dry now. Nothing but rocks at the bottom."

No wonder he'd been uneasy when Katherine backed and turned and maneuvered! Susan stood at the rear of the long car and observed with frozen horror that the gleaming left fenders of the car were actually not more than four feet from that sharp, jagged cut.

It was, as Cecil said, an irregular, gash-like cleft interrupting the smooth floor of the plateau. The ravine was narrow, not more than fifteen feet wide where it began at the cliff edge and narrowing to a point. Beyond it was the small plateau again, except that, there, it was not cleared except for a path that ran from the edge of the parking space, around the end of the short, sharp ravine and out again to a bench which was almost directly opposite the car. Katherine spoke quickly and loudly.

"There's a grand view from the other side of the Crescent," she said. "The view from the bench over there is better even than from the plateau on this side. Shall we walk around?"

But Sally Lee Sully, strolling toward them across the parking space, vetoed that. "We'd better get started up the mountain, if we're going."

"Right," agreed Cecil. "Weatherman to the contrary, it's going to be cloudy."

So they started, Katherine plunging ahead and becoming flushed and panting after the first half-mile. Norman trudged along easily beside Susan, smoking a pipe. Sally Lee Sully strolled behind them with an appearance of laziness and fatigue until you realized that she remained exactly twenty feet behind the whole way and might as easily have kept with them. Cecil stayed behind. It was the accustomed thing and occasioned no comment and no offers of company. As they reached a turn in the sharply climbing path that brought them out above the inn and the plateau, they could see him, clear and small below them. It was Norman who saw him first.

"There's Cecil—over on the Crescent. On the bench. See him? He's reading."

"He's always reading." That was Sally Lee.

They went on. And it was a pleasant enough climb. Except that it was cloudy. So cloudy that by the time they reached the top there was no view at all and nothing to do but sit on dampish boulders above a faintly moving, pearly gray blanket and smoke and rest before they started down again.

By the time they reached the inn it was twilight, with the car looming ghostily out of the mist, its sleek gray sides wet, and the windows of the inn lighted and showing distant-looking blobs of radiance.

"Light looks good," said Norman who was by that time merely a thick black bulk trudging beside Susan. "Hope they've got a fire. Hi, Katherine—I'd better turn on the car lights—did you lock the door?"

"Only the ignition. Do turn on the lights, Norm. I don't suppose anybody will be coming up tonight in this fog, though."

Norman vanished, a glow appeared before the car, and Katherine was the first to reach the inn. And at the sound of her step on the porch, the door flung open, letting out light and warmth, with Cecil outlined against the light welcoming them and exclaiming about the fog.

And it was Cecil who suggested that they have dinner at the inn before attempting the descent.

"You are all tired and cold. And the fog is bad. Anyway I've already ordered dinner."

Katherine hesitated and looked at Susan, and afterward Susan wondered what would have happened had she herself insisted on undertaking their trip down the mountain at once. Or rather when it would have happened.

But she did not insist. The open fire leaping in the huge fireplace, the smells of dinner, the table already laid and drawn up to the fire, and more than anything, the prospect of the fog's eventually lifting, were irresistible. And Norman, entering, looked at Katherine and looked at Cecil and closed the door behind him.

"The fog can't get worse," he said. "And it may lift a bit. Tell the girl to bring on the steaks, Cecil. I'm hungry as a bear." Then Norman added abruptly: "Golly, I forgot to bring in the champagne."

"Champagne!" Katherine's voice was strained.

Sally Lee Sully lifted languorous dark eyes to look at Katherine, and Norman said: "Of course. Champagne is the official betrothal toaster. I doubt very much if an engagement to marry is legal without champagne."

"Engagement," said Norman, facing her solidly. "Sally Lee Sully engaged to marry Cecil Vandeman. Announcement made by old friend of family, Norman Bridges." He paused. Cecil somehow was standing between Sally Lee Sully and Katherine—his hand was on Sally Lee but he looked at Katherine. Then Norman crossed to Katherine and forced her to look away from Cecil and at him. "Come now, dear—they've waited patiently till Cecil is better. Now he's well enough to marry—"

Katherine jerked away from him.

"He's not well enough!" she cried.

In the stricken, uncomfortable silence, the door from the kitchen opened brusquely and the waitress entered, laden tray in her hands.

"How do you do?" she said chattily to Norman, who was nearest the table. "Shall I serve dinner now?"

"All right," said Cecil. His hand on Sally Lee increased its pressure, as if comfortingly, before he left her. "I'll get the champagne," he said, obviously thankful for the interruption. And Norman nodded quickly: "Do. It's in the rumble seat."

Cecil picked up his hat and reached the door and paused there, looking at Katherine's rigid back, and Norman said: "Fog is bad, Cecil. Don't stumble and drop the champagne. The car lights are on, you can see all right. Look here, my girl, have you got some glasses?"

Cecil's eyes waited another instant for Katherine to turn. She did not move and he glanced then at Sally Lee, made a cheerful little gesture with his hand, and the door opened, letting in black fog, and closed.

"Goblets will do," said Norman to the waitress. "Bring 'em on. Anything will do when it's champagne."

Katherine whirled from the window.

"You had planned this all along," she said harshly. "You and Cecil. You were going to tell me like this when Sally Lee was here—and Susan—because you thought that in their presence I would say nothing."

"It was Cecil's plan—"

"And yours too, Norman. And Sally Lee's. Probably Sally Lee's plan first. She knew I would object."

"Suppose we did plan it, Katherine," Norman said with stubborn gentleness. "I have waited too."

Sally Lee looked at her ankles and drawled: "Don't be that way, Katherine. I won't eat Cecil."

"You!" said Katherine simply.

"The main thing," drawled Sally Lee, "is that Cecil loves me. And he's free, white, and twenty-one, in spite of the sick baby you've tried to make him."

It was a dreadful silence—dreadful to sit there and see Sally Lee's languid sweetness, to watch that dull red slowly sweep out of Katherine's face and her long angular hands double themselves as if she could strike Sally Lee's smiling, pretty face.

Finally Norman said fumblingly: "Now, Sally Lee—" And Katherine said in a choked way: "Did you hear that, Norman? Did you hear what she said? And I've put everything away, you and everything, to nurse and care for Cecil. Yet you say let them marry. Norman, is it possible you do not realize that she's marrying him only for his money?"

Sally Lee Sully showed herself suddenly and pettishly angry.

"I meant you were making him spineless and childish. He's not half the invalid you've made him think he is. You've tried to dominate him. Well, you can't any more. He loves me. Suppose I am marrying him for his money. It's going to make him happy. If you are so devoted to him I should think that would please you."

Katherine's clenched hands relaxed hopelessly. She said to Norman:

"You see what you've done."

"I've done nothing," said Norman, standing his ground solidly. "Be reasonable, Katherine. Sally Lee isn't marrying him just for his money. He wants her. And she'll make him a good wife."

"It divides the Vandeman fortune in half if Cecil—" Sally Lee Sully checked herself as if frightened at what her vicious little tongue had been about to say and looked from Katherine quickly and supplicatingly to Norman. "You see, Norm—if Cecil doesn't marry, the whole thing would come to Katherine."

"Be reasonable," said Norman pleadingly again. "You angered her, Katherine. After all, you didn't exactly welcome her into the family." He approached Katherine and put his hand on her arm but she jerked savagely away from him and went to the door, her sport shoes making heavy, angry footfalls. She opened the door and fog poured in and it was black beyond.

"Cecil ought to be coming," she said as if detached from the painful, ugly quarrel. She peered into the fog.

"He'll be back in a minute," said Norman, relievedly pouncing upon a new topic. "Hope the fog lifts before we go down the mountain. Ah, here come the glasses. And the steaks."

The waitress entered again, glasses clinking faintly and musically and the fragrance of broiling steaks filling the room.

Sally Lee Sully looked at the steaks smoking on the table, hesitated, shrugged, let her skirt drop over her beautiful knees, and rose. Her walk across to where Katherine stood, still peering into the fog beyond the open door, was to Susan's awakened eyes a thing of potent grace. Odd, she'd never perceived the danger in the girl before.

Sally Lee put her hand on Katherine's arm. She was all wooing, all tender and sweet. "K, dear, forgive me. I didn't mean anything—You've been so good to Cecil. I'll try to be as good a wife as you've been a sister."

Norman beamed. Katherine finally tore her seeking eyes from the fog and darkness and looked slowly and searchingly into the girl's flower-like face. And it was then that she said a very strange and dreadful thing.

"Sally Lee," she said, "you will never be Cecil's wife."

Under that searching, bright regard, Sally Lee shrank back.

And Norman said roughly: "Shut the door, Katherine. It's cold. Cecil will be here in a moment."

"He ought to be here now," said Katherine. "I'm going to look for him."

"Don't be silly, K, he's all right."

"He ought to have returned," she said stubbornly. "You know, Norm, he has no sense of direction. He's probably wandering about somewhere."

"Nonsense. He can see the lights from the inn."

It was just there, Susan realized later, that from somewhere, stealthily, cautiously, scarcely observed, there crept into the situation a strange sense of tension, of foreshadowing.

But it was a good ten minutes before it became definite. Observable. Tangible, even.

Ten minutes of discussion—of increasingly anxious watching, of Norman first and then Katherine vanishing into the fog and shouting from the edge of the porch into the whirling darkness beyond, soft and black and impenetrable, with not a gleam of light anywhere except from the open door and windows behind them.

But Cecil did not return. And did not reply.

And he was not at the dark and silent car, nor anywhere between the car and the inn; and the lights and the hurriedly summoned proprietor and the two servants and themselves could not discover him and could not make him hear. They were all somehow out in the fog and there were blobs of lights from electric torches and the streaming lights again from the car, and shouting voices everywhere and then that diapason of sound became suddenly still, silenced by one scream.

That was Katherine's scream when they found him.

He was at the bottom of the ravine, huddled on the rocks, dead.

It was the proprietor and Norman who crawled down there with flashlights and ropes. Mercifully the darkness and the fog veiled the thing from Katherine's eyes. And during those black moments while the men painfully, slowly, with difficulties which were too readily to be surmised, managed to remove the slender, broken body and carry it at last toward the inn, Susan sat in the blank dampness beside Katherine and held the woman's strong, angular hands.

Norman, panting, returned at last and put his arm around Katherine and drew her toward the inn. Susan and Sally Lee followed. The light gravel crunched under their feet.

All at once after that black interlude of horror they were again in the long dining room. The fire was stirred to flames. Katherine, looking like a sleepwalker, was sitting before it. The men, Norman and the proprietor and the fat, frightened cook, were talking—talking in circles, repeating themselves, exclaiming, saying how it happened. Sally Lee Sully was crouched, slim and white and silent. The waitress—white, now, and incoherent with excitement—was saying they ought to have turned on the light on the point beyond the Crescent.

And the whole thing was as the proprietor said: Cecil had gone across the open space toward the car. Had become confused in the fog and darkness. Had passed the car without knowing it. Had stepped over the edge of the ravine. It was all perfectly— terribly—clear.

"It's a cruel drop," said the proprietor. "But I never thought of anybody just walking over it like that. The lights ought to have been turned on."

"Lights?" said Norman.

"The light beyond the Crescent. Have it strung up on a wire. It is connected on the same switch with the porch light. But it was so foggy tonight—nobody here but you folks here in the dining room."

"Don't you make a habit of turning it on every night?"

But they didn't. Why should they? So few people came up at night. It was only during the summer that people from town came up for parties and liked to walk out and sit on the ledge beyond the ravine.

Norman, shuddering, was reproaching himself bitterly.

"I sent him out, Katherine. But I never thought—how could I? He walked out into the fog—aiming toward the car—he was excited, poor Cecil. Never had a head for direction. I ought to have realized the danger. It's all my fault."

Katherine finally spoke. "It's nobody's fault," she said. Her voice was heavy and slow, each word dropping like a weight. "Well—what are we going to do?"

Telephone? But there was no telephone.

"We're so far from town," said the innkeeper. "But I'll watch the—I'll watch while you send to town."

And the waitress sobbed and said again, if she'd only turned on the lights, but how was she to know?

"Him going out into pitch-dark and the fog besides," she said, wiping her eyes.

Something stirred in Susan and quite automatically began to function. The suddenness of the thing, the confusion and, submerging everything, the blinding, swirling fog had shocked and, in a sense, submerged her. Even now she spoke without conscious purpose. And she said only, in a small, clear voice:

"Darkness! But the lights of the car were turned on. He would have been guided by that."

There was an odd, short silence. Then they looked at her.

No one spoke. Under all those eyes Susan smoothed back her hair and heard herself saying quite definitely: "The lights of the car were on. Norman turned them on when we returned from the mountaintop." She paused and added because she couldn't help it and because it was so very obvious: "But there were no lights anywhere when we went to the porch to look for Cecil. There were certainly no lights at all, then."

It was a puzzle.

Not a very great puzzle, to be sure; one doubtless with the simplest of explanations. Norman had turned on the car lights. The doors of the car were not locked. For some trivial reason someone had turned out those lights.

But it was a puzzle that all at once assumed significance.

The car lights would have guided Cecil safely to the car. He would not have passed beyond it in the darkness. Those front lights would have made a blob of yellow that would have served as a beacon.

She thought that far and realized that no one was speaking.

But presently the tensely ruminative look in the waitress's face bore fruit. She said with a burst: "Oh, yes, there were lights. I saw them from the window."

"When did you see them?" asked Susan.

"I remember exactly. I was just going from this room into the kitchen after glasses and I looked out the window and saw a light. And it was right after Mr. Vandeman had gone out for the champagne. I'm sure about it."

"Why yes," said Katherine slowly. "The lights of the car were turned on. I'm sure Cecil could have seen them from the porch. And they were on, when he left. I could see the glow myself from the window as he went out the door. The light was dim and looked far away on account of the fog but quite clear enough to guide him. Who turned them off?"

Again no one spoke for a moment. Then Norman said: "I certainly turned on the lights. And when we stepped out on the porch to call for Cecil I remember thinking how dark it was. If Katherine saw the lights as Cecil left and they were gone when we went to call him—"

The proprietor interrupted anxiously.

"None of us touched your car, Mrs. Vandeman. I was in the kitchen the whole time after you arrived. The cook was there, too, and Jennie"—he indicated the waitress—"was coming and going from the dining room. None of us was anywhere near your car."

Katherine's hand made a weary gesture and Sally Lee Sully said suddenly:

"Perhaps Cecil himself turned out the lights."

There was another thoughtful moment. Then Katherine said: "You mean he reached the car, for some reason turned out the lights and then accidentally stepped over the edge?"

Katherine rose abruptly as if she could not bear talking.

"We'll never know what happened," she said, staring into the flames. "Never. Come—we'd better go down the mountain. It's impossible, of course, to take"—she did not say "Cecil"; instead she simply stopped and then continued: "The coupe is so small. I'll get hold of Dr. Benham. He'll know what to do."

But before they started Susan did a bit of private exploring— the odd little puzzle of the lights was still a puzzle.

The switch beside the door did control both the light on the long porch, a single bare bulb set into its sloping rustic roof, and another light high up in the trees above the bench on the far side of the ravine; too, the car lights were on now, streaming dully into the fog. The fog veiled their brilliance. Still it would have been impossible, even in the fog, to miss those lights.

And Susan herself had seen that resultant glow when Norman turned them on. And Katherine had seen it from the window at the time Cecil went out toward it. And Susan herself had seen that there was no light anywhere at the moment when all four of them stepped from the dining room to the porch in order to call Cecil.

Then had he reached the car? And if he had reached the car, why had he turned off the lights before returning to the inn?

Susan walked slowly across the gravel toward the car. Back at the inn were lights and muffled voices. But the mountain was silent and dark, and felt rather than seen. Off toward the right, veiled by that soft, damp blackness was the sharp edge of the plateau. Just before her was the car and beyond the car was the narrow wedge of blackness, cruel and masked by fog, dividing the plateau from the ledge beyond. She measured her steps, noted how the strong lights of the car were blurred and veiled and only gradually became perceptible as lights, and reached the car. Across that dark space which she knew lay at her feet and away up in the trees was the light; that, too, had it been lighted, would have been a guide to Cecil. Or rather not a guide but a warning. Then the confused sound of footsteps was on the gravel and shadows were emerging from the fog.

"Let me drive, K." That was Norman's voice.

And Katherine said wearily: "No, Norman. It will give me something to do. You and Sally Lee can ride in the rumble."

But when she had got into the car and fumbled for the ignition, she said quite suddenly to Susan: "I was wrong, Susan. I can't drive."

"I'll drive," offered Susan quickly.

Susan found the road and entered it, and very cautiously made the first of those fumbling, fog-blinded curves.

It wasn't going to be any fun, getting that long car down the mountain. It hadn't been so bad coming up. Cecil had been with them, then. Cecil.

But Cecil was dead now. In an accident. Cecil who had been the focus of a queer, dreadful quarrel. They were peaceful now, Norman and Katherine and Sally Lee. Peaceful now that Cecil was dead and they had him no longer to quarrel about.

Susan peered into the fog and turned and watched for the road. It was somehow hypnotic, that constant moving through dense swirling mists, that constant heightening of tension in all the nerves, that straining for perception, that groping, groping into fog. Groping into fog. Trying to feel out imperceptible things.

Murder!

The word suddenly entered and possessed Susan's consciousness. It was unexpected. And it was like an alarm.

Now why should she think of that? No reason at all. Murder.

If it was Cecil's death she was trying to connect with murder, that was all wrong. Cecil had stepped over a cliff while all four of them were together in that lighted dining room. Talking. Quarreling about Cecil.

But Cecil was not murdered.

Now look here, Susan, she thought, let's examine this. Don't dismiss it as if you were afraid of it; prove to yourself that there's no murder. No murder. No murder because he couldn't have been murdered when there was no one to murder him.

And there was no motive. No one who would profit by his death and no one to whom that death would be welcome.

Katherine, of course, would inherit the whole of the Vandeman fortune instead of only half of it, if Cecil died without heirs. Without a wife. But Katherine was devoted to Cecil. And she had enough money as it was. Sally Lee Sully stood to lose at Cecil's death. And Norman Bridges, unless he married Katherine, was not affected in any way. Although if he married Katherine, Cecil's death just now doubled Katherine's (and thus in a sense, Norman's own) fortune.

Katherine stirred and said abruptly: "But he's better off dead. Marriage with Sally Lee—" she did not finish.

The broken sentence fitted into a small groove in Susan's thoughts.

No motive. No murderer. Then there was no murder.

On through the fog, carrying consciousness of murder. Murder becoming part of the fog.

Against her will, against her reason, the thing persisted. Against—

If Cecil had turned out the lights of the car after leaving it, then where was the champagne? It should be in that case shattered somewhere in that deadly steep ravine. But was it?

The question was sharp and sudden like an unexpected flash of lightning.

Susan consciously and clearly began to think and build and remember. It was as if that flash of light had briefly illumined a dark room and she knew not what the objects it contained were, but merely that they were there.

And Susan knew that she had to go back. To go back now before others came. Before—a glow of yellow was rounding a curve twenty feet ahead. Susan put on brakes and clutched for the horn, and its long mellow notes echoed in unseen valleys. Susan's car stopped. The other car stopped. There were voices and men's figures before the lights.

And out of the fog came Jim Byrne. Out of the fog and up to the car.

"Susan?" he cried. "Good Lord! Why didn't you stay where you were till the fog lifted!"

Susan said something; she never knew what. Another man— Jim called him vaguely Landy—approached and Susan heard Katherine speaking to him.

"There was an accident," she was saying as if she knew him. "Cecil fell into the ravine."

Terse explanations, horrified low-voiced talk, Norman there, too, telling them. Somehow she must let Jim know that it was no accident. That it was murder. And that they must go back. That they must discover that evidence before it was destroyed.

Jim's blunted, agreeably irregular face loomed rather sternly from the blackness. His sensitive mouth looked tight, his chin, as always, faintly pugnacious.

Susan touched his hand. And as he looked directly at her, she said in a voice that was scarcely more than a whisper: "It's murder."

He heard it. His eyes became aware and his face very still. She whispered: "We must go back. Arrange it—somehow. And let me ride with you."

He arranged it. Smoothly and with his customary resource and aplomb. She believed that there was some general feeling that they were to bring the body down the mountain in Landy's sedan. No one objected. Norman took Susan's place at the wheel. With Jim and Landy at the side of the road watching lest the wheels go over the edge and shouting directions, he managed to reverse the long coupe.

And Susan, shaking a little, was beside Jim, in the front seat of the Landy sedan.

The moving rear light of the coupe ahead made a small red signal, warning them of curves. But the man Landy and Sally Lee were in the tonneau. Sally Lee was drenched with fog and chilled, and white, and very appealing. She had to ride inside, now that she could. Susan could hear Landy being comforting.

The trouble was Susan couldn't talk to Jim. The story came out but only in outline, only the surface of it, and she could not tell Jim that first they must make sure about the champagne bottles. That they must look for a string or a rope with a weight on one end. Or neither, but instead something unpredictable.

That because the motive was what she felt it was, they must prevent another murder. That was what made it so urgent. That was why they had to find evidence, conclusive evidence—somehow.

One murder and then, after a while, another. The murder of Cecil was only half that grim program. The second murder would complete it.

"He never had a head for direction," Sally Lee was saying plaintively.

Faintly, ironically, the little red gleam ahead led them over that blind, winding journey.

Once Susan said, under cover of Landy's heavier voice: "Why did you start up the mountain?"

"Nerves." He grinned at her and then sobered. "One of my fey nights. Fog and general unrest. I got your note; you hadn't returned."

There was the inn, lights in the windows and on the porch. Across, beyond the Crescent, the light in the trees made a blur. The coupe was already parked before it, and as the gravel spattered under the sedan tires the door opened. And still there was no chance to talk to Jim. Suppose she had made a mistake. Jim helped her out of the car.

"What shall I do?"

"Talk. Ask questions. Especially about the lights."

"You girls had better go inside to the fire," Landy was saying, speaking to both of them and looking at Sally Lee.

It was not difficult to approach, in the confusion and shifting lights, the rumble seat of the coupe and search for champagne bottles that *were not there*. Not difficult either to walk quietly in the shadows behind the parked cars toward the Crescent. The lights from the cars, the porch light, enabled her to pick her way along. Here was the place where the Vandeman car had been parked—here were its tire marks. That dark rift was the edge of the ravine. Across it and considerably to the right was the light in the trees.

She hesitated. She could, if she was very careful not to make a misstep, find her way along the path that skirted the ravine. The others had gone into the inn. The light among the trees over there would serve as a guide. But the fog was treacherous, inconceivably bewildering.

She took a few steps and stopped sharply. Was there a curious faint echo of crunching gravel? If so, it was silent now. Susan swallowed her heart and went on, feeling her way cautiously, step by step.

There were shrubs now as she passed the curve of the ravine and the path rose a little. Somewhere beyond the clouds there must be a rising moon, full and white, for the fog had taken on a kind of gray gleam. Her feet were yet on the path and it was easier than she'd expected. But she didn't like being alone in the fog.

Something white loomed out of it and she stopped dead still and terrified before she saw that it was only the bench. The bench where Cecil had sat reading during the afternoon.

Above her was the light and she could see it now as a light and not as just a bright glow. It was a bulb, shaded by a reflector, swathed in mist. As this side of the plateau was a little higher than the inn side, the light looked from the side of the inn much higher than it proved actually to be. For it was not more than twelve feet off the ground. It was a makeshift affair, strung as if for only temporary use on a drop-cord and hanging over a convenient branch with the slack taken up and tied in a loop.

Something rustled again in a dripping thicket nearby and Susan turned with a kind of gasp of comprehension and something very like terror. Her return over that path and around the black depth that was the ravine was, in spite of its caution, like a flight. Yet she knew that there was no one there in the fog. Everyone was at the inn. Once on the cleared space and headed toward the parked cars and the inn she lost some of her unreasoning terror. It was only murder that she was afraid of; the fact of it; the presence of it which was like a tangible thing.

The instrument of murder was there beyond that opened door, where light made a long, broad radiance.

She was panting though, when she reached the porch of the inn. What had they done? What had they decided? She controlled her breath and smoothed her hair back tightly under her brown beret and entered. And walked upon a tableau.

Katherine stood, tall and vigorous, though her long face was pale, before the fire. Sally Lee was seated languidly in a chair, looking very helpless and very beautiful. Norman was standing beside Sally Lee. Landy was leaning lazily over the back of a chair and looked perplexed. The innkeeper and the fat cook with his white apron twisted around his waist were looking worried and the waitress, Jennie, was peering in at the kitchen door.

And Jim was sitting casually on the edge of a table. He had just finished saying something, for there was about them an air of intent listening, and Jim was very definitely the focus of that strained attention. No one seemed to be aware of Susan's entrance but she knew that Jim had noted it. Norman cleared his throat and said:

"I don't understand you."

Jim flicked a glance toward Susan.

"It's a question of satisfying the coroner. It makes no difference to me of course. It's nothing to me—except a very regrettable affair. But you see, the—body *was removed*. And it was a death by violence. I'm only telling you that the coroner will be bound to ask questions. It's just as well to be perfectly clear in your minds about what happened. This business of the lights, now, seems to me confusing. Probably it isn't, really. In the excitement of the moment"—he turned suddenly and directly to Katherine.

"You turned on the car lights? When was that?"

"When we came down from the mountain. About six o'clock. But I didn't turn them on. Norman did it for me."

"Then it was you, Mr. Bridges, who turned on the lights?"

"Why, yes, of course," said Norman.

"You are sure? I mean, your sleeve didn't catch on the switch as you turned from the car and turn them off again—something like that?"

"Certainly, I'm sure. Anyway, Katherine saw the car lights

from the window just as Cecil left this room and went into the fog."

"That's right," said Jim agreeably. Evidently from the talk in the car and from the questions that had preceded Susan's entrance he had got a fairly complete version of the thing.

"Did anybody else see the lights after you arrived at the inn?"

Susan started to mention the waitress when the girl darted forward. "I did," she said eagerly. "Just after Mr. Vandeman went out the door."

"I see," said Jim. "Then what happened to the car lights between the time when Mrs. Vandeman and Jennie saw them, and the time when you opened the door and went out to call for Cecil? You have all said that there was no light anywhere then."

"That's just the point. There's only one thing that could have happened. Cecil must have turned them out."

"Why?" said Jim again, gently.

But Katherine's long face was beginning to look angry.

Norman said with decision: "We don't know. One never knows exactly how accidents happen. But since we were all here in this room when it must have happened (or in the kitchen), there is no other explanation. Cecil for some reason turned out those lights, started into the fog away from the car, perhaps turned back for something. We'll never know just what happened. Except that somehow—he misjudged the distances— missed his footing—"

Sally Lee looked up at Jim.

"Poor Cecil," she said. "He always got confused so easily." She dabbed her lovely eyes with her handkerchief and the Landy person looked altogether fatuous.

Jim said to her: "What did *you* do when Cecil did not return?"

Sally Lee looked blank and stopped dabbing her eyes. She said after a moment: "Well, it was like this. Katherine and Norman walked out on the porch and shouted. Pretty soon I went out too. There wasn't any light. Somebody said something about lights and Norman said he'd call the proprietor. Katherine said maybe Cecil was in the car and started across the space toward the car. Norman ran along the porch and knocked on the kitchen door, I think, and shouted something. Then—I don't know what happened. I started out toward the car and—it was very dark and I could hear people but couldn't see anything. Pretty soon I bumped into Katherine and we were all calling Cecil. It's pretty confused. I don't know what happened really. The innkeeper was out there, too."

"Were there any lights?"

Sally Lee looked thoughtful.

"After a while," she achieved presently. "Somebody turned on the lights of the car. And the innkeeper, I suppose, had some flashlights. And there was a light on the porch. And another up in the trees over there. That's all I can remember. Except that Katherine and I—and Miss Dare, I suppose—stood there together while they were climbing down into the ravine. And Katherine started to cry. Then they said he was dead and they were bringing—him up."

"I see," said Jim. "Does everybody agree to that—or has Miss Sully forgotten something?"

No one spoke for a moment. Then the proprietor said:

"I guess that's right."

Norman Bridges nodded.

"Exactly right, I think."

"Who finally turned on the porch light?"

Jennie stepped forward again.

"I did. He"—she looked at Norman—"pounded on the door from the porch and shouted that somebody was lost. My father"—(The cook, thought Susan parenthetically, or the innkeeper? The latter, for the girl added definitely, "Him," and pointed to the innkeeper)—"got some flashlights and went outdoors and the cook went too. I came in here to find out what had happened. Nobody was here. I went to the door and it was all dark outside except that just as I looked the car lights shone up all at once, as if somebody had just turned them on. They looked real near and I started out to see what had happened. Everybody was shouting and calling Cecil and pretty soon I saw the flashlights over beyond the Crescent and I thought about the light over there, so I ran back to the porch—the switch is right there beside the door—and turned it on."

"Lights," said Katherine suddenly, "are extremely confusing when there's such a dense fog."

Jim looked at her.

"Are these stories as you remember things, Mrs. Vandeman?"

Katherine hesitated. "I think so. I was very frightened. Terrified."

"Terrified?"

"I am always nervous about Cecil. I have cared for him so long. I—I was afraid he would become chilled, staying out in the fog so long."

"You didn't think of an accident?"

"No," said Katherine. "That is—yes, when he did not return. One's mind always flashes ahead to catastrophe."

Norman moved restively.

"Don't you think we'd better get under way," he suggested

rather diffidently. "We'll just tell the coroner the truth. That's all we can do. And we—well, we had to move the body. We couldn't just leave him there."

Jim said: "You were certain that he was dead?"

Katherine choked back a gasping cry and Norman said quickly: "Certainly. There was no doubt." He turned definitely to Katherine. "Warm enough to start again, dear? I think we'd better get down to town. There's nothing we can do here."

There was a general air of assent. Landy stood up and Sally Lee began to fasten her green sweater around her throat. And Jim looked at Susan.

Susan's heart leaped to her throat and pounded there. Time to act. Time to start that inexorable process going. And it had to be started. It had been a cruel and dreadful thing; terribly cruel, terribly simple, terribly brutal. It had been even stupid. Yet its very stupidity was baffling. But for one thing it would have succeeded. And that one thing was so trivial. So little. She took a long breath. Jim's eyes glowed and urged her to speak.

But she couldn't even then until he said quite clearly—so clearly that everyone in the room stopped and turned to look.

"Tell them what you know."

It was like Jim. And there was all at once a taut line about his jaw and sparks of light in his eyes like phosphorescence in a deep-lying sea. What he really said was: "Go ahead, Susie, spill it. I'm with you." But that was only with his eyes.

She said, under that compulsion: "Katherine, you said that when you were standing at the window and Cecil left, you could see the lights of the car?"

"Yes." Katherine looked tired and angry. "Let's not talk any more, Susan. It doesn't help. He's dead."

"Were the lights very clear?"

"Well"—Katherine considered—"of course, the car was at an angle with the inn so that I could see only the glow of the light. No, it wasn't exactly clear. But I knew, of course, what it was."

"You said that it seemed far away."

Katherine hesitated. "Why—yes. It did seem far away."

"Did you see two lights or one?" persisted Susan.

"I didn't see any lights," said Katherine, frowning. "There was only a kind of radiance. The way the car was facing I couldn't have seen the headlights themselves, if that is what you mean."

"But you saw a radiance, close to the ground, that seemed far away and was very dim in the fog? That's really all you could swear to seeing, isn't it?"

"I suppose so. What are you getting at, Susan?"

Susan turned to the waitress. "Tell us exactly why you are so sure you saw the lights from the car."

Jennie looked shrewd. "Because," she said quickly, "the light was close to the ground."

Something had happened in that long, firelit room. Something strange had passed over it and its chill breath had touched them all. No one moved. Susan said to the innkeeper, "When Cecil Vandeman stepped over the edge of the ravine he is supposed to have had some bottles of champagne with him. I suppose they would have dropped and been broken in the fall. Did you see anything of the kind?"

"N-no," said the innkeeper. He looked perplexed and very worried. There was something going on here that he didn't understand. "But there may be something. We can look in the morning."

Susan felt inexpressibly tired. She said wearily: "You might look, too, for some thread. Thrown probably into the bushes somewhere."

The chill, queer thing that had entered that room became possessive, like a spell. Susan was aware that Jim slipped very gently from the table and was standing so that he faced the others and was between them and Susan. His hand was in his pocket. And Katherine said:

"What do you mean, Susan?"

"I mean," said Susan slowly, "that Cecil was murdered."

Jim said very quietly: "You are perfectly sure, Susan?"

Susan turned to Sally Lee Sully.

"Do you know," she said, "that an accessory to murder, either before or after the fact, is criminally liable?"

"Is—*what*—"

"Can be tried for murder. That includes—concealing evidence."

There was another silent—yet packed—moment while Sally Lee considered it. Then suddenly, pale and deadly in her beauty, she whirled to Norman Bridges.

"Tried for murder!" she screamed. "I *can't* be—I *can't* be—He did it! I don't know how, but he did it!"

Confusion. Shouts. A rush of movement. Norman's wide hands closing down across Sally Lee's beautiful, treacherous mouth. Men's figures intervening, and the firelight blotted out intermittently.

"He did it," screamed Sally Lee again frantically. "That's why he threw the champagne bottles out of the car. He hated Cecil. He was jealous. He wanted me. But I had nothing to do with the murder. Nothing—nothing—"

They were holding Norman who was struggling, and Susan said to Sally Lee: "Why do you think he wanted you?"

Above its white and selfish terror, Sally Lee's face was scornful—not of men but of Susan's ignorance. "He wanted the money too," she cried sharply. "He was going to marry Katherine."

"Why?"

"To get the money, of course."

Jim said abruptly, cutting through the confusion: "These are only accusations. You have no proof."

Sally Lee paused. An accessory—tried for murder. Concealing evidence. Her eyes glittered; nothing soft about them now, nothing languorous. She cried:

"He threw the champagne bottles, three of them, out of the car on the way down the mountain after Cecil's death. He told me not to tell. He made love to me, when Katherine didn't know. But I"—she hesitated, then plunged on: "but he could never have got me without money. I know my market, and he knew it."

In the shocked silence Katherine moved and said with a kind of groan: "That was why, Susan. That was why I needed you. There was something—I didn't know quite what. I wanted your advice."

Susan thought: Cecil first. Then Katherine. She said to Katherine: "Come, Katherine, we'll go home."

But they were not to go yet. Not before Jim had asked certain questions. Had put together logically and with conclusiveness the thing that had thrust itself with such dreadful persistence upon Susan.

"The proof," she said to Jim. "I don't know." She considered slowly. They were on the porch, cool air touching her cheek. Inside there were preparations.

"There's the electric light bulb. Fingerprints are on it."

"What bulb?"

Susan dug into that queer subterranean storehouse where all things are assembled and labeled, to emerge as conclusions.

"He turned on the car lights. We saw the glow. But Katherine and I and then Sally Lee entered the house. While the lights were on, he ran around the path and let down the light on the point. (It's on a drop-cord with the slack taken up in a loop. All he had to do was pull a string he had previously tied to the loop.) By that time we had reached the house. He turned out the car lights as he passed, leaving the light (then not burning) across the ravine. The fog was so thick that the light (when he turned it on as he entered the house) made only a bright glow and as it was about two feet off the ground, anybody would think, seeing that low light off in the fog, that it was the lights of a car. Particularly if that idea was fixed in one's mind. If you were told it was the light from a car. If you expected it to be that. But Katherine, you see, said it seemed far away."

"Wait. Was the light on the point beyond the ravine burning then—when you came down the mountain?"

"No. He had to let it down first. But he reached the house after we had entered it. The switch is just beside the door. He could have turned it on as he entered."

"The porch light would have been turned on too. They are on the same switch. Someone would have seen it."

"That's where his fingerprints must be. You see he had to un-screw the bulb before turning on the light. It would be very sim-ple, the work of an instant. The whole thing is simple; it was only a matter of accomplishing promptly every step in the process at the right time. There was really only one point of danger in the whole thing."

"Wait," said Jim again, looking thoughtful. "Let's go chrono-logically. So far it's all clear. You are all in the house: the lights of the car are turned out but across the ravine a light is shining which, owing to the fog and distance and its being so close to the ground, looks very like the lights of a car. Now what?"

"Well—the waitress saw it and, naturally, merely registered that it was a low light; hence car lights. Remember that the fog actually changed and confused everything; and we would all make allowances for it. Also, Katherine saw that light and, fortunately from the murderer's viewpoint, saw it just as Cecil left the house."

"He left to get the champagne?"

"Yes. They'd quarrelled—Norman and Cecil had evidently talked of announcing the engagement; had planned to have dinner up here, and Norman must have suggested bringing the champagne. That was evident too. His only problem was to get Cecil to go to the car, and that wasn't a problem. Both men would offer to get the champagne. He would let Cecil go. Of course, if Cecil himself had already brought in the champagne Norman would have made some other pretext to take Cecil into the fog. The next step was simple; the only necessary thing was to do it. He waited until he knew Cecil would have reached the ravine. He had said as Cecil went out the door: 'The car lights are on,' thus fixing the idea in Cecil's mind—to go straight for the glow of light."

"But it might have failed."

"No. Not when he had succeeded with the preparations and had actually got Cecil started. Cecil was worried, upset on account of the quarrel. He was always easily confused about directions. And once really into the fog—no, it was pretty sure to succeed. But if it hadn't, he would have tried some other way."

"It's pretty complicated," he said and reflected. "No," he said, then. "It's just a series of trivialities, nothing about it that was difficult. And—if it worked—almost proof against detection. And I can see how it would appeal to a mind accustomed to detail and acutely aware of the need to make it look like an accident." He looked at Susan thoughtfully. "Go on."

"Then—he went to the door. Casually—as if to glance out at the fog. And by doing so, had a chance to press the switch for the outside lights again. Thus when we opened the door there was no light anywhere. So what more likely than to assume what we did assume—that Cecil had reached the car, had for some reason turned out the lights and become confused starting back toward the inn. When we stood there in the darkness calling for Cecil, and Cecil didn't reply, he knew that his plan had worked. Of course, Cecil might be still alive—he couldn't know. But it was a deadly fall. It was just then Norman reached his dangerous moment. And that was to accomplish three things before the porch light and, simultaneously, the other light was turned on by somebody. He had to screw that bulb up there tight in the socket again, he had to pound on the kitchen door and shout for the innkeeper, he had to run along the path, push the bench up to the light, climb on the back of the bench and loop up the drop-cord again so that, when the switch was turned on, the light would be high in the tree again. It was his only dangerous moment. And, of course, he had as nearly as he was able, rehearsed it."

"Rehearsed?"

"When the waitress came into the room and saw him she said, 'How do you do?' As if she recognized him. As if he'd been up here before—and recently. You can ask her in order to verify it. But I'm sure. I'm sure, too, that if you'll telephone the weather bureau they'll tell you that their real forecast was cloudy weather. Not fair, as Norman reported."

"The light," said Jim, "would have silhouetted the car."

"It's too far to one side. You can look tomorrow. The car tracks will still be there."

The door opened. They had an instant's view of people moving about and a lovely, graceful figure against the light.

"So that was the motive," said Jim.

"Yes," said Susan. "It was—I don't know—it was just there. Between them."

"It was a gamble on her selfishness," said Jim. "It was a risk." He paused. Fog swirled in and around them and, outside, it was quiet and cold. Presently he said: "Not such a gamble, perhaps. 'Oh, serpent heart, hid with a flowering face' "—he quoted absently, stopped and laughed unsteadily—"Shakespeare said everything. Get into the car, Sue. I'll—see to the rest."

THE DANCE
F. Scott Fitzgerald

Generally regarded as one of America's great writers of the twentieth century, F. Scott Fitzgerald (1896-1940), it is not well known that he began his writing career as a mystery writer. In 1909, at the age of thirteen, he wrote the murder story, "The Mystery of the Raymond Mortgage," which was published in the September 1909 issue of *Now and Then*, the publication of St. Paul Academy. The careful reader will discover that it was flawed by an oversight by the young author: the title document is never mentioned in the text. It was published again in 1960 by Random House in a scarce pamphlet of 750 copies.

In Fitzgerald's masterpiece, *The Great Gatsby* (1925), the climactic scene features Jay Gatsby being shot to death by George Wilson, the cuckolded husband of Gatsby's mistress, when he is told that Gatsby killed his wife by hitting her with his car, though he was not at the wheel.

Fitzgerald, briefly as famous as Ernest Hemingway, was an endless source of gossip when he and his beautiful wife Zelda threw notorious headline-making parties attended by the literati and other stars of the artistic world. The end of the apparently enviable life of wealth and fame came when Zelda had a breakdown in 1930, another two years later, from which she never recovered. They tried to keep their marriage together but Scott had become an alcoholic and finally left her (and their son) in 1937 to move to Hollywood to write screenplays. He was only forty-four when he died in 1944.

"The Dance" is an unusual story because it is told in the first person by a young woman and is set in the small-town South, not to mention being the only mystery short story Fitzgerald ever wrote, aside from his pubescent effort. It was originally published in the June 1926 issue of *The Red Book Magazine* (now *Redbook*); it was first collected in *Bits of Paradise* (New York, Scribner's, 1973), which also contained stories by Zelda Fitzgerald.

The Dance
F. Scott Fitzgerald

ALL MY LIFE I have had a rather curious horror of small towns: not suburbs; they are quite a different matter—but the little lost cities of New Hampshire and Georgia and Kansas, and upper New York. I was born in New York City, and even as a little girl I never had any fear of the streets or the strange foreign faces—but on the occasions when I've been in the sort of place I'm referring to, I've been oppressed with the consciousness that there was a whole hidden life, a whole series of secret implications, significances and terrors, just below the surface, of which I knew nothing. In the cities everything good or bad eventually comes out, comes out of people's hearts, I mean. Life moves about, moves on, vanishes. In the small towns—those of between five and twenty-five thousand people—old hatreds, old and un-forgotten affairs, ghostly scandals and tragedies, seem unable to die, but live on all tangled up with the natural ebb and flow of outward life.

Nowhere has this sensation come over me more insistent-ly than in the South. Once out of Atlanta and Birmingham and New Orleans, I often have the feeling that I can no lon-ger communicate with the people around me. The men and the girls speak a language wherein courtesy is combined with vi-olence, fanatic morality with corn-drinking recklessness, in a fashion which I can't understand. In *Huckleberry Finn* Mark Twain described some of those towns perched along the Mis-sissippi River, with their fierce feuds and their equally fierce re-vivals—and some of them haven't fundamentally changed be-neath their new surface of flivvers and radios. They are deeply uncivilized to this day.

I speak of the South because it was in a small Southern city of this type that I once saw the surface crack for a minute and something savage, uncanny, and frightening rear its head. Then the surface closed again—and when I have gone back there since, I've been surprised to find myself as charmed as ever by the magnolia trees and the singing Negroes in the street and the sensuous warm nights. I have been charmed, too, by the boun-tiful hospitality and the languorous easy-going outdoor life and the almost universal good manners. But all too frequently I am the prey of a vivid nightmare that recalls what I experienced in that town five years ago.

Davis—that is not its real name—has a population of about twenty thousand people, one-third of them colored. It is a cot-ton-mill town, and the workers of that trade, several thousand gaunt and ignorant "poor whites," live together in an ill-reputed section known as "Cotton Hollow." The population of Davis has varied in its seventy-five years. Once it was under consideration for the capital of the State, and so the older families and their kin form a proud little aristocracy, even when individually they have sunk to destitution.

That winter I'd made the usual round in New York until about April, when I decided I never wanted to see another invitation again. I was tired and I wanted to go to Europe for a rest; but the baby panic of 1921 hit father's business, and so it was suggested that I go South and visit Aunt Musidora Hale instead.

Vaguely I imagined that I was going to the country, but on the day I arrived the Davis *Courier* published a hilarious old picture of me on its society page, and I found I was in for another season. On a small scale, of course: there were Saturday-night dances at the little country club with its nine-hole golf course, and some informal dinner parties and several attractive and attentive boys. I didn't have a dull time at all, and when after three weeks I wanted to go home, it wasn't because I was bored. On the contrary I wanted to go home because I'd allowed myself to get rather interested in a good-looking young man named Charley Kincaid, without realizing that he was engaged to another girl.

We'd been drawn together from the first because he was almost the only boy in town who'd gone North to college, and I was still young enough to think that America revolved around Harvard and Princeton and Yale. He liked me too—I could see that; but when I heard that his engagement to a girl named Marie Bannerman had been announced six months before, there was nothing for me except to go away. The town was too small to avoid people, and though so far there hadn't been any talk, I was sure that—well, that if we kept meeting, the emotion we were beginning to feel would somehow get into words.

Marie Bannerman was almost a beauty. Perhaps she would have been a beauty if she'd had any clothes, and if she hadn't used bright pink rouge in two high spots on her cheeks and powdered her nose and chin to a funereal white. Her hair was shining black; her features were lovely; and an affection of one eye kept it always half-closed and gave an air of humorous mischief to her face.

I was leaving on a Monday, and on Saturday night a crowd of us dined at the country club as usual before the dance. There was Joe Cable, the son of a former governor, a handsome, dissipated and yet somehow charming young man; Catherine Jones, a pretty, sharp-eyed girl with an exquisite figure, who under her rouge might have been any age from eighteen to twenty-five; Marie Bannerman; Charley Kincaid; myself and two or three others.

I loved to listen to the genial flow of bizarre neighborhood anecdote at this kind of party. For instance, one of the girls, together with her entire family, had that afternoon been evicted from her house for nonpayment of rent. She told the story wholly without self-consciousness, merely as something troublesome but amusing. And I loved the banter which presumed every girl to be infinitely beautiful and attractive, and every man to have been secretly and hopelessly in love with every girl present from their respective cradles.

"We liked to die laughin'" . . . "—said he was fixin' to shoot him without he stayed away." The girls "'clared to heaven"; the men "took oath" on inconsequential statements. "How come you nearly about forgot to come by for me—" and the incessant

Honey, Honey, Honey, Honey, until the word seemed to roll like a genial liquid from heart to heart.

Outside, the May night was hot, a still night, velvet, soft-pawed, splattered thick with stars. It drifted heavy and sweet into the large room where we sat and where we would later dance, with no sound in it except the occasional long crunch of an arriving car on the drive. Just at that moment I hated to leave Davis as I never had hated to leave a town before—I felt that I wanted to spend my life in this town, drifting and dancing for-ever through these long, hot, romantic nights.

Yet horror was already hanging over that little party, was waiting tensely among us, an uninvited guest, and telling off the hours until it could show its pale and blinding face. Beneath the chatter and laughter something was going on, something secret and obscure that I didn't know.

Presently the colored orchestra arrived, followed by the first trickle of the dance crowd. An enormous red-faced man in mud-dy knee boots and with a revolver strapped around his waist, clumped in and paused for a moment at our table before going upstairs to the locker-room. It was Bill Abercrombie, the sheriff, the son of Congressman Abercrombie. Some of the boys asked him half-whispered questions, and he replied in an attempt at an undertone.

"Yes. . . . He's in the swamp all right; farmer saw him near the crossroads store. . . . Like to have a shot at him myself."

I asked the boy next to me what was the matter.

"Trouble," he said, "over in Kisco, about two miles from here. He's hiding in the swamp, and they're going in after him tomorrow."

"What'll they do to him?"

"Hang him, I guess."

The notion of the forlorn Negro crouching dismally in a desolate bog waiting for dawn and death depressed me for a moment. Then the feeling passed and was forgotten.

After dinner Charley Kincaid and I walked out on the veranda—he had just heard that I was going away. I kept as close to the others as I could, answering his words but not his eyes—something inside me was protesting against leaving him on such a casual note. The temptation was strong to let something flicker up between us here at the end. I wanted him to kiss me—my heart promised that if he kissed me, just once, it would accept with equanimity the idea of never seeing him any more; but my mind knew it wasn't so.

The other girls began to drift inside and upstairs to the dressing room to improve their complexions, and with Charley still beside me, I followed. Just at that moment I wanted to cry—perhaps my eyes were already blurred, or perhaps it was my haste lest they should be, but I opened the door of a small card-room by mistake and with my error the tragic machinery of the night began to function. In the card-room, not five feet from us, stood Marie Bannerman, Charley's fiancée, and Joe Cable. They were in each other's arms absorbed in a passionate and oblivious kiss.

I closed the door quickly, and without glancing at Charley opened the right door and ran upstairs.

A few minutes later Marie Bannerman entered the crowded dressing room. She saw me and came over, smiling in a sort of mock despair, but she breathed quickly, and the smile trembled a little on her mouth.

"You won't say a word, honey, will you?" she whispered.

"Of course not." I wondered how that could matter, now that Charley Kincaid knew.

"Who else was it that saw us?"

"Only Charley Kincaid and I."

"Oh!" She looked a little puzzled; then she added: "He didn't wait to say anything, honey. When we came out, he was just going out the door. I thought he was going to wait and romp all over Joe."

"How about his romping all over you?" I couldn't help asking.

"Oh, he'll do that." She laughed wryly. "But, honey, I know how to handle him. It's just when he's first mad that I'm scared of him—he's got an awful temper." She whistled reminiscently. "I know, because this happened once before."

I wanted to slap her. Turning my back, I walked away on the pretext of borrowing a pin from Katie, the Negro maid. Catherine Jones was claiming the latter's attention with a short gingham garment which needed repair.

"What's that?" I asked.

"Dancing-dress," she answered shortly, her mouth full of pins. When she took them out, she added: "It's all come to pieces—I've used it so much."

"Are you going to dance here tonight?"

"Going to try."

Somebody had told me that she wanted to be a dancer—that she had taken lessons in New York.

"Can I help you fix anything?"

"No, thanks—unless—can you sew? Katie gets so excited Saturday night that she's no good for anything except fetching pins. I'd be everlasting grateful to you, honey."

I had reasons for not wanting to go downstairs just yet, and so

I sat down and worked on her dress for half an hour. I wondered if Charley had gone home, if I would ever see him again—I scarcely dared to wonder if what he had seen would set him free, ethically. When I went down finally he was not in sight.

The room was now crowded; the tables had been removed and dancing was general. At that time, just after the war, all Southern boys had a way of agitating their heels from side to side, pivoting on the ball of the foot as they danced, and to acquiring this accomplishment I had devoted many hours. There were plenty of stags, almost all of them cheerful with corn liquor; I refused on an average at least two drinks a dance. Even when it is mixed with a soft drink, as is the custom, rather than gulped from the neck of a warm bottle, it is a formidable proposition. Only a few girls like Catherine Jones took an occasional sip from some boy's flask down at the dark end of the veranda.

I liked Catherine Jones—she seemed to have more energy than these other girls, though Aunt Musidora sniffed rather contemptuously whenever Catherine stopped for me in her car to go to the movies, remarking that she guessed "the bottom rail had gotten to be the top rail now." Her family were "new and common," but it seemed to me that perhaps her very commonness was an asset. Almost every girl in Davis confided in me at one time or another that her ambition was to "get away and come to New York," but only Catherine Jones had actually taken the step of studying stage dancing with that end in view.

She was often asked to dance at these Saturday night affairs, something "classic" or perhaps an acrobatic clog—on one memorable occasion she had annoyed the governing board by a "shimee" (then the scapegrace of jazz), and the novel and somewhat startling excuse made for her was that she was "so tight she didn't know what she was doing, anyhow." She impressed me as a curious personality, and I was eager to see what she would produce tonight.

At twelve o'clock the music always ceased, as dancing was forbidden on Sunday morning. So at eleven-thirty a vast fanfaronade of drum and cornet beckoned the dancers and the couples on the verandas, and the ones in the cars outside, and the stragglers from the bar, into the ballroom. Chairs were brought in and galloped up en masse and with a great racket to the slightly raised platform. The orchestra had evacuated this and taken a place beside. Then, as the rearward lights were lowered, they began to play a tune accompanied by a curious drum-beat that I had never heard before, and simultaneously Catherine Jones appeared upon the platform. She wore the short, country girl's dress upon which I had lately labored, and a wide sunbonnet under which her face, stained yellow with powder, looked out at us with rolling eyes and a vacant leer.

She began to dance.

I had never seen anything like it before, and until five years later, I wasn't to see it again. It was the Charleston—it must have been the Charleston. I remember the double drum-beat like a shouted "Hey! Hey!" and the unfamiliar swing of the arms and the odd knock-kneed effect. She had picked it up, heaven knows where.

Her audience, familiar with Negro rhythms, leaned forward eagerly—even to them it was something new, but it is stamped on my mind as clearly and indelibly as though I had seen it yesterday. The figure on the platform swinging and stamping, the excited orchestra, the waiters grinning in the doorway of the bar, and all around, through many windows, the soft languorous Southern night seeping in from swamp and cottonfield and lush foliage and brown, warm streams. At what point a feeling of tense uneasiness began to steal over me I don't know. The dance could scarcely have taken ten minutes; perhaps the first beats of the barbaric music disquieted me—long before it was over, I was sitting rigid in my seat, and my eyes were wandering here and there around the hall, passing along the rows of shadowy faces as if seeking some security that was no longer there.

I'm not a nervous type; nor am I given to panic; but for a moment I was afraid that if the music and the dance didn't stop, I'd be hysterical. Something was happening all about me. I knew it as well as if I could see into these unknown souls. Things were happening, but one thing especially was leaning over so close that it almost touched us, that it did touch us. . . . I almost screamed as a hand brushed accidentally against my back.

The music stopped. There was applause and protracted cries of encore, but Catherine Jones shook her head definitely at the orchestra leader and made as though to leave the platform. The appeals for more continued—again she shook her head, and it seemed to me that her expression was rather angry. Then a strange incident occurred. At the protracted pleading of some one in the front row, the colored orchestra leader began the vamp of the tune, as if to lure Catherine Jones into changing her mind. Instead she turned toward him, snapped out, "Didn't you hear me say no?" and then, surprisingly, slapped his face. The music stopped, and an amused murmur terminated abruptly as a muffled but clearly audible shot rang out.

Immediately we were on our feet, for the sound indicated that it had been fired within or near the house. One of the chaperons gave a little scream, but when some wag called out, "Caesar's in that henhouse again," the momentary alarm dissolved into laughter. The club manager, followed by several curious couples, went out to have a look about, but the rest were already moving around the floor to the strains of "Good Night, Ladies," which traditionally ended the dance.

I was glad it was over. The man with whom I had come went to get his car, and calling a waiter, I sent him for my golf clubs, which were in the stack upstairs. I strolled out on the porch and waited, wondering again if Charley Kincaid had gone home. Suddenly I was aware, in that curious way in which you become aware of something that has been going on for several minutes, that there was a tumult inside. Women were shrieking; there was a cry of "Oh, my God!," then the sounds of a stampede on the inside stairs, and footsteps running back and forth across the ballroom. A girl appeared from somewhere and pitched forward in a dead faint—almost immediately another girl did the same, and I heard a frantic male voice shouting into a telephone. Then, hatless and pale, a young man rushed out on the porch, and with hands cold as ice, seized my arm.

"What is it?" I cried. "A fire? What's happened?"

"Marie Bannerman's dead upstairs in the women's dressing-room. Shot through the throat!"

The rest of that night is a series of visions that seem to have no connection with one another, that follow each other with the sharp instantaneous transitions of scenes in the movies. There was a group who stood arguing on the porch, in voices now raised, now hushed, about what should be done and how every waiter in the club, "even old Moses," ought to be given the third degree tonight. That a Negro had shot and killed Marie Bannerman was the instant and unquestioned assumption—in the first unreasoning instant, anyone who doubted it would have been under suspicion. The guilty one was said to be Katie Golstien, the colored maid, who had discovered the body and fainted. It was said to be "that Negro they were looking for over near Kisco." It was any Negro at all.

Within half an hour people began to drift out, each with his little contribution of new discoveries. The crime had been committed with Sheriff Abercrombie's gun—he had hung it, belt and all, in full view on the wall before coming down to dance. It was missing—they were hunting for it now. Instantly killed, the doctor said—bullet had been fired from only a few feet away.

Then a few minutes later another young man came out and made the announcement in a loud, grave voice:

"They've arrested Charley Kincaid."

My head reeled. Upon the group gathered on the veranda fell an awed, stricken silence.

"Arrested Charley Kincaid!"

"Charley Kincaid!"

Why, he was one of the best, one of themselves.

"That's the craziest thing I ever heard of!"

The young man nodded, shocked like the rest, but self-important with his information.

"He wasn't downstairs, when Catherine Jones was dancing—he says he was in the men's locker-room. And Marie Bannerman told a lot of girls that they'd had a row, and she was scared of what he'd do."

Again an awed silence.

"That's the craziest thing I ever heard!" someone said again.

"Charley Kincaid!"

The narrator waited a moment. Then he added:

"He caught her kissing Joe Cable—"

I couldn't keep silence a minute longer.

"What about it?" I cried out. "I was with him at the time. He wasn't—he wasn't angry at all."

They looked at me, their faces startled, confused, unhappy. Suddenly the footsteps of several men sounded loud through the ballroom, and a moment later Charley Kincaid, his face dead white, came out the front door between the Sheriff and another man. Crossing the porch quickly, they descended the steps and disappeared in the darkness. A moment later there was the sound of a starting car.

When an instant later far away down the road I heard the eerie scream of an ambulance, I got up desperately and called to my escort, part of the whispering group.

"I've got to go," I said. "I can't stand this. Either take me home or I'll find a place in another car." Reluctantly he shouldered my clubs—the sight of them made me realize that I now couldn't leave on Monday after all—and followed me down the steps just as the black body of the ambulance curved in at the gate—a ghastly shadow on the bright, starry night.

The situation, after the first wild surmises, the first burst of unreasoning loyalty to Charley Kincaid, had died away, was outlined by the Davis *Courier* and by most of the State newspapers in this fashion: Marie Bannerman died in the women's dressing room of the Davis Country Club from the effects of a shot fired at close quarters from a revolver just after eleven forty-five o'clock on Saturday night. Many persons had heard the shot; moreover it had undoubtedly been fired from the revolver of Sheriff Abercrombie, which had been hanging in full sight on the wall of the next room. Abercrombie himself was down in the ballroom when the murder took place, as many witnesses could testify. The revolver was not found.

So far as was known, the only man who had been upstairs at the time the shot was fired was Charles Kincaid. He was engaged to Miss Bannerman, but according to several witnesses they had quarreled seriously that evening. Miss Bannerman herself had mentioned the quarrel, adding that she was afraid and wanted to keep away from him until he cooled off.

Charles Kincaid asserted that at the time the shot was fired he was in the men's locker room—where, indeed, he was found, immediately after the discovery of Miss Bannerman's body. He denied having had any words with Miss Bannerman at all. He had heard the shot but it had had no significance for him—if he thought anything of it, he thought that "some one was potting cats outdoors."

Why had he chosen to remain in the locker-room during the dance?

No reason at all. He was tired. He was waiting until Miss Bannerman wanted to go home.

The body was discovered by Katie Golstien, the colored maid, who herself was found in a faint when the crowd of girls surged upstairs for their coats. Returning from the kitchen, where she had been getting a bite to eat, Katie had found Miss Bannerman, her dress wet with blood, already dead on the floor.

Both the police and the newspapers attached importance to the geography of the country club's second story. It consisted of a row of three rooms—the women's dressing room and the men's locker-room at either end, and in the middle a room which was used as a cloak-room and for the storage of golf clubs. The women's and men's rooms had no outlet except into this chamber, which was connected by one stairs with the ballroom below, and by another with the kitchen. According to the testimony of three

Negro cooks and the white caddy-master, no one but Katie Golstien had gone up the kitchen stairs that night.

As I remember it after five years, the foregoing is a pretty
accurate summary of the situation when Charley Kincaid was
accused of first-degree murder and committed for trial. Other
people, chiefly Negroes, were suspected (at the loyal instigation
of Charley Kincaid's friends), and several arrests were made, but
nothing ever came of them, and upon what grounds they were
based I have long forgotten. One group, in spite of the disappearance of the pistol, claimed persistently that it was a suicide
and suggested some ingenious reasons to account for the absence of the weapon.

Now when it is known Marie Bannerman happened to die so
savagely and so violently, it would be easy for me, of all people, to
say that I believed in Charley Kincaid all the time. But I didn't. I
thought that he had killed her, and at the same time I knew that
I loved him with all my heart. That it was I who first happened
upon the evidence which set him free was due not to any faith in
his innocence but to a strange vividness with which, in moods of
excitement, certain scenes stamp themselves on my memory, so
that I can remember every detail and how that detail struck me
at the time.

It was one afternoon early in July, when the case against
Charley Kincaid seemed to be at its strongest, that the horror
of the actual murder slipped away from me for a moment and I
began to think about other incidents of that same haunted night.
Something Marie Bannerman had said to me in the dressing
room persistently eluded me, bothered me—not because I believed it to be important, but simply because I couldn't remember. It was gone from me, as if it had been a part of the fantas-

tic undercurrent of small-town life which I had felt so strongly that evening, the sense that things were in the air, old secrets, old loves and feuds, and unresolved situations, that I, an outsider, could never fully understand. Just for a minute it seemed to me that Marie Bannerman had pushed aside the curtain; then it had dropped into place again—the house into which I might have looked was dark now forever.

Another incident, perhaps less important, also haunted me. The tragic events of a few minutes after had driven it from everyone's mind, but I had a strong impression that for a brief space of time I wasn't the only one to be surprised. When the audience had demanded an encore from Catherine Jones, her unwillingness to dance again had been so acute that she had been driven to the point of slapping the orchestra leader's face. The discrepancy between his offense and the venom of the rebuff recurred to me again and again. It wasn't natural—or, more important, it hadn't seemed natural. In view of the fact that Catherine Jones had been drinking, it was explicable, but it worried me now as it had worried me then. Rather to lay its ghost than to do any investigating, I pressed an obliging young man into service and called on the leader of the band.

His name was Thomas, a very dark, very simple-hearted virtuoso of the traps, and it took less than ten minutes to find out that Catherine Jones's gesture had surprised him as much as it had me. He had known her a long time, seen her at dances since she was a little girl—why, the very dance she did that night was one she had rehearsed with his orchestra a week before. And a few days later she had come to him and said she was sorry.

"I knew she would," he concluded. "She's a right goodhearted girl. My sister Katie was her nurse from when she was born up to the time she went to school."

"Your sister?"

"Katie. She's the maid out at the country club. Katie Gols-tien. You been reading 'bout her in the papers in 'at Charley Kincaid case. She's the maid. Katie Golstien. She's the maid at the country club what found the body of Miss Bannerman."

"So Katie was Miss Catherine Jones's nurse?"

"Yes ma'am."

Going home, stimulated but unsatisfied, I asked my companion a quick question.

"Were Catherine and Marie good friends?"

"Oh, yes," he answered without hesitation. "All the girls are good friends here, except when two of them are tryin' to get hold of the same man. Then they warm each other up a little."

"Why do you suppose Catherine hasn't married? Hasn't she got lots of beaux?"

"Off and on. She only likes people for a day or so at a time. That is—all except Joe Cable."

Now a scene burst upon me, broke over me like a dissolving wave. And suddenly, my mind shivering from the impact, I remembered what Marie Bannerman had said to me in the dressing room: "Who else was it that saw?" She had caught a glimpse of someone else, a figure passing so quickly that she could not identify it, out of the corner of her eye.

And suddenly, simultaneously, I seemed to see that figure, as if I too had been vaguely conscious of it at the time, just as one is aware of a familiar gait or outline on the street long before there is any flicker of recognition. On the corner of my own eyes was stamped a hurrying figure—that might have been Catherine Jones.

But when the shot was fired, Catherine Jones was in full view of over fifty people. Was it credible that Katie Golstien, a woman of fifty, who as a nurse had been known and trusted by three generations of Davis people, would shoot down a young girl in cold blood at Catherine Jones's command?

"But when the shot was fired, Catherine Jones was in full view of over fifty people."

That sentence beat in my head all night, taking on fantastic variations, dividing itself into phrases, segments, individual words.

"But when the shot was fired—Catherine Jones was in full view—of over fifty people."

When the shot was fired! What shot? The shot we heard. When the shot was fired. . . . When the shot was fired. . . .

The next morning at nine o'clock, with the pallor of sleeplessness buried under a quantity of paint such as I had never worn before or have since, I walked up a rickety flight of stairs to the Sheriff's office.

Abercrombie, engrossed in his morning's mail, looked up curiously as I came in the door.

"Catherine Jones did it," I cried, struggling to keep the hysteria out of my voice. "She killed Marie Bannerman with a shot we didn't hear because the orchestra was playing and everybody was pushing up the chairs. The shot we heard was when Katie fired the pistol out the window after the music was stopped. To give Catherine an alibi!"

I was right—as everyone now knows, but for a week, until Katie Golstien broke down under a fierce and ruthless inquisition, nobody believed me. Even Charley Kincaid, as he afterward confessed, didn't dare to think it could be true.

What had been the relations between Catherine and Joe Cable no one ever knew, but evidently she had determined that his clandestine affair with Marie Bannerman had gone too far. Then Marie chanced to come into the women's room while Catherine was dressing for her dance—and there again there is a certain obscurity, for Catherine always claimed that Marie got the revolver, threatened her with it and that in the ensuing struggle the trigger was pulled. In spite of everything I always rather liked Catherine Jones, but in justice it must be said that only a simpleminded and very exceptional jury would have let her off with a mere five years.

And in just five years from her commitment my husband and I are going to make a round of the New York musical shows and look hard at all the members of the chorus from the very front row.

After the shooting she must have thought quickly. Katie was told to wait until the music stopped, fire the revolver out the window and then hide it—Catherine Jones neglected to specify where. Katie, on the verge of collapse, obeyed instructions, but she was never able to specify where she had hid the revolver. And no one ever knew until a year later, when Charley and I were on our honeymoon and Sheriff Abercrombie's ugly weapon dropped out of my golf-bag onto a Hot Springs golf-links. The bag must have been standing just outside the dressing room door; Katie's trembling hand had dropped the revolver into the very first aperture she could see.

We live in New York. Small towns make us both uncomfortable. Every day we read about the crime-waves in the big cities, but at least a wave is something tangible that you can provide against. What I dread above all things is the unknown depths, the incalculable ebb and flow, the secret shapes of things that drift through opaque darkness under the surface of the sea.

THE EPISODE OF THE
TANGIBLE ILLUSION
C. Daly King

His slim output prevents C(harles) Daly King (1895-1963) from being ranked at the top rung of detective fiction writers, but he has produced some masterly works, notably in *The Curious Mr. Tarrant*, selected by Ellery Queen for his *Queen's Quorum* as one of the 106 most important volumes of mystery short stories of all time, where it was described as containing "the most imaginative detective short stories of our time."

Trevis Tarrant, the amateur detective in the eponymous story collection, is a wealthy, cultured gentleman of leisure who believes in cause and effect; they "rule the world," he says. He takes it on himself to explain locked room mysteries and impossible crimes that involve such improbabilities as mysterious footsteps by an invisible entity heard even in broad daylight, horrible images of a hanged man haunting a modern house, headless corpses found on a heavily traveled highway, as well as dealing with apparent ghosts and other supernormal happenings. It entertains him to bring his gift of being able to see things clearly and solve mysteries by the use of inarguable logic. He is accompanied at all times by his valet, Katoh, a Japanese doctor and spy.

Born in New York City, he graduated from Yale University, received his master's degree in psychology from Columbia University, and a Ph.D. from Yale for an electromagnetic study of sleep. He was a practicing psychologist who wrote several books on the subject. In the 1930s, King divided his time between Summit, New Jersey, and Bermuda, where he wrote his detective novels. With the advent of World War II, he stopped writing mysteries and devoted the rest of his life to his work in psychology. As a mystery writer, King wrote six novels, the most critically being *Obelists at Sea* (1933), *Obelists en Route* (1934) and *Obelists Fly High* (1935).

"The Episode of the Tangible Illusion" was originally published in the February 1935 issue of *Mystery*; it was first collected in *The Curious Mr. Tarrant* (London, Collins Crime Club, 1935).

The Episode of the Tangible Illusion
C. Daly King

MARY THREW her golf bag into the rumble of the roadster. "Sorry to keep you waiting, Jerry. Whatever is the matter with Valerie? She looks like a perfect hag."

"Is that so?" I slipped the clutch into second and jerked the car brutally around the curve beside the clubhouse. Mary's my sister.

When the jerks stopped and we straightened out on the drive at about forty-five, she managed to sit up. "You're such a mooing calf about Val you can't see how terribly she looks. What *is* wrong with her, anyhow?"

"I don't know."

"And just after she's got into that darling house. How long has she been there? A couple of months, isn't it? Probably," Mary considered, "it's simply your hanging around so much. Your face at the window twice a day, darling, would give any girl jitters."

For once in her life, though, Mary was right. Something was desperately wrong with Valerie and I couldn't find out what it was. She wouldn't tell me, and if I pressed the question, she got so upset that I had to stop.

Valerie Mopish had come to Norrisville with her brother five years ago when she was eighteen. Although they were orphans and nobody knew them, they were so pleasant, especially Valerie, that they made friends everywhere; within a year they were in all the clubs and on intimate terms with the crowd to which Mary and I belonged. Why she liked me, heaven only knows, but she did, from the start. Why I liked her, is easy; she is the loveliest-looking girl that ever got into a one-piece bathing suit. She has golden-blonde hair and violet eyes—violet, mind you—and she's sweet and sort of fragrant; and she always wears high-heeled shoes and her ankles give you a feeling as if you were tied to a roller coaster.

After lunch I hung around for an interminable hour until I thought it would be all right to walk over and see Val. I came out of the woods and across the field just as she stepped onto the terrace that runs along one side of her new house. I vaulted over the low, stone railing and said, "'lo, Val. Marry me?"

She looked pale and there certainly were little circles under her eyes, but she smiled. "Sorry." And then the smile went out like a light, leaving just trouble. "Oh, Jerry, go away and forget about me. I—I—I can't."

We were pretty close together when she began; when she

ended, we were a good deal closer. As my arms went around her, she sort of collapsed and lay back in them. Then she raised her face and kissed me.

"Jerry, let me go. . . . Please."

I felt foolish, standing there all alone, so I sat down on the railing. Valerie had taken one of the big, wicker chairs and was patting at her hair.

"I called up Dr. Beckenforth yesterday and he's coming out to see me this afternoon; any minute now."

"Huh? Who's he?"

"He's the man who treated me when I had the nervous breakdown, before we moved to Norrisville. He's a psychiatrist."

"A who?"

"A whoozie-doctor, I suppose you'd call him. He got me over a lot of complexes and things once. . . . I know you care for me, Jerry, and I'm going to tell you about this. I think I ought to. . . . Before John and I moved out to Norrisville, I had what they call a nervous breakdown. You know that, but you don't know how bad it was. I felt terribly and I got morbid and it went on and on and got worse instead of better. Finally I began to hear things—"

"*Hear* things?"

"Things that weren't there. Oh, Jerry, it was awful. I knew I was going crazy and there wasn't anything I could do about it. . . . Then, finally, I had Dr. Beckenforth and he showed me how these hallucinations came out of my unconscious mind, and after about six months or so, he helped me to get rid of them. One of the things I heard was someone following me; he showed me why I heard that—because I wanted to—and that went away first. Bye and bye all the other horrors went, too, and I was cured. I never thought another, thing about it or worried at all until just recently."

"Why worry now?"

She said simply, "I've got 'em again."

"Oh come on, Val. If——"

"No," she hurried on, "there's no use saying it isn't so when it is. About a week after I moved in here, the day after John sailed in fact, I began to get frightened of nothing; that's the way it started before. And it's got worse and worse. And I'm so tired of trying to hide it and not tell anyone, and they all see it anyhow. I know there's nothing really to be afraid of, but I am. And now, now I've begun to hear the footsteps again."

A reasonable explanation occurred to me. "Of course you get nervous all alone here," I offered, "no one within a mile of you at night. Why don't you have Annie stay with you instead of going back to the big house every night? Or better yet, go back yourself for a while."

"I can't do that. I can't run away from it, or I'd be licked for the rest of my life. Don't you understand, Jerry? I'm not afraid of tramps prowling around or anything like that. It's just because I know there's no one here that it's so awful. When someone follows me up the stairs and there just isn't anyone there and I can hear him as plainly as I hear you now, I get so that I nearly scream. And then there are other things, too. It hasn't anything to do with living here alone; it would happen to me anywhere."

"Then it's only imagination," I remarked inadequately. "You'll be O.K. again in a jiffy. If you'd only marry me, I'll bet you'd never think of this stuff again. We'd go for a swell, long trip and——"

"I told you this, Jerry, so you'd know why I can't marry you. I can't get married until I'm absolutely sure there isn't something funny about me. And I don't see how I can be sure; maybe I'll never be sure. . . ."

I got up and crossed over to her chair. I said, "Listen, lady. Sooner or later you're going to marry me. Sooner is best, but later is a lot better than never. I don't care if you're goofy as a loon, which obviously you're not." I pushed her over into a corner of the big chair and perched on the edge. . . .

When I left, I was sure that Valerie, in spite of her obstinacy, was feeling a lot better.

Perhaps I should explain about Val's two houses. When she and John Mopish had come to Norrisville originally, they had picked up a place outside the town at a bargain price. It comprised roughly fifty acres of ground, mostly wooded, although there were some farm fields now disused, on which stood an old-fashioned residence, a cut above a farm house but far from modern. It wasn't exactly what they wanted but it was close enough and they moved in with two servants, a cook and a maid. No attempt was made to cultivate the farm.

Valerie, however, was very fond of modern things, appliances and whatnot, and the old house never suited her. So when building costs took a tumble, she decided to put up just the sort of house she had always dreamed of, on a remote part of the land. In a straight line, of course, it was no more than a quarter of a mile away from the former house but, due to the configuration of the ground and the woods that covered it, the actual journey came almost to a mile. She and her brother had mulled over the project for a year before the building was undertaken.

John, being an architect, had naturally drawn the plans and supervised the construction. Everything about it was ultramodern, but since John was really talented in his profession, it escaped being ridiculous and was a perfect example of what can actually be put into a house under modern conditions. It had flues for air conditioning, of course, in conjunction with its gas furnace; it had the usual electric refrigeration, and more unusual gadgets such as no-shadow lighting in the bathrooms and disappearing wallbeds on the small sleeping porch outside Val's own room. The doors of the little garage underneath opened automatically when you drove up to it and closed again after you were inside. Both inside and outside the style was modernistic, as were the entire furnishings.

Not only to save construction costs but because she wanted it only for herself, the house was very small. Beyond the terrace that stretched across the front was the big, sunken living room (radio and electric victrola built into the walls and a concealed modernistic bar, disclosed by a sliding section of panels) where Val could give a reasonable party when she wanted to. Besides this room there were on the first floor only an entrance hallway, with closets and a dressing room and lavatory off it, and the small but complete kitchen. Between the living room and the hallway a broad staircase led upward, its upper half spiralled.

The second floor had two comfortable bedrooms, each with a bath, and one smaller room that could be used as a study or a tiny library or for sports equipment or whatever. And that was all there was, with the exception of the garage and the cellar for furnace and storage space. Annie came over in the daytime to prepare the meals and attend to the cleaning, but otherwise, Val lived alone.

Nothing more happened for the next few weeks. Valerie seemed to be much the same—and I saw quite a bit of her. Then, late one afternoon I walked over to the new house for cocktails.

I had already come around the corner of the house and had

gone perhaps ten feet along the terrace, before I stopped whis-
tling in the middle of a bar and stood still with my mouth part
way open. On the wicker lounge Mary sat with her arms around
Valerie and Valerie was sobbing violently; not pretty sobbing but
great, wrenching sobs that seemed to come from way down inside of her somewhere.

I stood there for quite a long while, and then I said, "Huh?"

Mary looked up. "Oh, you're here, are you?"

"What's the matter?"

"I don't know what's the matter. She won't tell me. . . . Shut
up and go away."

Valerie had stopped sobbing and started gasping. "D-don't
make Jerry go. He knows ab-about it."

They were both busy now with powder and stuff out of
Mary's vanity case.

"It was terrible last night," Valerie said in a low voice. "It was
simply awful. And now tonight's almost here. When the afternoon began going and the sun started to set, I just—I guess I'm
no good."

"What was terrible last night?" Mary demanded.

"None of your business," I told her. "And if you open that trap
of yours about this——"

Valerie said, "Jerry!" and Mary looked as if she were going to
get mad, then decided not to. She smiled, "God will probably
forgive you; and I certainly realize you don't know what you're
doing. So far I haven't anything to open, in your elegant phrase,
my trap about."

"You won't have, either. . . . Val, you've got to come and spend
the night with us."

"I can't run away from it, Jerry."

"See here," Mary announced in her competent voice, "I don't

care what it's about if you don't want to tell me. But I'll stay here with Val tonight, if she wants me."

But Valerie shook her head. "It's sweet of you, Mary; you're swell to me. But I can't let you. Honestly."

The thing was impossible. I started to walk up and down. I growled for a while and then I spoke. "It's no go. You won't come with us and won't let Mary stay here. All right; then I'll stay. I'm here and I'm staying here."

It was Annie's day off and Val and I got our own supper in the little kitchen. She continued to apologize for her outbreak and to urge me to go home, but underneath it I sensed her nervousness increasing as the daylight faded.

After supper we had coffee out on the terrace, while the dusk deepened and a glorious moon, verging toward the full, came up above the eastern trees. We also had liqueurs. The evening was balmy with late Spring and I stretched back in my chair, enjoying myself thoroughly.

The time went before I knew it; it was nearly twelve o'clock when Val ground out a cigarette and stood up. She had been perfectly calm all evening, but now I could almost feel a wave of nervousness sweep across from where she stood. In the moonlight pouring down on the terrace I saw her shiver.

She gave a little shake. "I'm going up, Jerry." There was a forced tone in her voice that made it sound as if she had just avoided adding—to the execution chamber.

"You, you don't have to stay."

"So? . . . I'm staying, Val."

I followed her into the hallway and, at the foot of the stairs, took her hand and kissed it. It was a cold little hand. But she walked up the staircase steadily enough. "Don't you worry," I called after her, "I'll be right here in the living room all night long. And the lights will be on and I'll be awake. Just you give a yell if there's any nonsense." As she went around the turn of the stairs and disappeared, she forced a smile and gave a little wave with one hand.

If it was half as bad as she imagined, though, she was a brave kid, I thought, as I glanced into the kitchen and saw that the windows were closed and locked. I also turned the bolt inside the front door and inside the door of the steps leading down to the basement and garage. If there was any funny business around, I wasn't going to guess where it came from, any how. But of course there wasn't; how could there be? Valerie herself said she was sure nobody was prowling about her house. It was just imagination and overwrought nerves. Nothing at all would happen tonight and the reason it wouldn't happen would be because I was there. I made a note to advance this in the morning as an excellent reason why I should always be there.

Now I was in the living room, where I turned on the indirect lighting and secured all the windows except two of the French ones giving onto the terrace. I intended to sit down between these myself when I had picked out a book from the shelves across the room.

This I did, and by the time I had finished, it was after two in the morning. The slight noises of Valerie moving around up-stairs and drawing water in the bathroom, had long since ceased. I didn't feel like reading any more and the radio was in the wall right beside me. I turned the volume down low and fiddled with that for an hour.

I tired of that, too. I got up, lit a cigarette, and stood in one of the open windows looking out over the terrace. The moon had got into the west now but it was still shining brightly, a beautiful night, cool and fresh—and peaceful.

Then Valerie screamed.

It broke the quiet, like a ton of rock crashing into a still pool. I jerked up and stood in motionless surprise for a moment; to this day I don't know what happened to the cigarette. But I wasn't motionless for long; if I have any idea of what terror is, there was sheer terror in that cry.

I ran for the hallway, and as I ran, I shouted some stupid thing, like, "What's the matter?" I started to take the stairs two steps at a time, and stumbled; I wasn't familiar enough with that particular stairs. It is important to note that I plunged up them a step at a time, as fast as I could. Because a third of the way up before I had reached where they spiralled, *someone began to follow me!* There was no question about it at all; even in my haste to get to Valerie (and there was no question of that either) the pounding footsteps behind me were so clear and unmistakable that, when I reached the place where the stairs turned, I turned, with an arm drawn back to slug the fellow, who could not possibly have any business there.

And the stairs behind me were absolutely empty!

I couldn't wait; I ran on and dashed into Valerie's room. After the lights in the hall, it seemed pitch black but luckily I knew where the light switch was, and found it. She was sitting up in bed, clutching the blankets and sheets around her, and shaking with fear. I was a little jolted myself, after that business on the stairs.

"Where the devil is it?" I demanded fiercely. Without the slightest idea of what I meant.

But Valerie didn't answer. She had collapsed on the bed and

was pushing frightened sobs into the pillows. I suppose if I'd had any sense I'd have gone over to her and taken her in my arms, but I'm not a very wild sort of fellow and I've never been much in bedrooms with beautiful-looking girls like Valerie. So I just stood where I was and kept asking what it was all about. Not that it did me much good; all I could get out of her, even after the sobbing had subsided to whimpering, was that "It" had gone. Curiously enough, she asked me to turn the lights off in order to make sure of this.

Naturally I made a careful search of the room and went out on the adjacent sleeping porch. I found nothing and came back to look through the other two rooms and the bathrooms on the second floor. Nothing there, either. Valerie had quieted down now and insisted that she would be all right and go to sleep again. I wasn't especially satisfied to leave her but she insisted and, also, I was anxious to go through the rest of the house. I hadn't said anything about being followed as I ran up, but I couldn't see for the life of me how anyone could have come halfway up the stairs behind me and then vanished; there wasn't any place for him to jump to so suddenly. The more I thought of it, the less I understood.

So I went down, still a little reluctantly, and searched through the lower floor. Here again there were no results, no sign of anyone except myself having been in the house, and the windows and doors were all locked just as I had left them. I locked the two open windows in the living room and descended to the garage and the little cellar. The same answer over again; nothing disturbed, everything fastened on the inside.

I came back and opened one of the windows. Neither head nor tail could I make out of what had happened. Of course I didn't know what had frightened Valerie but what I myself had met on the staircase was beginning to make me doubt that over-wrought nerves could any longer be a complete explanation. I simply could not believe that the sounds behind me had been imagined; they had been as clear and distinct, as loud and plain, as any ordinary sounds I had ever heard; they had been unmistakable footsteps, heavy and solid.

And now I heard something else. No scream this time; what came to my ears was the sound of running feet above. For the second time I made for the hall.

I was just in time to see Valerie begin a rush down the stairs, her face once more a mask of terror. She came around the curving steps all right and halfway down the straight steps below them. The lights were on and I could see perfectly plainly. Just about where the footsteps that had followed me had ceased, she suddenly pitched forward, as if someone had given her a shove from behind. There was no person, nor anything else, near her.

She landed at the foot of the steps with a crash, unconscious. As I reached her and raised her body to a sitting position, I saw that her right leg was doubled up under her in a posture that could only mean it was broken. I looked around desperately for someone or something that had attacked her. I saw nothing whatsoever; the lights burned steadily and brightly, there was not a sound in the house.

I carried her into the living room and laid her on a lounge. I slid back the panel of the bar and drew a glass of water, grabbed a brandy bottle in the other hand. When I got back to the lounge, she was already stirring; and I gave her a sip of water first, then the straight brandy. She groaned, tried to sit up and clung to me. "Jerry, Jerry, something pushed me." She groaned again.

I was so upset that for some minutes I couldn't think what to do. Valerie had to have a doctor; I couldn't leave her alone, and

I mustn't be found with her at an hour like this. What a nasty thing conventions are, anyhow. I laid her back on the lounge as gently as I could and walked over to the telephone. I wouldn't have been much surprised if it had failed to work, but the dial-tone was clear and the little clicks came back in succession as I moved the disk.

"Hello," said a sleepy voice.

My tone was probably fairly strained and excited. "Get a doctor for Valerie! Get him out here as quick as you can! And get here yourself; you've got to get here before him. Do you—"

Mary is pretty quick on the trigger, I'll say that for her. And she isn't one of those silly females who ask a hundred questions when there is something to be done. She said sharply, "I'll get him. Coming, Jerry." And snapped the phone down.

Twenty minutes later Mary walked through the French window and I made another search of the house, once more a futile one. As I jumped over the rail of the terrace, a headlight beam shot up in the dim light above the woods to the south; so the doctor was coming, too.

I walked aimlessly through the trees in the general direction of home. I was bewildered and I was angry, but I hadn't anything on which to focus the anger. What the devil was going on? Something was attacking Valerie, but when you looked, nothing was there to hit back at. Imagination and tricky nerves were out now, definitely. I had heard the footsteps on the stairs and in full light I had seen Valerie thrown down the steps—by nothing. For a time I cursed with vigor and, strangely, it didn't relieve a single feeling. "What the hell, what the hell?" I groaned in a fury of futility. She had been hurt and she would be hurt again, unless something were done. But what could be done? Just the same, it had to be, it—

For no reason that I can think of, a picture formed itself all at once in my mind. Only a month before I had stood in a basement room in the Metropolitan Museum, in complete darkness, facing an ancient Aztec curse contained in an old, a very old manuscript. Several of us had gathered there on a crazy bet, to test the power of the ancient and magic script. A strange thing had happened there—or so it had seemed at the time. The picture I had now was that of the man who had so abruptly appeared at the height of the phenomenon, a clear-cut picture of his steady eyes, his unruffled, even amused calm, his complete unbluffableness.

I remember talking with him at his apartment later; being impressed with the terrific extent of his knowledge and experience. I remembered his profound and sane utterances on confused and complicated issues. His name was Tarrant, I recalled. . . .

I quickened my steps and my walking took on an intended direction.

I drove into New York in the sedan. At the door of Tarrant's apartment, Katoh, the little Japanese butler who was a doctor in his own country, answered my ring. Despite my disheveled appearance and the peculiar hour of my visit—it was just six-forty-five—his welcoming grin held no element of surprise.

"How do, Mister Phelan. Come in, please. Mr. Tarrant out now for ride in Park, but back soon. You have breakfast? Yiss."

While Katoh set another place beside the one already prepared, I had time to reflect on the strangeness of my mission and even to become somewhat embarrassed. After all, I had only met Tarrant once; he had been friendly, certainly, but there was no reason to suppose he would wish to interest himself in this affair of mine. Well, I'd put it up to him, anyhow; it was too late to reconsider now. Besides, Valerie's danger was more important than anything else. Then he came in.

He walked through the hallway and stopped in the living room entrance, in well-worn riding togs. He, at least, looked at me in surprise, then more keenly. "Well, Jerry Phelan. What brings you in so early? Something on your mind, you look worried and dragged out."

"I've spent the night fighting a ghost. And the ghost won."

Tarrant smiled. "It sounds promising," he commented. "But no more now. I'll jump into the shower and then we'll both have some breakfast. After that, I'd like to hear about it."

In an astonishingly short period he reappeared, this time in a lounging robe. We ate Katoh's delicious meal with only a few casual remarks interspersed. After we had finished, Tarrant got up and crossed the room for cigarettes, then stretched out in a big chair opposite me. "Go ahead," he invited, "tell me about it."

I told him about Valerie. Once started, there seemed to be quite a lot to tell, and he interrupted me occasionally with questions. "This Miss Mopish must be rich?" he ventured at one point.

"She is very well off," I replied, "though she isn't tremendously rich. She and her brother are orphans, you see, and they were in very poor circumstances, practically poverty-stricken, she told me, until some distant relative died and left her his whole estate which was considerable."

"Just to her? The brother got nothing?"

"No, John didn't get anything. He is still as poor as he ever was, but his profession will bring him in plenty some day, with the progress he's making now. Meantime Valerie is very generous with him; I'm sure she makes him a pleasant allowance. They always seem to be very fond of each other."

"I believe I've heard of him. Didn't he design those modern houses they were showing up at Radio City last month?"

"Yes, he did those. He's getting quite a reputation now. Three months ago he went over to Rome as a result of some prize he got. His design won a competition and they wanted him to come across and supervise the finishing touches on the building. . . . He's on his way back now; he'll be landing in another day or so."

I got back then to our real business and told him of Valerie's increasing nervousness after John's departure and how I had come to insist on staying with her the night before. To the best of my ability I described what had occurred, but in Tarrant's living-room, it didn't sound very convincing, even to me.

"But I tell you I heard those footsteps myself! I saw her pushed off the stairs, and I swear that nothing touched her!"

My obvious sincerity impressed him. "Of course," he admitted, "if you are really right about it, it's an amazing performance. There's no need in asking whether you could be mistaken; I can see you are convinced. . . . Well, I haven't any explanation I can offer you from this distance. I don't believe in haunted houses and I've never yet heard of a modernistic house equipped with ghosts."

The crucial moment had arrived. "Will you come out for a few days and see these things for yourself? You said once you were interested in peculiar happenings, and this one is the most peculiar I've ever seen. I can't get anywhere with it and I'm worried to death about Valerie."

"I wouldn't worry too much about the girl," Tarrant said. "Her brother will be back in a day or so to take care of her."

"No. He won't be any more use when he gets here, than I am. He lives at the big house, not with Valerie in the new one. I don't believe she will let him stay with her, anyhow; she has an idea that she has to fight the thing out alone. But it isn't just imagination she's fighting, it's something a good deal more dangerous than that." I knew I was imposing on him but he was the only one I could think of to turn to. "I wish you'd come, if you can."

For some moments he considered in silence. Then he seemed to have made up his mind. He gave an unusual whistle and his valet appeared in the doorway. "Katoh, pack a bag for each of us. We are going to spend a few days in the country."

We stood in the small hallway of Valerie's house. Valerie was upstairs in bed and Annie was with her. We had had luncheon at home with Mary who assured us that everything had been done that could be done. After luncheon we had come over to the new house and I had taken Tarrant up and introduced him. Valerie, of course, looked perfectly lovely sitting up in bed and I could see that my friend was even startled by her unexpected beauty. Whatever misgivings I may have had about bringing him into the affair vanished at once, for it was clear with the first few words that Valerie liked him and was prepared to trust him. And indeed his calm matter-of-factness and his low, steady voice were reassurance itself.

Now we stood in the hall below, Tarrant and Katoh and myself. Tarrant said, "That sister of yours is a fine girl, Jerry. Most attractive." Then more briskly, "Well, let's make a little experiment and see whether your ghost is still around. See if you can find a ladder, will you, Katoh?"

A tall step-ladder was discovered and placing it beside the stairs, Tarrant mounted it and perched on top. "Apparently the wraith is not afraid of light, so we might as well try to conjure him up now. Jerry, you had better tell them up above that we are making some experiments, so they won't be frightened. And, Katoh, you walk up the stairs while I sit here and observe."

The little Japanese gravely mounted the steps. And nothing at all happened. At the top he turned and came down again. "No ghost," he remarked blandly.

"Now you, Jerry."

I ran up the stairs, and there the footsteps were, about two treads behind me, clear and audible. Tarrant's arm shot out and extended part way across the step I had just passed. *The footsteps went under his arm and continued.* As I had done the night before, I stopped halfway up and turned on my pursuer. Although I had known what to foresee, the recurrence of the phenomenon was so impressive that I really expected to find someone at my back. As I stood there, Tarrant's expression for the first time held more than polite incredulity.

"Hmm," said Tarrant. "He's awake now, evidently. You heard that, of course, Katoh?"

"I hear." The valet's face was expressionless.

"All right, come on down, Jerry. Now I want you to do that again, only go all the way up, this time. Don't stop till you get to the hall upstairs. Katoh, you run up about three or four steps behind him."

We did this and I was followed again. Not only by Katoh. Between him and myself, other footsteps pounded up the stairs. It was a weird feeling, this business of an unknown behind you, and I had all I could do to keep from stopping once more and turning around. The thought of the valet, also behind me, was distinctly pleasant. It may sound incredible but near the top of the flight *he* increased his speed and reached vainly at the empty air at my back. That's how overwhelmingly natural the thing was. The footsteps followed me to the top.

As I watched Katoh returning to the ground floor, it seemed to me that at one point he made a peculiar movement. I looked at him queerly. "Did you feel a slight push on the way down?"

He shook his head. "No. No push."

Tarrant slid down the ladder and stood with his hands in his pockets. "There is no use doing any more of this. There's something here I don't understand. Under some circumstances I'd think of mass suggestion but I happen to know how to avoid that for myself. It's an impressive demonstration of magic." He looked over at the valet. "What do you think, Katoh?"

"Is mahg-ic. But not here. This more like jiu-jitsu, I think. Also might be dangerous."

"It is dangerous." Tarrant's tone was decisive. "There is something here far more objective than imagination. It is objective and it is in this house. Miss Mopish must be moved to the other place. I shall insist on it. We three will spend the night here and we'll spend it alone, except for whatever this intruder is."

Valerie finally consented. I never thought she would, but Tarrant is a persuasive talker. After twenty minutes or so, most of which was spent in pointing out that something was in the house and that it simply could not be a matter of her own subjective nervousness, she agreed.

I stayed a moment after Tarrant had left the room. "Jerry," said Valerie, "please take care of yourself tonight. I couldn't bear it if anything happened to you."

That made me feel grand. "I'll take care of whatever is around here," I said grimly, "if I can once get my hands on it."

That night we divided our forces. Katoh was stationed in

the entrance between the hallway and the living room, where he could observe all of the latter and at the same time be close to the foot of the stairs. I sat in Valerie's own room upstairs; and Tarrant roved through the house, now here, now there.

I was tired—I had had no sleep the previous night. We began our vigil about eleven in the evening and the hours dragged by interminably. Nothing happened; I just sat in the dark and waited. At first the fact that I didn't know what I was waiting for kept me keyed up but finally I decided to lie down on the bed and rest my body, anyhow. Of course I fell asleep.

I don't know how much later it was when I began dreaming of a forest fire. As the flames mounted higher and higher in dazzling brilliance, I woke and sat up. For a moment I had no idea where I was, nor was I concerned with that. Opposite the foot of Valerie's bed a full-length mirror was set in the wall and this mirror was mysteriously bright, although no light in the room was on. That was puzzling, though not especially terrifying; but something else was. In the center of the mirror, illuminated by the unexplained glow, was a clear and gruesome image of a scaffold with a human figure dangling from it!

I gasped and rubbed my eyes. Yes, there it was, no doubt about it. Even as I stared at it, it began to fade—just like a fade-out in the movies. I called to Tarrant, but when he came in, I hardly believed that I had seen anything real myself.

We sat discussing it in the darkness. I made no concealment of the fact that I had been asleep and that when I had first seen it, I had not been fully awake. It hadn't lasted long but it seemed to me that before it had faded out completely, I had been plenty awake. As we went on talking I still sat on the bed, supporting myself with one hand which was buried in the pillow on which my head had rested. Happening to glance down presently, I noticed that the pillow was becoming bright, as if a light were focused on it; and at almost the same instant Tarrant grunted with surprise.

We both saw it this time. The mirror glowed again and we were treated to a close-up of the same previous picture. An agonized face stared out at us, the noose knotted behind one ear, the rope leading upward.

As the image began to fade once more, Tarrant was out of his chair and pressing the electric light button across the room. Instantly the picture vanished. A moment later he was knocking with his fist over the now empty mirror, sounding it and the walls immediately beside it. There appeared no hint of any hollowness, however; both glass and wood gave a solid response to his pounding.

"I shall examine that mirror more carefully in the morning," he promised. "We can't do much now. Let us turn the lights out and see if there is any more."

But though we sat through the next two hours to daylight, no further display occurred. Nothing further of any kind occurred, in fact. The image of that face of agony kept haunting me, nonetheless, and I began to understand the added horror, were I convinced as Valerie had been, that the thing was being projected from my own morbid mind. Even the position of the bed would add to that illusion, for the mirror was directly opposite it and in the natural course of events reflected the bed and its occupant.

I also realized why she had wanted the lights turned off the night before, in order to see if "It" was still there.

The following day I spent at home in my own bed. Sound asleep. Mary drove Tarrant into Norrisville and he returned with various instruments, such as a yardstick, a saw, chisels, and a hammer. He also procured from Valerie the original plans of the house.

"What did you want all that stuff for?" I inquired the same evening, when I was told about it. "Were you looking for hidden passages or recesses in the house?"

"No," he assured me. "Even without the plans, you can see that there is no place anywhere for a secret passage large enough to be used by a monkey. And by the way, I took that mirror out and there was nothing behind it but solid wall. No signs of its being connected with any kind of mechanism at all."

"So what we saw was not the result of mechanical arrangement?"

"No, it wasn't. I am certain that there is no mechanical contrivance in the entire house in any way connected with the phenomena."

"So what? Damn it all, Tarrant, we're completely stymied. What in heaven's name can be causing those sights and sounds?"

"I believe I could tell you the answer to that now," he asserted calmly enough. "Half an hour's more work tomorrow and I'm sure I shall have the whole answer. . . . I'll need a good, high ladder, though."

"I'll see that you get the ladder. But what is the answer?"

He would say no more, however. "I shall tell all of you, say day after tomorrow, when Miss Mopish's brother arrives home. He will certainly be interested in the things that have been going on in his house."

I was bitten with a terrific curiosity, for I felt certain that Tarrant would not have claimed a solution he had not achieved. Nevertheless, try as I would, I failed to get any satisfaction. On the other hand, Tarrant, too, was disappointed. That very evening

Valerie received a radio from John, saying that he had been taken ill during the crossing and would have to be transferred directly from the ship to a hospital in New York. Two days later, when it was learned that he was really desperately sick and would be confined for a considerable period at least, Tarrant gave up his notion and summoned us to the new house to exorcise, as he said, the ghost. Valerie was brought back, in a chair, and Mary and Katoh and I were there, of course. Also, at the last moment, Tarrant insisted that Annie, Valerie's maid, should come.

The demonstration was simple.

We all trooped out into the hall after Tarrant and stood grouped about; I noticed at once that a step had been removed from the staircase and through the aperture could be seen a slanting strip of wood, backing it. Valerie's house was certainly well constructed.

"I want you, Mr. Phelan, to walk up those stairs, then turn around and walk down them."

I did so, climbing over the missing step. Somewhat to my own surprise no sound accompanied me other than my own footsteps on the hard wood.

"Now, Mr. Phelan, kindly run up the stairs as fast as you can. But when you come down, walk; please be sure of that, *walk.*"

This time there could be no question of it; three treads behind me the ghostly footsteps followed my own to the floor above. Tarrant watched my descent, then spoke quietly.

"One would hardly suppose that so simple a thing could be so terrifying. The sounds that followed Mr. Phelan are, of course, no more than an *echo.* Here"—through the missed step he tapped the slanting wood behind it—"is an ingenious sounding-board, so made that it reflects the echo downward; thus the echoed steps appear always to be just *behind* the person mounting the stairs. When they are taken at a walk, nothing happens; the echo functions only for running footsteps. I am sure that Miss Mopish could be guaranteed to run—at times, anyhow.

"But the staircase is more dangerous than yet appears. In a house where all the furnishings and all the fixtures, even the construction itself, is modernistic, the eye is led away and confused by curious angles, by surfaces and planes at unaccustomed slants. It is not remarkable, therefore, that, seen from this hallway, the various steps appear uniform. *But they are not uniform.* I have measured them carefully and at a point just below the turn in the stairs three steps in succession have such dimensions *as to cause one to slip there.* That is what happened to Miss Mopish a few nights ago. She was not pushed off the stairs—she slipped forward so suddenly that the impression was the same. It happened in a much less degree to my assistant when he came down the stairs and we are indebted to his excellent leg reflexes and his quick recognition for the first hint of what sort of thing was happening here."

He turned suddenly to Valerie, seated in her chair by the living room entrance. "Both Mr. Phelan and I have seen the apparitions in your mirror, Miss Mopish; you may dismiss entirely any notion that you manufactured them yourself. For these the arrangement is more difficult than in the matter of the stairs, but simple, once one gets on to it.

"At the end of your room upstairs are two French windows opening upon a sleeping porch and above each is a permanent transom of leaded glass. In these transoms are set four prisms. The most interesting are the two which contain tiny replicas of the images seen in the mirror; the other two simply concentrate the moonlight upon the pillow of the bed so that it will frequently happen that anyone sleeping there will be awakened. Then the image-prisms function, concentrating their light and images in the mirror. The angles, of course, are very carefully worked out, to correspond with certain positions of the moon in the sky. To the naked eye the moon's motion is imperceptible but, actually, it is always moving. The prisms, protected by the overhang of the roof, only function fully for a period of seconds, the image then fading out and making it more probable than ever that the vision was due to a disordered imagination. By the time a witness arrives, the picture is gone. I am certain these pictures have appeared at particular times, when the moon has been full, or nearly full, for example."

Valerie nodded.

"As a matter of fact the images are not nearly as clear as they seem to be in the middle of the night, with one's eyes accustomed to darkness after some hours' sleep. The lighting in the room overwhelms them completely; that is also why the sun, even should it occupy the same relative position as the moon, does not cause them in the daytime when the room is bright.

"There was a somewhat similar arrangement in a temple in Egypt in the old days, called *Het Abtit* or the House of the Net. I do not know whether your brother is interested in Egyptology but, if not, then he has struck upon a very similar arrangement. The temple arrangement ensured that at high noon upon one special day of each year the Net, for which the building was named, should be illuminated through the temple roof in such a fashion that its ordinary outlines vanished and a resplendent picture of the miracle of the Virgin Birth appeared in its place. In the present instance we find the same principles used for a far less worthy purpose. . . . I have taken the liberty of removing the prisms from your transoms. I do not know of any further phenomena in the house. Have there been any?"

"No," Valerie answered in a low voice, so low as to be scarcely audible. "That is all, the mirror and the stairs. It was enough."

"In the case of a girl only a few years recovered from so serious a breakdown as I understand occurred," Tarrant went on, looking about at the rest of us, "it will readily be appreciated how such apparently inexplicable events would work upon her. Especially as one of them, the footsteps, if not the other phenomena also, were devised to correspond with previous obsessions. She would naturally suppose a return of her former troubles, which this time, however, could be guaranteed not to yield to any subjective technique at all, since they depended upon quite objective arrangements, having nothing to do with her personal imagination. It was a cruel performance; fortunately we have discovered its nature in time."

From my interest in Tarrant's explanation I abruptly awoke to its implications. I cried out, "Why, the damned skunk! But what could he—but what—but why?"

"That is something I do not feel myself commissioned to find out, Jerry. But money has caused plenty of trouble and is still doing it. I do not know who is the beneficiary under Miss Mopish's will, nor do I wish to. I might also point out that, after a few years in a sanitarium, an administrator is usually appointed for the patient's estate."

I was so mad I could have knocked the stairs down with my bare hands; but Valerie was sobbing. So I went to her.

John Mopish died the following week in his New York hospital. And it was damn lucky for him that he did. I don't know whether Valerie was glad or sorry, for we never mention him. I do know, though, that she kept me waiting only a month, the darling.

HAIRCUT
Ring Lardner

Mainly known as a sports writer and humorist, Ring(gold) Wilmer Lardner (1885-1933) began his writing career in 1906 in Indiana but soon moved to a couple of Chicago newspapers before becoming the editor of *Sporting News*, a weekly baseball paper in St. Louis. While moving to numerous other newspapers, he also began to write fiction.

In 1914, he created Jack Keefe, a baseball pitcher who, along with his wife Florrie, appeared in a series of connected short stories in *The Saturday Evening Post* that quickly amassed a large and devoted following, being collected in *You Know Me, Al* (1916). As with most of his work, it is satirical, but soon the satire became darker and more extreme when he realized that his favorite team, the Chicago White Sox, were deliberately trying to lose the 1919 World Series to the Cincinnati Reds in what has become known as the infamous Black Sox scandal.

From that time on, the hilarity of his best fiction belied the savage satiric elements of his work as it turned more and more bitter. His friend F. Scott Fitzgerald said that Lardner had "stopped finding any fun in his work ten years before he died."

While many of Lardner's tales, such as "Alibi Ike," "Golden Honeymoon," and the *You Know Me, Al* stories, are classics of humor, none is as well-known as "Haircut," a masterpiece of dark humor notable for its subtle malevolence. It is certainly not a typical mystery story, as it takes a while before the reader recognizes that it is a crime story.

"Haircut" was originally published in the March 28, 1925, issue of *Liberty Magazine*; it was first collected in *The Love Nest and Other Stories* (New York, Charles Scribner's Sons, 1926).

Haircut
Ring Lardner

I GOT *another* barber that comes over from Carterville and helps me out Saturdays, but the rest of the time I can get along all right alone. You can see for yourself that this ain't no New York City and besides that, the most of the boys works all day and don't have no leisure to drop in here and get themselves prettied up.

You're a newcomer, ain't you? I thought I hadn't seen you round before. I hope you like it good enough to stay. As I say, we ain't no New York City or Chicago, but we have pretty good times. Not as good, though, since Jim Kendall got killed. When he was alive, him and Hod Meyers used to keep this town in an uproar. I bet they was more laughin' done here than any town its size in America.

Jim was comical, and Hod was pretty near a match for him. Since Jim's gone, Hod tries to hold his end up just the same as ever, but it's tough goin' when you ain't got nobody to kind of work with.

They used to be plenty fun in here Saturdays. This place is jam-packed Saturdays, from four o'clock on. Jim and Hod would show up right after their supper, round six o'clock. Jim would set himself down in that big chair, nearest the blue spittoon. Whoever had been settin' in that chair, why they'd get up when Jim come in and give it to him.

You'd of thought it was a reserved seat like they have sometimes in a theayter. Hod would generally always stand or walk up and down, or some Saturdays, of course, he'd be settin' in his chair part of the time, gettin' a haircut.

Well, Jim would set there a w'ile without openin' his mouth only to spit, and then finally he'd say to me, "Whitey"—my right name, that is, my right first name, is Dick, but everybody round here calls me Whitey—Jim would say, "Whitey, your nose looks like a rosebud tonight. You must of been drinkin' some of your aw de cologne."

So I'd say, "No, Jim, but you look like you'd been drinkin' somethin' of that kind or somethin' worse."

Jim would have to laugh at that, but then he'd speak up and say, "No, I ain't had nothin' to drink, but that ain't sayin' I wouldn't like somethin'. I wouldn't even mind if it was wood alcohol."

Then Hod Meyers would say, "Neither would your wife." That would set everybody to laughin' because Jim and his wife wasn't on very good terms. She'd of divorced him only they wasn't no chance to get alimony and she didn't have no way to take care of herself and the kids. She couldn't never understand Jim. He *was* kind of rough, but a good fella at heart.

Him and Hod had all kinds of sport with Milt Sheppard. I

don't suppose you've seen Milt. Well, he's got an Adam's apple that looks more like a mushmelon. So I'd shavin' Milt and when I'd start to shave down here on his neck, Hod would holler, "Hey, Whitey, wait a minute! Before you cut into it, let's make up a pool and see who can guess closest to the number of seeds."

And Jim would say, "If Milt hadn't of been so hoggish, he'd of ordered a half a cantaloupe instead of a whole one and it might not of stuck in his throat."

All the boys would roar at this and Milt himself would force a smile, though the joke was on him. Jim certainly was a card!

There's his shavin' mug, settin' on the shelf, right next to Charley Vail's. "Charles M. Vail." That's the druggist. He comes in regular for his shave, three times a week. And Jim's is the cup next to Charley's. "James H. Kendall." Jim won't need no shavin' mug no more, but I'll leave it there just the same for old time's sake. Jim certainly was a character!

Years ago, Jim used to travel for a canned goods concern over in Carterville. They sold canned goods. Jim had the whole northern half of the state and was on the road five days out of every week. He'd drop in here Saturdays and tell his experiences for that week. It was rich.

I guess he paid more attention to playin' jokes than makin' sales. Finally the concern let him out and he come right home here and told everybody he'd been fired instead of sayin' he'd resigned like most fellas would of.

It was a Saturday and the shop was full and Jim got up out of that chair and says, "Gentlemen, I got an important announcement to make. I been fired from my job."

Well, they asked him if he was in earnest and he said he was and nobody could think of nothin' to say till Jim finally broke the ice himself. He says, "I been sellin' canned goods and now I'm canned goods myself."

You see, the concern he'd been workin' for was a factory that made canned goods. Over in Carterville. And now Jim said he was canned himself. He was certainly a card!

Jim had a great trick that he used to play w'ile he was travelin'. For instance, he'd be ridin' on a train and they'd come to some little town like, well, like, we'll say, like Benton. Jim would look out the train window and read the signs on the stores.

For instance, they'd be a sign, "Henry Smith, Dry Goods." Well, Jim would write down the name and the name of the town and when he got to wherever he was goin' he'd mail back a postal card to Henry Smith at Benton and not sign no name to it, but he'd write on the card, well, somethin' like "Ask your wife about that book agent that spent the afternoon last week," or "Ask your Missus who kept her from gettin' lonesome the last time you was in Carterville." And he'd sign the card, "A Friend."

Of course, he never knew what really come of none of those jokes, but he could picture what *probably* happened and that was enough. Jim didn't work very steady after he lost his position with the Carterville people. What he did earn, doin' odd jobs round town, why he spent pretty near all of it on gin and his family might of starved if the stores hadn't of carried them along. Jim's wife tried her hand at dress-makin', but they ain't nobody goin' to get rich makin' dresses in this town.

As I say, she'd of divorced Jim, only she seen that she couldn't support herself and the kids and she was always hopin' that some day Jim would cut out his habits and give her more than two or three dollars a week.

They was a time when she would go to whoever he was workin' for and ask them to give her his wages, but after she done this once or twice, he beat her to it by borrowin' most of his pay in advance. He told it all round town, how he had outfoxed his Missus. He certainly was a caution!

But he wasn't satisfied with just outwittin' her. He was sore the way she had acted, tryin' to grab off his pay. And he made up his mind he'd get even. Well, he waited till Evans's Circus was advertised to come to town. Then he told his wife and two kiddies that he was goin' to take them to the circus. The day of the circus, he told them he would get the tickets and meet them outside the entrance to the tent.

Well, he didn't have no intentions of bein' there or buyin' tickets or nothin'. He got full of gin and laid round Wright's pool room all day. His wife and kids waited and waited and of course he didn't show up. His wife didn't have a dime with her, or nowhere else, I guess. So she finally had to tell the kids it was all off and they cried like they wasn't never goin' to stop.

Well, it seems, w'ile they was cryin', Doc Stair came along and he asked what was the matter, but Mrs. Kendall was stubborn and wouldn't tell him, but the kids told him and he insisted on takin' them and their mother in to the show. Jim found this out afterwards and it was one reason why he had it in for Doc Stair.

Doc Stair come here about a year and a half ago. He's a mighty handsome young fella and his clothes always look like he has them made to order. He goes to Detroit two or three times a year and w'ile he's there he must have a tailor take his measure and then make him a suit to order. They cost pretty near twice as much, but they fit a whole lot better than if you just bought them in a store.

For a w'ile everybody was wonderin' why a young doctor like

Doc Stair should come to a town like this where we already got old Doc Gamble and Doc Foote that's both been here for years and all the practice in town was already divided between the two of them.

Then they was a story got round that Doc Stair's gal had throwed him over, a gal up in the Northern Peninsula somewheres, and the reason he come here was to hide himself away and forget it. He said himself that he thought they wasn't nothin' like general practice in a place like ours to fit a man to be a good all round doctor. And that's why he'd came.

Anyways, it wasn't long before he was makin' enough to live on, though they tell me that he never dunned nobody for what they owed him, and the folks here certainly has got the owin' habit, even in my business. If I had all that was comin' to me for just shaves alone, I could go to Carterville and put up at the Mercer for a week and see a different picture every night. For instance, they's old George Purdy—but I guess I shouldn't ought to be gossipin'.

Well, last year, our coroner died, died of the flu. Ken Beatty, that was his name. He was the coroner. So they had to choose another man to be coroner in his place and they picked Doc Stair. He laughed at first and said he didn't want it, but they made him take it. It ain't no job that anybody would fight for and what a man makes out of it in a year would just about buy seeds for their garden. Doc's the kind, though, that can't say no to nothin' if you keep at him long enough.

But I was goin' to tell you about a poor boy we got here in town—Paul Dickson. He fell out of a tree when he was about ten years old. Lit on his head and it done somethin' to him and he ain't never been right. No harm in him, but just silly. Jim Kendall used to call him cuckoo; that's a name Jim had for anybody that was off their head, only he called people's head their bean. That was another of his gags, callin' head bean and callin' crazy people cuckoo. Only poor Paul ain't crazy, but just silly.

You can imagine that Jim used to have all kinds of fun with Paul. He'd send him to the White Front Garage for a left-hand-ed monkey wrench. Of course they ain't no such a thing as a left-handed monkey wrench.

And once we had a kind of a fair here and they was a baseball game between the fats and the leans and before the game started Jim called Paul over and sent him way down to Schrader's hard-ware store to get a key for the pitcher's box.

They wasn't nothin' in the way of gags that Jim couldn't think up, when he put his mind to it.

Poor Paul was always kind of suspicious of people, maybe on account of how Jim had kept foolin' him. Paul wouldn't have much to do with anybody only his own mother and Doc Stair and a girl here in town named Julie Gregg. That is, she ain't a girl no more, but pretty near thirty or over.

When Doc first came to town, Paul seemed to feel like here was a real friend and he hung around Doc's office most of the w'ile; the only time he wasn't there was when he'd go home to eat or sleep or when he seen Julie Gregg doin' her shoppin'.

When he looked out Doc's window and seen her, he'd run downstairs and join her and tag along with her to the different stores. The poor boy was crazy about Julie and she always treat-ed him mighty nice and made him feel like he was welcome, though of course it wasn't nothin' but pity on her side.

Doc done all he could to improve Paul's mind and he told me once that he really thought the boy was gettin' better, that they was times when he was as bright and sensible as anybody else.

But I was goin' to tell you about Julie Gregg. Old Man Gregg was in the lumber business, but got to drinkin' and lost the most of his money and when he died, he didn't leave nothin' but the house and just enough insurance for the girl to skimp along on.

Her mother was a kind of a half invalid and didn't hardly ever leave the house. Julie wanted to sell the place and move somewheres else after the old man died, but the mother said she was born here and would die here. It was tough on Julie, as the young people round this town—well, she's too good for them.

She's been away to school and Chicago and New York and different places and they ain't no subject she can't talk on, where you take the rest of the young folks here and you mention anything to them outside of Gloria Swanson or Tommy Meighan and they think you're delirious. Did you see Gloria in *Wages of Virtue*? You missed somethin'!

Well, Doc Stair hadn't been here more than a week when he come in one day to get shaved and I recognized who he was as he had been pointed out to me, so I told him about my old lady. She's been ailin' for a couple years and either Doc Gamble or Doc Foote, neither one, seemed to be helpin' her. So he said he would come out and see her, but if she was able to get out herself, it would be better to bring her to his office where he could make a complete examination.

So I took her to his office and w'ile I was waiting' for her in the reception room, in come Julie Gregg. When somebody comes in Doc Stair's office, they's a bell that rings in his inside office so he can tell they's somebody to see him.

So he left my old lady inside and come out to the front office and that's the first time him and Julie met and I guess it was what they call love at first sight. But it wasn't fifty-fifty. This young fella was the slickest lookin' fella she'd ever seen in this town and she went wild over him. To him she was just a young lady that wanted to see the doctor.

She'd came on about the same business I had. Her mother had been doctorin' for years with Doc Gamble and Doc Foote and with no results. So she'd heard they was a new doc in town and decided to give him a try. He promised to call and see her mother that same day.

I said a minute ago that it was love at first sight on her part. I'm not only judgin' by how she acted afterwards but how she looked at him that first day in his office. I ain't no mind reader, but it was wrote all over her face that she was gone.

Now Jim Kendall, besides bein' a jokesmith and a pretty good drinker, well, Jim was quite a lady-killer. I guess he run pretty wild durin' the time he was on the road for them Carterville people, and besides that, he'd had a couple little affairs of the heart right here in town. As I say, his wife could of divorced him, only she couldn't.

But Jim was like the majority of men, and women, too, I guess. He wanted what he couldn't get. He wanted Julie Gregg and worked his head off tryin' to land her. Only he'd of said bean instead of head.

Well, Jim's habits and his jokes didn't appeal to Julie and of course he was a married man, so he didn't have no more chance than, well, than a rabbit. That's an expression of Jim's himself. When somebody didn't have no chance to get elected or somethin', Jim would always say they didn't have no more chance than a rabbit.

He didn't make no bones about how he felt. Right in here, more than once, in front of the whole crowd, he said he was stuck on Julie and anybody that could get her for him was welcome to his house and his wife and kids included. But she wouldn't have nothin' to do with him; wouldn't even speak to him on the street. He finally seen he wasn't gettin' nowheres with his usual line so he decided to try the rough stuff. He went right up to her house one evenin' and when she opened the door he forced his way in and grabbed her. But she broke loose and before he could stop her, she run in the next room and locked the door and phoned to Joe Barnes. Joe's the marshal. Jim could hear who she was phonin' to and he beat it before Joe got there.

Joe was an old friend of Julie's pa. Joe went to Jim the next day and told him what would happen if he ever done it again.

I don't know how the news of this little affair leaked out. Chances is that Joe Barnes told his wife and she told somebody else's wife and they told their husband. Anyways, it did leak out and Hod Meyers had the nerve to kid Jim about it, right here in this shop. Jim didn't deny nothin' and kind of laughed it off and said for us all to wait: that lots of people had tried to make a monkey out of him, but he always got even.

Meanw'ile everybody in town was wise to Julie's bein' wild mad over the Doc. I don't suppose she had any idea how her face changed when him and her was together; of course she couldn't of, or she'd kept away from him. And she didn't know that we was all noticin' how many times she made excuses to go up to his office or pass it on the other side of the street and look up in his window to see if he was there. I felt sorry for her and so did most other people.

Hod Meyers kept rubbin' it into Jim about how the Doc had cut him out. Jim didn't pay no attention to the kiddin' and you could see he was plannin' one of his jokes.

One trick Jim had was the knack of changin' his voice. He could make you think he was a girl talkin' and he could mimic any man's voice. To show you how good he was along this line, I'll tell you the joke he played on me once.

You know, in most towns of any size, when a man is dead and needs a shave, why the barber that shaves him soaks him five dollars for the job; that is, he don't soak *him*, but whoever ordered the shave. I just charge three dollars because personally I don't mind much shavin' a dead person. They lay a whole lot stiller than live customers. The only thing is that you don't feel like talkin' to them and you get kind of lonesome.

Well, about the coldest day we ever had here, two years ago last winter, the phone rung at the house w'ile I was home to dinner and I answered the phone and it was a woman's voice and she said she was Mrs. John Scott and her husband was dead and would I come out and shave him.

Old John had always been a good customer of mine. But they live seven miles out in the country, on the Streeter road. Still I didn't see how I could say no.

So I said I would be there, but would have to come in a jitney and it might cost three or four dollars besides the price of the shave. So she, or the voice, it said that was all right, so I got Frank Abbott to drive me out to the place and when I got there, who should open the door but old John himself! He wasn't no more dead than, well, than a rabbit.

It didn't take no private detective to figure out who had played me this little joke. Nobody could of thought it up but Jim Kendall. He certainly was a card!

I tell you this incident just to show you how he could disguise his voice and make you believe it was somebody else talkin'. I'd of swore it was Mrs. Scott had called me. Anyways, some woman.

Well, Jim waited till he had Doc Stair's voice down pat; then he went after revenge.

He called Julie up on a night when he knew Doc was over in Carterville. She never questioned but what it was Doc's voice. Jim said he must see her that night; he couldn't wait no longer to tell her somethin'. She was all excited and told him to come to the house. But he said he was expectin' an important long distance call and wouldn't she please forget her manners for once and come to his office. He said they couldn't nothin' hurt her and nobody would see her and he just *must* talk to her a little w'ile. Well, poor Julie fell for it.

Doc always keeps a night light in his office, so it looked to Julie like they was somebody there.

Meanw'ile Jim Kendall had went to Wright's pool room, where they was a whole gang amusin' themselves. The most of them had drank plenty of gin, and they was a rough bunch even when sober. They was always strong for Jim's jokes and when he told them to come with him and see some fun they give up their card games and pool games and followed along.

Doc's office is on the second floor. Right outside his door they's a flight of stairs leadin' to the floor above. Jim and his gang hid in the dark behind these stairs.

Well, Julie come up to Doc's door and rung the bell and they was nothin' doin'. She rung it again and she rung it seven or eight times. Then she tried the door and found it locked. Then Jim made some kind of a noise and she heard it and waited a minute, and then she says, "Is that you, Ralph?" Ralph is Doc's first name.

They was no answer and it must of came to her all of a sudden that she'd been bunked. She pretty near fell downstairs and the whole gang after her. They chased her all the way home, hollerin', "Is that you, Ralph?" and "Oh, Ralphie, dear, is that you?" Jim says he couldn't holler it himself, as he was laughin' too hard.

Poor Julie! She didn't show up here on Main Street for a long, long time afterward.

And of course Jim and his gang told everybody in town, everybody but Doc Stair. They was scared to tell him, and he might of never knowed only for Paul Dickson. The poor cuckoo, as Jim called him, he was here in the shop one night when Jim was still gloatin' yet over what he'd done to Julie. And Paul took in as much of it as he could understand and he run to Doc with the story.

It's a cinch Doc went up in the air and swore he'd make Jim suffer. But it was a kind of a delicate thing, because if it got out that he had beat Jim up, Julie was bound to hear of it and then she'd know that Doc knew and of course knowin' that he knew would make it worse for her than ever. He was goin' to do somethin', but it took a lot of figurin'.

Well, it was a couple of days later when Jim was here in the shop again, and so was the cuckoo. Jim was goin' duck-shootin' the next day and had come in lookin' for Hod Meyers to go with him. I happened to know that Hod had went over to Carterville and wouldn't be home till the end of the week. So Jim said he hated to go alone and he guessed he would call it off. Then poor Paul spoke up and said if Jim would take him he would go along. Jim thought a w'ile and then he said, well, he guessed a half-wit was better than nothin'.

I suppose he was plottin' to get Paul out in the boat and play some joke on him, like pushin' him in the water. Anyways, he said Paul could go. He asked him had he ever shot a duck and Paul said no, he'd never even had a gun in his hands. So Jim said he could set in the boat and watch him and if he behaved himself, he might lend him his gun for a couple of shots. They made a date to meet in the mornin' and that's the last I seen of Jim alive.

Next mornin', I hadn't been open more than ten minutes when Doc Stair come in. He looked kind of nervous. He asked me had I seen Paul Dickson. I said no, but I knew where he was, out duck-shootin' with Jim Kendall. So Doc says that's what he had heard, and he couldn't understand it because Paul had told him he wouldn't never have no more to do with Jim as long as he lived.

He said Paul had told him about the joke Jim had played on Julie. He said Paul had asked him what he thought of the joke and the Doc had told him that anybody that would do a thing like that ought not to be let live.

I said it had been a kind of a raw thing, but Jim just couldn't resist no kind of a joke, no matter how raw. I said I thought he was all right at heart, but just bubblin' over with mischief. Doc turned and walked out.

At noon he got a phone call from old John Scott. The lake where Jim and Paul had went shootin' is on John's place. Paul had came runnin' up to the house a few minutes before and said they'd been an accident. Jim had shot a few ducks and then give the gun to Paul and told him to try his luck. Paul hadn't never handled a gun and he was nervous. He was shakin' so hard that he couldn't control the gun. He let fire and Jim sunk back in the boat, dead.

Doc Stair, bein' the coroner, jumped in Frank Abbott's fliver and rushed out to Scott's farm. Paul and old John was down on the shore of the lake. Paul had rowed the boat to shore, but they'd left the body in it, waitin' for Doc to come.

Doc examined the body and said they might as well fetch it

back to town. They was no use leavin' it there or callin' a jury, as it was a plain case of accidental shootin'.

Personally I wouldn't never leave a person shoot a gun in the same boat I was in unless I was sure they knew somethin' about guns. Jim was a sucker to leave a new beginner have his gun, let alone a half-wit. It probably served Jim right, what he got. But still we miss him round here. He certainly was a card!

Comb it wet or dry?

FINGERPRINTS DON'T LIE
Stuart Palmer

A prolific writer of books, short stories, journalism, and screenplays after holding such jobs as iceman, sailor, publicity man, apple picker, taxi driver, and editor, Charles Stuart Palmer (1905-1968) was a descendent of colonists who settled in Salem, Massachusetts, in 1634.

His best-known creation was the popular spinster-sleuth Hildegarde Withers. A schoolteacher in the early books, the thin, angular, horse-faced snoop devoted her energy to aiding Inspector Oliver Piper of the New York City Police Department, driving him slightly crazy in the process. She is noted for her odd, even eccentric, choice of hats. Palmer stated that she was based on his high school English teacher, Miss Fern Hackett, and on his father.

Miss Withers made her debut in *The Penguin Pool Murder* (1931), which was followed by thirteen more novels in the series, the last, *Hildegarde Withers Makes the Scene* (1969), being completed by Fletcher Flora after Palmer died. There also were three short story collections, with the first, *The Riddles of Hildegarde*

Withers (1947), being selected as a *Queen's Quorum* title. It was followed by *The Monkey Murders and Other Hildegarde Withers Stories* (1950), and *People vs. Withers and Malone* (1963), in conjunction with Craig Rice, which also featured Rice's series character, John J. Malone.

The film version of *The Penguin Pool Murder* was released in 1932 and spurred five additional comic mystery films, the first three featuring Edna May Oliver in a perfect casting decision, followed by Helen Broderick, and the last, *Forty Naughty Girls* (1937), with Zasu Pitts. Piper was played by James Gleason in all films.

The success of the series gained Palmer employment as a scriptwriter with thirty-seven mystery screenplays to his credit, mostly for such popular series as Bulldog Drummond, the Lone Wolf, and the Falcon.

"Fingerprints Don't Lie" was originally published in the November 1947 issue of *Ellery Queen's Mystery Magazine*; it was first collected in *The Monkey Murder and Other Hildegarde Withers Stories* (New York, Bestseller Mysteries, 1950).

Fingerprints Don't Lie
Stuart Palmer

THE TRAP—though the policemen who were setting it would have called it a "stakeout"—was set around noon. It was a little before two in the afternoon when a soft knock came at the front door of the little adobe cottage, and then another.

Before either of the two detectives could make up his mind about answering, the knob started to turn—hopefully but without result. Then there was the sound of footsteps scrunching around through the bedraggled little cactus garden to the rear of the place.

Young Rankin snorted. "This is going to be good!" He was a beefy man who bulged his blue serge, and he had a way of speaking faster than he thought. "It says in the book—"

Detective Tom Macy had been on the Las Vegas force for twenty-one years, and for his money nothing was any good except keeping out of trouble, getting off duty, and going home for supper. "All right, all right. So it says in the book they always return to the scene of the crime. Relax, eager-beaver."

Yet he too was alert, his gnarled red hand hovering near his holster, as there came the soft sound of scratching at the lock of the kitchen door. He caught Rankin's arm and drew him into the hall closet. They listened as the kitchen door opened and closed. There was the creak of light, cautious steps on the linoleum, then tinware rattled and cupboard doors opened. After a while the footsteps came past the breakfast nook and into the living room, and then stopped.

"Now!" Macy said, and they pounced. Rankin had his lead-heavy sap in the air, and narrowly managed to bring it down without damaging their prisoner, who turned out to be an angular spinster of uncertain years. She had no other weapon than her tongue, and needed none.

"I am Miss Hildegarde Withers!" she announced. "Take your big clumsy hands off me at once! What if I did enter this place? I have as much right in this cottage as you have, and perhaps more."

Rankin said that they would see about that. But Macy elbowed him firmly aside. "Lady, we're listening. But give it straight. We're Las Vegas police."

"In that case," Miss Withers said acidly, "I shall try to speak clearly and in words of one syllable. I am here, having interrupted a train journey from New York to Los Angeles, because a girl named Eileen Travis is supposed to be living here. For more than five weeks she has been establishing residence for a Nevada divorce. Her family back East has considerable influence with the powers that be, and they called on the New York police at Centre Street. You see, they were very worried about her—"

"Oh, so you claim to be a policewoman?" Rankin cut in.

"Nothing of the kind. My I.Q. is much too high, for one thing. I am a schoolteacher. But once in a while I fall heir to problems which are too far off the beaten track for Centre Street to bother with. Some friends of mine at Headquarters knew that I was en route to California for a vacation, so after Eileen's mother put the pressure on, she was told to telegraph me, and—"

Macy cleared his throat noisily. "Just why was the girl's mother worried about her?"

"I don't quite know. It was about some threats that George Travis, the girl's husband, was supposed to have made. The Kings County Grand Jury recently indicted him for violation of OPA rules—some sort of black market practices—and he felt that his wife was rushing through the divorce so that she would be able legally to testify against him at his forthcoming trial. On top of that, Eileen's mother phoned her long distance last week, and the girl acted strangely—she refused to talk." Miss Withers sniffed again. "Now you know as much as I do. By the way, where is the body?"

"Ah, ha!" cried Rankin jubilantly. "How'd you know about that?"

"I didn't, until you told me. But I suspected it. There's an odor of perfume, stale alcohol, tobacco, and cordite in this room. Besides, why should there be two detectives lurking in the house?"

Macy sighed, and indicated the bedroom door. "She's in there. Around midnight last night, close as we can figure, somebody let her have it with a shotgun, right smack in her pretty face. We're waiting for the ambulance now—only two in town, and both pretty busy." He gestured. "Sorry, but you'll have to come down to the station."

"Illegal, but to be expected. Meanwhile, of course, the real murderer is making tracks out of town. Never fear, I shall go quietly."

"I wish!" Rankin muttered fervently.

"But first," insisted the schoolteacher, "I think I ought to look at the body. Or has it been identified?"

Macy hesitated, and then said "Come on."

In the bedroom there were the grotesquely pitiful remains of a plump, tanned girl in a black négligée, sprawled all akimbo on a white goatskin rug. A lightweight shotgun lay nearby.

"That her?" Macy demanded. "I mean as far as you can tell, without any face."

Miss Withers knelt over the body. "New nylons. Shoes from I. Miller, New York. Négligée from Altman's—the expensive kind that you can draw through a ring. And speaking of rings—"

"We want to know, is that her or isn't it?" Rankin cut in.

"She must have been pretty," Miss Withers said. "Once."

Rankin sighed. "Sure musta. Don't see a figure like that once in a coon's age, even in this town."

"He's an expert," Macy said dryly. "These bachelors! Sure you never were out with her, Rank?"

"No such luck." Rankin was oddly blushing. "Well, ma'am?"

"I don't know if it's Eileen Travis or not," the schoolteacher admitted. "I never saw the girl. I just wanted to find out if there were any clues you'd missed."

Rankin looked angry, but Macy almost laughed. "And were there?"

"Only that her ring is missing." Miss Withers pointed to the narrow pale line around the ring finger of the dead girl's left hand.

"Pretty sharp," Macy said. "Only there was a ring there when we found her. This one." From his pocket he produced a heavy white-gold wedding ring. "It says, 'From G T to E H Jan 20 '44.'"

"From George Travis to Eileen Hampton," Miss Withers said. "He gave himself top billing, as they used to say in vaudeville. That tells us something about George, does it not?"

"You mean because he put his own initials first?" Macy looked at her with a new respect.

"Uh-hmmm." The schoolteacher had opened the closet door and was looking at the rows of expensive clothes, the big leather bag of golf clubs—everything well cared-for and expensive.

"Nothing in here," Macy said, "but the shotgun. And that's just an ordinary sixteen-gauge, not new, not old."

"Everybody around here has one," Rankin put in. "We use 'em for shooting doves and prairie jacks. Jackrabbits, that is."

They went back into the living room, and Macy showed Miss Withers the bottle of Scotch, part-full, which had been found on the coffee table, beside two glasses. There was also an ashtray with some cigarette butts and ashes, and a half-smoked perfecto, unchewed and still bearing the band decorated with the head and plump bust of a señorita.

"A fifty-center," Rankin said. "Boy, could I go for a box of those!"

"We figure," Macy explained, "that the girl had a caller. She gave him a drink—"

"The cigar means it was a man. A man she knew, or she wouldn't have had a drink with him dressed in that flimsy nightie," Rankin said.

"Yeh? Some of the tomatoes you run around with on your off time would—" Macy gestured broadly. "Sorry, ma'am. Anyway, we figure that this visitor puffs on his cigar and drinks his drink and then—"

"And then he pulls the shotgun out of his vest pocket and shoots his hostess smack in the face, is that it?" Miss Withers sniffed very dubiously. "Obliging of him to leave fingerprints. By the way, you're welcome to take mine, although I don't drink, smoke cigars, or shoot shotguns."

Rankin guffawed. "Oh, they're not women's prints. Mostly just fragments, but we got a complete thumbprint on one of the glasses, and it was a big one, even for a man. Too bad that dame's husband is in jail back East, or this would be duck soup."

"A man with black market connections," pointed out Miss Withers, "could arrange to have someone commit murder for him."

Macy shrugged. "Well, ma'am, we'll look into all that at the proper time. Let's go downtown." He led the way out through the back door, then stopped short. "What were you doing here in the kitchen when you came in?" he demanded curtly.

"Looking for clues. You can tell a lot about a person by her garbage can, and her shelves. Notice the ham, and biscuit dough, and cans of black-eyed peas? A hearty eater, that girl. And if you'll look in her garbage—"

"I don't see any sense in pawing through old orange rinds and coffee grounds," Macy protested.

"That's the point. There weren't—"

But he hurried her along to the battered sedan which had been parked in the alley. Macy drove around to the front and down the street, while Officer Rankin looked after them wistfully from a front window. "Guess this is the first time Rankin's been squeamish about being left alone with a blonde," Macy said as they drove.

The schoolteacher was staring back toward the lonely cottage. "If I were you I shouldn't worry too much about his solitude," she said.

"Why not?"

"Because I just saw a man step out from behind a billboard across the street heading for the cottage."

Macy drove on automatically for half a block, and then made a quick U-turn which bumped Miss Withers severely against the door. They roared up the street again, brakes screeching as they stopped. "If you're playing tricks—" Macy warned.

But then he saw the cottage door open. They hurried in, Miss Withers no more than three feet behind, and found Rankin rolling on the floor in an undignified but very realistic wrestling match. His opponent turned out to be a pale, unshaven gentleman of about thirty, dressed in a neat, dark, pin-stripe suit which had mopped up a great deal of dust from Eileen Travis's floor.

Seeing that the odds were now three to one against him, he stopped wrestling. But he wasn't talking.

"I do believe it's Mr. George Travis!" Miss Withers exclaimed. And as they all stared at her, she continued: "Elementary. The pallor of his face is the typical night-club tan of Manhattan. The clothing suggests Brooks Brothers. Besides, if you will notice the signet ring on his finger, you'll see the initials 'G T.'"

The stranger didn't deny it. "I want to see my wife . . . alone. That's why I waited until I thought you'd gone. Where's Eileen?'

"In here," Macy said softly, and showed him. "This is just the way the cleaning woman found her this morning. Not pretty, huh?"

Travis came out of the bedroom looking pale around the gills. "I—I flew out here to see her," he admitted. "I walked in and this hot-head jumped me. I didn't know she was dead."

"You know it now," Macy said. "Let's go. All of us."

"You're not going to leave her alone like that?" Travis protested.

"She won't mind," Rankin told him. "You worry about yourself."

The house was locked up tight, with a note on the door to the coroner which read "Back in twenty minutes" and they all rode downtown in the police car. Nobody did any talking, although Miss Withers wished that she could be alone with Travis for a moment. He looked like a sulky schoolboy, and she knew how to handle them. Once at the station a mousy but excited little secretary was called in to take down his statement that he had just got off the Los Angeles plane, that he had come out here in an effort to get his wife to postpone the divorce until after his trial, and that he knew nothing about her murder.

"I risked forfeiting my bond just to talk to her," he went on. "Not that it would have done much good. She was bitter because I made her sell most of her jewels to raise cash so I could hang on to my property. She figured this was her chance to get even. Eileen had a rotten temper—no maid ever stayed with her more than a month, and she even went after one of them with a riding crop."

"Okay, okay," Macy said. "We're holding you. Not for murder, not yet. But if you're wanted in New York—" They took him away.

Miss Withers confidently expected the same fate, but the officers only took her fingerprints, made a few notes, and let her go. "Don't leave town, though," Rankin warned her.

Macy smiled. "Try the Mesa—it's a pretty fair hotel."

Miss Withers nodded, and went to La Mesa. In a little corner room, ornamented with a spittoon and a reproduction of "The End of the Trail" showing a dejected redskin on a more dejected cayuse, she sat herself down and thought her own thoughts. Finally there came a knock at the door.

She opened it, facing a slick-haired young man who introduced himself as "Larry Koontz—I work down at the Wheel of Fortune." Miss Withers told him that she had not come to town to gamble—

The young man winked at her, lighted a cigarette, and said that he knew very well why she had come to town. "You're out here on this Travis case," he said. "You represent her family—"

"Do I?"

"Sure, I know. I got connections. You want to know the real lowdown?"

"Curiosity," admitted Miss Withers, "is my besetting sin."

"Huh? Well, anyway, I got the dope. I met Eileen down at the place I work. I'm a sort of shill—that means I play the dice games with the house money whenever there's a lull at the table. I can tell you all you want to know—" here he licked his thin lips—"if I get mine. I figure two grand would be about right."

Miss Withers had to admit that she was not in a position to lay any such honorarium on the line. He smiled. "You could get it from her folks, couldn't you?"

"I don't know. I'd have to have some idea—"

Mr. Koontz pondered. Then he opened his mouth, but before he could say anything, the telephone interrupted. The schoolteacher answered it, to hear the voice of the desk clerk. "Two gentlemen to see you."

"Sorry, but I'm busy at the moment," she said.

"They're on their way up. It's the police."

"Police? But—"

Miss Withers heard the door close, and when she looked around Mr. Koontz had disappeared. She had barely time to adjust her hair and assume an innocent expression, when Detectives Macy and Rankin came into the room. They looked grimly unpleasant. "Now don't tell me you found that my fingerprints matched those on the murder gun!"

They didn't tell her anything. "We want to know why you got into town yesterday and only went out to the Travis girl's apartment this afternoon," Rankin demanded.

"Very simple. I hadn't her address, only the phone number. It took some time to get any information out of the telephone company." She sniffed. "If you gentlemen would turn your suspicions upon Mr. George Travis—after all, he could have committed the murder last night, driven back to Los Angeles, and then flown in on the first plane this morning."

"We thought of that," Macy said wearily.

"But his prints didn't match the ones on the gun and glasses," Rankin finished.

"Fingerprints!" retorted Miss Withers scornfully. "Police put so much faith in technicalities like that that they forget to study motives and personalities. Not to speak of wedding rings."

They both stared at her. "Come, come!" Miss Withers chided, "Don't tell me you didn't notice that the ring you took from the dead girl's finger was too wide for the mark it was supposed to have left!"

"Go on," Macy said.

"You might start wondering why somebody took a narrow wedding ring off Eileen's finger and put on a wide one," the schoolteacher snapped. "In my opinion the girl wasn't wearing her own wedding ring while she was here waiting for her divorce. Or else—" Here she stopped short. "If it's not asking too much, could you tell me whether or not you've officially announced the murder of Eileen Travis?"

They shook their heads.

"Then," continued Miss Withers, "I suggest that you don't. Give out the story that the body has tentatively been identified as somebody else—any girl on your list of missing persons. You can always issue a corrected statement later."

Macy nodded. "So the killer will think he got the wrong girl maybe?"

Miss Withers smiled. "Sometimes it helps to toss a monkey wrench into the machinery."

"Could be, if Sheriff Kehoe will go for the idea." Macy seemed friendlier now. "You know, ma'am, we phoned New York about you, and they said at Centre Street that once in a while you made a lucky guess."

"Bless Inspector Piper's black Irish heart," murmured Miss Withers. Then she shrugged. "Well, here's another guess. Do you know a man named Larry Koontz, who is a shill at the Wheel of Fortune?"

Macy frowned and shook his head, but Rankin brightened. "Sure we do, Tom. That's Molly's husband—the girl who works in the sheriff's office. They busted up over some dame, and she's been crying her eyes out."

"Really? Things like that make me resigned to my state of single blessedness. Do you know where Mr. Koontz lives?"

They didn't, but said that they could easily find out. "We'll give you a ring," Macy promised.

Alone again, Miss Withers went down to dinner, came back again, and finally was in the midst of giving her hair its requisite hundred strokes preparatory for bed when the call came.

"Hello? Hello, Detective Rankin? Well, did you find Mr. Koontz's address?"

"Why, yes, ma'am, we did." There was an unpleasant overtone in the voice of Detective Rankin. "He was living out at the Iris Apartments. But he moved—a few minutes ago. Or rather, they moved him. Over to Callahan's Mortuary."

"What?"

"Acting on your tip, Macy and I went out there. The door was open, the lights were all on, and there was Koontz in the kitchenette with an icepick between his shoulder blades."

There was a moment of silence. "Oh, dear!" said Miss Withers.

"Oh dear is right. You can say the rest at the station. We're downstairs, so get a move on."

Miss Withers moved, getting into her dress again and taking two aspirins, fancying that this might be a hectic night. Neither Macy nor Rankin had much to say on the way to the station. "It seems odd to me that none of the neighbors heard or noticed anything," the schoolteacher finally offered.

"Lady, nobody in this town is ever home between ten o'clock and two or three in the morning. The visitors are playing, and the natives are working in the joints." Rankin pulled the car up outside police headquarters. In spite of all the haste Miss Withers found herself cooling her heels in a shabby outer office for some time.

At last the inner door opened and she was beckoned inside, where she faced Detectives Macy and Rankin, a beak-nosed sexagenarian with a sheriff's star pinned to the front of his Stetson, and a thin, freckled woman with red eyes whom she recognized as the one who had transcribed her statement earlier that day. "This is Molly Koontz," the sheriff said. "Ma'am, suppose you tell us why you were so interested in her late husband just before he got stabbed."

"Gladly," answered the schoolteacher, "if you'll answer a question for me, or have Mrs. Koontz answer it." Taking silence for consent, she told of her brief meeting with the shill who worked at the Wheel of Fortune, and who had had so little good fortune himself. "He knew the answer to all this, or he thought he did," she concluded.

The sheriff nodded noncommittally. "Now," said Miss Withers, "it's my turn. Forgive me, Mrs. Koontz, for prying into your family troubles but I understand that you and your husband separated over another girl."

"Girl! You mean girls. Larry played the field."

"Was one of those women Eileen Travis?"

Molly Koontz shrugged. "I dunno. We broke up a couple of months ago. Only we stayed in touch, sort of. Larry used to take me to dinner now and then, or borrow a few dollars when he got to gambling."

"Well, can you name any girl he was interested in?"

"No—only there was one little number who kept phoning him—one of those southern girls who say 'honey-chile' and 'lil ol' me.' Her name was Thelma something."

"Thelma Pringle," Detective Rankin put in. "She's on our Missing Persons list."

"Maybe," Molly said. "I can tell you one thing. Any girl Larry went for was on the *zoftig* side—you know, plump. And well-dressed. Larry went for the dressy ones."

Sheriff Kehoe yawned and stood up, signaling that the session was concluded. "By the way," pressed Miss Withers, "did anyone happen to check Koontz's fingerprints with those on the murder gun?"

"We did," Macy said. "And they weren't. But the prints on the icepick matched the prints on the shotgun and glasses."

"Of course!" Miss Withers cried. "Then—" But the sheriff gestured, and she found herself propelled toward the door by Macy.

"Thanks for trying to help," he said, as he led her down the hall, unlocking the door of another office. "You better spend the night here. That couch in the corner isn't too bad."

"But you can't—"

"Lady, whenever a cop hears anybody say anything about 'you can't do this to me!' he just laughs. Now take it easy. Maybe you'll go to sleep and dream up a solution to this case." He started out, then came back to remove a spare .38 pistol and a pair of handcuffs from the desk drawer. He indicated the door of the washroom, and went out, locking the door firmly from the outside.

Miss Hildegarde Withers sat herself down indignantly upon the rickety couch, and then caught sight of the telephone on the desk. She lifted the receiver and said, "I want to call New York City, collect!"

But the operator, stationed at a switchboard somewhere in the building, said genially but firmly, "Take it easy, ma'am. Tomorrow is another day."

"Really!" Miss Withers slammed down the phone. Leaving the harsh overhead light burning, she flung herself down on the couch, closing her eyes in order to concentrate better.

In her mind's eye she saw the partially-smoked cigar which had left no ashes in the tray, the thin white line around the dead girl's finger. She saw the two whisky-stained glasses, the Scotch bottle, the shotgun, the icepick planted between the dapper shoulders of the man who thought he knew two thousand dollars' worth about the crime. But these clues kept mixing themselves up with other things that didn't matter, like the dead cactus around the adobe cottage, the black-eyed peas in the kitchen, the garbage can without any orange rinds, the golf clubs with the heads in their neat socks, the nylon hose, and the wedding ring. . . .

Then she jerked awake at the sound of rapping at the door. She realized that she had a stiff neck and that daylight surprisingly filled the room. But the puzzle was all neatly solved. She knew the name of the murderer—and why. It was as easy as that. She was smiling pleasantly when she opened the door to Detective Macy.

"Mornin', ma'am," he said. "After you get fixed up a little, could you join us in the sheriff's office, please? Somebody we want you to meet." He waited patiently while Miss Withers washed her face and did what she could to straighten her hair. Then he led the way down the hall.

"When did the Travis woman give herself up?" the schoolteacher asked.

Macy stopped dead in his tracks. "How'd you know that?"

"Isn't it obvious? It was clear from the beginning that it was not her body in the bedroom, in spite of the New York clothes. The girl who lived in that cottage had stocked the kitchen with the makings of meals preferred south of the Mason-Dixon line. New Yorkers breakfast on coffee and orange juice, and there was no sign of an orange or an orange peel in the place."

Macy nodded. "I get it. Well, Eileen Travis read about the murder in the Los Angeles papers last night, and she hopped in her car and drove up here. She confessed—"

"Not to the murders?"

Macy laughed jovially. "No, ma'am. But here we are. Come in."

Sheriff Kehoe still sat at his desk, with his Stetson on the back of his head. Officer Rankin leaned against the window, and in the one comfortable chair sat a lovely, lush girl in a bright purple jacket and flannel slacks.

"Mrs. Travis," said the sheriff, half-arising, "this is the lady your mother hired to look you up and see if you were all right."

Eileen said coolly, "You may tell mother that I'm fine."

"Are you?" asked Miss Hildegarde Withers. "I wonder."

"We're sorry, Miss Withers, that we had to keep you here all night," the sheriff went on. "But we didn't want any more killings, and the New York police asked us to take special care of you."

"Thank you so much. And now, what is all this about Mrs. Travis's confession?" Miss Withers beamed brightly at them all.

"I simply admitted," Eileen burst forth, "that I'd taken a cottage here to establish legal residence, and then hired a girl I met in a gambling house to live there in my name."

"A girl with a southern accent, named Thelma Pringle?"

Eileen nodded. "I knew it wasn't strictly legal, but I didn't want to be stuck here when I could be in Los Angeles. And besides, I had good reason to believe that George would stop at nothing to keep me from getting my decree—to keep me from being able to testify against him legally later on."

"You said 'stuck here'?" questioned the sheriff ominously.

"I didn't mean that." Eileen flashed her soft dark eyes at him. "It's just that I don't gamble, and I love ocean swimming. . . ."

"We got pools," the sheriff said glumly. He looked at Detective Macy. "Better get George Travis up here, right away."

Eileen was open-mouthed. "You mean my husband is actually in town? Then that proves—"

Sheriff Kehoe wasn't listening to her. "And ask Molly to come in with her notebook," he called after the departing detective. There was a long, tense period of waiting, during which Miss Withers saw that Officer Rankin was having difficulty in keeping his eyes off Eileen's slim, bare, brown ankles.

Finally George Travis, even more disheveled and unshaven than before, was ushered into the room. He glared morosely at his wife.

"Hello, George," she said, in a low voice that dripped with acid. "Isn't it a shame that your hired hoodlum shot the wrong girl?"

Travis said nothing, but sank down quickly on a hard chair, his head in his hands. A moment later Detective Macy came in with Molly, who was still puffy-eyed. But she had her pencil and notebook.

"Now that we are all here, nice and cosy-like," began the sheriff, "we'll start at the beginning and see if we can straighten this out."

"I suggest," Miss Withers interrupted pleasantly but firmly, "that we start at the end instead. It will save a lot of time. You see, I know who the murderer is."

She met their blank stares with a bright smile. "It all came to me when I was asleep."

"Dreams, yet!" Detective Rankin muttered softly.

But the schoolteacher had the floor. "It's obvious that Mr. Koontz was killed to cover up the first murder, so when we solve the killing of Thelma Pringle we solve them both. Shall we take up the most important clue—the cigar?"

Rankin moved as if to silence her, but Detective Macy was nodding slowly, and the sheriff made no move. "The cigar," went on Miss Withers, "was obviously a plant. It was left as a false clue, having been smoked beforehand. Moreover, the killer was not used to cigars, for he forgot to remove the band and he held it in his lips, like a cigarette, leaving no teeth marks as real cigar smokers do. I've watched Inspector Piper, back home, mangle a cigar so that I didn't know if he was chewing or smoking it."

The sheriff nodded, looking at his own well-filled ashtray. "Moreover," Miss Withers continued, "Thelma Pringle was not killed by mistake, in place of Eileen here. She was killed by somebody who knew her and who wanted her dead. She was shot in the face with a shotgun, either by someone who wanted to spoil her looks or who wanted to prevent identification, at least temporarily—"

There was a brief period of silence, broken when Molly Koontz dropped her pencil and had to grope for it.

"Now look here," the sheriff said, "you're trying to tell us that the killer walked in with a shotgun, had a drink with the girl, and then—"

"The drinks could have been set up afterward," Miss Withers pointed out. "There was a distinct reek of whisky in the garbage."

"But the girl would have yelled for help if she saw somebody come at her with a shotgun," Detective Rankin put in.

"Who would have heard her? The murder was committed at an hour when almost everybody in Las Vegas is away from home. I have my own theory as to how the gun came into the house. It could have been butt-down in a golf bag, with a golf-club stocking over the muzzle. But never mind that for a moment. The point is—*the murderer of Thelma Pringle was a woman!*"

"A woman who left a man's full-size fingerprints?" Rankin argued.

"Some women have large hands." Miss Withers looked at Molly Koontz, who had forgotten to take notes. The woman suddenly jumped to her feet.

"I didn't do it, I didn't! You can take my prints—"

"Relax, Molly," the sheriff said. "We already got 'em off the compact in your desk, and you didn't do it."

"I wasn't suggesting that she did," Miss Withers said, "even though her husband had been mixed up with Thelma Pringle. However, I think that they got the idea of blackmail separately. You see, the murder was well planned—designed to throw an even heavier weight of guilt on George Travis. The killer did not know that Travis was out on bond, but she did know that if a body identified as that of his wife was found in Las Vegas, he would be suspected of having instigated the murder. Even if the identity of the corpse came to light, it would still appear that his agents had merely struck down the wrong woman. Only one person had a motive to involve George Travis in *more* trouble than he was already in—and that person came into the cottage with a shotgun and killed the girl who was trying to blackmail her, thus killing two birds with one stone."

"Very neat," the sheriff said. "But if you're—"

"I certainly am," Miss Withers cried breathlessly. "Eileen Travis, I accuse you of a double murder."

It should have been a rousing climax, but it fell flat as a pancake. Eileen was shaking her head, almost pityingly. Macy's expression was sorrowful, and Rankin was almost laughing. The sheriff smiled a weary, patient smile. "All done, ma'am?"

"Isn't—isn't that enough?"

"Plenty. Very ingenious, too. Only I think that you ought to know, ma'am, that when she came in Mrs. Travis insisted we take her fingerprints, and they don't match the ones on the gun, glasses, or icepick!"

Miss Withers felt slightly faint. "But they *have* to!" she protested.

"Officer Rankin here is our fingerprint expert," the sheriff said. "He's read all the books."

Rankin beamed.

"But there must be some mistake!" cried Miss Withers.

"There is, and you've made it." The sheriff looked at the big silver watch the size of a teacup. "Miss Withers, there's a plane out of here at nine o'clock, which gives you just half an hour. Macy, you see that she gets placed and on that plane and out of my hair!"

Sheriff Kehoe was standing up now, his voice rising to a deep baritone roar. Miss Withers, the bitter taste of defeat in her mouth, backed hastily out of the door.

There was a long silence. The sheriff sat down again, lighted a cigar, and mopped his forehead. "Now, like I said, we'll start at the beginning, and see if we can straighten this out. You first, Mrs. Travis. We'll take your statement, and Molly will type it out so you can sign it and go."

Eileen spoke carefully and slowly, for some time. Her statement was in the typewriter when the telephone on the sheriff's desk rang shrilly. He picked it up. "Kehoe. What? Oh, Macy. What's the matter, did you let her miss the plane?"

There was a short pause, and then the sheriff heaved a deep sigh of relief. "Good, good. I'm glad you reported—it's a load off my mind." He started to hang up, and then jammed the instrument against his ear "What? What final request?"

The others in the room all strained their ears, but they could hear only a jumble of sounds from the other end of the line. At last the sheriff put down the phone, and said, "Rankin!"

"Yes, sheriff?"

"You're supposed to be our fingerprint expert. This case is at a dead end because we can't find any suspect whose prints fit those on the murder weapons and the drinking glass. Tell me, is there any way a person could deliberately leave false prints?"

The burly young detective swallowed. "There—there's a photographic process on gelatin, but it's easy to detect because it doesn't leave pore marks. . . ."

But the sheriff wasn't listening. He turned slowly toward Eileen Travis, who still leaned back in the one easy chair, her bare brown ankles crossed, a cigarette dangling from her full lush mouth. She stared back at him, letting the ashes fall to the floor.

"Mrs. Travis," he asked with ceremonious politeness, "would you mind very much if I asked you to take off your shoes?"

She opened her mouth, but no words came.

"It's been suggested by the lady who just left," continued Sheriff Kehoe, "that fingers are not the only portions of the human body that have distinctive skin patterns. With your permission—or without it—we'd like to take your *toeprints!*"

THE WITNESS IN THE METAL BOX
Melville Davisson Post

The technical skill that Melville Davisson Post (1869-1930) brought to his short stories helped make him the most commercially successful magazine writer of his time. Born in West Virginia, he practiced criminal and corporate law for eleven years before devoting himself to writing fulltime. He died at the age of sixty-one after falling from a horse. He played an important role in the development of the detective story and, while his name may be familiar only to devoted readers of detective fiction, he was regarded as the best American mystery short story writer of the early twentieth-century by no less an authority than Ellery Queen.

It is difficult to create a memorable character but Post succeeded in doing it twice. The more likely to be remembered today is Uncle Abner, the backwoods protector of the innocent in what is now West Virginia during Thomas Jefferson's presidency. Abner, known for his integrity and sense of justice, believed that evil would be defeated due to the omnipresence of God. His cases were collected in *Uncle Abner: Master of Mysteries* (1918).

A more conventional figure and undoubtedly of greater significance is Randolph Mason, a brilliant but utterly unscrupulous lawyer. Born in Virginia but practicing in New York, Mason recognizes that there is not always a strong correlation between justice and the law. In the past, criminals had tried to avoid capture but, in the Mason stories, the paramount concern is the avoidance of punishment. These stories were often based on genuine legal loopholes, eventually bringing about numerous changes to criminal procedure. There were three collections based on the character, beginning with *The Strange Schemes of Randolph Mason* (1896).

Both *Uncle Abner: Master of Mysteries* and *The Strange Schemes of Randolph Mason* were selected for *Queen's Quorum* as being among the 106 most important collections of detective short stories in history.

Post's deep familiarity with the law is evident in "The Witness in the Metal Box," which was originally published in the November 1929 edition of *The American Magazine*; it was first published in book form in *Best American Mystery Stories of the Year*, edited by Carolyn Wells (New York, John Day, 1931).

The Witness in the Metal Box
Melville Davisson Post

I SHALL always remember this famous case.

To me there were romance and mystery and wonder in it. It stands out Homeric in my youthful fancy.

It was tried, as the lawyers say, before Judge Edmond Lewis and a jury, but it was tried, also, before Virginia. For the county came into that trial. The people filled the courtroom to the doors, crowded the county seat, and overran the taverns.

Old Edmond Lewis and his court, and the litigants and their attorneys, were, for the term of that trial, famous. They passed from the tavern to the courtroom through a lane of excited faces. Those who could not force a standing in the courtroom were at least determined to see the actors in the drama, even if they could not see the drama staged.

In this respect I had a great advantage.

My grandfather was a relative of Judge Edmond Lewis and I went in with him. I was a small boy, holding to my grandfather's hand. But I was old enough to understand the great event, and I missed nothing of its drama. We had a chair inside the court's railing by the judge's bench, where the lawyers and the officials were assembled.

There were famous men of Virginia in that courtroom.

Judge Edmond Lewis was a large figure in this portion of the commonwealth west of the mountains. There was something big and undisturbed about him, something almost Oriental in its immobility. He filled the huge armchair behind the judge's bench, and his very presence gave the proceedings in his court a serenity as of some majestic justice above the affairs of men, and of which he was, here, merely the vice regent.

And the litigants were romantic figures:

One could not look at Blackmer Harrington and at once withdraw the eye. The man held one's attention, he was so markedly the desperate adventurer; a tall, hawk-faced man in the maturity of life, with a cruel, relentless face that mirrored a will determined to go its way against any barrier. It was a face moving through adventure tales that are read in storybooks, sprawling by the fire; a face to sack a city, or to run a pirate ship in a boiling sea under the Jolly Roger!

It held me with a dreadful fascination.

And the other! One fell back on the storybooks in vain, to equal her. She came like a fairy thing from the city of Zeus, bringing the wonder of that city with her. For she had, in fact, come overseas from France to defend her inheritance in this court, and she brought into this frontier of Virginia the dress and the manner of that far-off, vaguely imagined land of elegant demeanor. This seems overdrawn for the truth, and I write it here with some misgivings. But it was the profound impression of my youthful fancy, and one cannot disentangle actuality from that golden glamour.

The case I knew thoroughly in detail, for I had heard it discussed in every direction before it came up in the court. It was the most important litigation of the time. There was a great estate to turn on the issue of it, and there was something more than that bare decision to stimulate one's interest. The facts about the case were not involved:

The suit in itself was over the will of Alexander Harrington. It was supposed at the time that he had died intestate, leaving his great properties to pass by operation of law to his daughter, for he had no other child. This daughter had been sent for her education to France, and was there when her father died. But to the amazement of the county, this younger brother of Alexander came forward with a will leaving the estate to him, with some minor provisions for the daughter.

It was a brief will on a single sheet of paper, written by the dead man, and signed after his manner, "A. Harrington," with an immense, intricate flourish under the signature. It was this signature that stamped it as authentic. That big arabesque of a scrawl could not be imitated. It was known to everybody. The deeds and contracts executed by the dead man and lodged about in the courts all bore that distinguishing evidence of the signature. There was no living man who could duplicate that scrawl.

Mr. Dabney Mason, the clerk of the circuit court, and an authority, held the thing impossible, and this was also the certain opinion of every scrivener in Virginia; that free-hand, intricate flourish, entangling itself below the name, was the sole artistry of the dead man. There could be no two opinions on that point. It was the signature of Alexander Harrington at the foot of this testament, and as it was thus a holograph will, it required no witnesses.

Harrington had endured no long illness at his death. He had been stricken in the fields at harvest, and had got down from his horse in the shade of an oak tree; from there, unconscious, he had been carried into his house. As the daughter was in France and there was no near relative but this younger brother, word of the illness was sent over the mountains and the man arrived. Alexander Harrington remained for some time in life, but only in periods of fitful consciousness.

It was not known what talk the two men may have had together after the brother arrived, but this was hardly an important feature, as the will was of an earlier date. If it had been of this date, it would scarcely have stood before a jury: the incapacity of the testator was too apparent.

But the question did not come up. After Harrington's death, the brother called in some of the representative men of the county, and this will was found among the dead man's papers. It came, therefore, into the court with all the safeguards of the law about it and the required formalities to make it legal: a holograph will found among the important papers of the testator, in his possession, at his death.

It seemed no intricate case to try.

There was only the validity of the will to prove, and, after that, to meet whatever attack the contestant might bring up. And no one could see any firm ground for an attack. The stock ones in such cases could hardly be seriously urged: senility in the testator or undue influence. But who could be found to say that Alexander Harrington had any weakness of the mind? He was not advanced in age, and there was no abler man of business. And how could undue influence in this brother be even vaguely shadowed? He lived at a distance over the mountains, or went adventuring about the world, and the testator was here upon his estates.

There seemed no possible point of entry against the testament.

This was the consensus. But here was Colonel Braxton appearing for the daughter, and the experts about the courtroom wagged their heads. One never knew the issue when this eccentric lawyer was involved—a gold eagle from the mint, assailed by him, would be in doubt!

It was not the case, it was the man behind it that perplexed the experts.

I remember my grandfather and old Edmond Lewis talking in the judge's room in the crowded tavern. They could see nothing here but the formalities of a trial. What could Braxton do, or any other lawyer? A jury might be moved in its emotions to the daughter's aid. But clearly there was no issue for a jury. There must be some evidence against the will for the jury to consider, exclusive of innuendoes and vague doubts.

Braxton knew this. But he was an enigma, even to the judges. What did the man have up his sleeve?

It was anterior to the time when judges were considered such feeble creatures that the facts of a case could not be talked of before them, and I have heard Judge Lewis state the facts in more than one involved matter, for my grandfather's comment. He cleared the brush out, as old Edmond used to say.

To me, on the morning of this trial, the scene was a thrilling thing.

The whole country was present, as though the hills and valleys had emptied themselves into the county seat. The crowd seemed to press in on the courthouse. Long before the court convened, the room was crowded. It was difficult for the sheriff to make a way for the court and the litigants to enter. I sat on a step of the judge's bench, beside my grandfather's chair, with a feeling of immense importance, as though I, too, were a part of this tremendous drama.

I overlooked no detail of that scene: the vast sea of faces, the jury in their chairs, the big, placid body of the judge leaning forward on the bench, and below him the clerk, Mr. Dabney Mason, dressed like a Bond Street print, in his English clothes. And the litigants and their attorneys! It was like a romance of Arthur. Who would win when they presently shocked together in this arena—this adventurer or this damsel in distress?

I cannot tell you how the thing thrilled me. There was a fascination about this Black-Sheep Harrington, as they used to call him, with his hawk face and his adventure legends; and his counsel, young Pennington Carlisle, was a model held up for us all; a brilliant, rising lawyer who filled the courthouse when he spoke. He had no equal before a jury, or before the people, when in a political campaign he took the stump in Virginia.

I had a sinking of the heart when I turned to the other lawyer's table.

What could this Colonel Braxton do for the lovely creature who sat beside him? A big man, like the judge, filling his chair, a handkerchief spread over his shirt front to screen it from the ash of his cigar; his eyes half closed, his body relaxed and inert, as thought it rested at ease after some exertion.

The man required to be awakened!

This was no time to drowse idly in a chair. I thought Destiny had mixed her figures. The adventurer with his ruthless face should have come in with this attorney, and the brilliant Carlisle should have championed the girl. This Colonel Braxton was no knight-errant for romance, unless—and I got a thrill with the idea—unless he were a magician appearing for a fairy princess. I hugged the notion with a consuming joy. That was it—a magician! And, in truth, to saner minds the absurd conception had a sort of color.

The lawyer had a small metal box on his table. And it was the only thing he had. Paper and law books cluttered the table before young Pennington Carlisle; cases from Virginia and the English courts, to refute every possible point that could be made against him, and he had witnesses waiting to be sworn: to establish the legal formalities about the will and to prove the signature of the testator.

But this Colonel Braxton had only his metal box!

The amazement in the thing reached beyond one small boy seated on a step of the judge's bench. It extended to the sea of faces; to the very officers of the court. What had this mysterious thing to do with the case at issue, this circular metal box sitting on a lawyer's table?

The thing became more conspicuous when the clerk called the witnesses to be sworn. The adventurer stood up with the reputable citizens that Pennington Carlisle had called to establish the legal formalities about the will. They took the oath, and the judge turned to Colonel Braxton.

"Call your witnesses!" he said.

The lawyer took the smoldering cigar out of his mouth and laid it down carefully on the table. He looked vaguely about the courtroom as though it had, but now, come to his attention.

"I have no witnesses, Your Honor," he replied, "except the witness in this box . . . and I fear it cannot stand up to be sworn."

He put out his hand, touched the mysterious object beside him, and was silent.

That was all he said, and that was all we knew about his case.

I know that old Edmond Lewis, like every other man in that courtroom, was profoundly puzzled. He spoke of it with my grandfather. What was Braxton about with this confounded mystery? But my grandfather was equally in the dark.

I had a sense of a superior understanding of this thing.

I had got a light flashed on it in the drama of the courtroom: This Colonel Braxton was the magician out of a storybook. He would not be breaking lances with young Pennington Carlisle. He would entrap him with some enchantment. He had come in with his metal box to restore to the fairy princess her houses and her lands; and presently we should see the working of his sorcery. I could hardly wait for the time to pass.

I alone understood the thing. And in a certain fashion I was right!

I watched the case move forward, from my place on the step of the judge's bench. And it was the opinion of the experts that Pennington Carlisle managed the thing with skill. He established the legal requirements about the will, to cover any attack on it from the point of its holograph requirements; the testament, itself, was already before the court. He proved the signature by the most reliable persons in the community. And then he put Blackmer Harrington on the stand.

His purpose, behind the legal pretension, was, in fact, to show the confidence of the testator in his brother, and to exclude any wonder at the bequest of the estate to him rather than to the daughter. He brought forward the fact that the claimant had for some years acted as the trusted agent of the dead man in the sale of wild lands east of the mountains.

Such lands were the principal subject of speculation at this time in Virginia. They were purchased in great surveys for a trifling sum and peddled out in small tracts to the settlers. Blackmer Harrington handled this business for his brother; had, in fact, exclusive control of it and—as Carlisle skillfully drew out—the complete confidence of the dead man, as shown by the options and power of attorney in blank sent to him to use as the requirements of these transactions demanded. The confidence of the testator in his brother was, in consequence, evident beyond question.

The motive for the testament was more difficult to disclose. It was not Carlisle's intention to bring it out. He was too clever to do that. He would shadow it out vaguely, and let it lie, confident in the gossip and the imagination of the jury to supply what the lure of the idea required to fill it. His diplomatic instincts were sound here. But the horse he rode bolted.

The witness, once on the way, could not be pulled up. He elaborated the great aspect of his adventure; the lure that had won his brother to him; the plan to seize some islands in the West Indies and add them to the Republic. This estate was to be used to that magnificent end. That was the motive for the devise to him. Again and again he had laid the plans before his brother, and finally in the end had won him. It was a vast, splendid dream, that required, for reality, only funds and a man of courage.

Once seized, the American Government would annex the territory, and by that much the Republic would be advanced on its manifest destiny. As he warmed to his subject he grew more voluble. And the manner and the declaration of the man reached a certain element in the courtroom, and got a visible reaction. A vast empire extending itself into the sea fired their fancy. It had been a dream of the early men and it remained vaguely in their descendants.

And yet one could see Pennington Carlisle uneasy in his chair.

But he could not stop the thing that he had unwittingly set going. Finally he did break in to ask if the witness knew that the will had been executed. Harrington replied that he did not know it, until the will was found among his brother's papers after his death. He had convinced the dead man; but he did not know of that success until the testament was found.

And so Carlisle finally got his witness silenced.

My grandfather and Judge Lewis talked together gravely in the chamber behind the courtroom at the noon recess.

"Edmond," my grandfather said, "it will never do for Harrington to win this case. The wild fool will involve the country in a war, with some filibuster into the South or some piracy on the sea."

Judge Lewis stroked his big face with his hand.

"But what can I do?" he replied. "This intention is not an issue here. The sole issue is the validity of this will. What the prevailing litigant does with the estate he gains is not before me."

But my grandfather was not to be thus silenced.

"The welfare of the nation is before us all," he said. "What did Marshall do, or the great Virginia judges, when a doctrine of law threatened the whole people? The courts take their authority from the people, and in the ultimate exercise of that authority they must protect them."

"Yes," said Lewis, "'in the ultimate exercise of that authority.' But this is a trial court and not a court of last resort. If this feature of the case is to be considered, it is for the Supreme Court of Virginia to consider it. I cannot consider it."

"And they cannot consider it," replied my grandfather. "It will not be in the record, and so this dangerous fool will go out into the grainfields with his torch."

He stood up before the window, a tall, imperious old man with a grave, deep-lined face.

"In my father's house," he said, "there used to be a little circular glass window on which three names had been scratched with the diamond setting of a ring; 'Aaron Burr,' 'Harman Blennerhassett,' and 'Daniel Davisson.' It was a meeting of conspirators; but my father, Daniel Davisson, was not one of them. Burr was a relative and a guest, but he told him the truth. 'You're an infernal fool,' he said, 'and Tom Jefferson will hang you!'"

He turned about to Judge Lewis.

"And here, Edmond, is another infernal fool that you ought to hang, instead of giving the creature a treasure chest and a letter of marque."

I understood even then, in my early youth, the magnitude of this discussion.

My grandfather saw the welfare of the whole country in this case and Judge Edmond Lewis saw the exact limitations of the law in it. Both were right, and even at this day I do not know which opinion should have prevailed. Here was the law as Judge Lewis saw it, confined to a single issue. It could not go beyond that issue. It was better to look hardship in the face than to break down the rules of law—he saw that as clearly as Lord Eldon saw it.

They went back into the courtroom.

The same scene remained. But the case had now a larger meaning. What my grandfather had said to Judge Edmond Lewis had moved the whole drama up out of the mere adjustments of romance.

It had now a sort of national aspect.

I do not mean that the impending wrong, to the girl, sitting by her attorney, tugged any the less desperately at my heart. She was as entrancing as a dream, as a painted picture, and she was helpless before this blind stride of the law . . . unless the magician with his magic box could save her. . . .

What was in that box?

When Carlisle, for the will, finished with his case, Judge Lewis asked Colonel Braxton if he wished to cross-examine Harrington.

The big lawyer did not at once reply. He sat for some moments looking at the floor, as in reflection, idle and irrelevant to the matter at hand. Then he turned toward young Pennington Carlisle.

"I might ask him a question," he said.

The tone was gentle and apologetic, as though he were seeking a favor.

Carlisle laughed. "You have my permission, Colonel," he said.

"Thank you, Pennington. It's just a little thing I wanted to know."

Carlisle thought he saw an opening for a checkmate, and he stepped into it.

"About the signature to the will, Colonel?"

Colonel Braxton looked up with wide-open eyes, as in utter astonishment.

"Oh, no," he said, "it's the dead man's signature."

"Undue influence then?"

"Oh, no!" Colonel Braxton's astonishment seemed to increase. "There was no undue influence about the making of this testament . . . no undue influence, Pennington."

"Incapacity in the testator?"

"Oh, no!" The words whined like a refrain in some absurd opera. "You couldn't believe that, Pennington; nobody could believe that . . . I couldn't make the jury believe that."

An aspect of victory enveloped Carlisle. He had, by the clever trick of drawing these admissions, covered his case to the wall; cut from under his opponent all the possible supports that could be set up in such a case. He had nothing more to fear!

"It's just a little thing I wanted to ask the witness—for my own information, Pennington," the big lawyer added.

Carlisle made a courteous, ironic gesture of assent. "I would waive almost any rule of evidence," he said, "in order to add to the information of this bar."

There was a ripple of suppressed laughter. And Carlisle took his tribute with a triumphant smile. How could he know, in the arrogance of his visible victory, that he was trifling with disaster!

Colonel Braxton seemed not to realize the innuendo. "Thank you, Pennington," he said, and he turned to Harrington.

The adventurer, like his counsel, was in that pleasant mood of victory when one bears, in a genial fashion, with an irrelevant annoyance.

"I wanted to ask you," Colonel Braxton went on, "if you had ever seen a sodded field plowed?"

Everybody was astonished. What had the plowing of a sodded field to do with the issues of this case?

Carlisle's eyebrows lifted, and the witness smiled. "Why, yes, Colonel," Harrington replied; "when I was a boy on my father's estate, I have seen the negroes plow the pasture land."

"Then," continued the lawyer, "you can tell me what happens when the plow crosses a small, narrow, sodded ditch."

The witness replied that if the ditch were small and narrow the plow would jump it, leaving the sod at the bottom of the ditch undisturbed.

Colonel Braxton nodded in assent.

"Ah, yes," he said. "I thought that would be true. . . . I'm not much of a farmer. . . . I wanted to be certain."

That courtroom was full of persons who were very much farmers, and they were beyond doubt certain. The witness was precisely correct.

"Then," the lawyer went on, "it is always possible to tell whether such a small, narrow ditch or depression was present in the sodded field before it was plowed, or made after it was plowed?"

The witness replied that this was surely true, because, if it were made after the plowing, it would be in the broken ground, but if it existed before the plowing, the plow would jump it, and the undisturbed sod would remain at the bottom of the ditch or depression across the entire field.

"Ah . . . yes," Colonel Braxton reflected in his gentle drawl. "But I'm not much of a farmer . . . and I wanted to be certain."

He sat down.

We were all certain. But what had this simple illustration of the plow to do with the contestant's case?

Old Edmond Lewis was no less puzzled than the lad on the

step of his bench below him. I think he would have ruled out this irrelevant inquiry if Carlisle had asked it. But to Carlisle, in his security, this idle discussion of husbandry was of no importance. And, so far as we could see, he was clearly right.

The whole courtroom was astonished.

It was incredible. . . . It was beyond belief; but the case was ended. Here was Harrington leaving the witness chair. Here was Colonel Braxton gone back to his chair. Here was Carlisle on his feet, making his motion to exclude the evidence and direct a verdict.

The case was ended!

It was a rout . . . a debacle!

Judge Lewis turned to Colonel Braxton. He seemed to move heavily, like a man under pressure. And when he spoke, his voice was harsh:

"Do you wish to be heard on this motion?"

"No." The big lawyer was now standing up.

"Then you admit the validity of the will?"

"The will," replied Colonel Braxton, "is a forgery."

The tension on everybody in that courtroom was tremendous.

"A forgery!" exclaimed the judge. "You have introduced no evidence of forgery."

"The evidence," replied Colonel Braxton, "is on the face of the paper itself. But it takes a good eye to see it, and, in consequence, I have sent to Baltimore for the best eye that could be purchased."

The man had changed. The leisure aspect had vanished; the stoop of the shoulders; the drawl in the voice.

He opened the metal box on his table and took out a big lens.

He got the will from the clerk.

"The signature is genuine," he said, "but the writing above

the signature is forged. The signature was on this paper before the writing was added, and one does not sign his name first, and then after that, write his will above it.

"Look, Your Honor." He carried the papers and the lens across to the judge's bench and put them down before him. "This paper has been folded a number of times. These folds are across the signature, and extend from it under the body of this writing. And look, Your Honor, how the illustration of the plow on the sodded field parallels the pen on the field of this sheet of paper. When the sheet of paper was flat and unbroken by the folds, the pen ran smooth with no break in its furrow, as in the lettering and the scroll of this signature. But in the body of this writing above the signature, wherever the pen came to a crease of the fold, it jumped it, precisely as the plow jumps a narrow ditch, and it left the paper unmarked at the bottom of the fold precisely as the plow left the sod untouched at the bottom of the ditch. This signature was written when the sheet of paper was flat, and the writing above it after the sheet was folded."

Judge Edmond Lewis stooped over the paper with the lens in his big hand. Then he beckoned to my grandfather, went down to Carlisle's table, and called the jury.

The whole court crowded around him.

And there, under the magnification of the lens, lay the story of the forgery, so clear that the simplest man could see it. Carlisle saw it, and he was appalled. His client had taken one of the powers of attorney sent him, signed in blank by his brother, for it was folded like a letter, and above that signature he had traced this will, and lodged it among the dying man's papers when he came to attend him at his death. It was all there, standing out on the white field under the magnification of the lens.

It was tremendous.

The whole sea of faces packed into the courtroom was alight with victory. But there was no sound.

I stood up with a wild beating of the heart.

The magician had won for the fairy princess! And I looked to see the big figure of the lawyer vanish in some shattering wonder that would split the courtroom.

MAN BITES DOG
Ellery Queen

Every mystery reader who recognizes that the detective story has a history that dates back longer they've been alive undoubtedly knows that Ellery Queen is the joint nom de plume of two Brooklyn cousins, Frederic Dannay (born Daniel Nathan; 1905-1982) and Manfred B(ennington) Lee (born Manford Lepofsky; 1905-1971). Their brilliant marketing idea was to also name their detective Ellery Queen, reasoning that if readers forgot the name of the author, *or* the name of the character, they might remember the other. It worked, as Ellery Queen ranks among the handful of best-known names in the history of mystery fiction.

Lee was a full collaborator on the fiction created as Ellery Queen, but Dannay on his own was also one of the most important figures in the mystery world. He founded *Ellery Queen's Mystery Magazine* in 1941 and it remains, more than eighty years later, the preeminent periodical in the genre. He also formed one of the first great collections of detective fiction first editions, the rare contents leading to reprinted stories in the magazines and anthologies he edited.

Queen was as brilliant at producing puzzles in their short stories as the novels and managed to stay *au courant* with changing tastes in the literature. While nearly a clone to S. S. Van Dine's Philo Vance in their earliest work as they focused almost entirely on puzzles, they become more modern in outlook and came to develop more fully rounded characters in later years while writing stories that reflected the events and mores of the time.

The present story is set at the 1939 World Series. It was written long before the teams were chosen but the rivals were the New York Yankees and the San Francisco Giants. Queen was astute enough to feature the Yankees, though in the actual series they faced the Cincinnati Reds. The Joe DiMaggio-led Yankees, incidentally, swept the Reds.

"Man Bites Dog" was originally published in the June 1939 issue of *Blue Book*; it was first collected in *The New Adventures of Ellery Queen* (New York, Frederick Stokes, 1940).

Man Bites Dog
Ellery Queen

ANYONE OBSERVING the tigerish pacings, the gnawings of lip, the contortions of brow, and the fierce melancholy which characterized the conduct of Mr. Ellery Queen, the noted sleuth, during those early October days in Hollywood, would have said reverently that the great man's intellect was once more locked in titanic struggle with the forces of evil.

"Paula," Mr. Queen said to Paula Paris, "I'm going mad."

"I hope," said Miss Paris tenderly, "it's love."

Mr. Queen paced, swathed in yards of thought. Queenly Miss Paris observed him with melting eyes. When he had first encountered her, during his investigation of the double murder of

Blythe Stuart and Jack Royle, the famous motion-picture stars,[1] Miss Paris had been in the grip of a morbid psychology. She had been in a deathly terror of crowds. "Crowd phobia" the doctors called it. Mr. Queen, stirred by a nameless emotion, determined to cure the lady of her psychological affliction. The therapy, he conceived, must be both shocking and compensatory; and so he made love to her.

And lo! although Miss Paris recovered, to his horror Mr. Queen found that the cure may sometimes present a worse problem than the affliction. For the patient promptly fell in love with her healer; and the healer did not himself escape certain excruciating emotional consequences.

"Is it?" asked Miss Paris, her heart in her eyes.

"Eh?" said Mr. Queen. "What? Oh, no. I mean—it's the World Series." He looked savage. "Don't you realize what's happening? The New York Giants and the New York Yankees are waging mortal combat to determine the baseball championship of the world, and I'm three thousand miles away!"

"Oh," said Miss Paris. Then she said cleverly: "You poor darling."

"Never missed a New York series before," wailed Mr. Queen. "Driving me cuckoo. And what a battle! Greatest series ever played. Moore and DiMaggio have done miracles in the outfield. Giants have pulled a triple play. Goofy Gomez struck out fourteen men to win the first game. Hubbell's pitched a one-hit shutout. And today Dickey came up in the ninth inning with the bases loaded, two out, and the Yanks three runs behind, and slammed a homer over the right-field stands!"

"Is that good?" asked Miss Paris.

1   Related in *The Four of Hearts*, by Ellery Queen. Frederick A. Stokes Company, 1938.

"Good!" howled Mr. Queen. "It merely sent the series into a seventh game."

"Poor darling," said Miss Paris again, and she picked up her telephone. When she set it down she said: "Weather's threatening in the East. Tomorrow the New York Weather Bureau expects heavy rains."

Mr. Queen stared wildly. "You mean—"

"I mean that you're taking tonight's plane for the East. And you'll see your beloved seventh game day after tomorrow."

"Paula, you're a genius!" Then Mr. Queen's face fell. "But the studio, tickets . . . *Bigre!* I'll tell the studio I'm down with elephantiasis, and I'll wire Dad to snare a box. With his pull at City Hall, he ought to—Paula, I don't know what I'd do. . . ."

"You might," suggested Miss Paris, "kiss me . . . goodbye."

Mr. Queen did so, absently. The he started. "Not at all! You're coming with me!"

"That's what I had in mind," said Miss Paris contentedly.

And so Wednesday found Miss Paris and Mr. Queen at the Polo Grounds, ensconced in a field box behind the Yankees' dugout.

Mr. Queen glowed, he reveled, he was radiant. While Inspector Queen, with the suspiciousness of all fathers, engaged Paula in exploratory conversation, Ellery filled his lap and Paula's with peanut hulls, consumed frankfurters and soda pop immoderately, made hypercritical comments on the appearance of the various athletes, derided the Yankees, extolled the Giants, evolved complicated fifty-cent bets with Detective-Sergeant Velie, of the Inspector's staff, and leaped to his feet screaming with fifty thousand other maniacs as the news came that Carl Hubbell, the beloved Meal Ticket of the Giants, would oppose Señor El Goofy Gomez, the ace of the Yankee staff, on the mound.

"Will the Yanks murder that apple today!" predicted the Sergeant, who was an incurable Yankee worshiper. "And will Goofy mow 'em down!"

"Four bits," said Mr. Queen coldly, "say the Yanks don't score three earned runs off Carl."

"It's a pleasure!"

"I'll take a piece of that, Sergeant," chuckled a handsome man to the front of them, in a rail seat. "Hi, Inspector. Swell day for it, eh?"

"Jimmy Connor!" exclaimed Inspector Queen. "The old Song-and-Dance Man in person. Say, Jimmy, you never met my son, Ellery, did you? Excuse me. Miss Paris, this is the famous Jimmy Connor, God's gift to Broadway."

"Glad to meet you, Miss Paris," smiled the Song-and-Dance Man, sniffing at his orchidaceous lapel. "Read your *Seeing Stars* column, every day. Meet Judy Starr."

Miss Paris smiled, and the woman beside Jimmy Connor smiled back, and just then three Yankee players strolled over to the box and began to jeer at Connor for having had to take seats behind that hated Yankee dugout.

Judy Starr was sitting oddly still. She was the famous Judy Starr who had been discovered by Florenz Ziegfeld—a second Marilyn Miller, the critics called her; dainty and pretty, with a perky profile and great honey-colored eyes, who had sung and danced her way into the heart of New York. Her day of fame was almost over now. Perhaps, thought Paula, staring at Judy's profile, that explained the pinch of her little mouth, the fine lines about her tragic eyes, the singing tension of her figure.

Perhaps. But Paula was not sure. There was immediacy, a defense against a palpable and present danger, in Judy Starr's tautness. Paula looked about. And at once her eyes narrowed.

Across the rail of the box, in the box at their left, sat a very tall, leather-skinned, silent and intent man. The man, too, was staring out at the field, in an attitude curiously like that of Judy Starr, whom he could have touched by extending his big, ropy, muscular hand across the rail. And on the man's other side there sat a woman whom Paula recognized instantly. Lotus Verne, the motion-picture actress!

Lotus Verne was a gorgeous, full-blown redhead with deep mercury-colored eyes who had come out of Northern Italy Ludovica Vernicchi, changed her name, and flashed across the Hollywood skies in a picture called *Woman of Bali*, a color film in which loving care had been lavished on the display possibilities of her dark, full, dangerous body. With fame, she had developed a passion for press agentry, borzois in pairs, and tall brown men with muscles. She was arrayed in sun yellow and she stood out among the women in the field boxes like a butterfly in a mass of grubs. By contrast little Judy Starr, in her flame-colored outfit, looked almost old and dowdy.

Paula nudged Ellery, who was critically watching the Yankees at batting practice. "Ellery," she said softly, "who is that big, brown, attractive man in the next box?"

Lotus Verne said something to the brown man, and suddenly Judy Starr said something to the Song-and-Dance Man; and then the two women exchanged the kind of glance women use when there is no knife handy.

Ellery said absently: "Who? Oh! That's Big Bill Tree."

"Tree!" repeated Paula. "Big Bill Tree?"

"Greatest left-handed pitcher major-league baseball ever saw," said Mr. Queen, staring reverently at the brown man. "Six feet three inches of bull whip and muscle, with a temper as sudden as the hook on his curve ball and a change of pace that fooled the greatest sluggers of baseball for fifteen years. What a man!"

"Yes, isn't he?" smiled Miss Paris.

"Now what does that mean?" demanded Mr. Queen.

"It takes greatness to escort a lady like Lotus Verne to a ball game," said Paula, "to find your wife sitting within spitting distance in the next box, and to carry it off as well as your muscular friend Mr. Tree is doing."

"That's right," said Queen softly. "Judy Starr *is* Mrs. Bill Tree."

He groaned as Joe DiMaggio hit a ball to the clubhouse clock.

"Funny," said Miss Paris, her clever eyes inspecting in turn the four people before her: Lotus Verne, the Hollywood siren; Big Bill Tree, the ex-baseball pitcher; Judy Starr, Tree's wife; and Jimmy Connor, the Song-and-Dance Man, Mrs. Tree's escort. Two couples, two boxes . . . and no sign of recognition. "Funny," murmured Miss Paris. "From the way Tree courted Judy you'd have thought the marriage would outlast eternity. He snatched her from under Jimmy Connor's nose one night at the Winter Garden, drove her up to Greenwich at eighty miles an hour, and married her before she could catch her breath."

"Yes," said Mr. Queen politely. "Come on, you Giants!" he yelled, as the Giants trotted out for batting practice.

"And then something happened," continued Miss Paris reflectively. "Tree went to Hollywood to make a baseball picture, met Lotus Verne, and the wench took the overgrown country boy the way the overgrown country boy had taken Judy Starr. What a fall was there, my baseball-minded friend."

"What a wallop!" cried Mr. Queen enthusiastically, as Mel Ott hit one that bounced off the right-field fence.

"And Big Bill yammered for a divorce, and Judy refused to

give it to him because she loved him, I suppose," said Paula soft-ly. "And now this. How interesting."

Big Bill Tree twisted in his seat a little; and Judy Starr was still and pale, staring out of her tragic, honey-colored eyes at the Yankee bat boy and giving him unwarranted delusions of grandeur. Jimmy Connor continued to exchange sarcastic greetings with Yankee players, but his eyes kept shifting back to Judy's face. And beautiful Lotus Verne's arm crept about Tree's shoulders.

"I don't like it," murmured Miss Paris a little later.

"You don't like it?" said Mr. Queen. "Why, the game hasn't even started."

"I don't mean your game, silly. I mean the quadrangular situation in front of us."

"Look, darling," said Mr. Queen. "I flew three thousand miles to see a ball game. There's only one angle that interests me—the view from this box of the greatest li'l ol' baseball tussle within the memory of gaffers. I yearn, I strain, I hunger to see it. Play with your quadrangle, but leave me to my baseball."

"I've always been psychic," said Miss Paris, paying no atten-tion. "This is—bad. Something's going to happen."

Mr. Queen grinned. "I know what. The deluge. See what's coming."

Someone in the grandstand had recognized the celebrities, and a sea of people was rushing down on the two boxes. They thronged the aisle behind the boxes, waving pencils and papers, and pleading. Big Bill Tree and Lotus Verne ignored their pleas for autographs; but Judy Starr with a curious eagerness signed paper after paper with the yellow pencils thrust at her by people leaning over the rail. Good-naturedly Jimmy Connor scrawled his signature, too.

"Little Judy," sighed Miss Paris, setting her natural straw straight as an autograph-hunter knocked it over her eyes, "is flustered and unhappy. Moistening the tip of your pencil with your tongue is scarcely a mark of poise. Seated next to her Lotus-bound husband, she hardly knows what she's doing, poor thing."

"Neither do I," growled Mr. Queen, fending off an octopus which turned out to be eight pleading arms offering scorecards.

Big Bill sneezed, groped for a handkerchief, and held it to his nose, which was red and swollen. "Hey, Mac," he called irritably to a red-coated usher. "Do somethin' about this mob, huh?" He sneezed again. "Damn this hay fever!"

"The touch of earth," said Miss Paris. "But definitely attractive."

"Should 'a' seen Big Bill the day he pitched that World Series final against the Tigers," chuckled Sergeant Velie. "He was sure attractive that day. Pitched a no-hit shutout!"

Inspector Queen said: "Ever hear the story behind that final game, Miss Paris? The night before, a gambler named Sure Shot McCoy, who represented a betting syndicate, called on Big Bill and laid down fifty grand in spot cash in return for Bill's promise to throw the next day's game. Bill took the money, told his manager the whole story, donated the bribe to a fund for sick ball players, and the next day shut out the Tigers without a hit."

"Byronic, too," murmured Miss Paris.

"So then Sure Shot, badly bent," grinned the Inspector, "called on Bill for the payoff. Bill knocked him down two flights of stairs."

"Wasn't that dangerous?"

"I guess," smiled the Inspector, "you could say so. That's why you see that plug-ugly with the smashed nose sitting over there right behind Tree's box. He's Mr. Terrible Turk, late of Cicero, and since that night Big Bill's shadow. You don't see Mr. Turk's right hand, because Mr. Turk's right hand is holding onto an automatic under his jacket. You'll notice, too, that Mr. Turk hasn't for a second taken his eyes off that pasty-cheeked customer eight rows up, whose name is Sure Shot McCoy."

Paula stared. "But what a silly thing for Tree to do!"

"Well, yes," drawled Inspector Queen, "seeing that when he popped Mr. McCoy Big Bill snapped two of the carpal bones of his pitching wrist and wrote finis to his baseball career."

Big Bill Tree hauled himself to his feet, whispered something to the Verne woman, who smiled coyly, and left his box. His bodyguard, Turk, jumped up; but the big man shook his head, waved aside a crowd of people, and vaulted up the concrete steps toward the rear of the grandstand.

And then Judy Starr said something bitter and hot and desperate across the rail to the woman her husband had brought to the Polo Grounds. Lotus Verne's mercurial eyes glittered, and she replied in a careless, insulting voice that made Bill Tree's wife sit up stiffly. Jimmy Connor began to tell the one about Walter Winchell and the Seven Dwarfs . . . loudly and fast.

The Verne woman began to paint her rich lips with short, vicious strokes of her orange lipstick; and Judy Starr's flame kid glove tightened on the rail between them.

And after a while Big Bill returned and sat down again. Judy said something to Jimmy Connor, and the Song-and-Dance Man slid over one seat to his right, and Judy slipped into Connor's seat; so that between her and her husband there was now not only the box rail but an empty chair as well.

Lotus Verne put her arm about Tree's shoulders again.

Tree's wife fumbled inside her flame suède bag. She said suddenly: "Jimmy, buy me a frankfurter."

Connor ordered a dozen. Big Bill scowled. He jumped up and ordered some, too. Connor tossed the vendor two one-dollar bills and waved him away.

A new sea deluged the two boxes, and Tree turned round, annoyed. "All right, all right, Mac," he growled at the red-coat struggling with the pressing mob. "We don't want a riot here. I'll take six. Just six. Let's have 'em."

There was a rush that almost upset the attendant. The rail behind the boxes was a solid line of fluttering hands, arms, and scorecards.

"Mr. Tree—said—six!" panted the usher; and he grabbed a pencil and card from one of the outstretched hands and gave them to Tree. The overflow of pleaders spread to the next box. Judy Starr smiled her best professional smile and reached for a pencil and card. A group of players on the field, seeing what was happening, ran over to the field rail and handed her scorecards, too, so that she had to set her half-consumed frankfurter down on the empty seat beside her. Big Bill set his frankfurter down on the same empty seat; he licked the pencil long and absently and began to inscribe his name in the stiff, laborious hand of a man unused to writing.

The attendant howled: "That's six, now! Mr. Tree said just six, so that's all!" as if God himself had said six; and the crowd groaned, and Big Bill waved his immense paw and reached over to the empty seat in the other box to lay hold of his half-eaten frankfurter. But his wife's hand got there first and fumbled round; and it came up with Tree's frankfurter. The big brown man almost spoke to her then; but he did not, and he picked up the remaining frankfurter, stuffed it into his mouth, and chewed away, but not as if he enjoyed its taste.

Mr. Ellery Queen was looking at the four people before him with a puzzled, worried expression. Then he caught Miss Paula Paris's amused glance and blushed angrily.

The groundkeepers had just left the field and the senior umpire was dusting off the plate to the roar of the crowd when Lotus Verne, who thought a double play was something by Eugene O'Neill, flashed a strange look at Big Bill Tree.

"Bill! Don't you feel well?"

The big ex-pitcher, a sickly blue beneath his tanned skin, put his hand to his eyes and shook his head as if to clear it.

"It's the hot dog," snapped Lotus. "No more for you!"

Tree blinked and began to say something, but just then Carl Hubbell completed his warming-up, Crosetti marched to the plate, Harry Danning tossed the ball to his second-baseman, who flipped it to Hubbell and trotted back to his position yipping like a terrier.

The voice of the crowd exploded in one ear-splitting burst. And then silence.

And Crosetti swung at the first ball Hubbell pitched and smashed it far over Joe Moore's head for a triple.

Jimmy Connor gasped as if someone had thrust a knife into his heart. But Detective-Sergeant Velie was bellowing: "Wha'd I tell you? It's gonna be a massacree!"

"What is everyone shouting for?" asked Paula.

Mr. Queen nibbled his nails as Danning strolled halfway to the pitcher's box. But Hubbell pulled his long pants up, grinning. Red Rolfe was waving a huge bat at the plate. Danning trotted back. Manager Bill Terry had one foot up on the edge of the Giant dugout, his chin on his fist, looking anxious. The infield came in to cut off the run.

Again fifty thousand people made no single little sound. And Hubbell struck out Rolfe, DiMaggio, and Gehrig.

Mr. Queen shrieked his joy with the thousands as the Giants came whooping in. Jimmy Connor did an Indian wardance in the box. Sergeant Velie looked aggrieved. Señor Gomez took his warm-up pitches, the umpire used his whiskbroom on the plate again, and Jo-Jo Moore, the Thin Man, ambled up with his war club.

He walked. Bartell fanned. But Jeep Ripple singled off Flash Gordon's shins on the first pitch; and there were Moore on third and Ripple on first, one out, and Little Mel Ott at bat.

Big Bill Tree got half out of his seat, looking surprised, and then dropped to the concrete floor of the box as if somebody had slammed him behind the ear with a fast ball.

Lotus screamed. Judy, Bill's wife, turned like a shot, shaking. People in the vicinity jumped up. Three red-coated attendants hurried down, preceded by the hard-looking Mr. Turk. The bench-warmers stuck their heads over the edge of the Yankee dugout to stare.

"Fainted," growled Turk, on his knees beside the prostrate athlete.

"Loosen his collar," moaned Lotus Verne. "He's so p-pale!"

"Have to git him outa here."

"Yes. Oh, yes!"

The attendants and Turk lugged the big man off, long arms dangling in the oddest way. Lotus stumbled along beside him, biting her lips nervously.

"I think," began Judy in a quivering voice, rising.

But Jimmy Connor put his hand on her arm, and she sank back.

And in the next box Mr. Ellery Queen, on his feet from the instant Tree collapsed, kept looking after the forlorn procession, puzzled, mad about something; until somebody in the stands squawked: "SIDDOWN!" and he sat down.

"Oh, I knew something would happen," whispered Paula.

"Nonsense!" said Mr. Queen shortly. "Fainted, that's all."

Inspector Queen said: "There's Sure Shot McCoy not far off. I wonder if—"

"Too many hot dogs," snapped his son. "What's the matter with you people? Can't I see my ball game in peace?" And he howled: "Come o-o-on, Mel!"

Ott lifted his right leg into the sky and swung. The ball whistled into right field, a long long fly, Selkirk racing madly back after it. He caught it by leaping four feet into the air with his back against the barrier. Moore was off for the plate like a streak and beat the throw to Bill Dickey by inches.

"Yip-ee!" Thus Mr. Queen.

The Giants trotted out to their positions at the end of the first inning leading one to nothing.

Up in the press box the working gentlemen of the press tore into their chores, recalling Carl Hubbell's similar feat in the All-Star game when he struck out the five greatest batters of the American League in succession; praising Twinkle-toes Selkirk for his circus catch; and incidentally noting that Big Bill Tree, famous ex-hurler of the National League, had fainted in a field box during the first inning. Joe Williams of the *World-Telegram* said it was excitement, Hype Igoe opined that it was a touch of sun—Big Bill never wore a hat—and Frank Graham of the *Sun* guessed it was too many frankfurters.

Paula Paris said quietly: "I should think, with your detective instincts, Mr. Queen, you would seriously question the 'fainting' of Mr. Tree."

Mr. Queen squirmed and finally mumbled: "It's coming to a pretty pass when a man's instincts aren't his own. Velie, go see what really happened to him."

"I wanna watch the game," howled Velie. "Why don't you go yourself, maestro?"

"And possibly," said Mr. Queen, "you ought to go too, Dad. I have a hunch it may lie in your jurisdiction."

Inspector Queen regarded his son for some time. Then he rose and sighed: "Come along, Thomas."

Sergeant Velie growled something about some people always spoiling other people's fun and why the hell did he ever have to become a cop; but he got up and obediently followed the Inspector.

Mr. Queen nibbled his fingernails and avoided Miss Paris's accusing eyes.

The second inning was uneventful. Neither side scored.

As the Giants took the field again, an usher came running down the concrete steps and whispered into Jim Connor's ear. The Song-and-Dance Man blinked. He rose slowly. "Excuse me, Judy."

Judy grasped the rail. "It's Bill. Jimmy, tell me."

"Now, Judy—"

"Something's happened to Bill!" Her voice shrilled, and then broke. She jumped up. "I'm going with you."

Connor smiled as if he had just lost a bet, and then he took Judy's arm and hurried her away.

Paula Paris stared after them, breathing hard.

Mr. Queen beckoned the red-coat. "What's the trouble?" he demanded.

"Mr. Tree passed out. Some young doc in the crowd tried to pull him out of it up at the office, but he couldn't, and he's startin' to look worried—"

"I knew it!" cried Paula as the man darted away. "Ellery Queen, are you going to sit here and do *nothing?*"

But Mr. Queen defiantly set his jaw. Nobody was going to jockey him out of seeing this battle of giants; no, ma'am!

There were two men out when Frank Crosetti stepped up to the plate for his second time at bat and, with the count two all, plastered a wicked single over Ott's head.

And, of course, Sergeant Velie took just that moment to amble down and say, his eyes on the field: "Better come along, Master Mind. The old man wouldst have a word with thou. Ah, I see Frankie's on first. Smack it, Red!"

Mr. Queen watched Rolfe take a ball. "Well?" he said shortly. Paula's lips were parted.

"Big Bill's just kicked the bucket. What happened in the second inning?"

"He's . . . *dead?*" gasped Paula.

Mr. Queen rose involuntarily. Then he sat down again. "Damn it," he roared, "it isn't fair. I won't go!"

"Suit yourself. Attaboy, Rolfe!" bellowed the Sergeant as Rolfe singled sharply past Bartell and Crosetti pulled up at second base. "Far's I'm concerned, it's open and shut. The little woman did it with her own little hands."

"Judy *Starr?*" said Miss Paris.

"Bill's wife?" said Mr. Queen. "What are you talking about?"

"That's right, little Judy. She poisoned his hot dog." Velie chuckled. "Man bites dog, and—zowie."

"Has she confessed?" snapped Mr. Queen.

"Naw. But you know dames. She gave Bill the business, all right. C'mon, Joe! And I gotta go. What a life."

Mr. Queen did not look at Miss Paris. He bit his lip. "Here, Velie, wait a minute."

DiMaggio hit a long fly that Leiber caught without moving in his tracks, and the Yankees were retired without a score.

"Ah," said Mr. Queen. "Good old Hubbell." And as the Giants trotted in, he took a fat roll of bills from his pocket, climbed onto his seat, and began waving greenbacks at the spectators in the reserved seats behind the box. Sergeant Velie and Miss Paris stared at him in amazement.

"I'll give five bucks," yelled Mr. Queen, waving the money, "for every autograph Bill Tree signed before the game! In this box right here! Five bucks, gentlemen! Come and get it!"

"You nuts?" gasped the Sergeant.

The mob gaped, and then began to laugh, and after a few moments a pair of sheepish-looking men came down, and then two more, and finally a fifth. An attendant ran over to find out what was the matter.

"Are you the usher who handled the crowd around Bill Tree's box before the game, when he was giving autographs?" demanded Mr. Queen. "Yes, sir. But, look, we can't allow—"

"Take a gander at these five men. . . . You, bud? Yes, that's Tree's handwriting. Here's your fin. Next!" and Mr. Queen went down the line, handing out five-dollar bills with abandon in return for five dirty scorecards with Tree's scrawl on them.

"Anybody else?" he called out, waving his roll of bills.

But nobody else appeared, although there was ungentle badinage from the stands. Sergeant Velie stood there shaking his big head. Miss Paris looked intensely curious.

"Who didn't come down?" rapped Mr. Queen.

"Huh?" said the usher, his mouth open.

"There were six autographs. Only five people turned up. Who was the sixth man? Speak up!"

"Oh." The red-coat scratched his ear. "Say, it wasn't a man. It was a kid."

"A *boy?*"

"Yeah, a little squirt in knee pants."

Mr. Queen looked unhappy. Velie growled: "Sometimes I think society's takin' an awful chance lettin' you run around loose," and the two men left the box. Miss Paris, bright-eyed, followed.

"Have to clear this mess up in a hurry," muttered Mr. Queen. "Maybe we'll still be able to catch the late innings."

Sergeant Velie led the way to an office, before which a policeman was lounging. He opened the door, and inside they found the Inspector pacing. Turk, the thug, was standing with a scowl over a long, still thing on a couch covered with newspapers. Jimmy Connor sat between the two women; and none of the three so much as stirred a foot. They were all pale and breathing heavily.

"This is Dr. Fielding," said Inspector Queen, indicating an elderly white-haired man standing quietly by a window. "He was Tree's physician. He happened to be in the park watching the game when the rumor reached his ears that Tree had collapsed. So he hurried up here to see what he could do."

Ellery went to the couch and pulled the newspaper off Bill Tree's still head. Paula crossed swiftly to Judy Starr and said: "I'm horribly sorry, Mrs. Tree," but the woman, her eyes closed, did not move. After a while Ellery dropped the newspaper back into place and said irritably: "Well, well, let's have it."

"A young doctor," said the Inspector, "got here before Dr. Fielding did, and treated Tree for fainting. I guess it was his fault—"

"Not at all," said Dr. Fielding sharply. "The early picture was compatible with fainting, from what he told me. He tried the usual restorative methods—even injected caffeine and picrotoxin. But there was no convulsion, and he didn't happen to catch that odor of bitter almonds."

"Prussic!" said Ellery. "Taken orally?"

"Yes. HCN—hydrocyanic acid, or prussic, as you prefer. I suspected it at once because—well," said Dr. Fielding in a grim voice, "because of something that occurred in my office only the other day."

"What was that?"

"I had a two-ounce bottle of hydrocyanic acid on my desk—I sometimes use it in minute quantities as a cardiac stimulant. Mrs. Tree," the doctor's glance flickered over the silent woman, "happened to be in my office, resting in preparation for a metabolism test. I left her alone. By a coincidence, Bill Tree dropped in the same morning for a physical check-up. I saw another patient in another room, returned, gave Mrs. Tree her test, saw her out, and came back with Tree. It was then I noticed the bottle, which had been plainly marked DANGER—POISON, was missing from my desk. I thought I had mislaid it, but now . . ."

"I didn't take it," said Judy Starr in a lifeless voice, still not opening her eyes. "I never even saw it."

The Song-and-Dance Man took her limp hand and gently stroked it.

"No hypo marks on the body," said Dr. Fielding dryly. "And I am told that fifteen to thirty minutes before Tree collapsed he ate a frankfurter under . . . peculiar conditions."

"I didn't!" screamed Judy. "I didn't do it!" She pressed her face, sobbing, against Connor's orchid.

Lotus Verne quivered. "She made him pick up her frankfurter. I saw it. They both laid their frankfurters down on that empty seat, and she picked up his. So he had to pick up hers. She poisoned her own frankfurter and then saw to it that he ate it by mistake. Poisoner!" She glared hate at Judy.

"Wench," said Miss Paris *sotto voce*, glaring hate at Lotus.

"In other words," put in Ellery impatiently, "Miss Starr is convicted on the usual two counts, motive and opportunity. Motive—her jealousy of Miss Verne and her hatred—an assumption—of Bill Tree, her husband. And opportunity both to lay hands on the poison in your office, Doctor, and to sprinkle some on her frankfurter, contriving to exchange hers for his while they were both autographing scorecards."

"She hated him," snarled Lotus. "And me for having taken him from her!"

"Be quiet, you," said Mr. Queen. He opened the corridor door and said to the policeman outside: "Look, McGillicuddy, or whatever your name is, go tell the announcer to make a speech over the loud-speaker system. By the way, what's the score now?"

"Still one to skunk," said the officer. "Them boys Hubbell an' Gomez are hot, what I mean."

"The announcer is to ask the little boy who got Bill Tree's autograph just before the game to come to this office. If he does, he'll receive a ball, bat, pitcher's glove, and an autographed picture of Tree in uniform to hang over his itsybitsy bed. Scram!"

"Yes, sir," said the officer.

"King Carl pitching his heart out," grumbled Mr. Queen, shutting the door, "and me strangulated by this blamed thing.

Well, Dad, do you think, too, that Judy Starr dosed that frank-furter?"

"What else can I think?" said the Inspector absently. His ears were cocked for the faint crowd shouts from the park.

"Judy Starr," replied his son, "didn't poison her husband any more than I did."

Judy looked up slowly, her mouth muscles twitching. Paula said gladly: "You wonderful man!"

"She didn't?" said the Inspector, looking alert.

"The frankfurter theory," snapped Mr. Queen, "is too screwy for words. For Judy to have poisoned her husband, she had to unscrew the cap of a bottle and douse her hot dog on the spot with the hydrocyanic acid. Yet Jimmy Connor was seated by her side, and in the only period in which she could possibly have poisoned the frankfurter a group of Yankee ball players was *standing before her* across the field rail getting her autograph. Were they all accomplices? And how could she have known Big Bill would lay his hot dog on that empty seat? The whole thing is absurd."

A roar from the stands made him continue hastily: "There was one plausible theory that fitted the facts. When I heard that Tree had died of poisoning, I recalled that at the time he was autographing the six scorecards, *he had thoroughly licked the end of a pencil* which had been handed to him with one of the cards. It was possible, then, that the pencil he licked had been poisoned. So I offered to buy the six autographs."

Paula regarded him tenderly, and Velie said: "I'll be a so-and-so if he didn't."

"I didn't expect the poisoner to come forward, but I knew the innocent ones would. Five claimed the money. The sixth, the missing one, the usher informed me, had been a small boy."

"A kid poisoned Bill?" growled Turk, speaking for the first time. "You're crazy from the heat."

"In spades," added the Inspector.

"They why didn't the boy come forward?" put in Paula quickly. "Go on, darling!"

"He didn't come forward, not because he was guilty but because he wouldn't sell Bill Tree's autograph for anything. No, obviously a hero-worshiping boy wouldn't try to poison the great Bill Tree. Then, just as obviously, he didn't realize what he was doing. Consequently, he must have been an innocent tool. The question was—and still is—of whom?"

"Sure Shot," said the Inspector slowly.

Lotus Verne sprang to her feet, her eyes glittering. "Perhaps Judy Starr didn't poison that frankfurter, but if she didn't then she hired that boy to give Bill—"

Mr. Queen said disdainfully: "Miss Starr didn't leave the box once." Someone knocked on the corridor door and he opened it. For the first time he smiled. When he shut the door they saw that his arm was about the shoulders of a boy with brown hair and quick clever eyes. The boy was clutching a scorecard tightly.

"They say over the announcer," mumbled the boy, "that I'll get a autographed pi'ture of Big Bill Tree if . . ." He stopped, abashed at their strangely glinting eyes.

"And you certainly get it, too," said Mr. Queen heartily. "What's your name, sonny?"

"Fenimore Feigenspan," replied the boy, edging toward the door. "Gran' Concourse, Bronx. Here's the scorecard. How about the picture?"

"Let's see that, Fenimore," said Mr. Queen. "When did Bill Tree give you this autograph?"

"Before the game. He said he'd only give six—"

"Where's the pencil you handed him, Fenimore?"

The boy looked suspicious, but he dug into a bulging pocket and brought forth one of the ordinary yellow pencils sold at the park with scorecards. Ellery took it from him gingerly, and Dr. Fielding took it from Ellery, and sniffed its tip. He nodded, and for the first time a look of peace came over Judy Starr's still face and she dropped her head tiredly to Connor's shoulder.

Mr. Queen ruffled Fenimore Feigenspan's hair. "That's swell, Fenimore. Somebody gave you that pencil while the Giants were at batting practice, isn't that so?"

"Yeah." The boy stared at him.

"Who was it?" asked Mr. Queen lightly.

"I dunno. A big guy with a coat an' a turned-down hat an' a mustache, an' big black sunglasses. I couldn't see his face good. Where's my pi'ture? I wanna see the game!"

"Just where was it that this man gave you the pencil?"

"In the—" Fenimore paused, glancing at the ladies with embarrassment. Then he muttered: "Well, I hadda go, an' this guy says—in there—he's ashamed to ask her for her autograph, so would I do it for him—"

"What? What's that?" exclaimed Mr. Queen. "Did you say 'her'?"

"Sure," said Fenimore. "The dame, he says, wearin' the red hat an' red dress an' red gloves in the field box near the Yanks' dugout, he says. He even took me outside an' pointed down to where she was sittin'. Say!" cried Fenimore, goggling. "That's her! That's the dame" and he leveled a grimy forefinger at Judy Starr.

Judy shivered and felt blindly for the Song-and-Dance Man's hand.

"Let me get this straight, Fenimore," said Mr. Queen softly. "This man with the sunglasses asked you to get this lady's autograph for him, and gave you the pencil and scorecard to get it with?"

"Yeah, an' two bucks too, sayin' he'd meet me after the game to pick up the card, but—"

"But you didn't get the lady's autograph for him, did you? You went down to get it, and hung around waiting for your chance, but then you spied Big Bill Tree, your hero, in the next box and forgot all about the lady, didn't you?"

The boy shrank back. "I didn't mean to, honest, Mister. I'll give the two bucks back!"

"And seeing Big Bill there, your hero, you went right over to get *his* autograph for *yourself*, didn't you?" Fenimore nodded, frightened. "You gave the usher the pencil and scorecard this man with the sunglasses had handed you, and the usher turned the pencil and scorecard over to Bill Tree in the box—wasn't that the way it happened?"

"Y-yes, sir, an'. . . ." Fenimore twisted out of Ellery's grasp, "an' so I—I gotta go." And before anyone could stop him he was indeed gone, racing down the corridor like the wind.

The policeman outside shouted, but Ellery said: "Let him go, officer," and shut the door. Then he opened it again and said: "How's she stand now?"

"Dunno exactly, sir. Somethin' happened out there just now. I think the Yanks scored."

"Damn," groaned Mr. Queen, and he shut the door again.

"So it was Mrs. Tree who was on the spot, not Bill," scowled the Inspector. "I'm sorry, Judy Starr. . . . Big man with a coat and hat and mustache and sunglasses. Some description!"

"Sounds like a phony to me," said Sergeant Velie.

"If it was a disguise, he dumped it somewhere," said the Inspector thoughtfully. "Thomas, have a look in the Men's Room behind the section where we were sitting. And Thomas," he added in a whisper, "find out what the score is." Velie grinned and hurried out. Inspector Queen frowned. "Quite a job finding a killer in a crowd of fifty thousand people."

"Maybe," said his son suddenly, "maybe it's not such a job after all. . . . What was used to kill? Hydrocyanic acid. Who was intended to be killed? Bill Tree's wife. Any connection between anyone in the case and hydrocyanic acid? Yes—Dr. Fielding 'lost' a bottle of it under suspicious circumstances. Which were? That Bill Tree's wife could have taken that bottle . . . *or Bill Tree himself.*"

"Bill Tree!" gasped Paula.

"Bill?" whispered Judy Starr.

"Quite! Dr. Fielding didn't miss the bottle until *after* he had shown you, Miss Starr, out of his office. He then returned to his office with your husband. Bill could have slipped the bottle into his pocket as he stepped into the room."

"Yes, he could have," muttered Dr. Fielding.

"I don't see," said Mr. Queen, "how we can arrive at any other conclusion. We know his wife was intended to be the victim today, so obviously she didn't steal the poison. The only other person who had opportunity to steal it was Bill himself."

The Verne woman sprang up. "I don't believe it! It's a frame-up to protect *her*, now that Bill can't defend himself!"

"Ah, but didn't he have motive to kill Judy?" asked Mr. Queen. "Yes, indeed; she wouldn't give him the divorce he craved so that he could marry *you*. I think, Miss Verne, you would be wiser to keep the peace. . . . Bill had opportunity to steal the bottle of poison in Dr. Fielding's office. He also had opportunity to hire

Fenimore today, for he was the *only* one of the whole group who left those two boxes during the period when the poisoner must have searched for someone to offer Judy the poisoned pencil.

"All of which fits for what Bill had to do—get to where he had cached his disguise, probably yesterday; look for a likely tool; find Fenimore, give him his instructions and the pencil; get rid of the disguise again; and return to his box. And didn't Bill know better than anyone his wife's habit of moistening a pencil with her tongue—a habit she probably acquired from *him?*"

"Poor Bill," murmured Judy Starr brokenly.

"Women," remarked Miss Paris, "are *fools.*"

"There were other striking ironies," replied Mr. Queen. "For if Bill hadn't been suffering from a hay-fever attack, he would have smelled the odor of bitter almonds when his own poisoned pencil was handed to him and stopped in time to save his worthless life. For that matter, if he hadn't been Fenimore Feigenspan's hero, Fenimore would not have handed him his own poisoned pencil in the first place.

"No," said Mr. Queen gladly, "putting it all together, I'm satisfied that Mr. Big Bill Tree, in trying to murder his wife, very neatly murdered himself instead."

"That's all very well for *you,*" said the Inspector disconsolately. "But *I* need proof."

"I've told you how it happened," said his son airily, making for the door. "Can any man do more? Coming, Paula?"

But Paula was already at a telephone, speaking guardedly to the New York office of the syndicate for which she worked, and paying no more attention to him than if he had been a worm.

"What's the score? What's been going on?" Ellery demanded of the world at large as he regained his box seat. "Three to three!

What the devil's got into Hubbell, anyway? How'd the Yanks score? What inning is it?"

"Last of the ninth," shrieked somebody. "The Yanks got three runs in the eighth on a walk, a double, and DiMag's homer! Danning homered in the sixth with Ott on base! Shut up!"

Bartell singled over Gordon's head. Mr. Queen cheered.

Sergeant Velie tumbled into the next seat. "Well, we got it," he puffed. "Found the whole outfit in the Men's Room—coat, hat, fake mustache, glasses and all. What's the score?"

"Three-three. Sacrifice, Jeep!" shouted Mr. Queen.

"There was a rain check in the coat pocket from the sixth game, with Big Bill's box number on it. So there's the old man's proof. Chalk up another win for you."

"Who cares? . . . *ZOWIE.*"

Jeep Ripple sacrificed Bartell successfully to second.

"Lucky stiff," howled a Yankee fan nearby. "That's the breaks. See the breaks they get? See?"

"And another thing," said the Sergeant, watching Mel Ott stride to the plate. "Seein' as how all Big Bill did was cross himself up, and no harm done except to his own carcass, and seein' as how organized baseball could get along without a murder, and seein' as how thousands of kids like Fenimore Feigenspan worship the ground he walked on—"

"Sew it up, Mel!" bellowed Mr. Queen.

"—and seein' as how none of the newspaper guys know what happened, except that Bill passed out of the picture after a faint, and seein' as everybody's only too glad to shut their traps—"

Mr. Queen awoke suddenly to the serious matters of life. "What's that? What did you say?"

"Strike him out, Goofy!" roared the Sergeant to Señor Gomez, who did not hear. "As I was sayin', it ain't cricket, and the old man would be broke out of the force if the big cheese heard about it. . . ."

Someone puffed up behind them, and they turned to see Inspector Queen, red-faced as if after a hard run, scrambling into the box with the assistance of Miss Paula Paris, who looked cool, serene, and star-eyed as ever.

"Dad!" said Mr. Queen, staring. "With a murder on your hands, how can you—"

"Murder?" panted Inspector Queen. "What murder?" And he winked at Miss Paris, who winked back.

"But Paula was telephoning the story—"

"Didn't you hear?" said Paula in a coo, setting her straw straight and slipping into the seat beside Ellery's. "I fixed it all up with your dad. Tonight all the world will know is that Mr. Bill Tree died of heart failure."

They all chuckled then—all but Mr. Queen, whose mouth was open.

"So now," said Paula, "your dad can see the finish of your precious game just as well as *you*, you selfish oaf!"

But Mr. Queen was already fiercely rapt in contemplation of Mel Ott's bat as it swung back and Señor Gomez's ball as it left the Señor's hand to streak towards the plate.

THE CLUE OF THE TATTOOED MAN
Clayton Rawson

One of the most outstanding practitioners of the impossible crime story was also one of America's most famous illusionists. Clayton Rawson (1906-1971) was a member of the American Society of Magicians and wrote on the subject frequently; he also was one of the four founding members of the Mystery Writers of America and created its motto: "Crime Does Not Pay—Enough."

He used his extensive knowledge of stage magic to create elaborate locked room and impossible crime novels and short stories. Under his own name, all his fiction featured the Great Merlini, a professional magician and amateur detective who opened a magic shop in New York City's Times Square where he often is visited by his friendly rival, Inspector Homer Gavigan of the NYPD, when he is utterly baffled by a seemingly impossible crime.

Merlini's adventures are recounted by freelance writer Ross Harte. There are only four Merlini novels, two of which have been adapted for motion pictures. *Miracles for Sale* (1939) was based on Rawson's first novel, *Death from a Top Hat* (1938). In this film, the protagonist is named Mike Morgan, played by Robert Young; it was directed by Tod Browning. The popular Mike Shayne series used Rawson's second book, *The Footprints on the Ceiling* (1939), as the basis for *The Man Who Wouldn't Die* (1942), with Lloyd Nolan starring as Shayne, who consults a professional magician for help.

The other Merlini books are *The Headless Lady* (1940), *No Coffin for the Corpse* (1942), and *The Great Merlini* (1979), a complete collection of Merlini stories. Under the pseudonym Stuart Towne, Rawson wrote four pulp novellas about Don Diavolo that were later published in book form: *Death Out of Thin Air* (1941) and *Death from Nowhere* (1949).

"The Clue of the Tattooed Man" was originally published in the December 1946 issue of *Ellery Queen's Mystery Magazine*; it was first collected in *The Great Merlini* (Boston, Gregg Press, 1979).

The Clue of the Tattooed Man
Clayton Rawson

THE GREAT Merlini looked at his watch for the umpteenth time just as Inspector Gavigan's car pulled up before the Hotel Astor.

"I've got a good notion to turn you into a rabbit," the magician said as he got in. "I've been waiting here for you ever since eleven o'clock."

"You're a mindreader," Gavigan said in a tired voice. "You should know why we're late."

"I see," Merlini said. "Murder."

"I've seen you make better guesses," Gavigan said gloomily. "It's murder, all right. But it's also attempted suicide, a gambling charge, a vanishing man, a nine-foot giant, a . . ." His voice trailed off as though he didn't believe it himself.

"And dope, too," Merlini said. "Gavigan, you've been hitting the pipe."

The inspector growled. "Brady, you tell him. I'm a nervous wreck."

Brady seemed just as glum. "Well, it's like this. We get a phone call at 11:40 from a guy who says his wife has been murdered. He's in a phone booth in the lobby near the Garden. We step on the gas getting up there because he sounds like he might have suicide in mind. He does. We find a commotion in the drug store off the lobby and the druggist is scrapping with a tall, skinny guy who bought a bottle of sleeping tablets and then started to eat them like they was peanuts. So we send the Professor down to Bellevue to keep a date with a stomach pump."

"A Professor?" Merlini asked. "What of—romance languages, mathematics, nuclear physics—?"

"I never heard any worse guesses," Brady replied. "His name's Professor Vox. The circus opened at the Garden this week and he's a ventriloquist in the sideshow. So we go upstairs and before we can get into room 816 where the body is we have to wade through a crap game that is going on in the corridor outside—a cowboy, a juggler and three acrobats. I know then I won't like the case and a minute later I'm positive—the ventriloquist's wife is a snake-charmer. And she has been strangled with a piece of cloth a foot wide and about twenty feet long."

"And that," Merlini put in, "gives you a Hindu as a suspect."

"Wrong again. It's a turban all right, but it belongs to a little fat guy who is billed as Mohammed the Magician but whose real name is Jimmy O'Reilly and who makes up like a Hindu with greasepaint. What's more, he has taken it on the lam and so we figure as soon as we catch him the case is solved. But then we question the crap players. And we find that their game starts at 11 p.m., that Zelda, the Snake-charmer, goes into her room a few minutes later and that the magician never goes near her room at all."

"Maybe," Merlini said, producing a lighted cigarette from thin air, "he was already there—waiting."

"I hope not because this is on the eighth floor, the only window is locked on the inside, the crap players insist he didn't leave by the only door, and the only way out is to vanish into thin air."

"It's a good trick," Merlini said noncommittally. "If you can do it."

"Yeah," Brady went on even more glumly. "And pinning it on him in court would be a good trick too because what happens next is that the crap players all agree there was one guy who went into the murder room between the time they last saw the snake-charmer and the time we show up. He went in at 11:15, stays for maybe ten minutes, and comes out again. They swear his identification is a cinch because his face looks like a crazy-quilt. He is Tinto—The Tattooed Man.

"And he's also missing. We send out a call to have him picked up. And while we wait we turn up two more hot suspects—both guys who are scared to death of snakes and hate the snake-charmer because she sometimes gets funny and leaves a snake or two in their rooms for a joke. They both look like I feel at this point—definitely not normal. One is Major Little, a midget who is almost so small he could have walked past that crap game without being noticed—only not quite. The other is a guy who is about as noticeable as an elephant; he's a beefy nine-foot giant named Goliath.

"So now we got murder, attempted suicide, a crap game, a vanishing magician, two freaks with motives and no alibis—they claim they were asleep—and a walking picture gallery who is the only guy who could have done it. Two minutes later Tinto walks in—a tall, underfed-looking egg with a face like a WPA post-office mural. And he says he had a date to meet Zelda in front of the Hotel Astor at a quarter to eleven and waited there over an hour—only she didn't show up. He can't prove it and four witnesses say different. So we charge him."

"Well," Merlini said, "your excuse for keeping me waiting is one I haven't heard before—I'll give you that. There's one little thing I don't like about it though."

"One little thing!" Gavigan exploded. "My God! All of it is—" He stopped abruptly. "Okay, I'll bite. What didn't you like?"

"Your skepticism concerning Tinto's story. I think he was in front of the Hotel Astor at the time of the murder—just as he claims."

"Oh, you do, do you?" Gavigan said darkly. Then suddenly he blinked. "So that's it! Now we got a magician as a material witness. You saw him there at the time of the murder—while you were waiting for me."

Merlini nodded. "Yes, I did. But why so unhappy about it? That should tell you who killed Zelda. Since I myself saw Tinto at the Hotel Astor at the time of the murder," Merlini explained, "it's obvious that the tattooed man seen by the crap players was a phony. In other words, someone was impersonating Tinto— imitating his facial peculiarities the same way Jimmy O'Reilly imitates a Hindu—with greasepaint.

"Who? Well, Brady described Tinto as 'tall and underfed' and that eliminates the fat little magician, the midget, and the hefty nine-foot giant. It leaves only the 'tall, skinny' Professor Vox.

"The motive—his discovery that Tinto was dating his wife—is also obvious.

"There's another way of pinning the guilt on Professor Vox. Since the crap players swore that the tattooed man was 'the only guy' to go into and out of the murder room before the cops arrived, how come Vox knew his wife was dead? Answer: only if he were the counterfeit tattooed man—therefore, only if he were the murderer."

THE PHONOGRAPH MURDER
Helen Reilly

Helen Reilly (1891-1962) was part of a mysterious family. Born Helen Margaret Kieran, her brother, James Kieran, also wrote a mystery, *Come Murder Me* (1952), and two of her four daughters also had successful writing careers, as both Ursula Curtiss and Mary McMullen each had about twenty detective novels to their credit.

A family friend, William McFee, urged her to write and she became one of the first women to write straightforward police procedural novels, setting them in the Manhattan Homicide Squad. It was so unusual for women to write this kind of book in the 1930s and 1940s that many readers assumed they were written by a male using a pseudonym.

Reilly did use a pseudonym, Kieran Abbey, for three crime novels.

The outstanding mystery critic and historian Howard Haycraft praised Reilly's novels as "among the most convincing that have been composed on the premise of actual police procedure," aided, no doubt, by the fact that she was one of the few "outsiders" permitted to review the Homicide Squad's files.

Reilly's ongoing series character was Inspector Christopher McKee, who Ursula Curtiss described as her "rather sinister godfather." Following service in World War I, McKee joined the New York Police Department and, by the mid-1940s, had risen to head the department. Totally dedicated to his work, he can appear brusque because he doesn't believe he has the time for social niceties. His attitude toward murderers and blackmailers is one of implacable hatred.

In most of his more than thirty cases, beginning in 1930 with *The Diamond Feather*, McKee is assisted by his friend and fellow bachelor, Inspector Todhunter.

"The Phonograph Murder" was originally published in the January 25, 1947, issue of *Collier's*. It is Reilly's only short story.

The Phonograph Murder
Helen Reilly

GEORGE BONFIELD made up his mind on the night that the maid, Hannah Swenson, came to the door of the bedroom and told him that the thermostatic control on the electric clock on the stove was out of order.

Bonfield and his wife were alone in the first-floor bedroom of the house in West Thirteenth Street which they owned and in which they had lived for the thirty years since their marriage. At fifty-six George Bonfield was a slight, wiry man with a gentle face and thinning hair. Louise Bonfield had put on flesh with the years but she had a shapely head, a fine profile, and rich blue-black hair that she wore fastened in a knot at the nape of her neck.

Louise was getting ready for bed. She had been threatened with an attack of gallstones and was still under the doctor's care. She always went to bed at around nine on the nights when George was going to the office to work.

Louise was sitting on the edge of the bed, taking off her shoes, and George was brushing his hair in front of the bureau. As Louise slipped off her stockings and folded them neatly, she said, "Dr. Seebold's a perfectly *wonderful* man, George. He says that if I'm careful I'm good for another twenty years."

Twenty years. The words did something to George Bonfield. He stared into the mirror and went on mechanically brushing his hair. Time was done up in bundles. There were fifty-two weeks in a year, seven days in a week, twenty-four hours in a day. And there would be twenty more years of it.

Louise said, "George, no matter how busy you are tomorrow, I want you to see the insurance people. In three months your endowment will mature, and we've got to begin to make definite plans about investing the money. I've got some very definite ideas."

George said, "Yes," obediently. Louise always did have definite ideas. She had had ideas about their daughter's first love affair; she had had ideas about not buying the farm in Dutchess County but putting his aunt's bequest into steel; she had had ideas about the serviceable dark wallpaper for the dining room.

Louise's voice flowed smoothly, inexorably. "Steel, perhaps, or aircraft, or maybe—" She went on, devouring his $30,000 endowment to the last crumb. "And, George, there's another thing I want to speak to you about."

She slipped a nightgown over her head. "That Randall account. Don' let it run another week. Either Randall pays or you take the matter to a lawyer. Does he think paper and time and layouts grow on trees? You've been culpably weak with him!"

She got into bed. The springs creaked. She settled herself on her pillows. "My magazine, there on the chair, hand it to me, George. I'm reading a lovely story." She sighed comfortably, and yawned.

"Yes, dear." George Bonfield gave her the magazine. As he did so his hand came in contact with hers. Her skin was soft and a little moist. He shivered, and fought down a sudden sickening soul-shaking wave of nausea. He turned away, saying to himself with an odd quiver of surprise, "Why—why, I hate her."

There was a knock. The door opened and the maid, Hannah, stuck her head into the room. Hannah was a big, rawboned Swedish girl with a dish face and round blue eyes—not bright, and rather excitable, but willing and kind.

Hannah said, "The electric clock on the stove. It won't work."

Louise spoke severely. "You probably didn't set it properly, Hannah. Or you've been fooling with it. It worked all right this morning."

George said dully, "I'll have a look at it, Hannah."

Louise said, from her pillows, "Don't take too long, George; you've got a good night's work to do. Now, Hannah, remember, when you bring me my orange juice at eleven don't wake me, and be careful to see that the front door is bolted before you go to bed. Mr. Bonfield will ring when he gets home, and you can let him in."

"Yes, ma'am," the maid said.

George followed her out of the room. The front door was an old point of issue between himself and Louise. Servants objected, and rightly, to being dragged down from the top of the house in the middle of the night to let him in. The bolt and chain weren't necessary. There was a perfectly good lock on the door. Bolts and bars . . . He shivered again. Suddenly they surrounded him.

He went downstairs and examined the electric clock. It was then, as he stood beside the stove in the kitchen, that the idea came to him. He fingered the clock. It was an interesting device. He began swinging the dials.

Hannah said, "Will we have to call the stove people, Mr. Bonfield?"

George Bonfield said slowly—and his voice seemed to come from a long distance away—"No, Hannah. I can fix it tomorrow. I'm—rather good with my hands."

He stared down at them for a long moment, got his hat, and left the house.

His office was on the second floor of a building on West Forty-second Street. It consisted of a waiting room, another room where Joe Tyler and the two stenographers worked, and George's own room beyond. His advertising agency was small and unpretentious, but it did a good pedestrian business that brought in a steady profit.

As usual on the nights they worked, Joe Tyler was waiting for him. Tyler was a big eager giant with an enormous admiration for his boss. George said hello to Joe, gave him the copy for the radiator folders, went into his office, closed the door, and settled down in the chair behind his desk. He made no attempt to get at the remainder of the outline. George had much more important things to think about.

There was no danger of his being interrupted—Joe wouldn't dream of opening the door while his boss was engaged in creative endeavor. George smiled bitterly. He was about to embark on a creation of another kind.

That was on October the ninth. At the beginning of the following week, George Bonfield bought the clock. It wasn't an electric clock. It was a simple cheap alarm clock with a bell on the top.

He had an appointment that day with a client in Newark. The client's office was on Broad Street. There were plenty of drug stores on Broad Street, but he didn't buy the clock in any of them. He bought it in Jersey City. Bonfield put the clock in the bottom drawer of the desk in his office. He locked the drawer.

His next purchase, which required more care since it could be traced more easily, was a small portable phonograph. He had to wait to acquire this. Yet he couldn't wait too long. The endowment, the $30,000 to which he had looked forward for so long, was due in less than a month; and it was going to take a good bit of time to get things exactly right.

Five days after he bought the alarm clock, his opportunity came. An old client of his in New England telegraphed from Boston asking George to come up for a promotion conference. Louise grumbled mildly, and redoubled her instructions to Hannah about locking the house at night and keeping small boys away from the front steps in the daytime.

George was away two days. It was on the morning of the second day that he stopped on his way to the station at a store he had already located and bought the small phonograph in the neat unobtrusive blue case. He deposited the phonograph, carefully wrapped in brown paper, in the checkroom in Grand Central on his way to the office from the train. Joe Tyler mustn't see it.

Red Lytell sent George tickets for the football game at the stadium on Saturday afternoon. Under the plea of work to be finished, Bonfield gave the tickets to a grateful Joe, and the faithful assistant safely disposed of, George retrieved the phonograph from Grand Central. On the way back to the office he stopped at a crowded five-and-ten and bought four balls of cord of various strengths and thicknesses.

The office was deserted. Once he got a fright when a cleaning woman tried to gain entrance by the door leading from his room directly into the hall, but he remained quiet. As the door was locked from the inside, the woman presently went away. Removing the bell from the alarm clock and placing the phonograph on the desk, Bonfield experimented with all four varieties of cord until five o'clock. There was a queer little thread of exultation running through him as he put the alarm clock, phonograph, and cord into the bottom drawer. He locked the drawer and went home.

Louise was more trying than usual that night. She had sent back the shirts he had chosen for himself and had bought him others of her own choosing. Over pickles and cold beef, she said, "Don't pick and choose, my dear. Eat the fat; fat's good for you. Those other shirts were far too bright, George, and the material was too thin. What did the insurance people say?"

When he told her that everything was in order as far as the endowment was concerned, she spent the rest of the evening calculating percentages until she went to bed at nine. She required a good deal of sleep.

It was George who tiptoed into the bedroom at eleven that night with the glass of orange juice she sipped whenever she happened to wake up during the night. It was Hannah's day off. Louise insisted that orange juice gave her a wonderful throat, warded off coughs and colds. He tiptoed out of the room and examined the windows and the front door before he went to bed himself.

Twice that week, when Joe was away from the office and the stenographers had left, George put the experiment into operation again, deciding finally on a thin white string that had the proper tensile strength. It was a delicate operation: too much slack wouldn't do, and too little might break the string. That mustn't happen.

He had two purchases still to make. One, the glass cutter, was insignificant. He bought it at a hardware store in Brooklyn. The other purchase, on which success depended, was more difficult. He must never by any chance be connected with it.

The Rosy Cheek Tomato people supplied him with the opportunity to procure it. Late in the month he went to Philadelphia to see about some trade paper displays. That attended to, he sought a shop that handled radios and phonographs. There was the usual row of booths where you could try records out. You could also have your own voice recorded.

George had a record made of his voice. He left the shop with the small disc in his brief case.

Nothing remained but the spadework and the question of getting rid of the various implements safely. That took a good deal of figuring. The time would be short and the implements mustn't be tied to him in any way. But they were innocent in themselves, and deposited separately, they ought to arouse no suspicion in a city as big as New York.

His endowment was due in two weeks, then in one. The time for action was approaching. He had calculated minutes and distances to a hair, traveling to and fro on the Eighth instead of the Seventh Avenue subway. He had studied the various streets at night, weighing the hazards he might have to encounter.

The time for action came. Everything was in readiness. The annuity was due on Saturday. He had a choice of Wednesday,

Thursday, or Friday. His client, Frank Morrison, vice-president of Darling Soaps, would have suited equally well on any one of the three.

George chose Thursday on account of the weather. The forecast for Thursday was "cloudy and colder tonight, rain tomorrow."

At two in the afternoon the sun was still shining. George Bonfield controlled his nervousness. At four the sun went behind the clouds. At six, when he went home on the Seventh Avenue subway, it was raining and he was in despair. Actual rain would be even more fatal than a clear starlit night. To his relief, the rain stopped at around seven.

Louise talked steadily during dinner. Her voice slashed at his ears. He made himself look at her, made himself answer, keeping his voice normal and indifferent. She showed no surprise when he told her he had to go back to the office. He explained that Morrison of Darling Soaps wanted the material for a new campaign by morning, and that he might be late.

Louise said, "Don't make a noise coming home, and if it's wet out be sure and take off your rubbers before Hannah lets you in."

"Yes, dear." George Bonfield didn't look at his wife. He turned away, picked up his hat, and walked out into the hall.

Back at the office on the second floor of the building in West Forty-second Street, Joe was waiting for him. Bonfield laid out the evening's work. "You'll have to keep at these folders, Joe. Morrison is in a hurry. We've got to get them finished tonight. I'll get busy with the front material. It's tricky stuff, so don't disturb me and don't let me be disturbed."

Joe said cheerfully, "I'll keep at it, Mr. Bonfield," and Bonfield went into his office and closed the door. He locked it, as he sometimes did when he wanted to remain uninterrupted. He had to run the risk of a question from Joe about the copy, but he had gone over the folders carefully and there should be no questions. He had spent three solid hours the previous night completing the entire Darling Soap campaign to the last dot and dash. He locked the door leading into the hall. That was at 9:20.

The period of waiting was the hardest. He didn't dare walk around because he was supposed to be engrossed in the papers on his desk. Once he heard Joe approach the water cooler, but Joe didn't come near the inner office.

At 9:55 Bonfield opened the bottom drawer of the desk and took out the alarm clock, minus bell, the phonograph in the blue case, and the record. He adjusted the string and set the clock.

At 10:02 he left the inner office silently, by way of the door opening directly on the corridor. He locked this door behind him with his key and glanced quickly up and down the hall. He went down the fire stairs and emerged cautiously into the lower hall. The watchman ought to be in the basement. George Bonfield's heart stood still at the sound of approaching footsteps. Ten feet separated him from the front door. If he was seen now, everything would be ruined. He held his breath. The footsteps receded.

Out in the cold night air he wiped the sweat from his forehead and pulled the second hat with which he had provided himself lower over his eyes. It was a green hat which some customer had left in his office months before. His own hat and topcoat were in the outer office.

He made his way swiftly to the Eighth Avenue subway, head down, collar turned up around his throat. Pedestrians were scarce. But it wasn't raining. He kept glancing up at the sky anxiously.

He got off the downtown express at Fourteenth Street. The

house in which he lived was on the south side of Thirteenth, but there was an alley from Twelfth leading into the bowels of the block. He entered the alley noiselessly.

He paused near the clothes dryer and surveyed the house. It was dark except for a light high up on the roof, the skylight over Hannah's room. He went up the path to the back door. The wind swayed the ailanthus and sent leaves fluttering down. He must be careful afterward about those leaves.

The glass cutter was in his pocket. So was the tape. He put his gloves on and attached the tape to a pane in the rear door. He cut the pane carefully and with the aid of the tape lifted it clear without noise. He put in his gloved hand and turned the key.

He opened the door, stepped into the kitchen and listened. There wasn't a sound. He crept into the narrow front hall and went to the front door. He took the chain off and unlocked the door. Holding himself tightly, every nerve taut, he tiptoed toward Louise's bedroom. . . .

It was 10:24 when George Bonfield entered his house by the rear door. It was 10:45 when he left the house by the same route. He was back in his office at 10:53 p.m.

He took off the green hat and shook it. There were no leaf fragments clinging to it. There were no leaf fragments on his shoes. He hung the hat in the closet and looked with dull wonder at his face in the mirror. He massaged his eyeballs, and listened. Yes, Joe was at work; the typewriter was clicking along evenly. He rustled a paper on his own desk. A horrible inertia possessed him.

He took the alarm clock, the record, and the phonograph from the desk, and again left his office. The lavatory was at the back of the building in the middle of a long hall. All the other offices were dark. He moved as rapidly as he could.

He smashed the record into small pieces and disposed of them through a window in the middle of the corridor; he got rid of the alarm clock through the window at the northern end, waiting until the jangling of a passing truck concealed the noise of its fall. This done, he proceeded to the other end of the hall. Opening the window there, he leaned out. Holding the phonograph well away from the wall, he gave it a swing and let it fall into the deep crevice between the buildings.

For a moment, as the neat blue case disappeared from sight, he wondered whether his disposition of the three things had been wise. He shrugged his doubts away and returned to his office. Assembling the scattered sheets of the Darling Soap campaign already prepared, he settled down to wait.

It was 11:12 p.m. when the call went into the precinct. The call was made by Mr. Gamble who lived next door to the Bonfields. Promptly at eleven Mr. Gamble was roused by piercing screams issuing from the red-brick house next to his own. He rushed out, a coat thrown hastily over his pajamas, and found Hannah Swenson, the maid, shrieking at the top of her lungs, at the Bonfield front door. He pushed her aside and ran along the hall. One glance was enough for Gamble. The police arrived within a few minutes.

They found Louise Bonfield lying on the floor of the bedroom. She had been struck over the head with a heavy brass candlestick from the mantel. She had also been choked. There were purplish areas on her plump throat. The room was in disorder. The desk drawers had been pulled out and their contents scattered. A beaded purse, empty, had been thrown down on a chair.

The police discovered the pane of glass that had been removed from the back door. A brass clock had fallen from the mantel. The glass had smashed, and the hands had stopped at 10:35.

The maid, Hannah Swenson, was interrogated. At best none too bright, she was a wreck, but the police managed to gather, from a story interrupted by moans and shudders and fresh outbursts of weeping, an approximation of what had happened.

Hannah Swenson had discovered her mistress' body at 11:00 p.m. when she entered the room with the glass of orange juice that she prepared for Mrs. Bonfield every night. The maid, coming down the back stairs to get the orange juice ready, must have been heard by the killer after he had done his dreadful work and while he was rifling the desk. His escape through the door at the back of the house was cut off by Hannah. He had fled through the front door.

The medical examiner arrived, took one look at the wildly laughing Hannah, and ordered her to St. Vincent's for the night, where she could receive proper care. The West Side precinct sent detectives around to notify the husband, and the investigation continued. . . .

In his inner office on the second floor of the building on Forty-second Street, George Bonfield heard the tramp of approaching feet as two big men came down the corridor. There was a murmur of voices in the other room, and Joe Tyler's shocked cry. The door opened.

George Bonfield was not an actor. It was one of the things that had worried him. He found he had no occasion to worry. The blood left his heart, and his legs gave way under him at the first sight of the law. But the detectives were considerate, and he recovered himself.

Bonfield returned with the detectives to the house on Thirteenth Street. Hannah Swenson was already gone.

He steeled himself when he was asked to make a formal identification of his wife. The bedroom was full of big men, some in uniform, some not. Flash bulbs went off, and there was a lot of noise. Everyone was very nice to Bonfield.

"If you'll step this way, sir?" Two attendants from the morgue were standing at either end of a long wicker basket. George walked slowly toward it. He looked down at Louise. Her eyes were closed. Hair veiled the bruises on her temple, and folds of linen obscured her injured throat.

He said in a whisper, "Yes, that's my wife." He stepped back, and the basket was borne away.

A tall slender man in loose gray tweeds, with cavernous brown eyes deeply set in the sockets of a fine head, entered the room accompanied by a stenographer. The newcomer was Inspector Christopher McKee of the Manhattan Homicide Squad. The Inspector listened to the precinct men, and read the maid's testimony. He spoke only once to George Bonfield. "You were at your office all evening, Mr. Bonfield?"

George Bonfield said, "Yes," and an icy shiver went through him. He waited. The tall man nodded and turned away.

It wasn't until the next morning at nine that Bonfield was questioned in detail. He knew it had to come. Joe Tyler was with him at the time. Joe had come to see if he could be of assistance.

Inspector McKee was there, together with two or three detectives. They asked Bonfield to step into the bedroom with them. Bonfield forced himself to show emotion—but not too much. It was the lieutenant from the local precinct who took charge. He explained the situation.

"The way we figure it, Mr. Bonfield, is that your wife was

killed by a burglar who entered this room without realizing it was a bedroom. His intention was evidently to rob. Your wife surprised him. He snatched the candlestick from the mantel, knocking down the clock as he did so. He was searching the desk when the maid surprised him. His retreat by the way he had entered the house was cut off. He made his escape by the front door. Now, about this desk—"

George Bonfield cleared his throat. He said that his wife kept money in the beaded purse. She had no jewelry, and her stock certificates and other valuables were in a safe-deposit box at the bank.

"Now, you yourself, Mr. Bonfield? You'll understand that this is just routine. We will also have to question the maid further when she's well enough. It's simply to get a complete picture of the case. Will you tell us exactly what you did last night?"

It had come, as he knew it must come—a circle of men, eyes fastened on him intently. George Bonfield crossed one knee over the other and began to talk. It was hard to keep his voice level and unhurried. The deadly fatigue which weighed him down was a help. Every time he had tried to fall asleep he had kept on seeing Louise's face.

"My wife and I had dinner at around half-past seven and, as usual on the nights I work, I left the house at around half-past eight. I had a lot of work to do." He described the campaign for the Darling Soap people. "After I left, I presume Louise did what she generally did—went to bed early."

"Were you alone in your office?"

"My assistant, Joe Tyler, was in the next room."

The detective brought Joe Tyler in. Joe corroborated Bonfield's testimony. He said that Mr. Bonfield entered his office at around 8:45 and that he was there until the police arrived. Joe was in the next room every single minute of the time, and he couldn't be mistaken.

The lieutenant said unexpectedly, "There's a door opening directly into the corridor from your office, isn't there, Mr. Bonfield?"

Bonfield knew all about that door, knew what they were thinking about it, and had prepared himself. He said quietly, "Yes, there's a door there. You mean you think I—?"

Joe Tyler sprang to his defense. Joe said excitedly, "Mrs. Bonfield was killed at ten thirty-five, wasn't she, Lieutenant? That's what it said in the paper—on account of the clock." The lieutenant nodded. "Then I can prove that Mr. Bonfield was in his office," Joe said. "I heard him moving around before that and after that, but at ten thirty-five he called Frank Morrison to tell him that the material would be ready in the morning. I heard him."

Bonfield was careful to keep his attitude and posture listless while the lieutenant put Joe through his paces as to memory, exactitude, and further details.

Joe said, "Sure, I remember the time. I remember it because we still had a lot of work to do. I knew Mr. Bonfield was worried about it, too, and I figured when I heard him say to Mr. Morrison, 'It's ten thirty-five now; another two hours and we'll have it licked. I'll have everything ready for you by morning,' that we still had a hell of a lot to do."

Obviously Bonfield couldn't have murdered his wife in the house on Thirteenth Street a minute or two after he made a telephone call from his office on West Forty-second Street. The conclusion was written on the faces surrounding him.

After a few purely routine questions about the house, the doors and windows, and the back yard, the police thanked him and took their departure.

An enormous weight fell from George Bonfield's shoulders. They didn't suspect him—couldn't suspect him on the evidence. They were very thorough. They had examined the maid's room, examined the office. They had gone through Bonfield's desk, and found everything in order. They had looked into the closet and seen the spare green hat. He had explained that it was a hat some customer had left there months before. They hadn't examined the crevices between the buildings, and the phonograph and the alarm clock had remained undiscovered.

Bonfield's nerves steadied. He was safe. For the first time in weeks he permitted himself to relax.

He knew there would be more red tape to be gone through, so he wasn't surprised or worried when he was summoned to the office of the head of the Manhattan Homicide Squad at four o'clock on the following afternoon.

There were half a dozen men in the room. Inspector McKee was seated behind a desk. Bonfield's statement had been taken down in shorthand, and typewritten copies of it were lying in front of the Inspector.

McKee said pleasantly, "Sorry to bring you here, Mr. Bonfield, but there are certain formalities."

The door opened, and a detective came in. He said, "It's okay, Inspector. I just talked to Morrison of Darling Soaps. He said that Mr. Bonfield called him at ten thirty-five. Mr. Bonfield said that he was within two hours of finishing, that he'd have the stuff complete by morning."

A little rustle went through the room. George settled himself in his chair. He felt larger. A new strength flowed through his blood. The world expanded. It was a wide, wide world. There was nothing he had neglected, nothing he hadn't foreseen. He had been very careful.

"Mr. Bonfield, if you'll just sign your name to these?" The Inspector pushed the statements toward him. Bonfield had the pen in his hand when the door opened again. It was only Hannah—big, stupid Hannah. He didn't really need her. All she could do was hammer home the points already established.

He listened idly while the Inspector took her, step by step, over the ground he himself knew so well. Hannah described the preparation of the orange juice at the usual time, her awful discovery when she entered the bedroom.

"And then what did you do?"

"I screamed. I threw open the window, and then I ran to the front door and unlocked it and ran out."

The Inspector looked at her. He said patiently, "But, Hannah, you couldn't have unlocked the front door at eleven o'clock. It was *already unlocked*. The murderer took the chain off and unlocked the door when he fled after killing Mrs. Bonfield at ten thirty-five."

"I don't care," Hannah persisted stolidly. "I did unlock the door after I ran out of the bedroom. It was locked when I found her."

Bonfield swallowed noisily. The crazy idiot! Of course, the door was unlocked when she got downstairs at a little before eleven. He had unlocked it with his own hands when he first entered the house at 10:24. Every moment of that interval was burned into his brain. The stupid, blundering fool! Had she lost her mind?

There was a red gauze in front of his eyes. Time and place disappeared, and there was only the necessity of getting Hannah to tell the truth. He was on his feet. He heard his own voice shouting. "The door *was* unlocked when you got downstairs. I know because I—"

He stopped. Everything stopped. He was impaled on a bright steel hook in a vacuum of silence. The Inspector was looking at him. So were the other men in the room. The Inspector spoke softly. "You know the door was unlocked because—Go on, Mr. Bonfield."

Bonfield licked dry lips. He couldn't go on, because there was no place to go. He had been so careful. It was such a little slip— and utterly damning.

Louise had beaten him in the end. He wasn't really surprised. But it was no use struggling any longer. He was exhausted. Blood pounded in his temples.

He said dully, "Yes, I killed her." He buried his face in his shaking hands. . . .

Later that afternoon Inspector McKee had a conference with the District Attorney. There was little to explain. George Bonfield had signed a confession.

"This," McKee said, "is what Bonfield did on the night of the killing: he went to his office on Forty-second Street and into his own inner room. His clerk, Joe Tyler, was in the outside room. When the time came, Bonfield arranged his contraption. It consisted of an alarm clock, a phonograph, and a record of his own voice. He set the alarm for ten thirty-five. He attached one end of a string to the clapper and the other end to the lever of the phonograph. Then he left the office, went down to Thirteenth Street, and killed his wife.

"He killed her, not at ten thirty-five—the smashed clock was a blind—but at around ten twenty-five. That done, he staged a fake robbery, and then called the soap man, Morrison, over the telephone in his wife's room at about ten thirty-four. Meanwhile, in his empty office, the clapper tripped the phonograph lever, the record revolved, and Joe Tyler listened to the identical telephone call, word for word, that Bonfield was then making from the house on Thirteenth Street. It was a perfect alibi."

"I'll say," the District Attorney agreed. "Tell me, McKee, did you suspect Bonfield before he broke?"

The Inspector shrugged. "The absence of fingerprints on the telephone in the Bonfield woman's bedroom looked queer. Someone had wiped it carefully for no apparent reason." He shrugged again. "I don't believe we would ever have got him, except for Mrs. Bonfield—and the wind."

The District Attorney frowned. "Mrs. Bonfield? The wind?"

"Mrs. Bonfield trained Hannah well. The maid was terrified of her. Lying in bed and listening to the wind, Hannah began worrying about the front door—whether or not she had locked it. Finally she couldn't stand it any longer. At not quite ten thirty Hannah crept down to the lower hall, found the door unlocked, locked it, put the chain on, and went back upstairs.

"She remained there until ten fifty-five, when it was time to get the orange juice ready. While she was in the lower hall locking the door, she didn't hear Bonfield and he didn't hear her. The house is pretty stout, and the wind was high. I guess that ties it up."

The Inspector reached moodily for his hat. "It's all yours, Counselor—and you're welcome to it." And McKee walked out of the room.

THE LIPSTICK
Mary Roberts Rinehart

As the creator of what is generally known as the "Had-I-But-Known" school (though that phrase never appeared in any of her books), Mary Roberts Rinehart (1876-1958) regularly had her plucky heroines put themselves in situations from which they needed to be rescued. That school of detective story has often been parodied and maligned, but it was so well handled that Rinehart was, for decades, one of the most successful and beloved mystery writers in America, producing the first mystery novel ever to appear on the bestseller list, *The Man in Lower Ten* (1909). She had written it as a serial for the first pulp magazine, *Munsey's*, which later serialized her novel *The Circular Staircase* (1908), which was released in book form before the first novel was released in that form.

Probably her most successful work is *The Bat*, the play she and Avery Hopwood adapted from *The Circular Staircase* in 1920, by which time she had become one of the highest-paid writers in America. The book had already served as the basis for a silent film, *The Circular Staircase* (1915) and then the play, which had some differences from the novel, inspired more than one film, including the silent *The Bat* (1926), and a sound version titled, *The Bat Whispers* (1930).

Rinehart's most famous character is Hilda Adams, whose propensity for getting involved in crimes and mysteries garnered her the nickname "Miss Pinkerton" after Allan Pinkerton, the famous real-life detective. She was encouraged in her sleuthing endeavors by George Patton, a small-time country detective who goes on to become a police inspector and is a recurring presence in the series. She overhears private conversations, listens to people who are sick or wounded so not at their peak strength, and provides information to Patton. It is her stated conviction that she is betraying no trust and, since criminals act against society, then society must use every means at its disposal to bring them to justice.

"The Lipstick" was originally published in the July 1942 issue of *Cosmopolitan*; it was first published in book form in *The Fourth Mystery Book*, edited anonymously (New York, Farrar & Rinehart, 1942).

The Lipstick
Mary Roberts Rinehart

I walked home after the coroner's inquest. Mother had gone on in the car, looking rather sick, as she had ever since Elinor's death. Not that she had particularly cared for Elinor. She has a pattern of life which divides people into conformers and non-conformers. The conformers pay their bills the first of the month, go to church, never by any chance get into anything but the society columns of the newspapers, and regard marriage as the *sine qua non* of every female over twenty.

My cousin Elinor Hammond had flouted all this. She had gone gaily through life, as if she wakened each morning wondering what would be the most fun that day; stretching her long lovely body between her silk sheets—how Mother resented those sheets—and calling to poor tired old Fred in his dressing room.

"Let's have some people in for cocktails, Fred."

"Anything you say, darling."

It was always like that. Anything Elinor said was all right with Fred. He worshiped her. As I walked home that day I was remembering his face at the inquest. He had looked dazed.

"You know of no reason why your—why Mrs. Hammond should take her own life?"

"None whatever."

"There was nothing in her state of health to cause her anxiety?"

"Nothing. She had always seemed to be in perfect health."

"She was consulting Dr. Barclay."

"She was tired. She was doing too much," he said unhappily.

Yet there it was. Elinor had either fallen or jumped from that tenth-floor window of Dr. Barclay's waiting room, and the coroner plainly believed she had jumped. The doctor had not seen her at all that day. Only the nurse.

"There was no one else in the reception room," she testified. "The doctor was busy with a patient. Mrs. Hammond sat down and took off her hat. Then she picked up a magazine. I went back to my office to copy some records. I didn't see her again until . . ."

The nurse was a pretty little thing. She looked pale.

"Tell us what happened next," said the coroner gently.

"I heard the other patient leave about five minutes later. She went out from the consulting room. There's a door there into the hall. When the doctor buzzed for the next case I went in to get Mrs. Hammond. She wasn't there. I saw her hat, but her bag was gone. Then—then I heard people shouting in the street, and I looked out the window."

"What would you say was her mental condition that morning, Miss Comings?" the coroner asked. "Was she depressed?"

"I thought she seemed very cheerful," the nurse said.

"The window was open beside her?"

"Yes. I couldn't believe it until I . . ."

The coroner excused her then. It was clear that she had told all she knew.

When Dr. Barclay was called, I was surprised. I had expected an elderly man, but he was only in the late thirties and good-looking. Knowing Elinor, I wondered. Except for Fred, who had no looks whatever, she had had a passion for handsome men.

Beside me, I heard Mother give a ladylike snort. "So that's it!" she said. "She had as much need for a psychiatrist as I have for a third leg."

But the doctor added little to what we already knew. He had not seen Elinor at all that morning. When he rang the buzzer and nobody came, he had gone into the reception room. Miss Comings was leaning out the window. All at once she began to scream. Fortunately, a Mrs. Thompson arrived at that time and took charge of her. The doctor had gone down to the street, but the ambulance had already arrived.

He was frank enough up to that time. Queried about the reason for Elinor's consulting him, he tightened. "I have many patients like Mrs. Hammond," he said. "Women who live on their nerves. Mrs. Hammond had been doing that for years."

"That is all? She mentioned no particular trouble?"

He smiled faintly. "We all have troubles," he said. "Some we imagine; some we magnify; some are real. But I would say that Mrs. Hammond was an unusually normal person. I had recommended that she go away for a rest. I believe she meant to do so."

His voice was clipped and professional. If Elinor had been attracted to him, it had been apparently a one-sided affair.

"You did not gather that she contemplated suicide?"

"No. Not at any time."

That is all they got out of him. He evaded them on anything Elinor had imagined or magnified. His relations with his patients, he said, were confidential. If he knew anything of value he would tell it, but he did not.

Mother nudged me as he finished. "Probably in love with her. He's had a shock. That's certain."

He sat down near us, and I watched him. I saw him come to attention when the next witness was called. It was the Mrs. Thompson who had looked after the nurse, a large mother-ly-looking woman.

She stated at once that she was not a patient. "I clean the doctor's apartment once a week," she said. "That day I needed a little money in advance, so I went to see him."

She had not entered the office at once. She had looked in and seen Elinor, so she had waited in the hall. She had seen the last patient, a woman, leave by the consulting room door and go down in the elevator. A minute or so later she heard the nurse scream.

"She was leaning out the window yelling her head off. Then the doctor ran in and I got her on a couch. She said somebody had fallen out, but she didn't say who it was."

Asked how long she had been in the hall, she thought about a quarter of an hour. She was certain no other patients had entered during that time. She would have seen them if they had.

"You found something belonging to Mrs. Hammond in the office, didn't you?"

"Yes, sir. I found her bag."

The bag, it seemed, had been behind the radiator in front of the window.

So that was that. Elinor, having put her hat on the table, had dropped her bag behind the radiator before she jumped. Somehow, it didn't make sense to me.

The verdict was suicide while of unsound mind. The window had been examined, but there was the radiator in front of it, and the general opinion seemed to be that a fall would have to be ruled out. Nobody mentioned murder. In the face of Mrs. Thompson's testimony, it looked impossible.

Fred listened to the verdict with blank eyes. His sister Margaret, sitting beside him dressed in mourning, rose. And Dr. Barclay stared straight ahead of him as though he did not hear it. Then he got up and went out, and while I put Mother in the car I saw him driving away, still with that queer fixed look on his face.

I was in a fine state of fury as I walked home. I had always liked Elinor, even when she had snatched Fred from under my nose, as Mother rather inelegantly said. As a matter of cold fact, Fred Hammond never saw me after he met her. He had worshiped her from the start, and his white stunned face at the inquest only added to the mystery.

The fools! I thought. As though Elinor would ever have jumped out of that window, even if she had been in trouble. She had never cared what people thought. I remembered almost the last time I had seen her. Somebody had given a suppressed-desire party, and Elinor had gone with a huge red *A* on the front of her white-satin dress.

Mother nearly had a fit when she saw it. "I trust, Elinor," she said, "that your scarlet letter does not mean what it appears to mean."

Elinor had laughed. "What do you think, Aunt Emma? Would you swear that never in your life—"

"That will do, Elinor," Mother said.

Elinor had been very gay that night, and she had enjoyed the little run-in with Mother. Perhaps that was one of the reasons I had liked her. She could cope with Mother. She wasn't an only daughter, living at home on an allowance which was threatened every now and then. And she had brought laughter and gaiety into my small world.

Mother was having tea when I got home. She sat stiffly behind the tea tray and inspected me. "I can't see why you worry about this, Louise. What's done is done. After all, she led Fred a miserable life."

"She made him happy, and now she's dead," I said. "Also, I don't believe she threw herself out that window."

"Then she fell."

"I don't believe that, either."

"Nonsense! What do you believe?"

But I had had enough. I went upstairs to my room. My mind was running in circles. Somebody had killed Elinor and had got away with it. Yet who could have hated her enough for that? A jealous wife? That was possible.

I could see the Hammond place from my window, and the thought of Fred sitting there alone was more than I could bear. Not that I had ever been in love with him, in spite of Mother's hopes. I dressed and went down to dinner, but I couldn't eat. Luckily it was Mother's bridge night, and after she and her three cronies were settled at the table I slipped out through the kitchen.

Annie, the cook, was making sandwiches and cutting cake. I told her to say I had gone to bed if I was asked for, and went out.

Fred's house was only two blocks away, set in its own grounds like ours, and as I entered the driveway I saw a man standing there looking at the place. I must have surprised him, for he turned around and looked at me. It was Dr. Barclay.

He didn't recognize me. He touched his hat and went out to the street, and a moment later I heard his car start. But if he had been in the house Fred did not mention it. I rang, and he opened the door. He seemed relieved when he saw me. "Thought you were the damned police again," he said. "Come in. I've sent the servants to bed."

We went into the library. It looked as if it hadn't been dusted for a month. Elinor's house had always looked that way: full of people and cigarette smoke and used highball glasses. But at least it had looked alive. Now—well, now it didn't. So it was a surprise to see her bag lying on the table. Fred saw me looking at it. "Police returned it today," he said.

"May I look inside it, Fred?"

"Go to it," he said dully. "There's no note there, if that's what you're thinking."

I opened the bag. It was crammed as usual: compact, rouge, coin purse, a zipper compartment with some bills in it, a memorandum book, a handkerchief smeared with lipstick, a tiny perfume vial, and some samples of dress material with a card pinned to them: *Match slippers to these.*

Fred was watching me, his eyes red and sunken. "I told you. Nothing."

I searched the bag again, but I could not find the one thing which should have been there. I closed the bag and put it back on the table.

Fred was staring at a photograph of Elinor in a silver frame. "All this police stuff," he said. "Why can't they just let her rest? She was beautiful, wasn't she, Lou?"

"She was indeed," I said.

"People said things. Margaret thought she was foolish and extravagant." He glanced at the desk, piled high with what looked like unopened bills. "Maybe she was, but what the hell did I care?"

He seemed to expect some comment, so I said, "You didn't have to buy her, Fred. You had her. She was devoted to you."

He gave me a faint smile, like a frightened small boy who has been reassured. "She was, Lou," he said. "I wasn't only her husband. I was her father too. She told me everything. Why she had to go to that damned doctor—"

"Didn't you know she was going, Fred?"

"Not until I found a bill from him," he said grimly. "I told her I could prescribe a rest for her, instead of her sitting for hours with that young puppy. But she only laughed."

He talked on, as if he were glad of an audience. He had made her happy. She went her own way sometimes, but she always came back to him. He considered the coroner's verdict an outrage. "She fell. She was always reckless about heights." And he had made no plans, except that Margaret was coming to stay until he closed the place. And as if the mere mention of her had summoned her, at that minute Margaret walked in.

I had never liked Margaret Hammond. She was a tall angular woman, older than Fred, and she merely nodded to me.

"I decided to come tonight," she said. "I don't like your being alone. And tomorrow I want to inventory the house. I'd like to have Father's portrait, Fred."

He winced at that. There had been a long quarrel about old Joe Hammond's portrait ever since Fred's marriage. Not that Elinor had cared about it, but because Margaret had wanted it she had held on to it. I looked at Margaret. Perhaps she was the nearest to a real enemy Elinor had ever had. She had hated the marriage; had resented Elinor's easy-going extravagant life. Even now, she could not help looking at the desk, piled with bills.

"I'd better straighten that for you, Fred," she said. "We'll have to find out how you stand."

"I know how I stand." He got up and they confronted each other, Fred with his back to the desk, as if even then he were trying to protect Elinor from Margaret's prying eyes.

Fred's sister shrugged and let it go.

It was warm that night. I walked slowly home. I had gone nearly half the way when I realized I was being followed. I stopped and turned. But it was only a girl. She spoke my name. "You're Miss Baring, aren't you?"

"Yes. You scared me half to death."

"I'm sorry. I saw you at the inquest today, and a reporter told me your name. Were you a friend of Mrs. Hammond's?"

"She was my cousin. Why?"

The girl seemed to make a decision. "Because I think she was pushed out that window," she said. "I'm in an office across the street, and I was looking out. I didn't know who she was, of course."

"Do you mean you saw it happen?"

"No. But I saw her at the window hardly a minute before it happened, and she was using a lipstick. When I looked out again she was—she was on the pavement." The girl shivered. "I don't think a woman would use a lipstick just before she did a thing like that, do you?"

"No," I said. "You're sure it was Mrs. Hammond you saw?"

"Yes. She had on a green dress, and I had noticed her hair. She didn't have a hat on. I—well, I went back tonight to see if the lipstick was on the pavement. I couldn't find it. But I'm pretty sure she still had it when she fell."

That was what I had not told Fred—that Elinor's gold lipstick was missing from her bag. "We might go and look again," I said. "Do you mind?"

The girl didn't mind, but she would not tell me her name. "Just call me Smith," she said.

I never saw her again, and unless she reads this she will probably never know that she took the first step that solved the case. Because we found the lipstick in the gutter. A dozen cars must have run over it. It was crushed flat, but Elinor's monogram was perfectly readable.

Miss Smith saw it and gasped. "So I was right," she said. The next minute she had hailed a bus and got on it.

It was late when I got to Dr. Barclay's office the next morning. The reception room was empty, so I went to the window and looked down. I tried to think that I was going to jump, and whether I would use a lipstick or not if I were.

The nurse came in. I gave her my name, and after a short wait she took me to the consulting room.

The doctor got up when he saw me, and I merely put Elinor's lipstick on the desk in front of him and sat down.

"I don't understand," he said.

"Mrs. Hammond was at the window in your reception room using that lipstick only a minute before she fell."

"I suppose you mean it fell with her."

"I mean that she never killed herself. Do you think a woman would rouge her mouth just before she meant to do—what we're supposed to think she did?"

He smiled wryly. "My dear girl, if you saw as much of human nature as I do, that wouldn't surprise you."

"So Elinor Hammond jumped out your window with a lipstick in her hand, and you watch the Hammond house last night and then make a bolt for it when I appear! If that makes sense—"

That shocked him. He hadn't recognized me before. "So it was you in the driveway. Well, I suppose I'd better tell you and trust you to keep it to yourself. I hadn't liked the way Mr. Hammond looked at the inquest. I was afraid he might—well, put a bullet in his head."

"You couldn't stop it standing in the driveway," I said skeptically.

He laughed at that. Then he sobered. "I see," he said. "Well, Miss Baring, whatever happened to Mrs. Hammond, I assure you I didn't do it. As for being outside the house, I've told you the truth. I was wondering how to get in when you came along. His sister had called me up. She was worried."

"I wouldn't rely on what Margaret Hammond says. She hated Elinor."

I got up and retrieved the lipstick. He got up too and surveyed me unsmilingly.

"You're a very young and attractive woman, Miss Baring. Why not let this drop? After all, you can't bring her back."

"I know she never killed herself," I said stubbornly, and went out.

I was less surprised than I might have been to find Margaret in the reception room when I reached it. She was standing close to the open window from which Elinor had fallen, and for a minute I thought she was going to jump herself.

"Margaret!" I said sharply.

She looked terrified when she saw me. "Oh, it's you, Louise," she said. "You frightened me." She sat down abruptly. "She must have slipped, Lou. It would be easy. Try it yourself."

But I shook my head. I had no intention of leaning out that window, not with Margaret behind me. She said she had come to pay Fred's bill for Elinor, and I let it go at that. Nevertheless, I felt shivery as I went down in the elevator.

I had trouble starting my car, which is how I happened to see her when she came out of the building. She looked over the pavement and in the gutter. So she either knew Elinor's lipstick had fallen with her or she had missed it out of the bag.

She didn't see me. She hailed a taxi and got into it. To this day, I don't know why I followed her.

I did follow her, however. The taxi went on into the residential part of town. On a thinly settled street it stopped and Margaret got out. She did not see me or my car. She was looking at a frame house with a narrow front porch, and as I watched, she went up and rang the bell.

She was inside the house for almost an hour. I began to feel idiotic. There were so many possible reasons for her being there; reasons which had nothing to do with Elinor. But when she finally came out I sat up in amazement.

The woman seeing her off on the porch was the Mrs. Thompson of the inquest.

I stooped to fix my shoe as the taxi passed me, but I don't believe Margaret even saw the car. Nor did Mrs. Thompson.

She sat down on the porch and was still there when I went up the steps.

She looked surprised rather than apprehensive. "I hope you're not selling anything," she said, not unpleasantly.

"I'm not selling anything," I said. "May I talk to you?"

"What about?" She was suspicious now.

"It's about a murder," I said. "There's such a thing as being accessory after the fact, and I think you know something you didn't tell at the Hammond inquest."

Her florid color faded. "It wasn't a murder," she said. "The verdict—"

"I know all about that. Nevertheless, I think it was a murder. What was Miss Hammond doing here if it wasn't?"

Mrs. Thompson looked startled, but she recovered quickly. "I never saw her before," she said. "She came to thank me for my testimony, because it showed the poor thing did it herself."

"And to pay you for it, I suppose?"

She flushed angrily. "Nobody paid me anything. And now you'd better go. If you think anybody can bribe me to lie, you're wrong. That's all."

She went in and slammed the door, and I drove back to town, puzzled over the whole business. Was she telling the truth, or had there been something she had not told at the inquest? Certainly I believed that the doctor had known more than he had told.

I was late for lunch that day, and Mother was indignant. "I can't imagine why, with nothing to do, you are always late for meals," she said.

"I've had plenty to do, Mother," I said. "I've been working on Elinor's murder."

She gave a ladylike squeal. "Murder? Who would do such a thing?"

"Well, Margaret for one. She always loathed her."

"Women in Margaret's position in life do not commit crimes," Mother said pontifically. "Really, I don't know what has happened to you, Louise. The idea of suspecting your friends—"

"She's no friend of mine. Elinor was."

"So you'll stir up all sorts of scandal. Murder indeed! I warn you, Louise, if you keep on with this idiotic idea you'll find yourself spread all over the newspapers. And I'll stop your allowance."

With this dire threat she departed, and I spent the afternoon wondering what Dr. Barclay and the Thompson woman knew or suspected, and in getting a wave at Elinor's hairdresser's.

The girl who set my hair told me something I hadn't known. "Here I was, waiting for her," she said. "She was always prompt. Of course she never came, and—"

"You mean you expected her here, the day it happened?"

"That's right," she agreed. "She had an appointment for four o'clock. When I got the paper on my way home I simply couldn't believe it. She'd always been so gay. Of course the last few weeks she hadn't been quite the same, but—"

"How long since you noticed a change in her?" I asked.

"Well, let me see. About Easter, I think. I remember I liked a new hat she had, and she gave it to me then and there! She said a funny thing, too. She said sometimes new hats were dangerous!"

I may have looked better when I left the shop, but my mind was doing pinwheels. Why were new hats dangerous? And why had Elinor changed since Easter?

Fred had dinner with us that evening. At least, he sat at the table and pushed his food around with a fork. Margaret hadn't come. He said she was in bed with a headache, and he spent most of the time talking about Elinor.

It was ghastly, of course. Even Mother looked unhappy. "I wish you'd eat something, Fred," she said. "Try to forget the whole thing. You made her very happy. Always remember that."

I asked him if anything had upset Elinor since Easter. He stared at me.

"I don't remember anything, Lou. Except that she started going to that damned psychiatrist then."

"Why did she go to him, Fred?" Mother inquired. "If she had any inhibitions I never noticed them."

If there was a barb in this, he wasn't aware of it. "You saw him," he said. "He is a good-looking devil. Maybe she liked to look at him. It would be a change from looking at me."

He went home soon after that. In spite of his previous protests, I thought he had resented the doctor's good looks and Elinor's visits to him. And I wondered if he was trying to build up a defense against her in his own mind; to remember her as less than perfect in order to ease his tragic sense of loss.

I slept badly, so I was late for breakfast the next morning. Mother had finished the paper, and I took it.

Tucked away on a back page was an item reporting that Mrs. Thompson had been shot the night before!

I read and reread it. She was not dead, but her condition was critical. All the police had been able to learn from the family was that she had been sitting alone on the front porch when it happened. Nobody had even heard the shot. She had been found by her husband when he came home from a lodge meeting at eleven o'clock. She was unconscious, and the hospital reported her as being still too low to make a statement.

So she had known something, poor thing. Something that

made her dangerous. And again I remembered Margaret going up the steps of the little house on Charles Street; Margaret searching for Elinor's lipstick in the street. Margaret, who had hated Elinor and who was now in possession of Fred, of old Joe Hammond's portrait, of Elinor's silk sheets, and—I suddenly remembered—of Fred's automatic, which had lain in his desk drawer for years.

I think it was the automatic which finally decided me.

Anyhow, I went to our local precinct stationhouse that afternoon and told a man behind a high desk that I wanted to see the person in charge. "He's busy," the man said, eying me indifferently.

"All right," I said. "If he's too busy to look into a murder, then I'll go downtown to Headquarters."

"Who's been murdered?"

"I'll tell *him* that."

There was an officer passing, and the man called him. "Young lady here's got a murder on her mind," he said. "Might see if the captain's busy."

The captain was not busy, but he wasn't interested either. When I told him it was about Elinor Hammond, he said he understood the case was closed, and anyhow, it hadn't happened in his district. As Mrs. Thompson was not in his district either, and as he plainly thought I was either out of my mind or looking for publicity, I finally gave up.

The man behind the desk grinned at me as I went out. "Want us to call for the corpse?" he inquired.

"I wouldn't ask you to call for a dead dog," I told him bitterly.

But there was a result, after all. I drove around the rest of the afternoon trying to decide what to do. When I got home I found Mother in the hall.

"There's a policeman here to see you," she hissed. "What have you done?"

I said, "I haven't done anything. It's about Elinor. I want to see this man alone, Mother."

"I think you're crazy," she said furiously. "It's all over. She got into trouble and killed herself. She was always headed for trouble. The first thing you know you'll be arrested yourself."

She followed me into the living room, and before I could speak to the detective there she told him I had been acting strangely for days and she was going to call a doctor and put me to bed.

"Suppose we let her talk for herself," he said. "Now, Miss Baring, what's all this about a murder?"

So I told him: about Elinor and the lipstick; about her appointment at the hairdresser's for shortly after the time she was lying dead on the pavement; about my conviction that Mrs. Thompson knew something she hadn't told.

"I gather you think Mrs. Hammond didn't kill herself. Is that it?"

"Does it look like it?" I demanded.

"Then who did it?"

"I think it was her sister-in-law."

Mother almost had a fit at that. She got up saying that I was hysterical.

But the detective did not move. "Let her alone," he said gruffly. "What about this sister-in-law?"

"I found her in Dr. Barclay's office yesterday," I said. "She insisted that Elinor had fallen out the window. Maybe it sounds silly, but she knew about the lipstick. She tried to find it in the street. I think she was in the office the day Elinor was killed.

I think the Thompson woman knew it. And I think Margaret Hammond shot her."

"Shot her?" he said sharply. "Is that the woman out on Charles Street?"

"Yes."

He eyed me steadily. "Why do you think Miss Hammond shot her?"

"Because she went there yesterday morning to talk to her. I followed her."

Mother started again. She couldn't understand my behavior. Margaret had been in bed last night with a headache. It would be easy to verify that. The servants . . .

The detective waited patiently and then got up. "I have a little advice for you, Miss Baring," he said. "Leave this to us. If you're right and there's been a murder and a try at another one, that's our job."

It was Mother who went to bed that afternoon, while I waited at the telephone. And when the detective finally called me, the news left me exactly where I had been before. Mrs. Thompson had recovered consciousness and made a statement. She did not know who shot her or why, but she insisted that Margaret had visited her merely to thank her for her testimony, which had shown definitely that Elinor had either fallen or jumped out the window. She had neither been offered nor given any money.

There was more to it, however. It appeared that Mrs. Thompson had been worried since the inquest and had telephoned Margaret to ask her if what bothered her was important. As a matter of fact, someone *had* entered the doctor's office while she was in the hall.

"But it was natural enough," the detective said. "It was the one individual nobody ever really notices. The postman."

"The postman?" I said weakly.

"Exactly. I've talked to him. He saw Mrs. Hammond in the office that morning. He remembers her. She had her hat off, and she was reading a magazine."

"Did he see Mrs. Thompson?"

"He didn't notice her, but she saw him."

"So he shot her last night!"

The detective laughed. "He took his family to the movies last night. And remember this, Miss Baring: that shot may have been an accident. Plenty of people carry guns now who never did before."

It was all very cheerio. Elinor had committed suicide, and Mrs. Thompson had been shot by someone who was practising for Hitler. Only I just didn't believe it. I believed it even less after I had a visit from Dr. Barclay that night.

Mother was still in bed refusing to see me, and I was listening to the radio when the maid showed him in.

"I'm sorry to butt in like this," he said. "I won't take much of your time."

"Then it's not a professional call?"

He looked surprised. "Certainly not. Why?"

"Because my mother thinks I'm losing my mind," I said rather wildly. "Elinor Hammond is dead, so let her lie. Mrs. Thompson is shot, but why worry? Remember the papers! Remember the family name! No scandal, please!"

"You're in bad shape, aren't you? How about going to bed? I'll talk to you later."

"So I'm to go to bed!" I said nastily. "That would be nice and easy, wouldn't it? Somebody is getting away with murder. Maybe two murders. And everybody tries to hush me up. Even the police!"

That jolted him. "You've been to the police?"

"Why not? Why shouldn't the police be told? Just because you don't want it known that someone was pushed out of your office window—"

He was angry, but he tried to control himself. "See here," he said. "You're dealing with things you don't understand. Why can't you stay out of this case?"

"There wasn't any case until I made one," I said furiously. "Why is everybody warning me off? How do I know you didn't do it yourself? You could have. Either you or the postman. And he was at the movies!"

"The postman!" he said, staring. "What do you mean, the postman?"

I suppose it was his astonished face which made me laugh. I laughed and laughed. I couldn't stop. Then I was crying too. I couldn't stop that either. Without warning he slapped my face.

It jerked my head back, but it stopped me. "That's the girl," he said. "You'd have had the neighbors in in another minute. You'd better go up to bed, and I'll send you some sleeping stuff from the drugstore."

"I wouldn't take anything you sent me on a bet."

He ignored that. "Believe it or not," he said, "I didn't come here to attack you! I came to ask you not to go out alone at night until I tell you that you may. I mean what I'm saying," he added. "Don't go out of this house alone at night, Miss Baring—any night."

"Don't be ridiculous!" I said, still raging. "Why shouldn't I go out at night?"

"Because it may be dangerous," he said shortly. "I particularly want you to keep away from the Hammond house."

He banged the front door when he went out, and I spent the next half hour hating him like poison. I was still angry when the phone rang. It was Margaret!

"I suppose we have you to thank for the police coming here tonight," she said. "Why can't you leave us alone? We're in trouble enough, without you making things worse."

"All right," I said recklessly. "Now I'll ask you one. Why did you visit Mrs. Thompson yesterday morning? And who shot her last night?"

She gasped and hung up the receiver.

It was a half hour later when the druggist's boy brought the sleeping tablets. I took them to the kitchen and dropped them in the coal range, while Annie watched me with amazement. She was fixing Mother's hot milk, I remember, and she told me that Clara, the Hammonds' cook, had been over.

"She says things are queer over there," she reported. "Somebody started the furnace last night, and the house was so hot this morning you couldn't live in it."

I didn't pay much attention. I was still shaken. Then I saw Annie look up, and Fred was standing on the kitchen porch.

"May I come in?" he asked. "I was taking a walk and I saw the light."

He looked better, I thought. He said Margaret was in bed, and the house was lonely. Then he asked if Annie would make him a cup of coffee.

"I don't sleep much, anyhow," he said. "It's hard to get adjusted. And the house is hot. I've been getting rid of a lot of stuff. Burning it."

So that explained the furnace.

I walked out with him when he left and watched him as he started home. Then I turned up the driveway again. I was near the house when it happened. I remember the shrubbery rustling, but I never heard the shot. Something hit me on the head. I fell, and after that there was a complete blackout until I heard Mother's voice. I was in my own bed with a bandage around my head and an ache in it that made me dizzy.

"The idea of her going out when you told her not to!" Mother was saying.

"I did my best," said a masculine voice. "But you have a very stubborn daughter."

It was Dr. Barclay. He was standing beside the bed when I opened my eyes. I remember saying, "You slapped me."

"And a lot of good it did," he retorted. "Now look where you are!"

I could see him better by that time. He looked very queer. One of his eyes was almost shut, and his collar was a wilted mess. I stared at him. "What happened?" I asked. "You've been in a fight."

"More or less."

"And what's this thing on my head?"

"That is what you get for disobeying orders."

I began to remember then—the scuffling in the bushes, and something knocking me down. He reached over and took my pulse.

"You've got a very pretty bullet graze on the side of your head," he said. "Also, I've had to shave off quite a bit of your hair." I suppose I wailed at that, for he shifted from my pulse to my hand. "Don't worry about that. It was very pretty hair, but it will grow again. At least, thank God, you're here!"

"Who did it? Who shot at me?"

"The postman, of course," he said, and to my fury went out of the room.

I slept after that. I suppose he had given me something. Anyhow, it was the next morning before I heard the rest of the story. Mother had fallen for Dr. Barclay completely, and she wouldn't let him see me until my best silk blanket cover was on the bed. Even then in a hand mirror I looked dreadful, with my head bandaged and my skin yellowish-gray. The doctor didn't seem to mind, however. He came in, big and smiling, with his right eye completely closed, and told me I looked like the wrath of heaven.

"You're not looking your best yourself," I said.

"Oh, that!" he observed, touching his eye gingerly. "Your mother put a silver knife smeared with butter on it last night. Quite a person, Mother."

He said I was to excuse his appearance, because he had been busy all night with the police. He'd go and clean up.

"You're not moving out of this room until I know what's been going on," I stormed. "I'm running a fever right now, out of pure excitement."

He put a big hand on my forehead. "No fever," he said. "Just your detective mind running in circles. All right. Where do I start?"

"With the postman."

So then he told me. Along in the spring, Elinor had come to him with a queer story. She said she was being followed. It made her nervous. In fact, she was frightened. It seemed that the man who was watching her wore a postman's uniform. She would be having lunch at a restaurant—perhaps with what she called a man friend—and he would be outside a window. He would turn up in all sorts of places. It sounded fantastic, but she swore it was true.

Some faint ray of intelligence came to me. "Do you mean it was this man Mrs. Thompson saw going into your office?"

"She's already identified him. The real letter carrier had been there earlier. He had seen Mrs. Hammond reading a magazine. But he had gone before the Thompson woman arrived. The one she saw was the one who—killed Elinor."

I knew before he told me. I felt sick. "It was Fred, wasn't it?"

"It was Fred Hammond. Yes." Dr. Barclay reached over and took my hand. "Tough luck, my dear. I was worried about it. I tried to get her to go away, but she wouldn't do it. And then she wore a dress at a party with a scarlet *A* on it, and I suppose that finished him."

"It's crazy!" I gasped. "He adored her."

"He had an obsession about her. He loved her, yes. But he was afraid he might lose her. And he was wildly jealous."

"But if he really loved her—"

"The line between love and hate is pretty fine. And it's just possible too that he felt she was never really his until—well, until no one else could have her."

"So he killed her!"

"He killed her," Dr. Barclay said slowly. "He knew that nobody notices the postman, so he walked into my office and—"

"But he was insane," I said. "You can't send him to the chair."

"Nobody will send him to the chair." The doctor hesitated. "I was too late last night. I caught him just as he fired at you, but he put up a real battle. He got loose somehow, and shot himself."

He went on quietly. There was no question of Fred's guilt, he said. Mrs. Thompson had identified his photograph as that of the postman she had seen going into the office and coming out shortly before she heard the nurse screaming. The bullet with which she had been shot had come from Fred's gun. And Margaret—poor Margaret—had been suspicious of his sanity for a long time.

"She came to see me yesterday after she learned the Thompson woman had been shot. She wanted her brother committed to an institution, but she got hysterical when I mentioned the police. I suppose there wasn't much of a case, anyhow. With Mrs. Thompson apparently dying and the uniform gone—"

"Gone? Gone how?"

"He'd burned it in the furnace. We found some charred buttons last night."

"Why did he try to kill Mrs. Thompson?" I asked. "What did she know? "

"She remembered seeing a postman going in and out of my office. She even described him. And Margaret found the uniform in the attic. She knew then.

"She collapsed. She couldn't face Fred. She locked herself in her room, trying to think what to do. But she had told Fred she was going to see Mrs. Thompson that day, and she thinks perhaps he knew she had found the uniform. She doesn't know, nor do I. All we do know is that he left this house that night, got out his car and tried to kill the only witness against him. Except you, of course."

"Except me!" I said.

"Except you," the doctor repeated dryly. "I tried to warn you, you may remember!"

"But why me? He had always liked me. Why would he try to kill me?"

"Because you wouldn't leave things alone. Because you were a danger from the minute you insisted Elinor had been murdered. And because you asked Margaret on the phone why she had visited Mrs. Thompson, and who had shot her."

"You think he was listening in?"

"I know he was listening in. He wasn't afraid of his sister. She would have died to protect him, and he knew it. But here you were, a child with a stick of dynamite, and you come out with a thing like that! That was when Margaret sent me to warn you."

"I'm sorry. I've been a fool all along."

The doctor's good eye twinkled. "I wouldn't go so far as that," he said. "That stubbornness of yours really broke the case. Not that I like stubborn women."

I had difficulty in getting him back to the night before. But he finally admitted that he had been watching the Hammond house all evening, and that when Fred came to our kitchen door he had been just outside. Fred had seemed quiet, drinking his coffee. Then I had walked out to the street with him.

It had looked all right at first. Fred had started down the street toward home, and he followed behind the hedge. But he lost him, and he knew he was on his way back. Fred had his revolver lifted to shoot me when he grabbed him.

Suddenly I was crying. It was all horrible: Elinor at the window, and Fred behind her; Mrs. Thompson resting after a hard day's work, and Fred shooting her. And I myself—

Dr. Barclay got out a grimy handkerchief and dried my eyes. "Stop it," he said. "It's all over now, and you're a plucky young woman, Louise Baring. Don't spoil the record." He rose abruptly. "I'm giving up your case. There'll be someone in to dress that head of yours."

"Why can't you do it?"

"I'm not that sort of doctor."

I looked up at him. He was haggard with strain. He was dirty, he needed a shave, and that eye of his was getting blacker by the minute. But he was big and strong and sane. A woman would be safe with him, I thought. Although she could never tell him her dreams.

"I don't see why you can't look after me," I said. "If I'm to look bald I'd prefer you to see it. After all, you did it."

He grinned. Then to my surprise he leaned down and kissed me lightly on the cheek. "I've wanted to do that ever since you slammed that lipstick down in front of me," he said. "And now will you please stop being a detective and concentrate on growing some hair on the side of your head? Because I'm going to be around for a considerable time."

When I looked up Mother was in the doorway, beaming.

TOO MANY SLEUTHS
Vincent Starrett

Along with Christopher Morley, one could make the case that (Charles) Vincent (Emerson) Starrett (1886-1974) was arguably America's greatest bibliophile. He was named a Grand Master by the Mystery Writers of America in 1958, more for his countless essays, biographical works, critical studies, and bibliographical pieces on a wide range of authors and subjects, than for his mystery fiction, though he wrote six well-regarded detective novels and scores of mystery short stories.

His non-fiction appeared in numerous journals and magazines but most famously in the "Books Alive" column in the *Chicago Tribune*, which he wrote for twenty-five years. Many of his best articles were collected in such treasured volumes as *Buried Caesars* (1923), *Penny Wise and Book Foolish* (1929), *Books Alive* (1940), *Bookman's Holiday* (1942), *Autolycus in Limbo* (1943), and *Books and Bipeds* (1947). He also wrote *Best Loved Books of the 20ᵗʰ Century* (1955), which covered fifty-two major works, and a memoir, *Born in a Bookshop* (1965), a must-read for bibliophiles.

His great affection for the printed word and crime fiction

made it almost inevitable that several of his fictional works fall into the bibliomystery category. They are infused with that rare combination of enthusiasm for the sub-genre plus profound knowledge of the subject.

His most famous is certainly "The Unique Hamlet," which features an inscribed copy of Shakespeare's most famous play. When it goes missing, Sherlock Holmes is called upon to locate it and return it to the rightful owner. It was privately printed in 1920 in a limited hardcover edition and was selected for *Queen's Quorum*, Ellery Queen's selection of the one hundred six most important volumes of detective fiction ever written.

Among his other bibliomystery stories are "A Volume of Poe" (1929) and the present story, which features a bookseller amateur detective.

"Too Many Sleuths" was originally published in the October 1927 issue of *Real Detective Tales and Mystery Stories*; it was first collected in *The Blue Door* (New York, Doubleday, 1930).

Too Many Sleuths
Vincent Starrett

1.

Miss Lambert's pretty maid paused in the doorway and addressed her mistress' back—that part of it that was visible above the faded brocade of an old chair.

"I won't be gone but a jiffy, Miss Lambert," she said. "I'll be back in no time at all. It's raining out, so I'm taking the umbrella." Her head inside the closing door, she added: "I'll be back in just a jiffy."

The straight, spinster back of Miss Harriet Lambert stiffened slightly. "You be careful of that umbrella, Lucy," said the voice of Miss Lambert, acidly. "It's the best umbrella I've got."

The article in question was the *only* umbrella Miss Lambert had, and so her observation, the maid knew, was strictly accurate.

The corners of the little maid's mouth drew downward for a moment. She made a wry face at the narrow shoulders of her mistress, rigidly encased in black satin, and showed a pink morsel of her tongue. "I'll be very careful, Miss Lambert," she promised, closing the door.

At the *click* of the latch, Miss Lambert rose to her feet and marched resolutely to the door that had just closed. Yes, the patent spring lock had snapped, and she was quite safe. She was locked in, and she was quite, quite safe. She listened for a moment and heard the outer door close after her vanishing servant. Then, returning to her seat before the wood fire that crackled in the grate, she resumed her tireless immobility.

Her eyes, somewhat faded like her dress, resumed their complacent consideration of the gew-gaws that decked her mantel. They were pretty little things, and they were *hers*. She smiled happily in the serene knowledge that they were hers. Pretty little things.

Lucy, too, was a pretty little thing; but it would be like her to leave the umbrella at the corner shop and have to go back for it. And, like as not, when she went back for it, it would be gone. That was the way things went. Still, rain or no rain, one must have one's evening paper. Life was so filled with deliciously horrible events that, otherwise, one would never hear about.

Miss Lambert shuddered pleasantly and thought of her jewels, hidden safely in the bedroom closet. Possibly, in the paper, there would be some new and hideous account of brutal murder, committed for just such treasures. Life was a dreadful thing. Times without number, old gentlewomen, living in single blessedness, had been horribly done to death for their pitiful little hoards, the savings of a lifetime. She lay back against her cushions and clutched the edges of her seat with tense, white fingers.

What her collection of brooches, rings, and pendants was worth she knew to the fraction of a dollar. It was worth twenty thousand dollars, if it was worth a penny.

Again she rose to her feet and tried the door, and again she was relieved to find it secure. It was exactly as she had left it a moment before. The patent spring lock still held against the bloody terrors that filled the outside world.

Miss Lambert returned to her seat before the fire and drowsed gently against her chair back. Her eyes traced the pattern of the rug upon which her feet rested, the delightful rug that had been given to her, years before, by Grandma Gilchrist. It was a lovely rug, and it was *hers*. Everything around her was hers. The umbrella had been a gift from Mr. Spurgeon, the lawyer, who would run upstairs to help her in case of trouble. All she had to do was knock upon the floor and Mr. Spurgeon, if he were at home, would run right up to her. It was a distressing thought that Mr. Spurgeon was not always at home, but Lucy would soon return. . . . And then the patter of the rain upon the little maid's umbrella became the rattle of many fingers upon a door that shut out all the newspapers of the world with spring locks of patent rings and brooches . . . and the rug that had been Grandma Gilchrist's rose up before her and bowed with the smile of Mr. Spurgeon the lawyer. . . .

Miss Lambert dozed against the faded brocade of the old chair back and did not wake until the sound of a key, in the lock behind her, told her that Lucy had returned with the evening paper.

She was really only partly awake when she half rose from her chair and turned, just in time to miss the full force of the blow that fell sidewise upon her head from behind. But it was sufficient to pitch her across the chair arm and to the floor, where she lay with sprawling arms clutching vaguely at the darkness that came and went within her brain.

She bleated feebly like a frightened sheep, and groped upward to her knees, reaching blindly for other knees that seemed to recede from her grasp. In the fleeting instant between the first blow and the second her brain bridged incredible intervals of time and thought, and she knew that she must knock upon the floor. With a dreadful joy she knew that at length her fears were being realized. It was, in its way, a moment of triumph.

And then, in an ecstasy of terror, she saw that the rug which had been Grandma Gilchrist's had reared itself upright and was rushing down upon her with the fury of a whirlwind.

2.

THE MURDER of Miss Harriet Lambert shocked the community. The morning newspapers were filled with it, and as usual there was a great deal of talk about the inadequacy of police protection in the outlying districts. Nonetheless, the police were doing their best to solve the mystery.

It really *was* a mystery. Two persons apparently had seen the murderer making his escape, without either quite suspecting what was going on. The fellow had been remarkably cool about it, and he was now very much at large. The two who had seen him and were prepared to identify him, if caught, were Robert

Spurgeon, the middle-aged lawyer who lived in the basement apartment beneath that of Miss Lambert, and Lucy Andrus, Miss Lambert's maid. So ran the newspaper accounts.

Spurgeon's story and that of Miss Andrus, as told to the police, were related at length in the news sheets. They were also related at length by Frederick Dellabough to his friend Troxell the bookseller. Dellabough, police reporter for the *Morning Telegram*, often took his problems to Troxell, and frequently received valuable assistance.

G. Washington Troxell—with a futile gesture he concealed a preliminary George—listened with attention to the reporter's account of the murder. A half inch of cigarette glowed intermittently under his straggling mustache; his whimsical little eyes seemed lost in rolls of surrounding pink tissue. To the ceiling, on three walls of his dusty little shop, he was surrounded by books—books old and new, books rare and fine, and books for which nobody with sense would pay a penny.

"Hmph!" observed Mr. Troxell, when he had heard the subject of the journalist's report. "I was just beginning to read about it."

Young Mr. Dellabough gestured deprecatingly. "I can tell you what's in the *Telegram*," he said. "I wrote it. The marvel is, Mr. Troxell, that she lived as long as she did. Three neighbors, called in by the maid's screams, saw her die—as well as Spurgeon and Lucy Andrus. All five heard her last words. They thought she was already dead, when suddenly she moved and tried to rise."

The reporter leaned forward in his chair. He spoke in a lower tone of voice, as if he had something secret to communicate. "It was hard to tell what she said, but it sounded like, 'The carpet . . . it rose up!' Next minute, she was really gone."

Washington Troxell stirred obesely in his seat. He was usually most flippant and cynical when he was most deeply moved. He glanced at a shelf of fairy tales, and back at the narrator.

"Magic carpet!" he murmured. "Very interesting."

"Of course she was raving," added Dellabough.

Mr. Troxell carefully removed his fragment of cigarette, burned his fingers, swore, and at length deposited the thing in a tray.

"Why?" he asked.

"It's crazy," answered the reporter, "perfectly crazy—unless she meant that the man came up through the floor, pushed the carpet aside, and then attacked her."

"What do Spurgeon and the maid think?"

"I'll tell you the whole story," said Dellabough. "About seven o'clock, Spurgeon was in his sitting room, immediately beneath that of Miss Lambert. He heard a noise in the room above. It was a distinct thump on the floor, as if the old lady had fallen out of her chair. An instant later there were three knocks on the floor—his signal. For months he had been subconsciously waiting for sounds of disaster. Miss Lambert was old and jumpy, and he had promised her that if she ever knocked on the floor he would run up to her. She was the sort of woman, you see, who is constantly afraid that something is going to happen to her."

The bookseller nodded. "I know them," he commented. "Something *ought* to happen to them."

"Well, something did, in this case," said the reporter. "Time and again, she told Spurgeon, and most of the neighbors too, that she *knew* something would happen to her. She almost insisted upon it. Of course, it was her jewels she was thinking about, and it was her jewels that the fellow got—thousands of dollars' worth of them, I guess. Old family stuff, you know. Anyway, she worried Spurgeon so much that he was always unconsciously listening for the knocks on the floor that would call him upstairs. He thinks she may have had some secret knowledge of a plot against her life—she always seemed so *certain.*"

"What did Spurgeon do when he heard her fall?"

"He jumped out of his chair and ran upstairs. At the head of the stairs he noticed that the inner corridor door stood open, although the outer door was closed. Miss Lambert's door was closed and locked; it locked with a spring lock. Well, he stood outside the door for a minute and listened; then, just as he put his hand on the knob and tried it, he heard another sound inside. He couldn't identify it, but it sounded like the breaking of sticks."

"Sticks? Was there a fireplace?"

"Yes, and there was a fire in it. You're thinking what *I* thought—that what he heard was somebody getting ready to burn something. But Spurgeon was excited and flustered, and he wondered if the sounds he had heard before might not have been perfectly natural ones. That is, he thought the servant was inside, breaking up some kindling for the fireplace, and that she had upset a chair, maybe—which would be the fall he had heard. Then he remembered the knocks, and didn't know what to think. There was a bell in the side wall, alongside the door, and he rang it three times without answer.

"Then he decided to break in; but just as he stood there, bracing himself, the outer door opened—the street door—and the maid came in. It seemed she had been out buying a paper for the old lady, and she was carrying the paper and a dripping umbrella. She saw Spurgeon at the door, and asked him what the trouble was. He told her what he had heard, and she thought at once, of course, that something had happened to Miss Lambert. All this takes time to tell, but actually it happened inside of a very few minutes."

"Was the maid excited?" asked Troxell, deeply interested. He was almost squirming with happiness. There was nothing he loved so much as a good mystery.

"She was very much excited. She got out her key, and Spurgeon took it and unlocked the door. I suppose they both expected somebody to spring out at them; but instead of that a very curious thing happened. Miss Lambert's sitting room lay before them, darkened except for the low fire in the grate, but there was a light going in the room beyond—that is, off to the right—which was Miss Lambert's bedroom. And just as they opened the door a well-dressed man came out of the bedroom, and turned and bowed to somebody he appeared to be leaving. He was so cool, and so polite, that they just stood there staring.

"His back was to them when he turned, and he was speaking. He said, 'Well, thank you very much, Miss Lambert, and I'm sorry to have been a trouble. I'll look in again, then, next week.' And with that he bowed again, turned, nodded in a friendly way to the two people in the doorway, pushed past them, and went quietly out into the street."

Washington Troxell hugged himself with pleasure. "Splendid!" he cried. "Perfectly splendid! The fellow was an artist. Of course, once in the street, he ran like hell."

Dellabough agreed gloomily. "He's probably still running," he observed. "Oh, yes, he was cool enough! Spurgeon and Miss Andrus, of course, were flabbergasted. They vaguely suspected something wrong, but apparently they had seen a friend leaving Miss Lambert with expressions of good-will. In a minute Spurgeon recovered his wits, groped around and found the switch in the sitting room, and flooded the place with light. Then they saw it."

"Absolutely beautiful," commented the bookseller.

"Not exactly," demurred Dellabough dryly. "The old lady's head had been pretty badly battered. I've seen the body."

"I mean the man's escape," said Troxell.

"Well, what do you think of the case?" demanded the reporter. "Have you any suggestions?"

"I suppose you have a description of the man? Spurgeon and Miss Andrus could have given you that."

"They did what they could. It was pretty dark, though, before Spurgeon snapped on the lights. Spurgeon saw a man a little taller than himself, and a little heavier, well featured and clean-shaven. Also a light overcoat, and—he *thought*—dark trousers. He thought the man was carrying something in his hand."

"Probably his hat," said Troxell.

Dellabough appeared surprised. "Why, yes," he agreed, "I suppose it was, now that you mention it. Funny it hadn't occurred to me."

"You were thinking about the jewels, or the weapon, I suppose. Those would be in his pocket. Or was the weapon found?"

"No, it wasn't. A hammer might have done the job—or a burglar's jimmy. Something like that. Something fairly heavy, anyway."

"How was the body lying?"

"Well, her feet were toward the door and her head toward the fireplace. But her head had been covered with a hearth rug. The injuries were frightful."

"Hmph!" said Washington Troxell. "There's your carpet, Dellabough! She wasn't dead when he covered her with the rug.

She saw it coming down on her, and it was the last thing she remembered."

The reporter applauded softly. "Muffed again," he observed. "I seem to miss all the easy ones. You're right, of course."

"But how about the maid's identification?" continued the bookseller. "How did it tally with Spurgeon's?"

"Approximately the same, except for three features. The maid thought he had a little mustache, a slightly crooked nose, and that he had some peculiarity in his gait."

"In his gait?" Troxell appeared surprised. "Was the corridor lighted?"

"Only faintly, I believe."

"She must have watched him pretty closely. He could hardly have taken half a dozen steps between Miss Lambert's bedroom and the door where the maid stood. The irregularity would have had to be pretty noticeable to be caught in that distance. It's odd that Spurgeon didn't see it, too."

Dellabough shrugged expressively.

"The fact is," he said, "both Spurgeon and Miss Andrus were completely bewildered, as I have suggested. They tried hard to remember what they had seen, and they may have thought—later—they saw things that they didn't. It's a common experience."

"Well, go on," said the bookseller.

"That's all."

"Surely not! What did Spurgeon and Miss Andrus do after the man had made his escape?"

"Oh! Spurgeon, as I said, snapped on the lights in the sitting room, and looked around him; and Miss Andrus ran into the bedroom. She called to Spurgeon that the place had been robbed."

"She didn't see the body as she crossed the room?"

"Apparently not. It was partly concealed by a chair."

"Even so, one would think that she would have looked at the chair. She undoubtedly left Miss Lambert sitting in it. I suppose her mind was on the jewels. Most women's minds are on jewels, or something similar. How did she know so quickly that the place had been robbed?"

"The box that had contained the jewels was on the bed in the bedroom, broken open and empty."

"I see! That was the 'breaking of sticks' that Spurgeon heard, I suppose."

"I suppose so. That's one that I got by myself."

G. Washington Troxell lighted a fresh cigarette, settled himself comfortably in his huge chair, and managed with an effort to cross his legs.

"I should really like to visit the scene," he said at last; "but of course that's out of the question. I can't and I won't. Besides, the actual sight of everything would probably upset my reasoning. I think much better at a distance from the scene. That way, I get only the essentials as reported by my clever friend Dellabough. Who knew about Miss Lambert's jewels?"

"Everybody in the place, I imagine," replied the reporter morosely. "She made no secret of her fears, anyway. She bothered everybody to death with them, and probably with her jewels too."

"It was a fearful joy she snatched from them," agreed the bookseller. "Well, there are a lot of things to be discovered. They have all occurred to you, no doubt?"

"Oh, no doubt!" grinned Dellabough. "Still, you might enumerate them. I may have missed one or two."

"It occurs to me," Washington Troxell lay back in his chair and blew a thin geyser of smoke at the ceiling of his shop—"it occurs to me that the murderer may have known where the jewels were kept. Certainly he found them without much difficulty. Who could have told him that? Or does the circumstance presuppose a previous acquaintance with the inside of the flat and the ways of its occupant? It occurs to me, also, that he chose an admirable time for his performance. He entered the apartment when its second occupant—the maid, Lucy Andrus—was out. Did he know that she would be out, or was it pure chance that took him there at so fortuitous a moment?"

Dellabough was scribbling furiously on a pad of paper that he had snatched from the bookseller's desk.

"If he knew that Lucy Andrus was out, how did he know it? Was it common knowledge that she went out every evening at that hour to get a paper?"

"I believe it *was*," interrupted Dellabough. "She did it every night, and probably the neighborhood knew it."

The bookseller nodded.

"But he should also have known that she would be back in a few minutes, and he should not have tarried until her arrival. However, perhaps he tried to time himself properly, and missed. Lucy's afternoon out would have been a better time, though. Is he a working man, who could not get away in the afternoon? That he is someone who knew about the jewels goes without saying. Who, other than the neighbors, might know about the jewels? What tradesmen come to the house? What plumbers? What friends? What neighbors, for that matter?"

"She had few friends," said Dellabough. "Very few visitors, I understand."

"So I should imagine. She talked people to death about herself, and so—finally—talked herself to death, as it were. One really can't feel particularly sorry for her, you know. She was a confounded nuisance, Dellabough, and there will be few to miss her, I suspect. Still, somebody murdered her, and murder is a practice that should either be discouraged or legalized."

He chuckled cynically.

"Finally, Mr. Frederick Dellabough, how did the murderer get into the apartment?"

"I thought of that," said Dellabough. "It's a facer. He had a key, that's certain. There was no sign of *force*, back, front, or at the windows."

"All right! Where did he get his key? Where and when did he have an opportunity to steal one, or to see one and have a duplicate made? Who gave him one?"

"Of course, there's an alternative," suggested the reporter.

"That he was *let* in? I know! It's a valid line of inquiry. Very well, who *let* him in? There are two alternatives there. If he was let in, he was let in by either Miss Lambert herself, or by Lucy Andrus before she went out. There are difficulties both ways. If Miss Lambert let him in, after the maid had gone out, then he was known to her. Otherwise, he would have struck her down at the door. And I can't quite conceive of the old lady letting *anybody* in, or even answering the doorbell. Certainly she didn't open the door, then calmly turn her back and stroll over to her chair.

"On the other hand, if he was let in by Lucy Andrus, how and when was it done? You may be sure that her mistress kept a sharp eye on Lucy, and knew what was going on most of the time. It would be possible, but exceedingly difficult, for the maid to introduce a man into the house. I think of only one way it could have been done with comparative safety. It *might* have been done just as the maid went out; that is, as Lucy Andrus opened the door to go out, the man might have slipped in. In that case, the murder must have occurred immediately after the maid's departure—even before she had got down the steps. The time element must be carefully checked. Spurgeon ought to be able to help there. If he happens to know the exact moment he heard the fall in the room above him, it can be checked against the time of the maid's departure. How long was she away? How long did Spurgeon stand in the corridor before he saw her come in? These are all pertinent and important questions, Dellabough." Mr. Troxell swelled out his chest and beamed amiably upon his friend.

"You think the maid is in on this, do you?" asked Dellabough, reaching for his hat.

"Good God, no!" exploded G. W. Troxell. "I merely think she *may* have been. I'm suggesting lines of inquiry that may lead only to eliminations; but eliminations have their value. It's a good thing, Dellabough, that you have *me* to come to in matters of this sort. If you hadn't, you'd be selling box lunches to the factory girls."

"All right, all *right!*" said Dellabough soothingly. "And, say— many thanks!"

He went happily away. Mr. Dellabough of the *Telegram* also thought it was a good thing that he knew G. Washington Troxell. It saved him a great deal of thinking.

3.

THEN, TO complicate matters, a cloud of witnesses appeared; in point of fact, there were twelve of them. They came forward with a great clatter, after the blanket invitation of the police had been published by the press. All lived in the neighborhood of the Lambert apartment, and all had seen a man loitering in the street during the weeks that preceded the murder.

The information would have been more valuable if they had been able to agree about the man's appearance. When their stories had been heard and sifted there emerged a weird mixture of derby hats, green caps, motor caps, and gray felts that created a confused and indefinite impression as to the head covering worn by the lounger in the street. Gray spats and checked trousers even figured in one description, and there was a wide difference of opinion about the man's upper lip. He wore a large mustache, he wore a small mustache, and he wore no mustache at all.

Dellabough, who was not a novice, threw his hands into the air and consigned them all to perdition and the police.

The thirteenth person to come forward, however, was one Thomas Gray, an amiable youth who played billiards in a local cue parlor no great distance from the scene of the crime. Young Mr. Gray, with a shrewd notion in his head that information was paid for, came forward with a story to tell. It appeared that one of the occasional visitors at the cue parlor frequented by Thomas Gray had been trying to sell a pawn ticket, which pawn ticket—when presented with a sum of money—was good for one crescent diamond brooch. What was more, the occasional visitor in question bore a general resemblance to the man seen and described by Spurgeon and Lucy Andrus.

This time, Dellabough threw his hat into the air, and hurried off to the address that had been furnished the police by Gray. In the small flat three blocks removed from the Lambert apartment he found a posse of detectives and listened to discouraging news.

Mr. and Mrs. Otto Sandow, late of that address, had left only the day before, for parts unknown.

"He didn't leave the pawn ticket, I suppose?" inquired Dellabough facetiously.

"He *didn't*," agreed Detective Sergeant Grimwood, "but if the brooch is in the city we'll get it without a ticket."

"*Can* you?" queried the reporter.

"We *can!*"

"How?" Mr. Dellabough was hoping for a lead that would enable *him* to find the piece of jewelry first.

Detective Sergeant Grimwood waved a jaunty hand. "Oh, there's *ways!*" he replied. After a moment he added: "We've got the pawnbrokers about where we want 'em, and when the word goes out what we're after, somebody'll come across with it."

The informant Gray stood idly by, half triumphant and half chagrined. His information had been a sensation, all right, but much good it had done anybody, to date! Dellabough eyed the billiard player with speculative glance.

"Say," he ventured, "is there any law against my talking to Mr. Gray?" The detective having guessed not, he addressed himself to the informant. "How much did Sandow want for the ticket?"

"Twenty dollars," said Gray, smiling.

"Hell!" observed the reporter. "I'd have given him *that* myself."

"So would I," said Gray, "if I'd had the twenty."

"Didn't he have any friends who could tell us where he's gone?"

"If he did, I don't know them. He didn't come into the parlor very often. Even Ed Lewis, the manager, didn't know him very well. He didn't play much; just hung around and watched the others."

"What did he look like?"

"Fairly tall, dark man, with a little black mustache. A German, I think."

"Anything wrong with his nose?"

"N-no, I don't think so. Mr. Grimwood asked me that, too. He had a big nose—big enough, anyway—and it was humped in the middle, if that's what you mean. Kind of a Jew nose."

"He certainly sounds like the man, doesn't he?" The reporter turned to the detective in charge.

"Oh, he's the man, all right," said Grimwood. "He answers to the description—near enough, anyway. Descriptions are never accurate. And he pawned a diamond brooch, that's certain. And finally, he's skipped. That's good enough to work on, I guess."

"How about his walk? He didn't limp, did he? Or *did* he?"

"Not that I ever noticed," answered Gray.

"He may have limped purposely, while Spurgeon and the maid were looking at him," suggested Grimwood.

"Or he may have hurt his leg while murdering the old woman," added Dellabough. "He pawned the brooch, I suppose, to get money enough to skip. The fact that he tried to sell the ticket would suggest that he didn't intend to redeem it. Look here, Grimwood: He may have *sold* the ticket, at that! Gray didn't buy it, but maybe somebody else did."

"I know. We've got to work fast. I've already made a report. In an hour there'll be a dozen men working the pawnshops. My job is to get Sandow."

Dellabough went away to a telephone and made his own report.

"Well," said his editor, "keep after it. If we could beat the police it would be great stuff, you know."

Keep after what? The admonition was typical of the vague orders of swivel-chair commanders, thought the reporter. The police were after the Lambert family brooch. Grimwood—a good man—was after Sandow. Nobody suspected the maid, however—unless it was Troxell. All right, he would pump the maid.

He sought the scene of the crime, and found Lucy Andrus and a big policeman in charge of the premises.

"Ever hear of a man named Sandow?" he asked, when the preliminary courtesies had been observed.

"No, sir," answered Lucy Andrus, "I don't think I ever did."

"He looks like the man you saw coming out of Miss Lambert's bedroom," continued Dellabough. "As far as you know, you had never seen *that* man before, had you?"

"Oh, no, sir!"

"He didn't remind you of anybody who ever called on Miss Lambert?"

"Not a bit; no, sir. Not many people called on Miss Lambert."

"How about the people who delivered things to her? Grocery boys and that sort of thing."

"I knew them all; every one of them. I used to do all the shopping, you see. Sometimes I brought things home, and sometimes they were delivered; but I knew all the delivery boys."

She was a pretty girl, the reporter noted; he could well believe that all the delivery boys knew her.

"How long have you been working here, Miss Andrus?"

"More than a year, I guess."

"Who was here before you were?"

"There was a girl named Molly. I don't know her other name. Miss Lambert used to just talk about Molly."

"Why did Molly leave?"

"I don't know."

The reporter tried a new line. "Did any of *your* friends ever come here to see you?"

The maid hesitated. It was one of the simple questions that the police had forgotten to ask. The burly bluecoat, who was giving an imitation of an absentminded man looking out of a window, pricked up his ears and listened for the reply.

"Well," said Lucy Andrus reluctantly, "only one."

Dellabough smiled his most seductive smile. "Nobody suspects him, of course," he explained, more or less truthfully, "but it's necessary, you see, to find out about everybody who ever came here. That's why I ask. Who was your friend, Miss Andrus? Or, to be accurate, who *is* your friend?"

"He *ain't* my friend any *more*," answered the maid, accepting the question literally. "He *used* to be my friend, but we don't go together any more. His name is Oscar," she added: "Oscar Slaney."

Oscar Slaney! Something in the name puzzled the reporter. Yet he was certain he had never heard it before. Why, then, should it strike him with a peculiar significance? He was immensely sensitive, he knew, to impressions, and somehow the name filled him with a sense of familiarity. Had he read it in the paper at some time?

"When did you and—ah—Oscar—stop going together?" he asked.

"Oh, a long time ago! Months ago!"

"He used to come to the house to see you, did he?"

"He was only here once or twice. Miss Lambert let me have him."

So Miss Lambert had met this Slaney, in all probability. She would have known him by sight if he had come to her door. Dellabough remembered the reflections of G. Washington Troxell and felt that he was getting "warm."

"What was he?" he continued. "I mean, what did he *do?*"

Again the maid hesitated. "It ain't really against him, you know," she said at last. "He was—what you call a—a bookmaker."

Hoop-la! Mr. Dellabough's pulses leaped. Now he was *get-*

ting somewhere! Oscar Slaney was a bookmaker, a race-track gambler!

"He was a good enough man," added Lucy Andrus. "I stopped going with him because he had another girl."

A good enough man! That was amusing, thought Dellabough. Well, maybe he was. But—as a new thought struck him—bookmakers liked to hang out in billiard parlors! And Otto Sandow—!

Mr. Dellabough glanced furtively at the policeman in the window. No doubt the fellow was listening, for all his apparent preoccupation. He would report all that he heard to his superiors. And suddenly Mr. Frederick Dellabough knew why the name of Oscar Slaney had rung familiarly in his ears. It was the man's initials that had struck him. *O. S.* Oscar Slaney! Otto Sandow!

"O Sunshine!" murmured Mr. Dellabough to himself.

He drew a long breath and began a masterly retreat.

"Well, it's probably unimportant," he observed. "I suppose you haven't seen Mr. Slaney lately?"

The maid had not.

Greatly cheered, the reporter took his hat and his departure. There were sundry and divers ways, after all, of looking up bookmakers. To himself, as he railroaded toward the Loop, Dellabough admitted that he was a good reporter. He marshaled his arguments, then subdivided them and passed them in review before him. Thus revealed, they grouped themselves somewhat as follows:

(*a*) Otto Sandow is undoubtedly Oscar Slaney, or vice versa.

(*b*) As Oscar Slaney he visited Lucy Andrus, and met Miss Lambert.

(*c*) Lucy Andrus, wittingly or unwittingly, revealed to him the secret of Miss Lambert's wealth. Not that it was much of a secret!

(*d*) Slaney, or Sandow, had stolen or borrowed Lucy's key long enough to make a wax impression, and then had returned it.

(*e*) Months later, when he was no longer visiting Lucy Andrus, and was therefore less liable to be suspected, he had returned and let himself into the house, knowing, of course, just when Lucy would be out on her errand. Knowing, obviously, just where to find the jewels. Lucy must have told him where they were!

This last consideration, of course, might mean that the maid was implicated, as Troxell had seemed to suggest. If so, she probably knew now exactly where to find Sandow. Might not Lucy Andrus, indeed, *lead* him ultimately to Sandow? Wherefore, the thing to do was to watch Lucy Andrus.

His flow of ideas ended abruptly. However, he was satisfied with his progress.

Highly delighted by these evidences of his own perspicacity, the clever young man betook himself to a large downtown pool room, where he was known, and where he proceeded to lose three straight games of pool to a very inferior cue artist. He knew that it was an establishment frequented by sporting characters—and by bookmakers.

When this had all been accomplished he approached the friendly manager and engaged him in conversation.

"By the way," he said casually, "what's become of Oscar Slaney? That race-track fellow, you know! Didn't he used to drop in here occasionally?"

"He drops in now occasionally," answered the manager. "He

was here only a little while ago. I saw him shaking dice at the cigar counter. What do you want him for?"

"I don't—particularly," asserted Dellabough untruthfully. "I want a friend of his, and I can't find him. I thought maybe Slaney could give me a line on him."

Circuitously he approached the cigar stand and purchased a handful of cigars. While he elaborately lighted one he observed between puffs to the man behind the counter: "I thought I saw Slaney here, a little while ago. He didn't say where he was going, I suppose?"

The cigar clerk jerked a thumb at the telephone booth, on the other side of the room. "He's telephoning," he explained briefly.

"Oh, thanks," said Dellabough, and strolled to the other side of the room. God, what luck! he told himself.

Passing the booth, he glanced within and had a good look at his victim. He was a husky fellow, this Slaney! And he fulfilled the terms of the composite description. Why, Lucy Andrus in *her* description had almost photographed the man!

It was odd, the reporter reflected. The maid had actually described Slaney as the man she had seen emerging from Miss Lambert's room on the night of the murder; yet she had positively denied ever having seen the man before. Questioned, she had been slightly reluctant to mention Slaney's name; yet she had done so, after a moment of hesitation. Had she not been afraid she was putting his neck in a halter?

By Jove! If Slaney *limped* it would explain the maid's perfect knowledge of the man, even on the night of the crime! Wouldn't it? And it would also mean that she had lied when she said she didn't recognize the murderer.

Dellabough sauntered back and forth until the suspect

emerged from the booth, and at that instant contrived to be at the far end of the room. He followed Slaney slowly to the stairway, saw him descend, and followed at the same pace. He *didn't* limp. That was awkward.

In the street, the bookmaker struck out at a brisk pace that kept the reporter busy keeping him in sight. The business district, with its huge crowds, was no place for shadowing a man. Panic-stricken, Dellabough did his best, and on the boulevard, outside a great hotel, had the satisfaction of seeing his quarry meet a young woman.

Stalking the pair cautiously, he soon knew that the young woman was *not* Lucy Andrus. They moved over to a corner and, after a short wait, caught a north-bound bus. Dellabough, running hard, caught up with it and swung on board, much to the disgust of the conductor. As his victims had climbed to the top, the reporter went inside and took a seat near the last right-hand window, where he could see all who alighted.

The pair he was following got off at a street on the near North Side of the city, and strolled leisurely eastward. Dellabough alighted while the bus was in motion, again to the huge disgust of the conductor, and followed. The suspects turned up a flight of steps halfway along the block. Strolling past, the reporter noted the number of the house. At the next corner he turned and strolled back. The young man was coming down the steps. The young woman had gone inside.

Dellabough slowed his walk to a gentle saunter that was almost a crawl; then he noted that the young man was waiting for him. His heart beat rapidly. Slaney was definitely waiting for him to approach!

However, there could be no retreat; and, after all, he could hardly be suspected. He was too good a reporter to be caught following his man! Possibly Slaney wanted a match. Instinctively he groped for the box in his pocket. In a moment he was opposite the lowest step on which the suspect stood.

"Well," observed Oscar Slaney, truculently, "exactly what the hell do *you* want?"

Too good a reporter!

"Why—why" stammered Dellabough. Suddenly he stood upon his dignity. "I don't know what you are talking about," he said. "I'm not aware that I asked you for anything."

"Whistle it!" said Slaney, with a belligerent grin. "Try it on your radio! How does the chorus go? What the hell have you been following me for?"

Mr. Dellabough looked quickly about him for a policeman. There was none in sight. It was while his face was momentarily averted that his adversary went into action. With a smashing right from the shoulder, he caught Frederick Dellabough of the *Telegram* a blow upon the chin that stretched the reporter flat upon the pavement. Reaching down then, he dragged Mr. Dellabough of the *Telegram* to his feet and pasted him twice in the eye. Finally, he turned leisurely and ascended the steps again, and a moment later had entered the house.

From his sitting position on the sidewalk, Mr. Dellabough, dazed, noted again the number of the building, and realized that he would never forget it.

4.

AT THE office, the following morning, Dellabough's right eye became a subject of comment, mostly of a vulgar and boorish nature, he thought.

"Honestly, Fred; how *did* you get it?" asked one of his tormentors. It was the fourteenth repetition of the query.

Dellabough turned wearily on his persecutors.

"I was standing on a corner, minding nobody's business but my own, when a fellow walked up and *pinned* it on me," he said earnestly; "and if any of you cheerful, mouse-colored asses think you can decorate the other one, you've only got to try."

They let him alone.

But Dellabough had realized the depths of his folly. His valued powers now served to tell him how superb an idiot he had made of himself. That was not doing much for his vanity, but it was something, he felt, to know enough to retreat promptly. . . . It seemed absurdly obvious to him, now, that Slaney was *not* Sandow.

If Slaney were Sandow—and Sandow had committed the murder—he would hardly have allowed himself to be trailed to a house where he was known, even by a reporter. Lucy Andrus, probably still annoyed by the perfidy of her old flame, had—consciously or unconsciously—described him when asked to describe the murderer. The description had happened also to fit Sandow, nearly enough for a mistake to be made, and the circumstance that the initials of the two men were the same had completed the error. It was odd, however, that such a strange fortuity should have occurred. Possibly, the reporter thought, he had better see Troxell again.

His first move was in the direction of the antiquarian bookshop. Concealing nothing, not even his own humiliation—which could hardly have been concealed—he told Troxell all that had occurred.

The bookseller chuckled cynically, as usual.

"You should have told Slaney exactly what you wanted, having gone as far as you did," he observed. "If he is innocent, he could only have been anxious to prove it. As it is, if he is *not* innocent, you have let him know that he is suspected. He can now destroy the pawn ticket, and again change his residence."

"What do *you* think about his innocence?" asked Dellabough, caressing his eye.

G. Washington Troxell spread himself more comfortably over his chair. "Slaney undoubtedly was a friend of Lucy Andrus," he asserted. "He undoubtedly visited her at Miss Lambert's apartment. He *could* have known about the jewels, and he *could* have had access to Lucy's key. Those are all significant facts. They are much more significant than the similarity of initials. That could be coincidence. It involves no strain on the imagination. The actual resemblance between Slaney and Sandow is problematical. You haven't seen the man called Sandow. Most descriptions furnished by witnesses will fit anywhere from one to one million men."

He puffed at his cigarette reflectively.

"Nonetheless, Sandow is a significant figure, too, and the fact that he is known to have offered a pawn ticket for sale—a pawn ticket for a diamond brooch—is highly important. If it could be shown that the brooch was not Miss Lambert's there would be, of course, no shadow of suspicion against Sandow. It is, after a fashion, in his favor that he tried openly to sell the ticket. But it is a curious coincidence, if it *is* a coincidence, that these two men, Slaney and Sandow, supposing them to *be* two men, should have the same initials, should resemble each other after a fashion, and should be concerned—even by suspicion—in this case. It is odd that Sandow should have pawned a diamond brooch so soon after a lot of brooches and things were stolen. It is inevitable that one should wonder whether they might not be the same man. Does Slaney have a crooked nose?"

"He has a well-humped nose; but he *doesn't* limp."

"It is, of course, also conceivable that Lucy Andrus has deliberately thrown suspicion on Slaney, while appearing not to. She may have her own suspicions of him, which she is unwilling to admit. She may suspect that he was the man she saw in the apartment, that night, slightly disguised; or she may even *know* him to be the man. It is hard to get inside of a woman's mind. There's only one thing to do—get after Slaney again. You know the house he went to. If he's innocent he can clear himself."

"Ought I to tell the police about him?"

"Why not? It may save your other eye! Go *with* the police. Slaney won't punch Grimwood in the eye. And take Gray along, too. He'll know whether Slaney is Sandow. But *if* Slaney is Sandow, and *if* Sandow committed the murder, of course he won't be there when you arrive."

Dellabough got to his feet in a hurry. "I'm off, right now," he said.

He hurried away to the Detective Bureau and told his tale. Grimwood, as it happened, was not on hand, but he had no difficulty in interesting the officer in command. In a short time, with four brutal-looking plain clothes men, he was again on his way to the North Side residence.

While two of the detectives went up an alley behind the house, to head off flight at that point, the other two, with Gray and the reporter, ascended the front steps in a body and announced their presence. The young woman who had been Slaney's companion the day before opened the door. She screamed at sight of the quartet on the doorstep and fell back a pace.

"We want to talk with Slaney," said the spokesman gruffly, and pushed past her into the house.

From a rear room, as they entered, a man's voice called to know what was the matter. Then the man himself hurried down the corridor. At sight of Dellabough his face became a mask of anger.

"So it's *you* again?" he cried furiously. "Brought your gang with you this time, have you? Well, what the hell *do* you want?"

His eyes fell upon the face of Thomas Gray, and his features underwent a change.

"Why, hello, Gray," he said uneasily. But suddenly he burst out again: "Say, what is it all about, anyway? What am I wanted for?"

"You are Oscar Slaney," answered Dellabough dramatically. He wondered secretly whether his left eye was about to suffer.

"All right, I'm Oscar Slaney. What's that to you?"

"You are also Otto Sandow," accused the reporter. "Isn't he, Gray?"

Gray nodded. "Yes, he's Otto Sandow, all right," he agreed.

"All right," growled Slaney, "I'm Otto Sandow, too. What of it?"

"You pawned a diamond brooch some days ago."

For an instant the bookmaker stared. Then, "My God!" he burst out. "You think I killed that old woman! I've just tumbled!"

"Didn't you?" asked the foremost detective bluntly.

Slaney sat down in a chair. "No, I didn't," he replied, "but I know who's to blame for this. That damned cat up at the house— Lucy Andrus!"

"No," said Dellabough, loyally enough, "I'm to blame. I questioned her, and she told me of your former relations, that's all."

The young woman who had let them in continued to stare in horror. She had slumped into a chair and was looking at them out of frightened, incredulous eyes.

Slaney rose to his feet. "Look here," he said angrily, "this is all damned nonsense. I was an idiot, I suppose, to try to sell that ticket; but I needed some money in a hurry. I once knew the old lady, because I knew the maid, but that's all. I didn't kill her. I'm not in that business."

"What business *are* you in?" asked the detective quickly.

"I'm a bookmaker," was the defiant answer.

"Why did you need money in a hurry?"

The confessed bookmaker squirmed. "I was going to leave town," he admitted at length. "That makes it worse for me, I suppose. But it's true. I took a lot of losses lately, and I was clearing out for New York. I was selling everything I could."

"Why did you change your residence?" asked Dellabough.

Again the bookmaker squirmed. "I suppose I might as well make a clean breast of it," he said. "I wanted to get away from the fellows I owed money to."

"Who is this young woman?" the detective wanted to know.

"My wife," answered Slaney promptly. "Have you anything against *her?*"

"Nothing, nothing at all."

"Then leave her out of the conversation, you damned muddleheads!"

"It won't do you any good to take that tone, you know," retorted the second detective, speaking for the first time. "Where is the pawn ticket?"

"It's in my pocket. It's here!" The bookmaker plunged a thumb and finger into his vest pocket and brought out a yellow bit of pasteboard. "Take it," he continued. "Take it to Rosenthal's in Halsted Street, and get the brooch. It's one that belonged to my wife's mother. I've pawned it four times before. It *never* was Miss Lambert's. Lock me up, if you like, till you've got the brooch; but you'll never prove murder on me."

Dellabough, feeling vastly uncomfortable, took the pawn

ticket in his hands when the detective had finished examining it. The yellow pasteboard bore a date, and he saw that the date was two days earlier than the date of Miss Lambert's murder. He called attention to the fact.

"Sure, look it over," said Slaney. "You haven't got anything on *me*."

"The Andrus girl could have given it to him *before*," asserted the first detective in a whisper to his companion.

"What?" asked Dellabough.

The detective repeated his whisper. The reporter nodded. "That's so," he muttered.

"Well," said the first officer, at length, "we'll take you along, Slaney—or Sandow—whatever your name is—just for luck. Maybe you did it, and maybe you didn't; but we'll take you along anyway, just for luck."

The bookmaker, now cocky and assured, shrugged his shoulders. "Go ahead," he said. "It'll be *bad* luck for somebody."

Accompanied by both detectives, he went after his hat, and Dellabough rushed frantically out of the house to a telephone. When he had made his long report to the office he debated with himself for a moment. He was none too sure about Slaney, hang it all!

There was the police station, and there was Rosenthal's. At both places there would be news of considerable importance. But Dellabough was about convinced that Slaney had told the truth. That date on the pawn ticket almost proved it. What was needed right then, he decided, was advice. So he flagged a hurrying taxi-cab and was driven to the shop of G. Washington Troxell.

The bookseller admitted that it was a bit of a mess.

"You'll see that the police will hold him, though," he prophesied. "He'll be suspected until they've got somebody else. Don't waste time being sorry for Slaney, though; he's probably a first-class crook on several counts."

"He *may* be the murderer," said Dellabough hopefully.

Washington Troxell shook his head. "He *may* be, but I doubt it—now! Do you realize what that would mean? If Slaney really murdered Miss Lambert, it would mean that you and the police had lighted on the murderer purely by accident! His name was not mentioned until you got it out of Lucy Andrus. He was caught because, as Otto Sandow, he tried to sell a pawn ticket and Gray remembered the circumstance. You supplied the connection of names, and told the police. No, if Slaney's brooch turns out to be an innocent one, it ought to clear him."

Considerably agitated, he wheezed to his feet and waddled about the shop in elephantine fashion, smoking furiously.

"Look here, Dellabough," he said at last, "I'm very much puzzled still by Lucy Andrus's part in all this. I suggested that she may have deliberately cast suspicion on Slaney, without appearing to. Jealous, perhaps, because he married someone else. I wonder if she had heard of that? Marriage licenses are listed in the papers, and Miss Lambert read the papers with great diligence. She *would!* She was the *kind* to read deaths, births, and marriage licenses! She would have mentioned the Slaney license, too, if she had found it. Confound it, I *don't* believe Slaney had anything to do with it."

Dellabough gestured helplessly. "Who did then?" he asked, without expecting an answer.

"I don't know," snapped G. Washington Troxell. "But who *could* have committed the murder, if not Lucy Andrus's old flame? If the maid is in this *at all*, Dellabough, she's *deeply* concerned. She hasn't entered a nunnery since Slaney and she parted. She's a good-looking girl, you tell me, and she's still unmarried.

There's no reason to suppose that Slaney hasn't had a *successor*, is there?"

Dellabough whistled softly.

"Wild horses wouldn't drag *his* name out of her," he replied after a moment.

"Nor will wild guessing drag it out of the air," retorted Troxell. "A bit of adroit detective work, however, might reveal it. Now don't go off at half cock. You may discover that Lucy *does* have a young man, who has not yet been mentioned; even so, it isn't certain that he is a murderer. The point I make is that he *may* be. It's a valid line of thought, considering the circumstances. Somebody who was familiar with the apartment and who had a key committed the crime, I think. Either that or he was *let* in by the maid. Either way, the proverbial finger of suspicion points to Lucy Andrus."

A great white light seemed to burst suddenly over the reporter.

"Troxell!" he cried. "Do you suppose the maid herself might have done it?"

But the bookseller shook his head.

"Obviously, she *didn't*. She can undoubtedly account for her time. She went out after a paper. Spurgeon saw her return. They entered together, and the murder already had been committed. If she had murdered the old lady *before* she went out, Spurgeon would have caught her *leaving* the house. But he didn't. He saw her return, and she was definitely carrying a wet umbrella and a newspaper."

Mr. Dellabough fared forth into the street. Well, he would drift over to the Bureau and see what had happened to Slaney. Perhaps there would be word from the pawnshop searchers, too.

His mind raced. Troxell had seemed to be hinting at something. What was it? Troxell had seemed to have an idea. Well . . .

At the Detective Bureau a telephone call had been received from the man who had been dispatched to Rosenthal's. He had the brooch and was on his way to the station. The office of the chief of detectives was quiet, but it seemed charged with suppressed excitement. Dellabough joined the waiting group.

In half an hour an auto drew up outside the door, and the detective who had recovered the brooch swaggered in as if he had just found the lost books of Livy—although he had never heard of *those*. His superior snatched the piece of jewelry and devoured it with his eyes.

"That's it," observed Slaney easily. He sat quietly now in his chair, as if the spectacle had begun to amuse him. "What did Rosenthal say about it?"

The burly sleuth stared at his interrogator, then scowled.

"Well, what *did* he say, Burns?" echoed the chief of detectives.

"He said Slaney had pawned it with him twice before," admitted Burns. "He said his marks were scratched on the under surface, and his books would show the dates."

"Right," smiled Slaney. "And the books of Hoyne, the pawnbroker at 1216 Harrison Street, will show two other dates. All earlier than the murder of Miss Lambert," he concluded pleasantly.

The chief muttered something under his breath, which Dellabough interpreted as "Damn!"

"Well, do I go free?" asked the bookmaker.

The chief considered.

"I suppose so," he said at last. "We can't hold you. If it isn't a part of the Lambert jewelry we haven't anything to hold you on. You can go in the morning," he added, "if we don't get anything *else* on you."

"You want to show the brooch to Lucy Andrus, I suppose,"

sneered Slaney. "Well, show it to her. It's my wife's brooch." He shrugged.

Thomas Gray was greatly cast down. "Sorry I got you into this mess, Slaney," he murmured feebly.

"Go to hell!" said Slaney, with a malevolent frown.

Mr. Gray slid quietly out of the door. When he had been gone some ten minutes Mr. Dellabough followed in a state bordering on panic. He fairly ran to the bookshop of Washington Troxell.

Mr. Troxell had been doing some thinking of his own in the meantime, and out of his thinking had emerged a clear-cut idea.

Somebody connected intimately with the house had done it. Somebody connected intimately with the maid, in fact. It was the most plausible solution. If not Slaney, then who? Slaney's pawning of the brooch had been an untimely coincidence, perhaps. Its connection with the crime had been most timely, however. Gray had been very much on the job. The brooch had been pawned two days before the murder of Miss Lambert. Might not the pawning of the brooch have suggested the murder? Or, if the murder had been planned for some time, might not Slaney's action have given it a date? Slaney had openly attempted to sell the pawn ticket. How many men had heard him? If one of the men to whom he had offered the ticket had by any chance been considering the murder of Miss Lambert—for her jewels—an opportunity might have been suggested to involve an innocent man in the crime. And who, supposing all this to be true, had seized the theoretical opportunity? Only one man had come forward; a man who knew Slaney—a man who might even have known that Slaney had pawned the brooch before. But did that man know Lucy Andrus? Why not? He frequented a billiard room in the neighborhood, as surely as Slaney did.

"Well, well, well!" muttered Washington Troxell. "It begins to look as if we may have overlooked something." The *we* was strictly editorial. He was not thinking of Dellabough.

Then Dellabough burst in.

"Troxell," he panted, "I think I've got it!"

"Hm-m," said Mr. Troxell cautiously. *"What* have you got, Dellabough?"

"Who involved Slaney in all this?" demanded the reporter.

"Gray," said Washington Troxell calmly. "Thomas Gray—not the poet, of course, who wrote the Elegy!"

"Please don't be funny," begged Dellabough. "Who also hangs around billiard rooms in the vicinity, and might know Lucy Andrus?"

"Gray," admitted Troxell. "Gray, as sure as you're born."

"Who might have been offered a pawn ticket calling for a diamond brooch, and then have gone out and murdered Miss Lambert?" concluded Dellabough triumphantly.

"Gray—Thomas Gray," smiled Washington Troxell serenely. "I have just reached the same conclusion myself. It must have been telepathy. Gray is the answer to all your questions. He might even have known that Slaney was planning to skip the town. But you've got to associate him with Lucy Andrus, Dellabough! Where is Mr. Gray now?"

"He left the station ten minutes before I did. He heard Slaney practically cleared by the chief, and slid out as if he were ashamed of himself. I'll bet he's done a vanishing act himself!"

"I should not be at all surprised," agreed Troxell.

"I'm off," said the reporter. "Goodbye!"

"Where?"

"I don't know. New York, Washington, Paris, Berlin! Wherever Gray has started for."

"Oh, take it easy, Dellabough," urged the bookseller. "He can't have gone far in the time he's had. And anyway, you've got to connect him with—"

He paused. Frederick Dellabough had disappeared.

5.

IN LEICESTER, where the fishing smacks put in, there is a small hotel and lunchroom, not far from the docks, which is largely frequented by hearty, sea-blown gentlemen engaged in the capture and sale of fish. It is a picturesque place, with sloping gables and a lamp before the door. The lunchroom occupies the first part of the lower floor, and the sleeping rooms—such as they are—are upstairs, overlooking the water and the tall masts of ships lying in the bay. The *front* upstairs window, however, overlooks the streets.

From this window it was possible for Thomas Gray to survey the approach to the hotel. Not that he entertained any particular fears; but there was no telling what might happen. He was very glad to be away from it all at last, and particularly to be away from Slaney. The bookmaker's glance, as his erstwhile acquaintance had left the Detective Bureau only a few days before, had been malevolent to a degree. Gray was certain that Slaney would thrash him within an inch of his life if he ever caught him. On the whole, he was very lucky to have got away as cheaply as he had. Slaney might even have killed him. A bad man, that Slaney! Leicester, fortunately, was a long way from Chicago.

In leisurely fashion he went down to dinner, and afterward quietly smoked his pipe in a corner of the converted barroom. As twilight drew on, he strolled out into the street for a whiff of the sea air and a glance at the pretty girls who sometimes stood around and talked with the young fishermen.

When he had taken four strides beyond the hotel doorway, a rapid step sounded behind him, and he turned. For a moment his heart stopped beating. A heavy hand was on his shoulder; another hand gripped a murderous pistol, the muzzle of which was almost against his breast. A pair of sinister eyes looked into his, from beneath the shade of a soft felt hat.

"Slaney!" he gasped.

The bookmaker's lips tightened in a smile. "Yep, Slaney," he replied, and dropped his weapon into his side pocket. "Are you coming along quietly, Gray?"

The prisoner's lips became a whitish color. "Do you intend to murder me, Slaney?" he asked. "It was a dirty trick, all right, but—that's going too far, isn't it?" He licked his lips.

The bookmaker sneered. "*What* was a dirty trick?" he asked.

"Why—mixing *you* in that murder. So help me God, Slaney, I thought you did it. I thought I was only doing my duty."

"Come over here," said the gambler, drawing his victim out of the center of the road. "One word out of you to anybody who passes, and I'll drill you." After a moment he continued: "No, you didn't think I did it; and you didn't think you were doing your duty. You know damn well who did it, and so do I. Do you think I came all this distance to punch your jaw for squealing on *me?*"

The informant drew a long breath. "You've got me guessing," he said.

"You had me guessing for awhile, and you've got the police guessing yet," observed Slaney. He added casually: "What did you do with the jewels?"

Thomas Gray squealed like a trapped rabbit. "Good God, Slaney, what do you mean? Do you think—do you think—I—?"

"Sure! I think you croaked the old lady, and then blamed it

on *me*. I figured it all out the night I spent in a cell; and then I knew what I was going to do when I got out. Until the real murderer is caught, the police are going to suspect me; every move I make will be watched. I've turned detective, Gray. Get a laugh out of that, if you can! Not official. Nobody knows where I am, or what I'm doing. This is all on my own. But I've got the murderer of Miss Harriet Lambert, and tonight I'm taking him back to Chi. Maybe I'll get a reward; maybe I'll get a kick in the pants and 'thank you.' But the damn police won't be on *my* neck any longer."

"You're crazy!"

"Know how I found you? I didn't go home when the police turned me loose in the morning. They figured I would, and their man was to pick me up at the house, I suppose, and keep track of me. I crossed them. I went to *your* house, and I watched *you*. I followed you to the train. I was on the same train that brought you here. I've been watching you for three days—ever since you left Chicago. Now I've got you. The police'll be hunting for *me*, by this time. Maybe they'll find us both, but I don't think so. We'll take a train tonight, and we'll go back and give ourselves up. Then they can take their choice."

"You're crazy as hell, Slaney!"

"I suppose you've got an alibi, eh?"

"Of course, I've got an alibi!"

"What'd you run away for?"

"To get away from *you*."

The bookmaker laughed sardonically. "Well, I guess you didn't do it," he answered. "Have you got the jewels on you?"

"My God, I tell you I didn't take them! I never saw them."

"Never knew Lucy Andrus either, I suppose?"

"I've seen her, that's all. I never spoke to her in my life."

Slaney shrugged. He dropped his hand into his pocket and shoved the nozzle of his weapon into the other's side, through the cloth. "March!" he said laconically. "We're going up to your room, and you can pack what you've got. Be sure to put the jewels in. And remember, one yelp out of you as we go through the hotel, and I'll ventilate you so quick you'll never know what hit you."

The informant threw up his hands with a gesture of despair. The pair moved slowly toward the hotel doorway, where Slaney drew back and pushed his companion before him. "Right through and upstairs," he warned.

"Good God!" moaned Thomas Gray. But he moved forward as directed.

They crossed the room in leisurely fashion and tramped up the curving stairflight. In Gray's rooms, the bookmaker calmly seated himself while the other packed.

"That's all," said the informant sullenly, at length.

"Are the jewels in?" asked Slaney.

"Everything I've got is in. I tell you I haven't got the jewels. I didn't kill—"

"Not so loud," cautioned Slaney. "If the landlord thought you were a murderer there's no telling what might happen. You might have to stay here, in jail, till you were extradited."

"You'll pay for this," asserted Gray. "I've got an alibi, and I'll prove it when we get back."

"What's your alibi?"

"Will you let me go if I tell you?"

"Certainly not!"

"What's the use of telling you then?"

"Hurry up!" said Slaney. "Ready? All right, down we go. I'll take the bag. Pay your bill as you go out. Tell the landlord I brought you word that your sister was ill. Something like that. Remember, I've still got the *gat* in my pocket."

An elderly carriage, of old-fashioned make, stood at the door as they emerged.

"Where to?" asked Slaney briskly.

"Fifty cents to the station, boss."

"Right!" the bookmaker said. "In you go, Gray. We're off at last. Won't mother be surprised to see us?" He laughed heartily.

Gray scowled, but had no reply to make.

With a flourish, they drove up to the station and descended. At the same instant, a young man who had just emerged from the doorway of the place turned a startled glance upon them and hurriedly drew back. A taller man joined him.

"What's wrong, Dellabough?" asked the tall man. "Seen a ghost?"

The reporter stabbed at the doorway with his finger. "He's there," he whispered. "He's there, and he's coming in. And he isn't alone! *Grimwood*, listen: he's with Slaney!"

"What the devil!" cried the detective.

"Don't you see it? They've joined forces! They were *both* in it, from the first. We're just in time. They were clearing out."

The big detective grunted. "Things sure happen, once they start," he muttered. "It's a good thing we dropped in here to ask questions. Good hunch of *yours* to follow Gray, too. Easy now, Dellabough! Let 'em get inside. They can't run far, once they're inside."

They slipped behind the door, which stood open, and awaited the coming of the two suspects. Footsteps crossed the threshold, and Gray and Slaney entered the station, the latter lugging the former's bag. Grimwood stepped quickly out of his concealment and closed the door. At the sound the newcomers halted and whirled.

"Well, boys," said the Chicago detective genially, "let's all go back together; you and me and Mr. Dellabough." He waited for the riot.

But the bookmaker and his companion stood helpless with astonishment.

Slaney's wits, however, were quick. In an instant he guessed what had happened. Dellabough, too, had suspected Gray, and had found his trail. He had brought Grimwood with him, to make the capture. No doubt they now suspected *him* again. It was a beautiful burlesque. A slow smile curved his lips under the little black mustache. He staggered to a bench and sat down, dropping Gray's bag with a crash. He bent over and roared with vulgar laughter. He seemed about to throw a convulsion. Suddenly, while the remaining trio stared, he stopped laughing and stood up.

"Excuse *me*, Sarge," he begged, addressing Grimwood with flippant gravity. "But—they don't do this any better in the movies. It's so funny, I almost believe Gray didn't do that little job in Chicago. I shouldn't be surprised if the old lady wasn't dead at all. Go back together? I should say we will! Buy the tickets, Grimwood; four of them. Let the city of Chicago stand the expense. Or the *Morning Telegram*—it's got plenty of money."

He slapped the detective boisterously upon the shoulder, and extended his wrists.

"Handcuffs?" he asked jovially. "No need, though! I'll go along. And say—there's just four of us, and it's a long way to Chi. What about a stateroom, and a nice long game of pinochle?"

6.

MEANWHILE, IN Chicago another great mind had been functioning. The fattest of the bevy of detectives—that is, G. Washington Troxell, antiquarian bookseller—had been thinking again. He regretted the unseemly departure in haste of his friend Dellabough; but that was the way with Dellabough. He was all legs.

When two days had passed into eternity, and still the reporter had not returned, Mr. Troxell, his thoughts as yet his own, decided to act alone. He could hardly take the trail himself. He never had and he never would. Cerebration was his forte, not physical exercise. Had a murder mystery ever been solved by telephone? he wondered.

He shuffled to his instrument, and with great puffing found a number in the only book in his shop that was not for sale. It was the number of the telephone of the late Miss Lambert. He gave it to the operator, and with a sigh settled back in the small chair.

A feminine voice answered.

"Ah—I should like to speak to Miss Lucy Andrus," said G. Washington Troxell.

The voice said, "This is Miss Andrus, talking."

"This is a friend, Miss Andrus." Mr. Troxell lowered his own voice impressively. *"Listen!* Pack your things and get out of town as quickly as you can. *They've got Gray!"*

For a moment there was a silence of significant portent. It might mean anything. Had she already fled? Then the voice of Miss Andrus, puzzled and vaguely alarmed, replied.

"They've got *what?"* it asked.

"Gray," said Mr. Troxell. "Tom Gray!"

His quick ear caught her murmured words: "What under the sun?" Aloud, she asked: "What number did you want?"

338 · VINCENT STARRETT

"Don't you understand?" cried the bookseller irritably. "Tom Gray has been captured! *Arrested!*"

"I suppose you think it's funny to do this," answered the voice from the Lambert apartment. "There's a policeman here, and I'll call him in a minute. I don't know Tom Gray, and I don't care if he *has* been arrested."

Mr. Troxell heard her receiver *click* on its hook; then heard the voice of the operator, also feminine, inquiring, "Number, please?" He swore audibly and hung up.

Well, that was that! She didn't know Tom Gray. What was more, she *didn't*. The bookseller was sure of that. If she had known him she would have betrayed herself, even over the telephone, unless she were the world's greatest actress. He would have liked to see her face. It was a pity he was so unwieldy. He would have liked to make the announcement in person. No, she didn't know Thomas Gray, and that was certain.

He ambled back to his own chair and slumped into it. Dellabough was on a wild-goose chase; that, too, was certain; another one. When would they end?

Everybody in turn seemed to have been under suspicion, yet nobody had committed the murder. Suppose—suppose—?

Somewhere deep in the furrows of his mind a new idea was forming. With infinite patience, he went over every inch of the case from the beginning. There was only one thing left to investigate. Suppose—suppose—?

Once more he puffed over to the telephone, and this time he called the *Morning Telegram*. When would Mr. Dellabough be back?

The *Telegram* didn't know.

"My God!" moaned Washington Troxell; "must I go myself?"

There were the police, of course. There were always the police. So he called the police. Think of calling the police!

"Send me a good man," said G. Washington Troxell; "one who knows something about the Lambert case."

At detective headquarters, the message was reported to the chief. "Troxell?" he echoed. "That's Dellabough's fat friend. He runs a bookshop over in Dearborn Street, near the bridge. He solves all Dellabough's mysteries for him. Wonder what he wants!"

"He wants a detective," answered the telephone operator.

"Really!" said the chief ironically. "Would you call *me* a detective, Riley? Because—I'm going over, myself."

After all, he thought, the old scoundrel might have happened onto something. Dellabough had solved that Logan Square murder, and he had certainly got his "dope" from Troxell. The old villain could *think*, all right.

The chief of detectives stepped into his private car, gave the necessary order, and was driven to the bookshop. Mr. Troxell met him in the doorway; led him to a chair.

"Glad to see you, Chief," said the bookseller cheerily. "I've often heard of you from my friend Dellabough. Didn't expect I'd ever see you in my shop, though. I may have something for you, if you care to listen. You see," he continued, lighting his cigarette, "I'm Dellabough's *brain*. Dellabough, to put it in another way, is my *legs*. I do the thinking; Dellabough does the hustling. When he tries to think by himself, he's lost; and when I try to hustle by myself, I'm—I'm graveled! Sedentary life, you know—suboxidized—and that sort of thing. In short, too fat."

"What's on your mind?" asked the chief of detectives, affably enough. Privately, he decided that the old pirate was mad as a lark.

"I'll tell you the story chronologically, if you don't mind. I'll begin at the beginning of the case, and you must follow me carefully."

The chief helped himself to a cigar. "Fire away," he said.

Mr. Troxell fired away. Briefly and concisely, he sketched the outstanding features of the crime, and from them proceeded to the processes that had led him to suspect, in turn, Lucy Andrus, Otto Sandow, Oscar Slaney, and Thomas Gray. It was a scholarly recital.

"There was reason for every suspicion," he argued. *"Good* reason. But in the end a lot of thinking would seem to have been wasted. After talking with Miss Andrus over the telephone, I am convinced that Mr. Gray had no hand in the murder. Mr. Sandow, or Slaney, is definitely out of consideration. The maid is not. She is still at the bottom of everything. By heaven, I've been right about *that* from the beginning, and I'm right about it now. Today, for the first time, it occurred to me to question her original story!

"Suppose, Mr. Chief of Detectives, Lucy Andrus lied. Suppose she didn't see a man emerging from Miss Lambert's bedroom the evening of the crime. Suppose when she entered the apartment she saw just what she expected to see—the body of Miss Lambert lying on the rug in the sitting room. Suppose that, and what follows?"

"We can't suppose that," objected the chief. "If we do, we must suppose that Spurgeon also lied."

"That's what follows!" observed Mr. Troxell triumphantly. "If Lucy lied, Spurgeon lied! And if Spurgeon lied—?"

The chief's eyes were slowly kindling.

"If Spurgeon lied," he answered slowly, "then Spurgeon himself is probably—"

"The murderer!" said Mr. Troxell. "Why not? He must be a hell of a lawyer to be living in a basement apartment; or else he must be a very clever lawyer, playing his own game. And if Spurgeon lied, you see how everything straightens itself out? Nothing happened as we think it happened. The maid went out: Spurgeon, using a key of his own, but furnished by the maid, let himself in, and killed the old lady. Then he and Lucy Andrus cooked up this beautiful tale between them, and everybody went hunting for a young man who never existed!"

"Of course, there's nothing to connect him with it, except his proximity," argued the chief. "He *could* have done it. That's all we can say."

"There's nothing to connect *anybody else* with it," said Troxell. "We've tried that, and you see where we've got. Spurgeon is all we have left. If we hadn't been singularly gullible we'd have looked into *his* life before this. But he told a plausible tale. The maid bore him out—with just enough dissimilarity to make it *more* plausible—and we all fell for the story. Then Gray came along with *his* story about Slaney—or Sandow. It was an unfortunate coincidence, but it helped us to forget Spurgeon. And Lucy lied when she was questioned about Sandow. Naturally we were glad to pick on Slaney. He was a gambler, and a man of no standing. But he proved that he had pawned the brooch two days before the murder, and he had to be turned loose. I'll bet he could have proved an alibi if he'd had to."

"He *did* prove one," said the chief dryly.

"There you are! Then Gray—but why talk about Gray? He was a false alarm."

"Perhaps," commented the chief. "Grimwood is after him down East, however."

"Why did *he* run away, I wonder? Was he afraid of Slaney?"

"He may be part of the plot," said the chief. "We're only guessing about Spurgeon."

"Nobody's in the plot but Spurgeon and Lucy Andrus," snapped Troxell, "and the sooner you get after that precious pair, the sooner you'll be seeing your name in the papers. Who was bothered to death, daily, by this ridiculous old female, Harriet Lambert? Spurgeon! Who knew all about her old-maid fears and her damned jewels? Spurgeon! Who probably wished her dead a hundred times before he actually killed her? Spurgeon! And, of course, the maid. Why, the old woman drove them both crazy with her tongue. They'd have been justified in murdering her if she hadn't had a penny!"

The chief stood up, laughing.

"I won't go that far, Mr. Troxell," he said, "but I'll go as far as that apartment, anyway—and right away. Would you care to come along?"

The bookseller hesitated.

"In my car, of course," added the chief.

"Hang it, I suppose I owe it to Dellabough," grumbled Troxell. "And, as a matter of fact, I'd *like* to. All right, I'll go."

He shuffled after his hat, shaking his head sadly, while his heart rejoiced within him. "I'm a damned old fool, I guess," muttered G. W. Troxell.

He found the back seat very comfortable, however, and his talk was a torrent of nonsense until the house was reached.

The chief of detectives ascended the stairs and was admitted by the uniformed policeman in charge of the murdered woman's apartment, who stared at sight of so great a dignitary of the force. Mr. Troxell followed with what speed he could muster.

"Where is Miss Andrus, Parkinson?" asked the chief.

"She's here, sir. She's in the kitchen. Shall I call her?"

"Yes, call her."

Parkinson called her. She stared at the intruders with hard, suspicious eyes.

"Miss Andrus," said the chief suavely, "does Mr. Spurgeon intend to marry you?"

Miss Andrus, it appeared, had been steeled against every question but the one that had been asked. She reached out suddenly and seized the back of a chair to steady herself. A wave of color rushed to her face and receded, leaving it white.

"What—what do you mean?" she stammered.

"I should think it would be the least he would do, in the circumstances. He is probably a man of some property, and by making you his wife he would be making you, in prospect, his widow. A man's widow should be provided for. He will certainly hang for the murder of Miss Lambert."

Miss Andrus decided to sit down.

"I don't know what you are talking about," she said. But she said it poorly.

"Let us go down to Mr. Spurgeon," said the chief.

"I shan't move!" shrieked the maid, suddenly vocal.

"Very well, Officer Parkinson will stay with you. Mr. Troxell and I will descend."

They had proceeded, however, only halfway down the flight to the basement when the girl rushed after them, with Parkinson in close pursuit. She flung herself recklessly down the steps, before any movement could be made to stop her, and, passing Troxell and the chief like a kitten, flung herself in at the door leading to Spurgeon's apartment. In another moment she had recoiled, gasping and staring, and had fallen unconscious in the doorway.

Looking over her prostrate body into the room whose door

she had opened, the chief of detectives and the antiquarian bookseller saw, hanging from a rafter of the low-ceilinged room, the gently oscillating body of a man.

"*Spurgeon!*" said Washington Troxell.

7.

AT THE last, at any rate, Spurgeon had been a gentleman. His careful confession, a document covering many pages, exonerated Lucy Andrus. He had forced her to aid him, he said, and she had agreed only because she loved him. There were cynics who doubted it—among them G. Washington Troxell—but there was nothing for the police to do but free the maid.

"She drove them both crazy," said Troxell stubbornly. "Whose idea it was, in the first place, we shall never know; but they were partners. Lucy Andrus was no meek follower of a master mind, or any of that rot. She knew where the jewels were, you may be sure, and you may be sure that she told Spurgeon. *Is* he a lawyer, by the way? That should be looked into! Yes, Harriet deserved all that she got, Dellabough. She cried for it until she got it. She wasn't *happy* until she got it. There are a lot of women like that . . . I've known three," he added reflectively.

"I have no doubt she drove *Spurgeon* crazy," responded Dellabough. "His confession was the confession of a madman. That knocking on the floor preyed upon his mind and made him mad."

He had returned the day after the suicide of Spurgeon, and his gratitude to Troxell was pathetic. Troxell had called up the *Telegram* and had given his paper all the facts.

"Possibly it was a prospective marriage with Lucy that drove him mad," remarked the bookseller cynically. "That *and* the murder," he added. "It was the thumping of the chair legs on the floor, as he drove them down onto his victim, that suggested the 'knocking' to him. But his remarks about Lucy were too good to be true. Methought the gentleman did protest too much."

"Gee, hasn't it all been a mess, though?" cried the reporter.

"Too many sleuths!" smiled the bookseller. "And too much imagination. Thought is a dangerous business; it is to be practised safely only in a book or in a bookshop. What with your imagination and mine, and Grimwood's and Gray's—and finally Slaney's, by Jove!—all working at once, there was bound to be a mess. Did you succeed in buying off Slaney and Gray, by the way? Or are they going to sue you and the city and the *Morning Telegram?*"

Mr. Dellabough put his fingertips swiftly to his temples. His grimace was eloquent.

"Wow! What a time I had with those two men!" he said.

A PASSAGE TO BENARES
T. S. Stribling

One of the half-dozen most successful American writers between World War I and World War II, Thomas Sigismund
Stribling (1881-1965) wrote a staggering number of short stories (he claimed 10,000, while writing as many as seven a day)
and more than a dozen novels.

He is best-remembered today for his epic trilogy featuring
Miltiades "Milt" Vaiden and the Vaiden family (many based
on his own family), beginning with *The Forge* (1931), *The Store*
(1932), which won the Pulitzer Prize, and *Unfinished Cathedral*
(1933). They were controversial, especially in the South, as they
attacked the social, political, and economic inequalities between
Blacks and whites, foretelling the demise of the Old South. All
three books were bestsellers during the Great Depression and
Stribling became Doubleday's most successful author.

Stribling's popularity inspired the adaptation of his works
for other media, most notably his novel *Birthright* (serialized in
1921 and published as a book the following year), which the fa-

mous Black director Oscar Micheaux adapted into a silent film in 1924 and again as a sound film in 1939.

In the mystery world, Stribling is noted for the series character who appears in dozens of short stories, Henry Poggioli, Ph.D., a psychologist-criminologist. The first collection of stories featuring the self-described "half-Italian, half-American" sleuth was *Clues of the Caribbees* (1929), which Ellery Queen selected for *Queen's Quorum* as one of the 106 greatest detective story collections ever published.

Queen proclaimed their "provocative quality is both arresting and rewarding—not only as intellectual exercises but as philosophically mature concepts of crime."

After he stopped writing novels, the last published in 1938, he continued writing short stories, including many about Poggioli, mainly for *Ellery Queen's Mystery Magazine*; the later stories were collected in *Dr. Poggioli: Criminologist* (Norfolk, Virginia, Crippen & Landru, 2004).

"A Passage to Benares" was originally published in the February 20, 1926, issue of *Adventure*; it was first collected in *Clues of the Caribbees* (New York, Doubleday, 1929).

A Passage to Benares
T. S. Stribling

IN PORT of Spain, Trinidad, at half-past five in the morning, Mr. Henry Poggioli, the American psychologist, stirred uneasily, became conscious of a splitting headache, opened his eyes in bewilderment, and then slowly reconstructed his surroundings. He recognized the dome of the Hindu temple seen dimly above him, the jute rug on which he lay; the blur of the image of Krishna sitting cross-legged on the altar. The American had a dim impression that the figure had not sat thus on the altar all night long—a dream, no doubt; he had a faint memory of lurid nightmares. The psychologist allowed the thought to lose itself as he got up slowly from the sleeping rug which the cicerone had spread for him the preceding evening.

In the circular temple everything was still in deep shadow, but the gray light of dawn filled the arched entrance. The white man moved carefully to the door so as not to jar his aching head. A little distance from him he saw another sleeper, a coolie beggar stretched out on a rug, and he thought he saw still another farther away. As he passed out of the entrance the cool freshness of the tropical morning caressed his face like the cool fingers of a woman. Kiskadee birds were calling from palms and saman trees, and there was a wide sound of dripping dew. Not far from the temple a coolie woman stood on a seesaw with a great stone attached to the other end of the plank, and by stepping to and fro she swung the stone up and down and pounded some rice in a mortar.

Poggioli stood looking at her a moment, then felt in his pocket for the key to his friend Lowe's garden gate. He found it and moved off up Tragarette Road to where the squalid East Indian village gave way to the high garden walls and ornamental shrubbery of the English suburb of Port of Spain. He walked on more briskly as the fresh air eased his head, and presently he stopped and unlocked a gate in one of the bordering walls. He began to smile as he let himself in; his good humor increased as he walked across a green lawn to a stone cottage which had a lower window still standing open. This was his own room. He reached up to the sill and drew himself inside, which gave his head one last pang. He shook this away, however, and began undressing for his morning shower.

Mr. Poggioli was rather pleased with his exploit, although he had not forwarded the experiment which had induced him to sleep in the temple. It had come about in this way: On the foregoing evening the American and his host in Port of Spain, a Mr. Lowe, a bank clerk, had watched a Hindu wedding procession enter the same temple in which Poggioli had just spent the night. They had watched the dark-skinned white-robed musicians smiting their drums and skirling their pipes with bouffant cheeks. Behind them marched a procession of coolies. The bride was a little cream-colored girl who wore a breast-plate of linked gold coins over her childish bosom, while anklets and bracelets almost covered her arms and legs. The groom, a tall, dark coolie, was the only man in the procession who wore European clothes, and he, oddly enough, was attired in a full evening dress suit. At the incongruous sight Poggioli burst out laughing, but Lowe touched his arm and said in an undertone:

"Don't take offense, old man, but if you didn't laugh it might help me somewhat."

Poggioli straightened his face.

"Certainly, but how's that?"

"The groom, Boodman Lal, owns one of the best curio shops in town and carries an account at my bank. That fifth man in the procession, the skeleton wearing the yellow *kapra*, is old Hira Dass. He is worth something near a million in pounds sterling."

The psychologist became sober enough, out of his American respect for money.

"Hira Dass," went on Lowe, "built this temple and rest house. He gives rice and tea to any traveler who comes in for the night.

It's an Indian custom to help mendicant pilgrims to the different shrines. A rich Indian will build a temple and a rest house just as your American millionaires erect libraries."

The American nodded again, watching now the old man with the length of yellow silk wrapped around him. And just at this point Poggioli received the very queer impression which led to his night's adventure.

When the wedding procession entered the temple the harsh music stopped abruptly. Then, as the line of robed coolies disappeared into the dark interior the psychologist had a strange feeling that the procession had been swallowed up and had ceased to exist. The bizarre red-and-gold building stood in the glare of sunshine, a solid reality, while its devotees had been dissipated into nothingness.

So peculiar, so startling was the impression, that Poggioli blinked and wondered how he ever came by it. The temple had somehow suggested the Hindu theory of Nirvana. Was it possible that the Hindu architect had caught some association of ideas between the doctrine of obliteration and these curves and planes and colors glowing before him? Had he done it by contrast or simile? The fact that Poggioli was a psychologist made the problem all the more intriguing to him—the psychologic influence of architecture. There must be some rationale behind it. An idea how he might pursue this problem came into his head. He turned to his friend and exclaimed:

"Lowe, how about staying all night in old Hira Dass's temple?"

"Doing what?" with a stare of amazement.

"Staying a night in the temple. I had an impression just then, a——"

"Why, my dear fellow!" ejaculated Lowe, "no white man ever stayed all night in a coolie temple. It simply isn't done!"

The American argued his case a moment:

"You and I had a wonderful night aboard the *Trevemore* when we became acquainted."

"That was a matter of necessity," said the bank clerk. "There were no first-class cabin accommodations left on the *Trevemore*, so we had to make the voyage on deck."

Here the psychologist gave up his bid for companionship. Late that night he slipped out of Lowe's cottage, walked back to the grotesque temple, was given a cup of tea, a plate of rice, and a sleeping rug. The only further impression the investigator obtained was a series of fantastic and highly colored dreams, of which he could not recall a detail. Then he waked with a miserable headache and came home.

Mr. Poggioli finished his dressing and in a few minutes the breakfast bell rang. He went to the dining room to find the bank clerk unfolding the damp pages of the Port of Spain *Inquirer*. This was a typical English sheet using small, solidly set columns without flaming headlines. Poggioli glanced at it and wondered mildly if nothing worth featuring ever happened in Trinidad.

Ram Jon, Lowe's Hindu servant, slipped in and out of the breakfast room with peeled oranges, tea, toast, and a custard fruit flanked by a half lemon to squeeze over it.

"Pound sterling advanced a point," droned Lowe from his paper.

"It'll reach par," said the American, smiling faintly and wondering what Lowe would say if he knew of his escapade.

"Our new governor general will arrive in Trinidad on the twelfth."

"Surely that deserved a headline," said the psychologist.

"Don't try to debauch me with your American yellow journalism," smiled the bank clerk.

"Go your own way if you prefer doing research work every morning for breakfast."

The bank clerk laughed again at this, continued his perusal, then said:

"Hello, another coolie kills his wife. Tell me, Poggioli, as a psychologist, why do coolies kill their wives?"

"For various reasons, I fancy, or perhaps this one didn't kill her at all. Surely now and then some other person—"

"Positively no! It's always the husband, and instead of having various reasons, they have none at all. They say their heads are hot, and so to cool their own they cut off their wives'!"

The psychologist was amused in a dull sort of way.

"Lowe, you Englishmen are a nation with fixed ideas. You genuinely believe that every coolie woman who is murdered is killed by her husband without any motive whatever."

"Sure, that's right," nodded Lowe, looking up from his paper.

"That simply shows me you English have no actual sympathy with your subordinate races. And that may be the reason your empire is great. Your aloofness, your unsympathy—by becoming automatic you become absolutely dependable. The idea, that every coolie woman is murdered by her husband without a motive!"

"That's correct," repeated Lowe with English imperturbability.

The conversation was interrupted by a ring at the garden-gate bell. A few moments later the two men saw through the shadow Ram Jon unlock the wall door, open it a few inches, parley a moment, and receive a letter. Then he came back with his limber, gliding gait.

Lowe received the note through the open window, broke the envelope, and fished out two notes instead of one. The clerk looked at the inclosures and began to read with a growing bewilderment in his face.

"What is it?" asked Poggioli at last.

"This is from Hira Dass to Jeffries, the vice-president of our bank. He says his nephew Boodman Lal has been arrested and he wants Jeffries to help get him out."

"What's he arrested for?"

"Er—for murdering his wife," said Lowe with a long face.

Poggioli stared.

"Wasn't he the man we saw in the procession yesterday?"

"Damn it, yes!" cried Lowe in sudden disturbance, "and he's a sensible fellow, too, one of our best patrons." He sat staring at the American over the letter, and then suddenly recalling a point, drove it home English fashion.

"That proves my contention, Poggioli—a groom of only six or eight hours' standing killing his wife. They simply commit uxoricide without any reason at all, the damned irrational rotters!"

"What's the other letter?" probed the American, leaning across the table.

"It's from Jeffries. He says he wants me to take this case and get the best talent in Trinidad to clear Mr. Hira Dass's house and consult with him." The clerk replaced the letters in the envelope. "Say, you've had some experience in this sort of thing. Won't you come with me?"

"Glad to."

The two men arose promptly from the table, got their hats, and went out into Tragarette Road once more. As they stood in the increasing heat waiting for a car, it occurred to Poggioli that the details of the murder ought to be in the morning's paper. He took the *Inquirer* from his friend and began a search through its closely printed columns. Presently he found a paragraph without any heading at all:

"Boodman Lal, nephew of Mr. Hira Dass, was arrested early this morning at his home in Peru, the East Indian suburb, for the alleged murder of his wife, whom he married yesterday at the Hindu temple in Peru. The body was found at six o'clock this morning in the temple. The attendant gave the alarm. Mrs. Boodman Lal's head was severed completely from her body and she lay in front of the Buddhist altar in her bridal dress. All of her jewelry was gone. Five coolie beggars who were asleep in the temple when the body was discovered were arrested. They claimed to know nothing of the crime, but a search of their persons revealed that each beggar had a piece of the young bride's jewelry and a coin from her necklace.

"Mr. Boodman Lal and his wife were seen to enter the temple at about eleven o'clock last night for the Krishnian rite of purification. Mr. Boodman, who is a prominent curio dealer in this city, declines to say anything further than that he thought his wife had gone back to her mother's home for the night after her prayers in the temple. The young bride, formerly a Miss Maila Ran, was thirteen years old. Mr. Boodman is the nephew of Mr. Hira Dass, one of the wealthiest men in Trinidad."

The paragraph following this contained a notice of a tea given at Queen's Park Hotel by Lady Henley-Hoads, and the names of her guests.

The psychologist spent a painful moment pondering the kind of editor who would run a millionaire murder mystery, without any caption whatever, in between a legal notice and a society note. Then he turned his attention to the gruesome and mysterious details the paragraph contained.

"Lowe, what do you make out of those beggars, each with a coin and a piece of jewelry?"

"Simple enough. The rotters laid in wait in the temple till the husband went out and left his wife, then they murdered her and divided the spoil."

"But that child had enough bangles to give a dozen to each man."

"Ye-es, that's a fact," admitted Lowe.

"And why should they continue sleeping in the temple?"

"Why shouldn't they? They knew they would be suspected, and they couldn't get off the island without capture, so they thought they might as well lie back down and go to sleep."

Here the street car approached and Mr. Poggioli nodded, apparently in agreement.

"Yes, I am satisfied that is how it occurred."

"You mean the beggars killed her?"

"No, I fancy the actual murderer took the girl's jewelry and went about the temple thrusting a bangle and a coin in the pockets of each of the sleeping beggars to lay a false scent."

"Aw, come now!" cried the bank clerk, "that's laying it on a bit too thick, Poggioli!"

"My dear fellow, that's the only possible explanation for the coins in the beggars' pockets."

By this time the men were on the tramcar and were clattering off down Tragarette Road. As they dashed along toward the Hindu village Poggioli remembered suddenly that he had walked this same distance the preceding night and had slept in this same temple. A certain sharp impulse caused the American to run a hand swiftly into his own pockets. In one side he felt the keys of his trunk and of Lowe's cottage; in the other he touched several coins and a round hard ring. With a little thrill he drew these to the edge of his pocket and took a covert glance at them. One showed the curve of a gold bangle; the other the face of an old English gold coin which evidently had been soldered to something.

With a little sinking sensation Poggioli eased them back into his pocket and stared ahead at the coolie village which they were approaching. He moistened his lips and thought what he would better do. The only notion that came into his head was to pack his trunk and take passage on the first steamer out of Trinidad, no matter to what port it was bound.

In his flurry of uneasiness the psychologist was tempted to drop the gold pieces then and there, but as the sheet car rattled into Peru he reflected that no other person in Trinidad knew that he had these things, except indeed the person who slipped them into his pocket, but that person was not likely to mention the matter. Then, too, it was such an odd occurrence, so piquing to his analytic instinct, that he decided he would go on with the inquiry.

Two minutes later Lowe rang down the motorman and the two companions got off in the Hindu settlement. By this time the sheet was full of coolies, greasy men and women gliding about with bundles on their heads or coiled down in the sunshine in pairs where they took turns in examining each other's head for vermin. Lowe glanced about, oriented himself, then started walking briskly past the temple, when Poggioli stopped him and asked him where he was going.

"To report to old Hira Dass, according to my instructions from Jeffries," said the Englishman.

"Suppose we stop in the temple a moment. We ought not to go to the old fellow without at least a working knowledge of the scene of the murder."

The clerk slowed up uncertainly, but at that moment they glanced through the temple door and saw five coolies sitting inside. A policeman at the entrance was evidently guarding these men as prisoners. Lowe approached the guard, made his mission known, and a little later he and his guest were admitted into the temple.

The coolie prisoners were as repulsive as are all of their kind. Four were as thin as cadavers, the fifth one greasily fat. All five wore cheesecloth around their bodies, which left them as exposed as if they had worn nothing at all. One of the emaciated men held his mouth open all the time with an expression of suffering caused by a chronic lack of food. The five squatted on their rugs and looked at the white men with their beadlike eyes. The fat one said in a low tone to his companions:

"The sahib."

This whispered ejaculation disquieted Poggioli somewhat, and he reflected again that it would have been discretion to withdraw from the murder of little Maila Ran as quietly as possible. Still he could explain his presence in the temple simply enough. And besides, the veiled face of the mystery seduced him. He stood studying the five beggars: the greasy one, the lean ones, the one with the suffering face.

"Boys," he said to the group, for all coolies are boys, "did any of you hear any noises in this temple last night?"

"Much sleep, sahib, no noise. Police-y-man punch us 'wake this morning make sit still here."

"What's your name?" asked the American of the loquacious fat mendicant.

"Chuder Chand, sahib."

"When did you go to sleep last night?"

"When I ate rice and tea, sahib."

"Do you remember seeing Boodman Lal and his wife enter this building last night?"

Here their evidence became divided. The fat man remembered; two of the cadavers remembered only the wife, one only Boodman Lal, and one nothing at all.

Poggioli confined himself to the fat man.

"Did you see them go out?"

All five shook their heads.

"You were all asleep then?"

A general nodding.

"Did you have any impressions during your sleep, any disturbance, any half rousing, any noises?"

The horror-struck man said in a ghastly tone:

"I dream bad dream, sahib. When police-y-man punch me awake this morning I think my dream is come to me."

"And me, sahib."

"Me, sahib."

"Me."

"Did you all have bad dreams?"

A general nodding.

"What did you dream, Chuder Chand?" inquired the psychologist with a certain growth of interest.

"Dream me a big fat pig, but still I starved, sahib."

"And you?" at a lean man.

"That I be mashed under a great bowl of rice, sahib, but hungry."

"And you?" asked Poggioli of the horror-struck coolie.

The coolie wet his dry lips and whispered in his ghastly tones:

"Sahib, I dreamed I was Siva, and I held the world in my hands and bit it and it tasted bitter, like the rind of a mammy apple. And I said to Vishnu, 'Let me be a dog in the streets, rather than taste the bitterness of this world,' and then the policeman punched me, sahib, and asked if I had murdered Maila Ran."

The psychologist stood staring at the sunken temples and withered chaps of the beggar, amazed at the enormous vision of godhood which had visited the old mendicant's head. No doubt this grandiloquent dream was a sort of compensation for the starved and wretched existence the beggar led.

Here the bank clerk intervened to say that they would better go on around to old Hira Dass's house according to instructions.

Poggioli turned and followed his friend out of the temple.

"Lowe, I think we can now entirely discard the theory that the beggars murdered the girl."

"On what grounds?" asked the clerk in surprise. "They told you nothing but their dreams."

"That is the reason. All five had wild, fantastic dreams. That suggests they were given some sort of opiate in their rice or tea last night. It is very improbable that five ignorant coolies would have wit enough to concoct such a piece of evidence as that."

"That's a fact," admitted the Englishman, a trifle surprised, "but I don't believe a Trinidad court would admit such evidence."

"We are not looking for legal evidence; we are after some indication of the real criminal."

By this time the two men were walking down a hot, malodorous alley which emptied into the square a little east of the temple. Lowe jerked a bell-pull in a high adobe wall, and Poggioli was surprised that this could be the home of a millionaire Hindu. Presently the shutter opened and Mr. Hira Dass himself stood in the opening. The old Hindu was still draped in yellow silk which revealed his emaciated form almost as completely as if he had been naked. But his face was alert with hooked nose and brilliant black eyes, and his wrinkles did not so much suggest great age as they did shrewdness and acumen.

The old coolie immediately led his callers into an open court surrounded by marble columns with a fountain in its center and white doves fluttering up to the frieze or floating back down again.

The Hindu began talking immediately of the murder and his anxiety to clear his unhappy nephew. The old man's English was very good, no doubt owing to the business association of his latter years.

"A most mysterious murder," he deplored, shaking his head, "and the life of my poor nephew will depend upon your exertions, gentlemen. What do you think of those beggars that were found in the temple with the bangles and coins?"

Mr. Hira Dass seated his guests on a white marble bench, and now walked nervously in front of them, like some fantastic old scarecrow draped in yellow silk.

"I am afraid my judgment of the beggars will disappoint you, Mr. Hira Dass," answered Poggioli. "My theory is they are innocent of the crime."

"Why do you say that?" queried Hira Dass, looking sharply at the American.

The psychologist explained his deduction from their dreams.

"You are not English, sir," exclaimed the old man. "No Englishman would have thought of that."

"No, I'm half Italian and half American."

The old Indian nodded.

"Your Latin blood has subtlety, Mr. Poggioli, but you base your proof on the mechanical cause of the dreams, not upon the dreams themselves."

The psychologist looked at the old man's cunning face and gnome-like figure and smiled.

"I could hardly use the dreams themselves, although they were fantastic enough."

"Oh, you did inquire into the actual dreams?"

"Yes, by the way of professional interest."

"What is your profession? Aren't you a detective?"

"No, I'm a psychologist."

Old Hira Dass paused in his rickety walking up and down the marble pavement to stare at the American and then burst into the most wrinkled cachinnation Poggioli had ever seen.

"A psychologist, and inquired into a suspected criminal's dreams out of mere curiosity!" the old gnome cackled again, then became serious. He held up a thin finger at the American. "I must not laugh. Your oversoul, your *atman*, is at least groping after knowledge as the blindworm gropes. But enough of that, Mr. Poggioli. Our problem is to find the criminal who committed this crime and restore my nephew Boodman Lal to liberty. You can imagine what a blow this is to me. I arranged this marriage for my nephew."

The American looked at the old man with new ground for deduction.

"You did—arranged a marriage for a nephew who is in the thirties?"

"Yes, I wanted him to avoid the pitfalls into which I fell," replied old Hira Dass seriously. "He was unmarried, and had already begun to add dollars to dollars. I did the same thing, Mr. Poggioli, and now look at me—an empty old man in a foreign land. What good is this marble court where men of my own kind cannot come and sit with me, and when I have no grandchildren to feed the doves? No, I have piled up dollars and pounds. I have eaten the world, Mr. Poggioli, and found it bitter; now here I am, an outcast."

There was a passion in this outburst which moved the American, and at the same time the old Hindu's phraseology was sharply reminiscent of the dreams told him by the beggars in the temple. The psychologist noted the point hurriedly and curiously in the flow of the conversation, and at the same moment some other part of his brain was inquiring tritely:

"Then why don't you go back to India, Mr. Hira Dass?"

"With this worn-out body," the old Hindu made a contemptuous gesture toward himself, "and with this face, wrinkled with pence! Why, Mr. Poggioli, my mind is half English. If I should return to Benares I would walk about thinking what the temples cost, what was the value of the stones set in the eyes of Krishna's image. That is why we Hindus lose our caste if we travel abroad and settle in a foreign land, because we do indeed lose caste. We become neither Hindus nor English. Our minds are divided, so if I would ever be one with my own people again, Mr. Poggioli, I must leave this Western mind and body here in Trinidad."

Old Hira Dass's speech brought to the American that fleeting credulity in transmigration of the soul which an ardent believer always inspires. The old Hindu made the theory of palingenesis appear almost matter-of-fact. A man died here and reappeared as a babe in India. There was nothing so unbelievable in that. A man's basic energy, which has loved, hated, aspired, and grieved here, must go somewhere, while matter itself was a mere dance of atoms. Which was the most permanent, Hira Dass's passion or his marble court? Both were mere forms of force. The psychologist drew himself out of his reverie.

"That is very interesting, or, I should say moving, Hira Dass.

You have strange griefs. But we were discussing your nephew, Boodman Lal. I think I have a theory which may liberate him."

"And what is that?"

"As I have explained to you, I believe the beggars in the temple were given a sleeping potion. I suspect the temple attendant doped the rice and later murdered your nephew's wife."

The millionaire became thoughtful.

"That is good Gooka. I employ him. He is a miserably poor man, Mr. Poggioli, so I cannot believe he committed this murder."

"Pardon me, but I don't follow your reasoning. If he is poor he would have a strong motive for the robbery."

"That's true, but a very poor man would never have dropped the ten pieces of gold into the pockets of the beggars to lay a false scent. The man who did this deed must have been a well-to-do person accustomed to using money to forward his purposes. Therefore, in searching for the criminal I would look for a moneyed man."

"But, Mr. Hira Dass," protested the psychologist, "that swings suspicion back to your nephew."

"My nephew!" cried the old man, growing excited again. "What motive would my nephew have to slay his bride of a few hours!"

"But what motive," retorted Poggioli with academic curtness, "would a well-to-do man have to murder a child? And what chance would he have to place an opiate in the rice?"

The old Hindu lifted a finger and came closer.

"I'll tell you my suspicions," he said in a lowered voice, "and you can work out the details."

"Yes, what are they?" asked Poggioli, becoming attentive again.

"I went down to the temple this morning to have the body

of my poor murdered niece brought here to my villa for burial. I talked to the five beggars and they told me that there was a sixth sleeper in the temple last night." The old coolie shook his finger, lifted his eyebrows, and assumed a very gnomish appearance indeed.

A certain trickle of dismay went through the American. He tried to keep from moistening his lips and perhaps he did, but all he could think to do was to lift his eyebrows and say:

"Was there, indeed?"

"Yes—and a white man!"

Lowe, the bank clerk, who had been sitting silent through all this, interrupted. "Surely not, Mr. Hira Dass, not a white man!"

"All five of the coolies and my man Gooka told me it was true," reiterated the old man, "and I have always found Gooka a truthful man. And besides, such a man would fill the rôle of assailant exactly. He would be well-to-do, accustomed to using money to forward his purposes."

The psychologist made a sort of mental lunge to refute this rapid array of evidence old Hira Dass was piling up against him.

"But, Mr. Hira Dass, decapitation is not an American mode of murder."

"American!"

"I—I was speaking generally," stammered the psychologist. "I mean a white man's method of murder."

"That is indicative in itself," returned the Hindu promptly. "I meant to call your attention to that point. It shows the white man was a highly educated man, who had studied the mental habit of other peoples than his own, so he was enabled to give the crime an extraordinary resemblance to a Hindu crime. I would suggest, gentlemen, that you begin your search for an intellectual white man."

"What motive could such a man have?" cried the American.

"Robbery, possibly, or if he were a very intellectual man indeed he might have murdered the poor child by way of experiment. I read not long ago in an American paper of two youths who committed such a crime."

"A murder for experiment!" cried Lowe, aghast.

"Yes, to record the psychological reaction."

Poggioli suddenly got to his feet.

"I can't agree with such a theory as that, Mr. Hira Dass," he said in a shaken voice.

"No, it's too far-fetched," declared the clerk at once.

"However, it is worth while investigating," persisted the Hindu.

"Yes, yes," agreed the American, evidently about to depart, "but I shall begin my investigations, gentlemen, with the man Gooka."

"As you will," agreed Hira Dass, "and in your investigations, gentlemen, hire any assistants you need, draw on me for any amount. I want my nephew exonerated, and above all things, I want the real criminal apprehended and brought to the gallows."

Lowe nodded.

"We'll do our best, sir," he answered in his thorough-going English manner.

The old man followed his guests to the gate and bowed them out into the malodorous alleyway again.

As the two friends set off through the hot sunshine once more the bank clerk laughed.

"A white man in that temple! That sounds like pure fiction to me to shield Boodman Lal. You know these coolies hang together like thieves."

He walked on a little way pondering, then added, "Jolly good thing we didn't decide to sleep in the temple last night, isn't it, Poggioli?"

A sickish feeling went over the American. For a moment he was tempted to tell his host frankly what he had done and ask his advice in the matter, but finally he said:

"In my opinion the actual criminal is Boodman Lal."

Lowe glanced around sidewise at his guest and nodded faintly.

"Same here. I thought it ever since I first saw the account in the *Inquirer*. Somehow these coolies will chop their wives to pieces for no reason at all."

"I know a very good reason in this instance," retorted the American warmly, taking out his uneasiness in this manner. "It's these damned child marriages! When a man marries some child he doesn't care a tuppence for—— What do you know about Boodman Lal anyway?"

"All there is to know. He was born here and has always been a figure here in Port of Spain because of his rich uncle."

"Lived here all his life?"

"Except when he was in Oxford for six years."

"Oh, he's an Oxford man!"

"Yes."

"There you are, there's the trouble."

"What do you mean?"

"No doubt he fell in love with some English girl. But when his wealthy uncle, Hira Dass, chose a Hindu child for his wife, Boodman could not refuse the marriage. No man is going to quarrel with a million-pound legacy, but he chose this ghastly method of getting rid of the child."

"I venture you are right," declared the bank clerk. "I felt sure Boodman Lal had killed the girl."

"Likely as not he was engaged to some English girl and was waiting for his uncle's death to make him wealthy."

"Quite possible, in fact probable."

Here a cab came angling across the square toward the two men as they stood in front of the grotesque temple. The Negro driver waved his whip interrogatively. The clerk beckoned him in. The cab drew up at the curb. Lowe climbed in but Poggioli remained on the pavement.

"Aren't you coming?"

"You know, Lowe," said Poggioli seriously, "I don't feel that I can conscientiously continue this investigation, trying to clear a person whom I have every reason to believe guilty."

The bank clerk was disturbed.

"But, man, don't leave me like this! At least come on to the police headquarters and explain your theory about the temple keeper, Gooka, and the rice. That seems to hang together pretty well. It is possible Boodman Lal didn't do this thing after all. We owe it to him to do all we can."

As Poggioli still hung back on the curb, Lowe asked:

"What do you want to do?"

"Well, I—er—thought I would go back to the cottage and pack my things."

The bank clerk was amazed.

"Pack your things—your boat doesn't sail until Friday!"

"Yes, I know, but there is a daily service to Curaçao. It struck me to go—"

"Aw, come!" cried Lowe in hospitable astonishment, "you can't run off like that, just when I've stirred up an interesting murder mystery for you to unravel. You ought to appreciate my efforts as a host more than that."

"Well, I do," hesitated Poggioli seriously. At that moment

his excess of caution took one of those odd, instantaneous shifts that come so unaccountably to men, and he thought to himself, "Well, damn it, this is an interesting situation. It's a shame to leave it, and nothing will happen to me."

So he swung into the cab with decision and ordered briskly: "All right, to the police station, Sambo!"

"Sounds more like it," declared the clerk, as the cab horses set out a brisk trot through the sunshine.

Mr. Lowe, the bank clerk, was not without a certain flair for making the most of a house guest, and when he reached the police station he introduced his companion to the chief of police as "Mr. Poggioli a professor in an American university and a research student in criminal psychology."

The chief of police, a Mr. Vickers, was a short, thick man with a tropic-browned face and eyes habitually squinted against the sun. He seemed not greatly impressed with the titles Lowe gave his friend but merely remarked that if Mr. Poggioli was hunting crimes, Trinidad was a good place to find them.

The bank clerk proceeded with a certain importance in his manner.

"I have asked his counsel in the Boodman Lal murder case. He has developed a theory, Mr. Vickers, as to who is the actual murderer of Mrs. Boodman Lal."

"So have I," replied Vickers with a dry smile.

"Of course you think Boodman Lal did it," said Lowe in a more commonplace manner.

Vickers did not answer this but continued looking at the two taller men in a listening attitude which caused Lowe to go on.

"Now in this matter, Mr. Vickers, I want to be perfectly frank with you. I'll admit we are in this case in the employ of Mr. Hira Dass, and are making an effort to clear Boodman Lal. We felt confident you would use the well-known skill of the police department of Port of Spain to work out a theory to clear Boodman Lal just as readily as you would to convict him."

"Our department usually devotes its time to conviction and not to clearing criminals."

"Yes, I know that, but if our theory will point out the actual murderer—"

"What is your theory?" inquired Vickers without enthusiasm.

The bank clerk began explaining the dream of the five beggars and the probability that they had been given sleeping potions.

The short man smiled faintly.

"So Mr. Poggioli's theory is based on the dreams of these men?"

Poggioli had a pedagogue's brevity of temper when his theories were questioned.

"It would be a remarkable coincidence, Mr. Vickers, if five men had lurid dreams simultaneously without some physical cause. It suggests strongly that their tea or rice was doped."

As Vickers continued looking at Poggioli the American continued with less acerbity:

"I should say that Gooka, the temple keeper, either doped the rice himself or he knows who did it."

"Possibly he does."

"My idea is that you send a man for the ricepot and teapot, have their contents analyzed, find out what soporific was used, then have your men search the sales records of the drug stores in the city to see who has lately bought such a drug."

Mr. Vickers grunted a noncommittal uh-huh, and then began in the livelier tones of a man who meets a stranger socially:

"How do you like Trinidad, Mr. Poggioli?"

"Remarkably luxuriant country—oranges and grapefruit growing wild."

"You've just arrived?"

"Yes."

"In what university do you teach?"

"Ohio State."

Mr. Vickers's eyes took on a humorous twinkle.

"A chair of criminal psychology in an ordinary state university—is that the result of your American prohibition laws, Professor?"

Poggioli smiled at this thrust.

"Mr. Lowe misstated my work a little. I am not a professor, I am simply a docent. And I have not specialized on criminal psychology. I quiz on general psychology."

"You are not teaching now?"

"No; this is my sabbatical year."

Mr. Vickers glanced up and down the American.

"You look young to have taught in a university six years."

There was something not altogether agreeable in this observation, but the officer rectified it a moment later by saying, "But you Americans start young—land of specialists. Now you, Mr. Poggioli—I suppose you are wrapped up heart and soul in your psychology?"

"I am," agreed the American positively.

"Do anything in the world to advance yourself in the science?"

"I rather think so," asserted Poggioli, with his enthusiasm mounting in his voice.

"Especially keen on original research work—"

Lowe interrupted, laughing.

"That's what he is, Chief. Do you know what he asked me to do yesterday afternoon?"

"No, what?"

The American turned abruptly on his friend.

"Now, Lowe, don't let's burden Mr. Vickers with household anecdotes."

"But I am really curious," declared the police chief. "Just what did Professor Poggioli ask you to do yesterday afternoon, Mr. Lowe?"

The bank clerk looked from one to the other, hardly knowing whether to go on or not. Mr. Vickers was smiling; Poggioli was very serious as he prohibited anecdotes about himself. The bank clerk thought: "This is real modesty." He said aloud: "It was just a little psychological experiment he wanted to do."

"Did he do it?" smiled the chief.

"Oh, no, I wouldn't hear of it."

"As unconventional as that!" cried Mr. Vickers, lifting sandy brows.

"It was really nothing," said Lowe, looking at his guest's rigid face and then at the police captain.

Suddenly Mr. Vickers dropped his quizzical attitude.

"I think I could guess your anecdote if I tried, Lowe. About a half hour ago I received a telephone message from my man stationed at the Hindu temple to keep a lookout for you and Mr. Poggioli."

The American felt a tautening of his muscles at this frontal attack. He had suspected something of the sort from the policeman's manner. The bank clerk stared at the officer in amazement.

"What was your bobby telephoning about us for?"

"Because one of the coolies under arrest told him that Mr. Poggioli slept in the temple last night."

"My word, that's not true!" cried the bank clerk. "That is exactly what he did not do. He suggested it to me but I said No. You remember, Poggioli—"

Mr. Lowe turned for corroboration, but the look on his friend's face amazed him.

"You didn't do it, did you Poggioli?" he gasped.

"You see he did," said Vickers dryly.

"But, Poggioli—in God's name—"

The American braced himself for an attempt to explain. He lifted his hand with a certain pedagogic mannerism.

"Gentlemen, I—I had a perfectly valid, an important reason for sleeping in the temple last night."

"I told you," nodded Vickers.

"In coolie town, in a coolie temple!" ejaculated Lowe.

"Gentlemen, I—can only ask your—your sympathetic attention to what I am about to say."

"Go on," said Vickers.

"You remember, Lowe, you and I were down there watching a wedding procession. Well, just as the music stopped and the line of coolies entered the building, suddenly it seemed to me as if—as if—they had—" Poggioli swallowed at nothing and then added the odd word, "vanished."

Vickers looked at him.

"Naturally, they had gone into the building."

"I don't mean that. I'm afraid you won't understand what I do mean—that the whole procession had ceased to exist, melted into nothingness."

Even Mr. Vickers blinked. Then he drew out a memorandum book and stolidly made a note.

"Is that all?"

"No, then I began speculating on what had given me such a

strange impression. You see that is really the idea on which the Hindus base their notion of heaven—oblivion, nothingness."

"Yes, I've heard that before."

"Well, our medieval Gothic architecture was a conception of our Western heaven; and I thought perhaps the Indian architecture had somehow caught the motif of the Indian religion; you know, suggested Nirvana. That was what amazed and intrigued me. That was why I wanted to sleep in the place. I wanted to see if I could further my shred of impression. Does this make any sense to you, Mr. Vickers?"

"I dare say it will, sir, to the criminal judge," opined the police chief cheerfully.

The psychologist felt a sinking of heart.

Mr. Vickers proceeded in the same matter-of-fact tone: "But no matter why you went in, what you did afterward is what counts. Here in Trinidad nobody is allowed to go around chopping off heads to see how it feels."

Poggioli looked at the officer with a ghastly sensation in his midriff.

"You don't think I did such a horrible thing as an experiment?"

Mr. Vickers drew out the makings of a cigarette.

"You Americans, especially you intellectual Americans, do some pretty stiff things, Mr. Poggioli. I was reading about two young intellectuals—"

"Good Lord!" quivered the psychologist with this particular reference beginning to grate on his nerves.

"These fellows I read about also tried to turn an honest penny by their murder—I don't suppose you happened to notice yesterday that the little girl, Maila Ran, was almost covered over with gold bangles and coins?"

"Of course I noticed it!" cried the psychologist, growing white, "but I had nothing whatever to do with the child. Your insinuations are brutal and repulsive. I did sleep in the temple—"

"By the way," interrupted Vickers suddenly, "you say you slept on a rug just as the coolies did?"

"Yes, I did."

"You didn't wake up either?"

"No."

"Then did the murderer of the child happen to put a coin and a bangle in your pockets, just as he did the other sleepers in the temple?"

"That's exactly what he did!" cried Poggioli, with the first ray of hope breaking upon him. "When I found them in my pocket on the tram this morning I came pretty near throwing them away, but fortunately I didn't. Here they are."

And gladly enough now he drew the trinkets out and showed them to the chief of police.

Mr. Vickers looked at the gold pieces, then at the psychologist.

"You don't happen to have any more, do you?"

The American said No, but it was with a certain thrill of anxiety that he began turning out his other pockets. If the mysterious criminal had placed more than two gold pieces in his pockets he would be in a very difficult position. However, the remainder of his belongings were quite legitimate.

"Well, that's something," admitted Vickers slowly. "Of course, you might have expected just such a questioning as this and provided yourself with these two pieces of gold, but I doubt it. Somehow, I don't believe you are a bright enough man to think of such a thing." He paused, pondering, and finally said, "I suppose you have no objection to my sending a man to search your baggage in Mr. Lowe's cottage?"

"Instead of objecting, I invite it, I request it."

Mr. Vickers nodded agreeably.

"Who can I telegraph to in America to learn something about your standing as a university man?"

"Dean Ingram, Ohio State, Columbus, Ohio, U.S.A."

Vickers made this note, then turned to Lowe.

"I suppose you've known Mr. Poggioli for a long time, Mr. Lowe?"

"Why n-no, I haven't," admitted the clerk.

"Where did you meet him?"

"Sailing from Barbuda to Antigua. On the *Trevemore*."

"Did he seem to have respectable American friends aboard?"

Lowe hesitated and flushed faintly.

"I—can hardly say."

"Why?"

"If I tell you Mr. Poggioli's mode of travel I am afraid you would hold it to his disadvantage."

"How did he travel?" queried the officer in surprise.

"The fact is he traveled as a deck passenger."

"You mean he had no cabin, shipped along on deck with the Negroes!"

"I did it myself!" cried Lowe, growing ruddy. "We couldn't get a cabin—they were all occupied."

The American reflected rapidly, and realized that Vickers could easily find out the real state of things from the ship's agents up the islands.

"Chief," said the psychologist with a tongue that felt thick, "I boarded the *Trevemore* at St. Kitts. There were cabins available. I chose deck passage deliberately. I wanted to study the natives."

"Then you are broke, just as I thought," ejaculated Mr. Vickers, "and I'll bet pounds to pence we'll find the jewelry around your place somewhere."

The chief hailed a passing cab, called a plainclothesman, put the three in the vehicle and started them briskly back up Prince Edward's Street, toward Tragarette Road, and thence to Lowe's cottage beyond the Indian village and its ill-starred temple.

The three men and the Negro driver trotted back up Tragarette, each lost in his own thoughts. The plainclothesman rode on the front seat with the cabman, but occasionally he glanced back to look at his prisoner. Lowe evidently was reflecting how this contretemps would affect his social and business standing in the city. The Negro also kept peering back under the hood of his cab, and finally he ejaculated:

"Killum jess to see 'em die. I declah, dese 'Mericans—" and he shook his kinky head.

A hot resentment rose up in the psychologist at this continued recurrence of that detestable crime. He realized with deep resentment that the crimes of particular Americans were held tentatively against all American citizens, while their great national charities and humanities were forgotten with the breath that told them. In the midst of these angry thoughts the cab drew up before the clerk's garden gate.

All got out. Lowe let them in with a key and then the three walked in a kind of grave haste across the lawn. The door was opened by Ram Jon, who took their hats and then followed them into the room Lowe had set apart for his guest.

This room, like all Trinidad chambers, was furnished in the

sparest and coolest manner possible: a table, three chairs, a bed with sheets, and Poggioli's trunk. It was so open to inspection nothing could have been concealed in it. The plainclothesman opened the table drawer.

"Would you mind opening your trunk, Mr. Poggioli?"

The American got out his keys, knelt and undid the hasp of his wardrobe trunk, then swung the two halves apart. One side held containers, the other suits. Poggioli opened the drawers casually; collar and handkerchief box at the top, hat box, shirt box. As he did this came a faint clinking sound. The detective stepped forward and lifted out the shirts. Beneath them lay a mass of coins and bangles flung into the tray helter-skelter.

The American stared with an open mouth, unable to say a word.

The plainclothesman snapped with a certain indignant admiration in his voice: "Your nerve almost got you by!"

The thing seemed unreal to the American. He had the same uncanny feeling that he had experienced when the procession entered the temple. Materiality seemed to have slipped a cog. A wild thought came to him that somehow the Hindus had dematerialized the gold and caused it to reappear in his trunk. Then there came a terrifying fancy that he had committed the crime in his sleep. This last clung to his mind. After all, he had murdered the little girl bride, Maila Ran!

The plainclothesman spoke to Lowe:

"Have your man bring me a sack to take this stuff back to headquarters."

Ram Jon slithered from the room and presently returned with a sack. The inspector took his handkerchief, lifted the pieces out with it, one by one, and placed them in the sack.

"Lowe," said Poggioli pitifully, "you don't believe I did this, do you?"

The bank clerk wiped his face with his handkerchief.

"In your trunk, Poggioli—"

"If I did it I was sleepwalking!" cried the unhappy man. "My God, to think it is possible—but right here in my own trunk—" he stood staring at the bag, at the shirt box.

The plainclothesman said dryly: "We might as well start back, I suppose. This is all."

Lowe suddenly cast in his lot with his guest.

"I'll go back with you, Poggioli. I'll see you through this pinch. Somehow I can't, I won't believe you did it!"

"Thanks! Thanks!"

The bank clerk masked his emotion under a certain grim facetiousness.

"You know, Poggioli, you set out to clear Boodman Lal—it looks as if you've done it."

"No, he didn't," denied the plainclothesman. "Boodman Lal was out of jail at least an hour before you fellows drove up a while ago."

"Out—had you turned him out?"

"Yes."

"How was that?"

"Because he didn't go to the temple at all last night with his wife. He went down to Queen's Park Hotel and played billiards till one o'clock. He called up some friends and proved that easily enough." Lowe stared at his friend, aghast.

"My word, Poggioli, that leaves nobody but—you." The psychologist lost all semblance of resistance.

"I don't know anything about it. If I did it I was asleep. That's all I can say. The coolies—" He had a dim notion of accusing them again, but he recalled that he had proved to himself clearly and logically that they were innocent. "I don't know anything about it," he repeated helplessly.

Half an hour later the three men were at police headquarters once more, and the plainclothesman and the turnkey, a humble, gray sort of man, took the American back to a cell. The turnkey unlocked one in a long row of cells and swung it open for Poggioli.

The bank clerk gave him what encouragement he could.

"Don't be too downhearted. I'll do everything I can. Somehow I believe you are innocent. I'll hire your lawyers, cable your friends—" Poggioli was repeating a stunned "Thanks! Thanks!" as the cell door shut between them. The bolt clashed home and was locked. And the men were tramping down the iron corridor. Poggioli was alone.

There was a chair and a bunk in the cell. The psychologist looked at these with an irrational feeling that he would not stay in the prison long enough to warrant his sitting down. Presently he did sit down on the bunk.

He sat perfectly still and tried to assemble his thoughts against the mountain of adverse evidence which suddenly had been piled against him. His sleep in the temple, the murder, the coins in his shirt box—after all he must have committed the crime in his sleep.

As he sat with his head in his hands pondering this theory, it grew more and more incredible. To commit the murder in his sleep, to put the coins in the pockets of the beggars in a clever effort to divert suspicion, to bring the gold to Lowe's cottage, and then to go back and he down on the mat, all while he was asleep—that was impossible. He could not believe any human being could perform so fantastic, so complicated a feat.

On the other hand, no other criminal would place the whole booty in Poggioli's trunk and so lose it. That too was irrational. He was forced back to his dream theory.

When he accepted this hypothesis he wondered just what he had dreamed. If he had really murdered the girl in a nightmare, then the murder was stamped somewhere in his subconscious, divided from his day memories by the nebulous associations of sleep. He wondered if he could reproduce them.

To recall a lost dream is perhaps one of the nicest tasks that ever a human brain was driven to. Poggioli, being a psychologist, had had a certain amount of experience with such attempts. Now he lay down on his bunk and began the effort in a mechanical way.

He recalled as vividly as possible his covert exit from Lowe's cottage, his walk down Tragarette Road between perfumed gardens, the lights of Peru, and finally his entrance into the temple. He imagined again the temple attendant, Gooka, looking curiously at him, but giving him tea and rice and pointing out his rug. Poggioli remembered that he lay down on the rug on his back with his hands under his head exactly as he was now lying on his cell bunk. For a while he had stared at the illuminated image of Krishna, then at the dark spring of the dome over his head.

And as he lay there, gazing thus, his thoughts had begun to waver, to lose beat with his senses, to make misinterpretations. He had thought that the Krishna moved slightly, then settled back and became a statue again—here some tenuous connection in his thoughts snapped, and he lost his whole picture in the hard bars of his cell again.

Poggioli lay relaxed a while, then began once more. He

reached the point where the Krishna moved, seemed about to speak, and then—there he was back in his cell.

It was nerve-racking, tantalizing, this fishing for the gossamers of a dream which continually broke; this pursuing the grotesqueries of a nightmare and trying to connect it with his solid everyday life of thought and action. What had he dreamed?

Minutes dragged out as Poggioli pursued the vanished visions of his head. Yes, it had seemed to him that the image of the Buddha moved, that it had even risen from its attitude of meditation, and suddenly, with a little thrill, Poggioli remembered that the dome of the Hindu temple was opened and this left him staring upward into a vast abyss. It seemed to the psychologist that he stared upward, and the Krishna stared upward, both gazing into an unending space, and presently he realized that he and the great upward-staring Krishna were one; that they had always been one; and that their oneness filled all space with enormous, with infinite power. But this oneness which was Poggioli was alone in an endless, featureless space. No other thing existed, because nothing had ever been created; there was only a creator. All the creatures and matter which had ever been or ever would be were wrapped up in him, Poggioli, or Buddha. And then Poggioli saw that space and time had ceased to be, for space and time are the offspring of division. And at last Krishna or Poggioli was losing all entity or being in this tranced immobility.

And Poggioli began struggling desperately against nothingness. He writhed at his deadened muscles, he willed in torture to retain some vestige of being, and at last after what seemed millenniums of effort he formed the thought:

"I would rather lose my oneness with Krishna and become the vilest and poorest of creatures—to mate, fight, love, lust, kill, and be killed than to be lost in this terrible trance of the universal!"

And when he had formed this tortured thought Poggioli remembered that he had awakened and it was five o'clock in the morning. He had arisen with a throbbing headache and had gone home.

That was his dream.

The American arose from his bunk filled with the deepest satisfaction from his accomplishment. Then he recalled with surprise that all five of the coolies had much the same dream; grandiloquence and power accompanied by great unhappiness.

"That was an odd thing," thought the psychologist, "six men dreaming the same dream in different terms. There must have been some physical cause for such a phenomenon."

Then he remembered that he had heard the same story from another source. Old Hira Dass in his marble court had expressed the same sentiment, complaining of the emptiness of his riches and power. However—and this was crucial—Hira Dass's grief was not a mere passing nightmare, it was his settled condition.

With this a queer idea popped into Poggioli's mind. Could not these six dreams have been a transference of an idea? While he and the coolies lay sleeping with passive minds, suppose old Hira Dass had entered the temple with his great unhappiness in his mind, and suppose he had committed some terrible deed which wrought his emotions to a monsoon of passion. Would not his horrid thoughts have registered themselves in different forms on the minds of the sleeping men!

Here Poggioli's ideas danced about like the molecules of a crystal in solution, each one rushing of its own accord to take its appointed place in a complicated crystalline design. And so a complete understanding of the murder of little Maila Ran rushed in upon him.

Poggioli leaped to his feet and halloed his triumph.

"Here, Vickers! Lowe! Turnkey! I have it! I've solved it! Turn me out! I know who killed the girl!"

After he had shouted for several minutes Poggioli saw the form of a man coming up the dark aisle with a lamp. He was surprised at the lamp but passed over it.

"Turnkey!" he cried, "I know who murdered the child—old Hira Dass! Now listen—" He was about to relate his dream, but realized that would avail nothing in an English court, so he leaped to the physical end of the crime, matter with which the English juggle so expertly. His thoughts danced into shape.

"Listen, turnkey, go tell Vickers to take that gold and develop all the fingerprints on it—he'll find Hira Dass's prints! Also, tell him to follow out that opiate clue I gave him—he'll find Hira Dass's servant bought the opiate. Also, Hira Dass sent a man to put the gold in my trunk. See if you can't find brass or steel filings in my room where the scoundrel sat and filed a new key. Also, give Ram Jon the third degree; he knows who brought the gold."

The one with the lamp made a gesture.

"They've done all that, sir, long ago."

"They did!"

"Certainly, sir, and old Hira Dass confessed everything, though why a rich old man like him should have murdered a pretty child is more than I can see. These Hindus are unaccountable, sir, even the millionaires."

Poggioli passed over so simple a query.

"But why did the old devil pick on me for a scapegoat?" he cried, puzzled.

"Oh, he explained that to the police, sir. He said he picked on a white man so the police would make a thorough investigation and be sure to catch him. In fact, he said, sir, that he had willed that you should come and sleep in the temple that night."

Poggioli stared with a little prickling sensation at this touch of the occult world.

"What I can't see, sir," went on the man with the lamp, "was why the old coolie wanted to be caught and hanged—why didn't he commit suicide?"

"Because then his soul would have returned in the form of some beast. He wanted to be slain. He expects to be reborn instantly in Benares with little Maila Ran. He hopes to be a great man with wife and children."

"Nutty idea!" cried the fellow.

But the psychologist sat staring at the lamp with a queer feeling that possibly such a fantastic idea might be true after all. For what goes with this passionate, uneasy force in man when he dies? May not the dead struggle to reanimate themselves as he had done in his dream? Perhaps the numberless dead still will to live and be divided; and perhaps living things are a result of the struggles of the dead, and not the dead of the living.

His thoughts suddenly shifted back to the present.

"Turnkey," he snapped with academic sharpness, "why didn't you come and tell me of old Hira Dass's confession the moment it occurred? What did you mean, keeping me locked up here when you knew I was an innocent man?"

"Because I couldn't," said the form with the lamp sorrowfully, "Old Hira Dass didn't confess until a month and ten days after you were hanged, sir."

And the lamp went out.

DISCUSSION QUESTIONS

- Reading this anthology, did you learn anything about the Golden Age whodunit story that you didn't already know? If so, what?

- Which story's mystery did you find the most perplexing?

- Did any of the solutions stretch credibility?

- Were you able to solve any of the mysteries before the main character? If so, which ones?

- How did the cultural history of the era play into these stories? Did anything help date them for you?

- Did any stories surprise you in terms of subject, character, or setting? If so, which ones?

- Did any stories remind you of work from authors today? If so, which ones?

- What characteristics do you think made these authors so popular in their day? Do you think readers today still want the same things from their reading material?

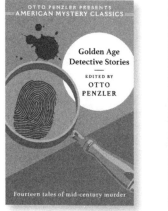

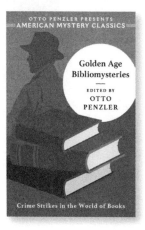

All titles are available in hardcover and in trade paperback.

Order from your favorite bookstore or from
The Mysterious Bookshop, 58 Warren Street, New York, N.Y. 10007
(www.mysteriousbookshop.com).

Charlotte Armstrong, *The Chocolate Cobweb.* When Amanda Garth was born, a mix-up caused the hospital to briefly hand her over to the prestigious Garrison family instead of to her birth parents. The error was quickly fixed, Amanda was never told, and the secret was forgotten for twenty-three years . . . until her aunt revealed it in casual conversation. But what if the initial switch never actually occurred? **Introduction by A. J. Finn.**

Charlotte Armstrong, *The Unsuspected.* First published in 1946, this suspenseful novel opens with a young woman who has ostensibly hanged herself, leaving a suicide note. Her friend doesn't believe it and begins an investigation that puts her own life in jeopardy. It was filmed in 1947 by Warner Brothers, starring Claude Rains and Joan Caulfield. **Introduction by Otto Penzler.**

Anthony Boucher, *The Case of the Baker Street Irregulars.* When a studio announces a new hard-boiled Sherlock Holmes film, the Baker Street Irregulars begin a campaign to discredit it. Attempting to mollify them, the producers invite members to the set, where threats are received, each referring to one of the original Holmes tales, followed by murder. Fortunately, the amateur sleuths use Holmesian lessons to solve the crime. **Introduction by Otto Penzler.**

Anthony Boucher, *Rocket to the Morgue.* Hilary Foulkes has made so many enemies that it is difficult to speculate who was responsible for stabbing him nearly to death in a room with only one door through which no one was seen entering or leaving. This classic locked room mystery is populated by such thinly disguised science fiction legends as Robert Heinlein, L. Ron Hubbard, and John W. Campbell. **Introduction by F. Paul Wilson.**

Fredric Brown, *The Fabulous Clipjoint.* Brown's outstanding mystery won an Edgar as the best first novel of the year (1947). When Wallace Hunter is found dead in an alley after a long night of drinking, the police don't really care. But his teenage son Ed and his uncle Am, the carnival worker, are convinced that some things don't add up and the crime isn't what it seems to be. **Introduction by Lawrence Block.**

John Dickson Carr, *The Crooked Hinge.* Selected by a group of mystery experts as one of the 15 best impossible crime novels ever written, this is one of Gideon Fell's greatest challenges. Estranged from his family for 25 years, Sir John Farnleigh returns to England from America to claim his inheritance but another person turns up claiming that he can prove he is the real Sir John. Inevitably, one of them is murdered. **Introduction by Charles Todd.**

John Dickson Carr, *The Eight of Swords.* When Gideon Fell arrives at a crime scene, it appears to be straightforward enough. A man has been shot to death in an unlocked room and the likely perpetrator was a recent visitor. But Fell discovers inconsistencies and his investigations are complicated by an apparent poltergeist, some American gangsters, and two meddling amateur sleuths. **Introduction by Otto Penzler.**

John Dickson Carr, *The Mad Hatter Mystery.* A prankster has been stealing top hats all around London. Gideon Fell suspects that the same person may be responsible for the theft of a manuscript of a long-lost story by Edgar Allan Poe. The hats reappear in unexpected but conspicuous places but, when one is found on the head of a corpse by the Tower of London, it is evident that the thefts are more than pranks. **Introduction by Otto Penzler.**

John Dickson Carr, *The Plague Court Murders.* When murder occurs in a locked hut on Plague Court, an estate haunted by the ghost of a hangman's assistant who died a victim of the black death, Sir Henry Merrivale seeks a logical solution to a ghostly crime. A spiritual medium employed to rid the house of his spirit is found stabbed to death in a locked stone hut on the grounds, surrounded by an untouched circle of mud. **Introduction by Michael Dirda.**

John Dickson Carr, *The Red Widow Murders.* In a "haunted" mansion, the room known as the Red Widow's Chamber proves lethal to all who spend the night. Eight people investigate and the one who draws the ace of spades must sleep in it. The room is locked from the inside and watched all night by the others. When the door is unlocked, the victim has been poisoned. Enter Sir Henry Merrivale to solve the crime. **Introduction by Tom Mead.**

Frances Crane, *The Turquoise Shop.* In an arty little New Mexico town, Mona Brandon has arrived from the East and becomes the subject of gossip about her money, her influence, and the corpse in the nearby desert who may be her husband. Pat Holly, who runs the local gift shop, is as interested as anyone in the goings on—but even more in Pat Abbott, the detective investigating the possible murder. **Introduction by Anne Hillerman.**

Todd Downing, *Vultures in the Sky.* There is no end to the series of terrifying events that befall a luxury train bound for Mexico. First, a man dies when the train passes through a dark tunnel, then it comes to an abrupt stop in the middle of the desert. More deaths occur when night falls and the passengers panic when they realize they are trapped with a murderer on the loose. **Introduction by James Sallis.**

Mignon G. Eberhart, *Murder by an Aristocrat.* Nurse Keate is called to help a man who has been "accidentally" shot in the shoulder. When he is murdered while convalescing, it is clear that there was no accident. Although a killer is loose in the mansion, the family seems more concerned that news of the murder will leave their circle. *The New Yorker* wrote than "Eberhart can weave an almost flawless mystery." **Introduction by Nancy Pickard.**

Erle Stanley Gardner, *The Case of the Baited Hook.* Perry Mason gets a phone call in the middle of the night and his potential client says it's urgent, that he has two one-thousand-dollar bills that he will give him as a retainer, with an additional ten-thousand whenever he is called on to represent him. When

Mason takes the case, it is not for the caller but for a beautiful woman whose identity is hidden behind a mask. **Introduction by Otto Penzler.**

Erle Stanley Gardner, *The Case of the Borrowed Brunette.* A mysterious man named Mr. Hines has advertised a job for a woman who has to fulfill very specific physical requirements. Eva Martell, pretty but struggling in her career as a model, takes the job but her aunt smells a rat and hires Perry Mason to investigate. Her fears are realized when Hines turns up in the apartment with a bullet hole in his head. **Introduction by Otto Penzler.**

Erle Stanley Gardner, *The Case of the Careless Kitten.* Helen Kendal receives a mysterious phone call from her vanished uncle Franklin, long presumed dead, who urges her to contact Perry Mason. Soon, she finds herself the main suspect in the murder of an unfamiliar man. Her kitten has just survived a poisoning attempt—as has her aunt Matilda. What is the connection between Franklin's return and the murder attempts? **Introduction by Otto Penzler.**

Erle Stanley Gardner, *The Case of the Rolling Bones.* One of Gardner's most successful Perry Mason novels opens with a clear case of blackmail, though the person being blackmailed claims he isn't. It is not long before the police are searching for someone wanted for killing the same man in two different states—thirty-three years apart. The confounding puzzle of what happened to the dead man's toes is a challenge. **Introduction by Otto Penzler.**

Erle Stanley Gardner, *The Case of the Shoplifter's Shoe.* Most cases for Perry Mason involve murder but here he is hired because a young woman fears her aunt is a kleptomaniac. Sarah may not have been precisely the best guardian for a collection of valuable diamonds and, sure enough, they go missing. When the jeweler is found shot dead, Sarah is spotted leaving the murder scene with a bundle of gems stuffed in her purse. **Introduction by Otto Penzler.**

Erle Stanley Gardner, *The Bigger They Come.* Gardner's first novel using the pseudonym A.A. Fair starts off a series featuring the large and loud Bertha Cool and her employee, the small and meek Donald Lam. Given the job of delivering divorce papers to an evident crook,

Lam can't find him—but neither can the police. The *Los Angeles Times* called this book: "Breathlessly dramatic . . . an original." Introduction by Otto Penzler.

Frances Noyes Hart, *The Bellamy Trial*. Inspired by the real-life Hall-Mills case, the most sensational trial of its day, this is the story of Stephen Bellamy and Susan Ives, accused of murdering Bellamy's wife Madeleine. Eight days of dynamic testimony, some true, some not, make headlines for an enthralled public. Rex Stout called this historic courtroom thriller one of the ten best mysteries of all time. **Introduction by Hank Phillippi Ryan.**

H.F. Heard, *A Taste for Honey*. The elderly Mr. Mycroft quietly keeps bees in Sussex, where he is approached by the reclusive and somewhat misanthropic Mr. Silchester, whose honey supplier was found dead, stung to death by her bees. Mycroft, who shares many traits with Sherlock Holmes, sets out to find the vicious killer. Rex Stout described it as "sinister . . . a tale well and truly told." **Introduction by Otto Penzler.**

Dolores Hitchens, *The Alarm of the Black Cat*. Detective fiction aficionado Rachel Murdock has a peculiar meeting with a little girl and a dead toad, sparking her curiosity about a love triangle that has sparked anger. When the girl's great grandmother is found dead, Rachel and her cat Samantha work with a friend in the Los Angeles Police Department to get to the bottom of things. **Introduction by David Handler.**

Dolores Hitchens, *The Cat Saw Murder*. Miss Rachel Murdock, the highly intelligent 70-year-old amateur sleuth, is not entirely heartbroken when her slovenly, unattractive, bridge-cheating niece is murdered. Miss Rachel is happy to help the socially maladroit and somewhat bumbling Detective Lieutenant Stephen Mayhew, retaining her composure when a second brutal murder occurs. **Introduction by Joyce Carol Oates.**

Dorothy B. Hughes, *Dread Journey*. A bigshot Hollywood producer has worked on his magnum opus for years, hiring and firing one beautiful starlet after another. But Kitten Agnew's contract won't allow her to be fired, so she fears she might be terminated more permanently. Together with the producer on a train journey from Hollywood to Chicago, Kitten becomes more terrified with each passing mile. **Introduction by Sarah Weinman.**

Dorothy B. Hughes, *Ride the Pink Horse*. When Sailor met Willis Douglass, he was just a poor kid who Douglass groomed to work as a confidential secretary. As the senator became increasingly corrupt, he knew he could count on Sailor to clean up his messes. No longer a senator, Douglass flees Chicago for Santa Fe, leaving behind a murder rap and Sailor as the prime suspect. Seeking vengeance, Sailor follows. **Introduction by Sara Paretsky.**

Dorothy B. Hughes, *The So Blue Marble*. Set in the glamorous world of New York high society, this novel became a suspense classic as twins from Europe try to steal a rare and beautiful gem owned by an aristocrat whose sister is an even more menacing presence. *The New Yorker* called it "Extraordinary . . . [Hughes'] brilliant descriptive powers make and unmake reality." **Introduction by Otto Penzler.**

W. Bolingbroke Johnson, *The Widening Stain*. After a cocktail party, the attractive Lucie Coindreau, a "black-eyed, black-haired Frenchwoman" visits the rare books wing of the library and apparently takes a headfirst fall from an upper gallery. Dismissed as a horrible accident, it seems dubious when Professor Hyett is strangled while reading a priceless 12th-century manuscript, which has gone missing. **Introduction by Nicholas A. Basbanes**

Baynard Kendrick, *Blind Man's Bluff*. Blinded in World War II, Duncan Maclain forms a successful private detective agency, aided by his two dogs. Here, he is called on to solve the case of a blind man who plummets from the top of an eight-story building, apparently with no one present except his dead-drunk son. **Introduction by Otto Penzler.**

Baynard Kendrick, *The Odor of Violets*. Duncan Maclain, a blind former intelligence officer, is asked to investigate the murder of an actor in his Greenwich Village apartment. This would cause a stir at any time but, when the actor possesses secret government plans that then go missing, it's enough to interest the local police as well as the American government and Maclain, who suspects a German spy plot. **Introduction by Otto Penzler.**

C. Daly King, *Obelists at Sea*. On a cruise ship traveling from New York to Paris, the lights of the smoking room briefly go out, a gunshot crashes through the night, and a man is dead. Two detectives are on board but so are four psychiatrists who believe their professional knowledge can solve the case by understanding the psyche of the killer—each with a different theory. **Introduction by Martin Edwards.**

Jonathan Latimer, *Headed for a Hearse*. Featuring Bill Crane, the booze-soaked Chicago private detective, this humorous hard-boiled novel was filmed as *The Westland Case* in 1937 starring Preston Foster. Robert Westland has been framed for the grisly murder of his wife in a room with doors and windows locked from the inside. As the day of his execution nears, he relies on Crane to find the real murderer. **Introduction by Max Allan Collins**

Lange Lewis, *The Birthday Murder*. Victoria is a successful novelist and screenwriter and her husband is a movie director so their marriage seems almost too good to be true. Then, on her birthday, her happy new life comes crashing down when her husband is murdered using a method of poisoning that was described in one of her books. She quickly becomes the leading suspect. **Introduction by Randal S. Brandt.**

Frances and Richard Lockridge, *Death on the Aisle*. In one of the most beloved books to feature Mr. and Mrs. North, the body of a wealthy backer of a play is found dead in a seat of the 45th Street Theater. Pam is thrilled to engage in her favorite pastime—playing amateur sleuth—much to the annoyance of Jerry, her publisher husband. The Norths inspired a stage play, a film, and long-running radio and TV series. **Introduction by Otto Penzler.**

John P. Marquand, *Your Turn, Mr. Moto*. The first novel about Mr. Moto, originally titled *No Hero*, is the story of a World War I hero pilot who finds himself jobless during the Depression. In Tokyo for a big opportunity that falls apart, he meets a Japanese agent and his Russian colleague and the pilot suddenly finds himself caught in a web of intrigue. Peter Lorre played Mr. Moto in a series of popular films. **Introduction by Lawrence Block.**

Stuart Palmer, *The Penguin Pool Murder*. The

first adventure of schoolteacher and dedicated amateur sleuth Hildegarde Withers occurs at the New York Aquarium when she and her young students notice a corpse in one of the tanks. It was published in 1931 and filmed the next year, starring Edna May Oliver as the American Miss Marple—though much funnier than her English counterpart. **Introduction by Otto Penzler.**

Stuart Palmer, *The Puzzle of the Happy Hooligan*. New York City schoolteacher Hildegarde Withers cannot resist "assisting" homicide detective Oliver Piper. In this novel, she is on vacation in Hollywood and on the set of a movie about Lizzie Borden when the screenwriter is found dead. Six comic films about Withers appeared in the 1930s, most successfully starring Edna May Oliver. **Introduction by Otto Penzler.**

Otto Penzler, ed., *Golden Age Bibliomysteries*. Stories of murder, theft, and suspense occur with alarming regularity in the unlikely world of books and bibliophiles, including bookshops, libraries, and private rare book collections, written by such giants of the mystery genre as Ellery Queen, Cornell Woolrich, Lawrence G. Blochman, Vincent Starrett, and Anthony Boucher. **Introduction by Otto Penzler.**

Otto Penzler, ed., *Golden Age Detective Stories*. The history of American mystery fiction has its pantheon of authors who have influenced and entertained readers for nearly a century, reaching its peak during the Golden Age, and this collection pays homage to the work of the most acclaimed: Cornell Woolrich, Erle Stanley Gardner, Craig Rice, Ellery Queen, Dorothy B. Hughes, Mary Roberts Rinehart, and more. **Introduction by Otto Penzler.**

Otto Penzler, ed., *Golden Age Locked Room Mysteries*. The so-called impossible crime category reached its zenith during the 1920s, 1930s, and 1940s, and this volume includes the greatest of the great authors who mastered the form: John Dickson Carr, Ellery Queen, C. Daly King, Clayton Rawson, and Erle Stanley Gardner. Like great magicians, these literary conjurors will baffle and delight readers. **Introduction by Otto Penzler.**

Ellery Queen, *The Adventures of Ellery Queen*. These stories are the earliest short works to feature Queen as a detective and are among the best of the author's fair-play mysteries. So many of the elements that comprise the gestalt of Queen may be found in these tales: alternate solutions, the dying clue, a bizarre crime, and the author's ability to find fresh variations of works by other authors. **Introduction by Otto Penzler.**

Ellery Queen, *The American Gun Mystery*. A rodeo comes to New York City at the Colosseum. The headliner is Buck Horne, the once popular film cowboy who opens the show leading a charge of forty whooping cowboys until they pull out their guns and fire into the air. Buck falls to the ground, shot dead. The police instantly lock the doors to search everyone but the offending weapon has completely vanished. **Introduction by Otto Penzler.**

Ellery Queen, *The Chinese Orange Mystery*. The offices of publisher Donald Kirk have seen strange events but nothing like this. A strange man is found dead with two long spears alongside his back. And, though no one was seen entering or leaving the room, everything has been turned backwards or upside down: pictures face the wall, the victim's clothes are worn backwards, the rug upside down. Why in the world? **Introduction by Otto Penzler.**

Ellery Queen, *The Dutch Shoe Mystery*. Millionaire philanthropist Abagail Doorn falls into a coma and she is rushed to the hospital she funds for an emergency operation by one of the leading surgeons on the East Coast. When she is wheeled into the operating theater, the sheet covering her body is pulled back to reveal her garroted corpse—the first of a series of murders **Introduction by Otto Penzler.**

Ellery Queen, *The Egyptian Cross Mystery*. A small-town schoolteacher is found dead, headed, and tied to a T-shaped cross on December 25th, inspiring such sensational headlines as "Crucifixion on Christmas Day." Amateur sleuth Ellery Queen is so intrigued he travels to Virginia but fails to solve the crime. Then a similar murder takes place on New York's Long Island—and then another. **Introduction by Otto Penzler.**

Ellery Queen, *The Siamese Twin Mystery*. When Ellery and his father encounter a raging forest fire on a mountain, their only hope is to drive up to an isolated hillside manor owned by a secretive surgeon and his strange guests. While playing solitaire in the middle of the night, the doctor is shot. The only clue is a torn playing card. Suspects include a society beauty, a valet, and conjoined twins. **Introduction by Otto Penzler.**

Ellery Queen, *The Spanish Cape Mystery*. Amateur detective Ellery Queen arrives in the resort town of Spanish Cape soon after a young woman and her uncle are abducted by a gun-toting, one-eyed giant. The next day, the woman's somewhat dicey boyfriend is found murdered—totally naked under a black fedora and opera cloak. **Introduction by Otto Penzler.**

Patrick Quentin, *A Puzzle for Fools*. Broadway producer Peter Duluth takes to the bottle when his wife dies but enters a sanitarium to dry out. Malevolent events plague the hospital, including when Peter hears his own voice intone, "There will be murder." And there is. He investigates, aided by a young woman who is also a patient. This is the first of nine mysteries featuring Peter and Iris Duluth. **Introduction by Otto Penzler.**

Clayton Rawson, *Death from a Top Hat*. When the New York City Police Department is baffled by an apparently impossible crime, they call on The Great Merlini, a retired stage magician who now runs a Times Square magic shop. In his first case, two occultists have been murdered in a room locked from the inside, their bodies positioned to form a pentagram. **Introduction by Otto Penzler.**

Craig Rice, *Eight Faces at Three*. Gin-soaked John J. Malone, defender of the guilty, is notorious for getting his culpable clients off. It's the innocent ones who are problems. Like Holly Inglehart, accused of piercing the black heart of her well-heeled aunt Alexandria with a lovely Florentine paper cutter. No one who knew the old battle-ax liked her, but Holly's prints were found on the murder weapon. **Introduction by Lisa Lutz.**

Craig Rice, *Home Sweet Homicide*. Known as the Dorothy Parker of mystery fiction for her memorable wit, Craig Rice was the first detective writer to appear on the cover of *Time* magazine. This comic mystery features two kids who are trying to find a husband for their widowed mother while she's engaged in sleuthing. Filmed with the same title in 1946 with Peggy Ann Garner and Randolph Scott. **Introduction by Otto Penzler.**

Mary Roberts Rinehart, *The Album*. Crescent Place is a quiet enclave of wealthy people in which nothing ever happens—until a bedridden old woman is attacked by an intruder with an ax. *The New York Times* stated: "All Mary Roberts Rinehart mystery stories are good, but this one is better." **Introduction by Otto Penzler.**

Mary Roberts Rinehart, *The Haunted Lady*. The arsenic in her sugar bowl was wealthy widow Eliza Fairbanks's first clue that somebody wanted her dead. Nightly visits of bats, birds, and rats, obviously aimed at scaring the dowager to death, was the second. Eliza calls the police, who send nurse Hilda Adams, the amateur sleuth they refer to as "Miss Pinkerton," to work undercover to discover the culprit. **Introduction by Otto Penzler.**

Mary Roberts Rinehart, *Miss Pinkerton*. Hilda Adams is a nurse, not a detective, but she is observant and smart and so it is common for Inspector Patton to call on her for help. Her success results in his calling her "Miss Pinkerton." *The New Republic* wrote: "From thousands of hearts and homes the cry will go up: Thank God for Mary Roberts Rinehart." **Introduction by Carolyn Hart.**

Mary Roberts Rinehart, *The Red Lamp*. Professor William Porter refuses to believe that the seaside manor he's just inherited is haunted but he has to convince his wife to move in. However, he soon sees evidence of the occult phenomena of which the townspeople speak. Whether it is a spirit or a human being, Porter accepts that there is a connection to the rash of murders that have terrorized the countryside. **Introduction by Otto Penzler.**

Mary Roberts Rinehart, *The Wall*. For two decades, Mary Roberts Rinehart was the second-best-selling author in America (only Sinclair Lewis outsold her) and was beloved for her tales of suspense. In a magnificent mansion, the ex-wife of one of the owners turns up making demands and is found dead the next day. And there are more dark secrets lying behind the walls of the estate. **Introduction by Otto Penzler.**

Joel Townsley Rogers, *The Red Right Hand*. This extraordinary whodunnit that is as puzzling as it is terrifying was identified by crime fiction scholar Jack Adrian as "one of the dozen or so finest mystery novels of the 20th century." A deranged killer sends a doctor on a quest for the truth—deep into the recesses of his own mind—when he and his bride-to-be elope but pick up a terrifying sharp-toothed hitch-hiker. **Introduction by Joe R. Lansdale.**

Roger Scarlett, *Cat's Paw*. The family of the wealthy old bachelor Martin Greenough cares far more about his money than they do about him. For his birthday, he invites all his potential heirs to his mansion to tell them what they hope to hear. Before he can disburse funds, however, he is murdered, and the Boston Police Department's big problem is that there are too many suspects. **Introduction by Curtis Evans**

Vincent Starrett, *Dead Man Inside*. 1930s Chicago is a tough town but some crimes are more bizarre than others. Customers arrive at a haberdasher to find a corpse in the window and a sign on the door: *Dead Man Inside! I am Dead. The store will not open today.* This is just one of a series of odd murders that terrorizes the city. Reluctant detective Walter Ghost leaps into action to learn what is behind the plague. **Introduction by Otto Penzler.**

Vincent Starrett, *The Great Hotel Murder*. Theater critic and amateur sleuth Riley Blackwood investigates a murder in a Chicago hotel where the dead man had changed rooms with a stranger who had registered under a fake name. *The New York Times* described it as "an ingenious plot with enough complications to keep the reader guessing." **Introduction by Lyndsay Faye.**

Vincent Starrett, *Murder on 'B' Deck*. Walter Ghost, a psychologist, scientist, explorer, and former intelligence officer, is on a cruise ship and his friend novelist Dunsten Mollock, a Nigel Bruce-like Watson whose role is to offer occasional comic relief, accommodates when he fails to leave the ship before it takes off. Although they make mistakes along the way, the amateur sleuths solve the shipboard murders. **Introduction by Ray Betzner.**

Phoebe Atwood Taylor, *The Cape Cod Mystery*. Vacationers have flocked to Cape Cod to avoid the heat wave that hit the Northeast and find their holiday unpleasant when the area is flooded with police trying to find the murderer of a muckraking journalist who took a cottage for the season. Finding a solution falls to Asey Mayo, "the Cape Cod Sherlock," known for his worldly wisdom, folksy humor, and common sense. **Introduction by Otto Penzler.**

S. S. Van Dine, *The Benson Murder Case.* The first of 12 novels to feature Philo Vance, the most popular and influential detective character of the early part of the 20th century. When wealthy stockbroker Alvin Benson is found shot to death in a locked room in his mansion, the police are baffled until the erudite flaneur and art collector arrives on the scene. Paramount filmed it in 1930 with William Powell as Vance. **Introduction by Ragnar Jónasson.**

Cornell Woolrich, *The Bride Wore Black.* The first suspense novel by one of the greatest of all noir authors opens with a bride and her new husband walking out of the church. A car speeds by, shots ring out, and he falls dead at her feet. Determined to avenge his death, she tracks down everyone in the car, concluding with a shocking surprise. It was filmed by Francois Truffaut in 1968, starring Jeanne Moreau. **Introduction by Eddie Muller.**

Cornell Woolrich, *Deadline at Dawn.* Quinn is overcome with guilt about having robbed a stranger's home. He meets Bricky, a dime-a-dance girl, and they fall for each other. When they return to the crime scene, they discover a dead body. Knowing Quinn will be accused of the crime, they race to find the true killer before he's arrested. A 1946 film starring Susan Hayward was loosely based on the plot. **Introduction by David Gordon.**

Cornell Woolrich, *Waltz into Darkness.* A New Orleans businessman successfully courts a woman through the mail but he is shocked to find when she arrives that she is not the plain brunette whose picture he'd received but a radiant blond beauty. She soon absconds with his fortune. Wracked with disappointment and loneliness, he vows to track her down. When he finds her, the real nightmare begins. **Introduction by Wallace Stroby.**